SENTINEL'S DILEMMA

George M. Gerstner

Hardcover ISBN: 979-8-9992537-0-5
Paperback ISBN: 979-8-9992537-1-2
eBook ISBN: 979-8-9992537-2-9
Audiobook ISBN: 979-8-9992537-3-6

Published by GMG Digital Technologies, Inc.

For my parents, who gave me my foundation
For my wife, who shares my journey
For my daughters, who are my future

Chapter 1

Antel Ralnar stood at attention as Senior Lieutenant Kalos Ranston addressed the assembled officers in the Mars base conference room. The red dust of the Martian landscape was visible through the viewport behind Ranston, casting a reddish glow across the room. Antel tried to focus on the briefing, though his mind kept drifting to the letter of assignment that had arrived earlier that morning. After all his training, he was finally going to Earth.

"Officers," Ranston began, activating the large display screen, "I'm here to brief you on the upcoming Earth expedition. The Council has given us approval to proceed with the next phase in our observation and study of Earth."

The screen displayed a map of Earth's North American region, labeled in Intallan. "Our landing site will be in this area the natives refer to as Denver. We believe they conduct their space-related military operations from this region, making it the perfect location to begin."

Antel studied the map intently, reflecting on the two years he'd spent learning English and taking accent reduction courses to ensure he would sound like a native of Earth. The opportunity to put that training to use sent a thrill of excitement through him.

"Our primary objective," Ranston continued, "will be to focus on Earth's current political environment and international power dynamics. This information will help our experts better understand how to deal with Earth when we eventually make our presence known."

The monitor shifted to a satellite view of a farmhouse. "The previous mission established this covert outpost disguised as a typical farmhouse outside Denver. This will serve as our base of operations."

Ranston's eyes scanned across the room, meeting each officer's gaze. "I must stress the importance of maintaining our cover. Our highest priority is the Standard Protocol, which forbids the people of Earth from learning of our true identities. Breaking cover risks our presence becoming public knowledge, which would constitute a serious breach with major legal consequences back home."

Antel nodded slightly. The memory of Nela's breakup flashed briefly in his mind. "I met someone," she had told him, but he pushed the thought away. Getting to Earth would put a welcome distance between them.

"Now, as for security..." Ranston continued, changing the display as he detailed the mission parameters. "While we don't expect complications, we need to be ready. Your role will be to provide security if trouble arises. While this sounds straightforward, the job is complex, as you must maintain your cover at all times."

"Remember," Ranston emphasized, "any use of force should be an absolute last resort. Every attempt should be made to handle situations without compromising our true origins."

A chuckle rippled through the room. None of the expedition members thought that was going to be realistic. If things got violent, no one expected their cover to remain intact for long.

"Mission duration is half an Earth year," Ranston concluded. "The Black Cat will be stationed on the far side of their moon. In an emergency, it can extract the team." He paused, surveying the officers once more. "Dismissed."

As the officers filed out, Antel felt a mixture of excitement and uncertainty. Soon, he would be among the few who had set foot on Earth itself.

"To Lieutenant Antel Ralnar," Junior Lieutenant Zhon Rell said as he raised his glass, "leader of the Earth expedition!"

Antel smiled, lifting his own glass in the Mars base's small recreation room. The news of his assignment had come through, and Zhon, his closest friend on the base, had insisted on celebrating.

"You know," Zhon continued, settling into his chair, "you're going to be one of the few to actually walk on their surface. I'm almost jealous. The best I can do is step outside of the Black Cat and breathe in Earth air, then get back on board. You get to roam free. At least I get to fly the Black Cat, so I can't complain too much."

"I still can't believe it's happening," Antel replied, taking a sip of his drink. "After all the training, we're actually going."

Zhon's expression shifted slightly. "Is it true what I heard about your team? That you've got Dr. Sallain as your lead scientist?"

Antel rolled his eyes. "Just my luck, right? Nela's graduate advisor. I hope he doesn't expect me to go out of my way to get research material for her."

"Ouch. That's going to be awkward."

"It doesn't matter," Antel said with forced confidence. "I'm over her. This mission is my priority now."

Zhon raised an eyebrow but didn't press further. "Well, at least you've got Sandun on your team. It'll be like your tour on Rimlus, except with fewer hostiles shooting at you."

"One can hope," Antel said, his mind already moving to the challenges ahead. "Have you seen the profiles on the rest of the team?"

"Briefly. Mostly solid. Emira Khen is supposed to be brilliant with languages—top of her class. Falron's technical skills are exceptional too."

"I'll need to review everyone's files tonight," Antel said. "We'll need to function seamlessly to pull this off."

"Always the professional," Zhon laughed. "You'll do fine. Just don't forget to enjoy yourself a little down there. I've heard Earth has some remarkable sights."

"This isn't a vacation, Zhon," Antel reminded him, though he couldn't help but smile. "We have a mission to complete."

"Of course, of course," Zhon conceded. "But when has that ever stopped you from appreciating a good view?"

Their conversation drifted to lighter topics as the evening wore on. Antel found himself actually relaxing for the first time in weeks. Whatever lay ahead on Earth, at least he wouldn't face it alone.

Expedition team members filed into the conference room, falling silent as they took their seats for their first briefing. Dr. Dahnt Sallain sat to Ranston's left, his neatly trimmed dark hair and slightly tanned skin giving him a stoic appearance.

Antel's jaw tightened involuntarily as Dr. Sallain took his seat. Despite their professional relationship, the sight of Nela's graduate advisor sent a familiar ache through his chest—a physical reminder of her rejection.

"Congratulations, team," Ranston began. "You've been carefully selected for the Earth landing mission. I've sent your mission orders, Terran names, cover stories, and notes to your datapads. Please review them thoroughly over the next few days." He gestured to his left. "Doctor, why don't you start us off with introductions? Include your Terran name."

Dr. Dahnt Sallain raised his hand to identify himself. "I'm Dr. Dahnt Sallain. I will be the lead researcher on the team, focusing on Earth's political structures and international relationships. My Terran name is Don Solomon." His stern tone left little room for pleasantries. Antel nodded stiffly, already sensing the challenge of working with Nela's graduate advisor.

A young woman with silvery-white hair tied in a regulation bun sat beside him, smiling warmly. "Ensign Emira Khen, linguist. Terran name is Emma Khan. I'll be handling language-related issues that might compromise our presence." Antel felt a moment of relief. Her enthusiasm would be a welcome counterbalance to Sallain's formality.

Next came a tall, broad-shouldered black man with an unmistakable Voran accent. "Hello, my friends! Junior Lieutenant Sandun Kandos, intelligence officer. I will go by Sean Cantor. I will be second in command and support the team with any 'spy stuff' we need." His emphasis on "spy stuff" drew chuckles from around the table. Antel suppressed a smile, grateful to have his old friend he served with on Rimlus on the team.

A slender woman with short brown hair introduced herself: "Serviceman 1st Class Liora Trandenn. Terran name: Lara Travers. I am the team's cultural and socio-political analyst." Antel noted her meticulous attention to detail, a quality that would serve them well.

"Ensign Irina Falron, technical specialist," said a woman with light blond hair. Small amounts of grease on her fingers betrayed her recent mechanical work. "I'll be handling technological repairs, hacking, and electronic warfare. On Earth, I will go by Irene Fallon." Antel's eyebrow raised slightly. Her hands-on approach suggested she preferred action to theory.

"Ensign Dalan Myros, medical officer. Terran name will be Dylan Myers." Myros had a friendly face with black hair and blue eyes, and a lighter Norgrany accent. Antel appreciated the medic's calm demeanor—a valuable trait when lives might depend on steady hands.

Finally, Antel sat up as all eyes turned to him. "Lieutenant Antel Ralnar, security officer. Terran name: Andrew Rall. My primary responsibility will be the safety and security of the team and our mission objectives."

"Excellent," Ranston said. "The Black Cat will depart for Earth in two Martian days. Use this time to prepare. Dismissed."

As the team filed out, Sandun caught up with Antel. "Well, my friend," he said, placing a hand on Antel's shoulder, "You feel ready for this?"

"The truth? No, not really. But that's never stopped me before."

"You can handle this," Sandun reassured him. "Besides, I'll be right there with you the whole time."

Antel returned a small smile. "I appreciate that. It's good to know I can count on you."

They walked together to an observation window overlooking the Martian landscape as the sun began to rise. The red desert stretched endlessly before them, a stark contrast to the blue and green world they would soon visit.

"Have you spoken to Nela since the mission was announced?" Sandun asked.

"No, and I don't plan to," Antel replied, his voice firmer than he intended. "It was her choice, so I'm going to make a clean break. The mission comes first now."

The docking bay of the base buzzed with activity as team members carried equipment and supplies through the airlock and loaded them onto the Black Cat for the journey to Earth. The process was painstakingly slow as the airlocks cycled between the base's breathable atmosphere and the thin Martian air outside, each pressure adjustment adding minutes to what would have been a simple loading operation on Arkonus.

Antel stood on the command deck of the Black Cat with Zhon, going through the final pre-launch checks.

"All systems green," Zhon reported. "We're ready when you are, Lieutenant."

Antel nodded, watching the loading operations through the viewport. Every detail needed to be perfect. Their mission was too important for errors. "What's our estimated travel time?"

"Just over four days at standard acceleration," Zhon replied. "The planets are in favorable alignment. When we return in half a Terran cycle, it might take a bit longer."

"Let's hope everything goes smoothly," Antel said. He couldn't shake the feeling that this mission would change everything.

Sandun entered the command deck, datapads in hand. "Final mission briefing materials from Ranston," he said, passing one to Antel. "Cover stories, intelligence reports, and contingency plans."

Antel skimmed through the files. "Anything unexpected?"

"Nothing major, but our cover story at the university has been refined. We'll be working closely with a Dr. Evelyn Carter in the history department. She's been briefed on our true nature by the previous team."

Antel raised an eyebrow. "How was she allowed to know our true origin?"

"Special exemption to the Standard Protocol," Sandun explained. "Apparently, she's been a valuable asset for gathering information on Earth's political systems. According to this, she's agreed to maintain secrecy."

"Let's hope she keeps her word," Antel said as he closed the datapad and looked out the viewport at the Martian landscape one last time. The red dust of the planet stretched endlessly before him, its rust-colored contours bathed in the pale glow of the distant sun. Antel's thoughts already drifted to the blue and green world they would soon visit, a stark contrast to the desolate beauty of Mars that had been his home these past months.

The ship's intercom crackled. "Lieutenant Ralnar, all team members are aboard and secured. Loading complete. We're awaiting your command to seal the hatches."

Antel pressed the response button. "Seal hatches and prepare for departure." He turned to Zhon. "Take us out, Junior Lieutenant."

"With pleasure," Zhon grinned, turning to his controls. "Initiating pre-launch sequence."

As they settled into their positions, Antel couldn't help but reflect on the significance of their mission. They were observers of a civilization that didn't know it was being watched. And it was his responsibility to ensure it stayed that way.

The Black Cat trembled slightly as its engines powered up. Outside the viewport, red dust swirled as the ship lifted from the Martian surface. Antel watched as the base grew smaller below them, his thoughts already on the world that awaited.

Earth. After all this time, he was finally going.

The Black Cat's engines thrummed steadily as Zhon guided the ship into a stable orbit around Mars. Antel, still sitting beside him on the bridge, watched the red planet slowly rotating below them. They were finally on their way to Earth. He wondered if he was truly ready for this mission or if he would be distracted by Nela's breakup with him.

"Orbital trajectory established, Lieutenant," Zhon reported.

"Thank you, Junior Lieutenant Rell," Antel replied, entering coordinates into the navigation system. "Setting course for Earth."

With their trajectory plotted, Zhon engaged the autopilot. The ship's gravitational wave drives hummed to life, accelerating them at a constant one g, giving the crew a comfortable simulation of normal gravity for the journey.

The Black Cat's decks, arranged like floors in a building as with all Rileean vessels, allowed the crew to move about normally while the gravitational wave drives maintained their steady one-g acceleration toward Earth.

Zhon reached for the ship's internal communications system. "Everyone, we are on our way. It is safe to unfasten your seat belts and move about."

Antel was still unbuckling his harness when Dr. Sallain's voice came over the comms.

"Lieutenant Ralnar, I need to discuss security protocols," Sallain said, his tone as dry as ever.

Antel sighed. He'd already reviewed procedures multiple times with the team. "I'll be right there, Doctor." He turned to Zhon. "Keep me posted on any issues that come up."

"You got it," Zhon replied with a slight grin. "But I'm more worried about you surviving four days of Dr. Sallain's briefings."

"I'll try not to strangle him," Antel joked. "No promises."

As Antel made his way through the ship's central ladder to the common area, he prepared himself for what was sure to be another tedious conversation. Sallain was waiting for him, sitting at the table with a datapad in hand.

"Lieutenant, I've been reviewing the Standard Protocol guidelines again," Sallain began before Antel could even sit. "I believe we need to implement additional restrictions on the team's communications with the locals."

Antel settled into his seat and exhaled. "Our protocols are already thorough, Doctor. What troubles you?"

"Serviceman Trandenn has been reviewing common Earth idioms. Given how many we've likely missed, we should limit contact with the natives to only myself."

Antel crossed his arms. "The team members are trained for this mission, Doctor. Their jobs require interaction with the locals. Trandenn analyzes culture, Khen studies language, and Kandos gathers intelligence. Keeping them isolated makes no sense."

"But the risks..."

"Will be managed," Antel interrupted firmly. "We'll proceed carefully, but everyone will fulfill their assigned duties."

"Fine," Sallain said, clearly displeased. "But I'm on record disagreeing with this plan."

As if punctuating their disagreement, the ship suddenly shuddered violently. The deck light flashed red as Antel was pulled sideways by the shifting forces.

"Bridge to Lieutenant Ralnar," Zhon's voice boomed over the intercom. "We've encountered an issue with engine four. I'm shutting down all engines temporarily."

The simulation of gravity disappeared when Zhon cut power, leaving them drifting in zero-g. The ship continued to spin slowly from the momentum. Antel's stomach lurched as his body suddenly felt weightless, his arms floating upward of their own accord. The familiar hum of the engines faded to an eerie silence, replaced by the soft pings and creaks of the hull as it adjusted to the temperature changes of space. Small objects—a stylus, a datapad, a water pouch—drifted lazily across the common area, catching light as they tumbled.

Antel grasped a nearby handhold, feeling the cool metal against his palm as his body's orientation shifted. The stars outside the viewport appeared to wheel past as the Black Cat continued its uncontrolled spin. Sallain, unprepared for the sudden shift, collided with a storage locker with a dull thud, his perfectly maintained appearance now disheveled as he struggled to regain his dignity in the disorienting environment.

"I'll check on it," Antel said, pushing off toward the access tunnel. This was exactly the kind of complication they didn't need so early in their journey.

The mission to Earth was officially underway, and already facing its first challenge. Antel only hoped it wasn't a sign of things to come.

Chapter 2

The Black Cat's sleek black hull settled silently in the clearing, over a thousand feet from the farmhouse that would serve as their outpost for the next several months. They landed silently in the late-night hours, the sleek black hull nearly invisible against the dark sky. The landing site was surrounded by tall trees, making it the perfect hiding place from anyone driving past on the country road.

The command deck sat about thirty-five dritts above the ground, nearly fifty feet in Terran measurements. From this height, only the farmhouse's weathered wooden roof was visible. The rest of the structure remained hidden by the forest. It was an ordinary house that looked remarkably similar to the rural homes in Rilee.

The property stretched outward, mostly hidden by night's veil. Behind the main house, completely obscured in shadow, Antel knew the rectangular work shed stood waiting, its simple structure concealing the sophisticated communication and computer equipment within.

Two hundred dritts in the opposite direction, about 287 Earth feet, the cylindrical metal grain bin occasionally reflected a faint silver glint of moonlight, its purpose as their antimatter generator perfectly disguised in the darkness.

The gravel driveway was a pale, winding thread cutting through the dense forest for nearly a thousand dritts before disappearing entirely into the blackness where it met the dirt road beyond. Midway along its curved path, the oval-shaped pond mirrored the trees behind it, its still surface occasionally rippling with nocturnal aquatic life.

The larger barn was merely a looming shape within its fenced enclosure, its closed doors blending into the night, the empty pasture around it invisible except as an absence of trees.

From this height, Antel appreciated the nighttime isolation of the outpost. No lights from other structures were visible, the surrounding forest creating an impenetrable barrier between their activities and any Terran observers. The expedition team's Earth Outpost was effectively invisible—just another patch of darkness in the rural landscape, utterly unremarkable to any passing observer.

The ship's ramp opened, and Antel stood at the top, scanning the trees to make sure there were no threats in the area. This planet might look like Arkonus, but it wasn't. As far as he was concerned, this was an alien planet, and he needed to remain vigilant.

When he was satisfied, Antel barked orders to the rest of the team. "Khen, Trandenn, get everything out of the ship and just leave it over there for now." Antel pointed at the tree line, well outside the thrust zone. After the ship was unloaded, the Black Cat was going to return immediately to orbit. Once it left, they could move the supplies into the house.

Dahnt hovered nervously, his eyes tracking each crate as if the crew were children handling priceless crystal artifacts. Antel thought it was ironic because, for a social science professor, he doubted there were any highly sensitive pieces of hardware. If anyone needed to be worried about sensitive equipment, it would be Ensign Myros. But Myros was handling his medical equipment by himself.

It didn't take the team long to remove all of the supplies from the ship's storage deck and place them a few yards from the ship. It took less time than it had taken to pack into the ship at Mars. To be fair, on Mars, they had the airlock slowing them down.

After the last crate was carried out of the ship, Antel visually scanned the forest one more time. Aside from small forest creatures, the area seemed safe enough. He walked up to one of the intercoms just inside the ramp and paged Zhon, who was sitting in the pilot's seat on the ship's bridge. "Junior Lieutenant Rell, the ship has been cleared. You will be cleared for takeoff as soon as you see me wave you off."

"Acknowledged, enjoy your vacation, sir," Zhon threw in a bit of humor.

"I wish it were a vacation. Have a good flight to orbit." Antel walked out and pressed the correct passcode on the control panel on the outside of the ship, and the ramp closed. He then walked over to where the others and the supplies were waiting.

Antel waved his arm to let Zhon know he was clear of the ship. When the team heard the engines hum gradually get louder until it reached full power, everyone, as per standard procedure, knelt down for stability as the Black Cat lifted off. A little dirt was kicked up, but the grassy ground held most of the earth in place.

The team stood back up and watched the ship continue into the sky. Once it was nothing more than a barely visible black dot in the dark sky, Antel ordered the team to continue transferring everything they had unloaded from the ship into the farmhouse.

The team moved efficiently under Antel's direction, their path illuminated only by the stars and the small tactical lights they had brought. With each trip between the supplies and the farmhouse, Antel found himself increasingly alert to the unfamiliar sounds of Earth's wildlife: the distant hoot of an owl, the rustling of leaves as small creatures scurried away from their approach. Though superficially similar to Rilee's forests, this wilderness still felt alien.

Stepping through the front door, Antel found himself in a pitch-black entryway, the wooden floors creaking softly beneath his feet. Throughout the house, there was the scent of old wood mingled with the mustiness of a building that had stood vacant for months.

As Sandun powered the antimatter generator, the interior of the farmhouse gradually revealed itself in a soft white glow.

To his right, a large living room emerged from the darkness, featuring comfortable furniture arranged around a stone fireplace. The draped windows appeared as black rectangles, the night outside complete and enveloping.

The central hallway stretched deeper into the house like a tunnel, passing a staircase that ascended into shadow. The walls held generic landscape paintings and what appeared to be photographs of the previous team.

The kitchen was adjacent to the living room. In the center of the kitchen stood a large wooden table, its surface reflecting the minimal light. It was large enough to seat all seven team members during their daily briefings. Moonlight spilled through a single uncurtained window, casting silver highlights on worn countertops and cabinet handles.

The eight bedrooms divided between the upper and lower floors remained mostly unexplored in the darkness, each a waiting silhouette of sparse furniture and storage compartments for personal equipment and supplies. The previous team had cleared out their belongings, leaving the spaces ready for new occupants to claim as their own.

"Rest up tonight," Antel told the team. "Tomorrow, we will begin preparing for our first meeting with Dr. Carter."

"Understood, sir," everyone grumbled back to Antel as they dragged their feet to their new quarters in the farmhouse to settle in for the night.

Antel decided to let them sleep in a bit longer. They had earned it. It wasn't as if they needed to be combat-ready. Tomorrow was going to be a busy day for them.

Antel stayed up a little longer to ensure everything was in place and the farmhouse was secured for the night. Everything was quiet, but his mind wrestled with questions. How much danger should he expect from the natives? Was he ready for this mission?

Excited to start the mission, Antel had been up for about an hour before the rest of the team when he finally called out, "Good morning, team."

He was wearing a flannel shirt buttoned to the neck and a pair of jeans. The shirt felt a little itchy, but he figured that once he was accustomed to it, it might start feeling comfortable.

Antel made a mental note that the expedition team's clothes were all brand new, and the natives might notice. The team might need to make them seem used.

"Maybe some drills crawling through the dirt could do the trick," Antel smiled as he thought of that idea as a joke.

Antel was already seated at the kitchen table, drinking a heated nutrient drink for breakfast. He couldn't wait until they could stock up on real food. He wasn't sure how much longer he could endure standard astronaut rations.

Soon, the team gathered around the table and took seats. Sandun decided to be helpful and warmed up the same nutrient drink for everyone else and passed them out.

"Okay, everyone, let's go over the plan for tomorrow," Antel started the briefing. "Khen, Trandenn, and Dr. Sallain will meet with Dr. Carter to discuss access to her resources," Antel explained, sipping his drink. "I will come as Sallain's graduate assistant from the University of..." He paused to look up the name on his datapad. "Chicago."

Antel pressed something on his datapad, which brought up a map on everyone else's datapads. "In case you're asked, here is where we are and where Chicago is."

"Kandos and Myros will remain here," Antel continued. "Myros will be ready if any injuries occur from any unexpected confrontations. Kandos, you will keep an eye out from space using our spy satellite we have in orbit."

"Understood," Sandun replied.

"We all need to stay alert," Antel added. "This is our first true exposure to the locals. Previous missions kept interactions with the natives to a minimum. It is our job to get a deeper understanding, and that will require getting up close and personal." He looked over at Emira and asked, "Did I get that expression right?"

"Perfect, sir," Emira replied.

"Excellent, thank you," Antel said. "Staying alert will help us avoid unnecessary attention. Speaking of which, it might be a good idea for you all to get out of those uniforms and put on Terran attire."

The group chuckled when they realized that they had put on their uniforms out of habit.

"Kandos," Antel looked up at Sandun. "The weapons?"

"Locked up and secure in that closet right there," Sandun reported. "The code is in everyone's messages. I recommend committing it to memory."

"Medical supplies?" Antel looked over at Myros.

"They're all still in the crates. I'll be unpacking them today," Dalan responded.

Antel moved on to his next question. "Communications and computer systems?"

"I'll be checking out the hardware the last team left us today," Emira said. "I will also be adding the computer systems to the work shed."

"Great. Looks like we're all set. Does anyone have anything to add?" Antel asked as he turned off his datapad.

"Yeah," Dalan put on a huge smile. "Try not to make it obvious you're conducting a military operation."

Everyone laughed. The team always appreciated the medic's good sense of humor. He had a knack for boosting morale and reducing the team's stress levels.

The team took the SUV. The large, red vehicle had been purchased by the previous team and left for Antel's team to use. It was an electric vehicle, but the previous team had retrofitted the batteries with Rileean antimatter power cells, much lighter and far more powerful. The power cells gave the vehicle enough range to drive to both coasts and return to the farmhouse before needing to recharge.

The Terran they were visiting on campus had given them a parking decal that allowed them to easily find a space to park. Thankfully, the driving rules in this country weren't too different from Rilee's. Dahnt walked ahead. As planned, Antel, Emira, and Irina followed along, acting as his graduate students.

Dr. Evelyn Carter was waiting for the team in the courtyard in front of the history department's main building. She was a distinguished-looking woman in her fifties with keen, intelligent brown eyes that seemed to evaluate everything they fell upon. Her shoulder-length silver-gray hair caught the sunlight. She wore what the team assumed was professional attire—a tailored blazer over a silk blouse, paired with a strand of polished amber beads that glowed warmly against the muted colors of her outfit. Her posture was straight but relaxed, conveying the confidence of someone comfortable in her academic domain.

She greeted them and led them into the building and to her office. "You must be my visitors," Dr. Carter said with a knowing smile. "It's the lost look in your eyes that gives you away."

Once everyone was comfortably seated inside her office, Dr. Carter closed the door and walked back to her desk chair. "I guess I should welcome you to Earth. I couldn't welcome you properly outside in case

I was overheard."

"Thank you, Dr. Carter," said Dahnt. Antel let him lead the conversation. "I would like to introduce our team." Dahnt introduced the team members in the room, first with their actual names, then went over their English names.

When she learned that Antel wasn't a social science expert and was there for security, she asked him politely, "Andrew, since this may not be as productive for you as it would be for your colleagues, would you like me to arrange a campus tour for you?"

Antel thought that was a brilliant idea and welcomed it. "That would be wonderful, thank you."

Dr. Carter raised a finger. "One sec." She picked up her desk phone. "Mrs. Davenport? Yes, could you please send one of your office student aides to give one of my visitors a campus tour?"

Dr. Carter waited for a short moment as the person on the other side of the call replied, then continued, "Thank you so much."

Dr. Carter, Dahnt, Irina, and Emira began discussing many topics. They looked like children showing off their fun stories. Antel enjoyed watching them, but it didn't take long for a knock to be heard on the door. It was the student sent by the department secretary to give Antel the tour.

"Hello? Dr. Carter? Mrs. Davenport asked me to give someone here a campus tour," the girl said.

"Yes." Dr. Carter motioned toward Antel. "Could you show Mr... I'm sorry, I forgot your name."

"Andrew Rall," Antel reminded her with a practiced smile.

"Ah, yes. Please give Mr. Rall a tour of campus, dear."

"Certainly," the girl answered.

Antel rose and followed her out of the office.

"Hello, I'm Sarah," she introduced herself as they stepped into the sunlight outside the building. She tucked a loose strand of wavy auburn hair back into her messy bun, her warm hazel eyes crinkling at the corners when she smiled. Though petite and slightly shorter than average, she radiated an infectious cheerfulness in her oversized sweater, well-worn jeans, and scuffed sneakers, practically bouncing on her toes with an enthusiasm that seemed to brighten the air around her.

"Hello, Sarah." Antel extended his hand, remembering Earth's greeting custom. "Please call me Andrew."

She gave his hand a quick, gentle shake. "Where are you from?"

"Chicago," he answered without hesitation, pleased with himself for the quick recall. "I'm a visiting graduate student."

Sarah nodded, adjusting the strap of her bag. "I'm a History Education major. When I finish my bachelor's degree, I plan to be a high school teacher."

"Sounds very noble," Antel replied, noting her enthusiasm.

"Thank you," she said, her expression softening with genuine appreciation. She looked at him for a moment, touched that a visiting graduate student would recognize the value in her career choice. "Most people just nod politely when I tell them. It's refreshing to meet someone who actually gets why teaching matters."

Antel followed Sarah across the campus. He took mental notes as they passed the various buildings. The library gave him a feeling of home. In Rilee, libraries were very popular. Historically they were just for books. Over the centuries, they evolved into community centers where people could gather and meet. Antel's parents met at a library. He was glad to see Earth had them too. Maybe with luck, the same evolution would occur here.

After an hour of walking around campus, they returned to the history building. Before arriving back, Sarah said, "Oh, I almost forgot. That over there is the engineering building. They do all kinds of cool stuff over there, including drones, robotics, and other high-tech cutting-edge research."

"I heard their latest project involves exciting satellite research." Despite giving Antel an hour-long tour, her enthusiasm still held firm.

"That's very interesting," Antel said, genuinely interested. "Tell me more."

Sarah's eyes lit up. "Well, my brother works with the engineering department on something that can detect stealth aircraft. He says it's going to be a game changer for air defense."

"Really?" Antel got a little nervous but kept a neutral expression. The Kallanians had developed a rudimentary form of that technology about 200 years ago, which is where experts had placed Earth's level of technology. It would make sense that they might be getting close to figuring out that technology right about now. Could their satellites detect the Black Cat despite its stealth emitters? He hoped that whatever they came up with wouldn't be ready for Rilee's more modern stealth technology.

Sarah nodded eagerly. "Absolutely. Something about advanced electromagnetic detection. I don't understand all the physics stuff, but it can apparently detect Chinese stealth jets even when regular radar can't."

"That's impressive. No faster-than-light communications or travel?" Antel asked. It was a serious question, but he posed it as a joke.

"You're funny," Sarah replied with a laugh. "No, nothing that sci-fi yet. Just practical applications."

Antel was relieved to hear that. "No chance our mission will be at risk of detection then," he thought. "Their technology couldn't possibly detect our stealth systems. They'd need subspace pings for that." He had to force himself not to smile at what sounded like a primitive version of what was available even at this moment around Earth's orbit. Years ago, the Rileean Empire had placed a stealth satellite in Earth's orbit to help with observing and studying the Earth. They would have found it by now if they had that technology.

"The coolest part," she continued as they entered the history building again and walked down the hall back to Dr. Carter's office, "is that they plan to design a whole network to watch over North America."

Antel's amusement diminished slightly. Even rudimentary stealth detection technology, with the help of a full network, might detect their presence. "How close are they to launching that?" he asked, trying to keep his tone casual.

"No idea," Sarah shrugged. "My brother says it could take years, if ever. You know… budget stuff. Besides, that part is probably classified."

"Oh, I know a lot about tight budgets," Antel said with a knowing smile. Military funding debates weren't so different on his world. The Rileean National Council constantly argued over defense spending. All it took was a skirmish with a rogue Kentan starship to remind them why it mattered.

"Don't worry," Antel reassured her. "I'm only interested because it's kind of related to my dissertation topic. Technology from a historical perspective." It wasn't completely a lie. He was here to help study Earth's technological development, after all.

"That sounds like a neat topic!" Her eyes lit up. "I know someone working on something similar. I should introduce you one day."

"That would be terrific." Antel wasn't sure how a Terran historian could help his mission when they already had Dr. Carter, but it couldn't hurt.

"Well, this is the end of the tour," Sarah said as they arrived just outside Dr. Carter's office. "I hope I was helpful."

"You were, thank you."

"And I hope to learn more about your thesis topic soon," she added.

"Oh, you will, I promise. Maybe with some time, you'll be teaching it to your students when you become that teacher." Little did she know how true that was. Antel assumed it was highly unlikely the Council would extend their studies of Earth past Sarah's lifetime.

"I might check it out in the next few days."

Chapter 3

Antel decided to go outside and enjoy the night air. The sun had set an hour ago, and the light breeze made him feel very comfortable.

He walked down the driveway farther from the farmhouse to a darker spot, away from the house lights, to get a better view of the stars. He knew Thanderen, the star Arkonus orbited, was somewhere due south in the sky, but he was disappointed he couldn't figure out which one it was.

"Doesn't matter anyway," Antel thought. "It's probably not bright enough to be seen from this distance."

Everyone else was inside, probably getting ready for bed if not already there. Only Dahnt was out. He said he needed to visit Dr. Carter at her home and wouldn't return until late. Dahnt declined when Antel asked if he needed an officer to accompany him. Since Earth seemed to be safer than everyone expected, Antel didn't press the issue. No one felt any danger.

Only Antel was outside. Everything was quiet. The only sounds were coming from the insects, making a soothing chirping noise. It almost sounded like the insects back in his hometown.

Antel closed his eyes, soaking in the chirping insects and gentle rustle of leaves when his communicator's sharp ping broke the silence. Antel's shoulders tensed at the unexpected alert, his relaxed posture instantly shifting to military alertness. He pulled it out of his pocket and took a look.

"What in the Universe?" Another signal was detected. Antel couldn't believe what he was seeing. The communicator was detecting yet another subspace signal. He adjusted the settings on his communicator, but the signal wouldn't clear up. It was encrypted, and his communicator couldn't figure out the encryption key.

"This can't be possible," Antel whispered, his brow furrowing as he examined the signal pattern. "Earth isn't expected to learn how to send faster-than-light communications for a century or two." Sarah had assured him they didn't have it. Yet, there it was. A signal. It couldn't be from Mars. His communicator wasn't powerful enough to pick that up. A bigger receiver would be needed for that. No, the source had to be much closer.

"The Moon? The Earth? Or..." a chill ran up his spine. "A starship in orbit?" No Rileean starships should be in orbit at the moment. Only the Black Cat was authorized to be here. If the Black Cat was sending a signal, they surely wouldn't encrypt it such that he couldn't decipher it.

No, not Rileean. "Oh, Universe! I hope that's not a Kentan signal," he said to himself. "If they're nearby, they would be violating the Interstellar Accords Treaty."

Antel took a deep breath. "I need to not jump to conclusions. Chances are better that its source is on Earth. But how? Do they have that technology already?" This might be a great question to ask Dr. Carter the next chance he got.

Antel considered whether he should inform Senior Lieutenant Ranston on Mars. His mission was to protect the expedition from any threat, and if he needed reinforcements, they wouldn't arrive for days anyway.

Besides, if he reported this to the Senior Lieutenant, the mission might get aborted, and the team would get recalled. Years of training for this mission would go to waste. "No, I think I'll investigate this further before I report this to Mars. If there's an unauthorized presence on Earth, I owe it to Ranston to catch whoever is potentially violating the Standard Protocol before he's forced to recall us."

Feeling determined, Antel went to the work shed that hid the advanced communications equipment. The first place to check was the most obvious. Maybe someone was making calls from right here. But when he arrived at the work shed's door, he found it locked.

He used his communicator to unlock the door via a short-range signal. The lights were off, and no one was inside. Well, the assumption that it wasn't as simple as a team member making calls proved right.

Antel pulled out a chair and sat in front of the subspace radio. He began reconfiguring the device. He tried various combinations to get the signal's encryption key. No luck. Nothing he tried was working.

"Just in case," Antel had a thought. "Let's record the signal." He flipped some switches on the recording computer that sat to the radio's right. "There. If the signal ends, at least I'll have something to work with."

Hours passed. Suddenly, a noise woke Antel. The sun's bright light came shining through the open door and got in his face. Junior Lieutenant Sandun Kandos was coming in.

"Sorry, Lieutenant," Sandun said softly. "I didn't mean to wake you."

"Quite all right," Antel lifted his head off the keyboard and rubbed his eyes. "I didn't realize I fell asleep."

"You look like you've been working on something all night," Sandun pointed at Antel's disheveled hair. "Everything okay? Can I help you with something?"

Antel thought about it for a moment. If anyone could decipher this message, it would be him. He was an intelligence officer, after all. "Okay, but we need to keep this between the two of us only."

"Um, okay, understood." Sandun wasn't sure where Antel was going with this, but he was his superior officer, so it wasn't like he had a choice. "May I ask why?"

Antel replayed the signal for Sandun. "What do you make of this?"

"Sounds like your typical subspace signal. What about it?"

"Can you decrypt it?"

"The radio should figure out the encryption key automatically."

"It didn't." Antel turned off the playback.

"Sorry? It didn't work?" Sandun's face wrinkled in confusion. "It always works."

"Not this time."

For the next hour, they reviewed the signal. Sandun did everything he could to decrypt it but got nowhere. Nothing he tried worked.

"I'm sorry, sir," Sandun said, feeling bad for disappointing Antel. "What do you think it's about?"

"I don't know," said Antel. "Could be someone on the team, an unauthorized starship in the area, or dare I say it, Kentans."

"We need more data," Sandun said. "This one transmission isn't going to tell us much."

"I agree. We need to set up something that will begin recording should this signal be picked up again."

"I'll get right on it," Sandun volunteered. "Are you sure we shouldn't let Senior Lieutenant Ranston know?"

"I don't want to risk our message getting intercepted."

Sandun wasn't comfortable with keeping this confidential, but he deferred to Antel's judgment.

The next few days went by with little excitement. The signal never came up again. Antel considered that maybe it was a naturally occurring event, but he knew that was unlikely as subspace waves didn't occur naturally. Or at least he didn't think they could.

Antel and Sandun took turns checking the equipment for new recordings under the guise of routine system maintenance.

On the third night, a brief signal was recorded by the stronger subspace receiver in the work shed, but it too couldn't be deciphered. "At least I know it's not naturally occurring. This would be too rare for that," Antel told Sandun when only the two of them were in the work shed alone. So far, both transmissions came during the night. That meant that someone on this planet was talking with someone farther out into the solar system, or it was just by chance that both signals were at night. At the power level he measured, he estimated it was probably near the planet the Terrans called Jupiter.

The next morning, Antel was awakened by a knock on his bedroom door. Hoping it wasn't an emergency because he wanted to sleep in a little bit, he got up and opened it to see who was there.

"Good morning, Lieutenant." It was Dahnt. "I hope I didn't wake you too early."

"Not a problem, Doctor," Antel yawned and rubbed his eyes. It was time to get up anyway. "What can I do for you?"

"I just received a message from Dr. Carter inviting us to her home later tonight for a social gathering she hosts once per semester. It will include some of her coworkers and their graduate students from her department."

"Sure, I'll be there," Antel assured him. "It will be good to meet some of her associates. Thank you." Antel didn't need to thank him. Although Dahnt was being polite, both knew that when Dahnt went out, especially to large groups, Antel or one of the other soldiers was required to accompany him for his safety. Antel had relaxed that rule recently given how safe the area turned out to be, but when it came to larger groups, perhaps it was prudent to accompany him this time.

Besides, Antel thought to himself, he could make use of the moment to perhaps ask Dr. Carter some questions of his own.

Later that night, Antel found himself in Dr. Evelyn Carter's home nursing a drink the Terrans called soda. He sampled small cubes of various flavors of cheese and small rolls of sliced meats as he tried to focus on all the conversations around him. Tonight, he needed to pretend to be a graduate student himself.

The gathering was casual. Dr. Carter's living room was filled with many of her colleagues and their graduate students. The room hummed with the guests' voices discussing many topics, mostly about sports or the weather. Light music was playing in the background to create a relaxing environment.

Dr. Carter had a small circle of people standing around her, participating in conversation. Dahnt had just asked her to give her opinion on the future possible alliances and rivalries she suspected would develop in the next few decades. Dr. Carter knew Dahnt had asked the question intentionally. He was trying to gain an understanding of how Earth's international political environment might evolve for the mission's sake. The others simply thought it was a novel topic of discussion and enjoyed offering their theories. Only Carter knew he was from off-world.

As the conversation continued, Dr. Carter noticed one of her favorite students entering the room. "Oh, Andrew," she said, using Antel's cover name, "I'd like you to meet someone." She gestured to the young woman who had just joined them. "This is Rebecca Miller, one of my most promising graduate students. Rebecca, this is Andrew Rall, a visiting student from Chicago."

"Please, call me Becky," she said with a warm smile, extending her hand. She was petite, standing an inch or two shorter than Antel, with a slim frame that made her appear almost delicate. Her warm brown eyes complemented her long black hair, which she'd pulled back in a loose, casual style that suited the informal gathering. Despite her small stature, she carried herself with a quiet confidence that immediately drew attention when she spoke.

Antel took her hand, hoping he was still using the proper Earth greeting custom correctly. "Nice to meet you, Becky."

"Rebecca's dissertation focuses on how technology has affected the course of history," Dr. Carter explained, a note of pride in her voice. "I think you'll find her perspective fascinating."

Ironic. Miss Miller was studying Earth's technological history, while his expedition's secondary mission was to study its current technological progress. The Universe probably planned this. Antel wondered if this was the student that his campus tour guide, Sarah, had told him about.

The conversation moved on to other topics. Antel was distracted for the rest of the night. As the gathering wound down and guests departed a few at a time, he lingered, hoping to get a moment of the professor's time alone to ask her some questions about technology. He expected to wait a long time before Dahnt would leave for the farmhouse, but to his pleasant surprise, he was one of the first few to leave.

Antel didn't have to wait long. Becky excused herself to help clean up in the kitchen while the others dispersed among the crowd. This was going to be his best opportunity.

"Dr. Carter," Antel kept his voice low once they had a moment alone. "May I ask you some technology-related questions?"

She understood that the emphasis on the phrase "technology-related" meant that the technology he was referring to was related to his world and didn't want to risk alerting anyone not privy to their arrangement.

"Sure, Lieutenant," she whispered as softly as she could. "How can I help?"

"What are the chances someone on Earth has discovered faster-than-light communications?" Antel just came right out and asked. No time to ease into the question. Someone could interrupt their conversation at any moment.

"Um, are we allowed to discuss technologies?" Dr. Carter was right to ask the question. The Standard Protocol was explained to her at the beginning, and it forbade talk about Arkonian technologies.

"Technically, this is about potential Earth technology."

"Clever loophole," she laughed. "Maybe being a lawyer suits you better than being a soldier."

He smiled at the comment.

"Oh, and please don't mention this conversation to anyone, not even any of my people."

"Your people?" Her brows furrowed. "Do you suspect someone on the expedition team of something?"

"I'm not sure yet. I can't rule anyone out."

Before she could answer his question, Becky returned from the kitchen with a steaming cup. "I made you your favorite, Earl Grey, Dr. Carter."

"Oh, thank you, dear," Carter reached with two hands to carefully take the warm cup from Becky. "That's my Rebecca for you. Always the kindest person I know."

"You're always welcome," Becky smiled at the compliment. "So whatcha talking about? Looks like a deep conversation."

"How new technologies are so hard to keep secret for very long." Dr. Carter was vague yet honest on purpose. "I would have to say the chances are low that it would remain a secret for more than a handful of years." Sandun had recently told her that the trick to deception is to be honest about it. He told her the Rileean intelligence agencies have a saying: deception equals truth minus fact. She was sure it made better sense in its original Intallan, but she got the point.

"That is so true," Becky felt right at home on this topic. Her dissertation was on "The Effects of Technology on History." "There's nuclear weaponry and rocket propulsion, just to name a few. It was only a matter of time before other countries figured it out. They just needed the idea." She had no idea the topic was specifically about subspace technology, but her point was relevant anyway.

Dr. Carter noticed one of her guests preparing to leave. "I think my favorite student answered your question better than I could have. If you'll excuse me, I need to say my goodbyes to someone." She patted

Antel on the shoulder and left him and Becky to thank the departing guest.

Antel felt a little uncomfortable being alone with Becky. He felt like an awkward teenager who wasn't sure what to say to a girl.

Becky could sense he was nervous, so she broke the silence to ease his anxiety. "Your perspectives on political movements are really interesting. I'd love to hear more about your research sometime."

"Oh, thank you," Antel replied, grateful for the academic focus. "I'd be interested in hearing more about your work on technology's impact on history as well."

"Why don't we grab coffee tomorrow? There's this great little place near campus where I usually do my writing. They make an amazing cappuccino," she suggested.

"Sure, that sounds good." Antel tried to keep his tone professional despite the slight flutter in his chest. "What time works best?"

"How about two? I have a bunch of morning classes, but I'm free after that."

"Two works perfectly," he said, trying to remember his schedule. He had regular weekly check-ins with Mars, but he was pretty sure he was free.

Antel came to the gathering only to inquire with Dr. Carter about the probabilities of his subspace signal's source being Terran in origin. He didn't expect to make coffee plans with Becky.

Antel started to worry. He felt some attraction for her. Maybe he should cancel. The smart thing to do would be to keep his distance from developing feelings for a Terran. Not to mention, he was just getting over Nela's breakup with him. This would only make his life complicated.

But he had already told her yes. Canceling now would be extremely rude, and he just wasn't that kind of person. And, Antel admitted to himself, he was looking forward to meeting up with her for coffee.

"This is going to be a monumentally bad idea," Antel thought to himself. "I don't know if I'll regret this more if I go or if I cancel."

Chapter 4

Antel checked the time on his communicator, disguised as a typical Terran smartphone, for the third time. The minutes crawled by painfully slowly. It didn't help that he had arrived far too early just to make sure he wouldn't be late.

"Why am I acting like a nervous schoolboy?" he mumbled to himself, drumming his fingers on the table.

He decided to wait until Rebecca joined him before ordering. Coffee was not something he looked forward to. He tried it during his first week on Earth and found the taste unpleasant. When he spotted hot chocolate on the menu, his interest was piqued. He'd tasted chocolate for the first time back on Mars, one of several Earth items previous missions had brought back, and had fallen in love with it. He hoped the liquid form would be just as delicious as the solid candy bars.

He sat at a corner table in the busy campus coffee shop, watching the afternoon crowd shuffle around with laptops, calculators, and textbooks. Most patrons spoke English, though he caught snippets of conversations in languages he didn't recognize.

His communicator buzzed. Antel opened the device only to find another signal sweep report from Sandun. Nothing detected so far. He closed the phone with a sigh and placed it back on the table, his eyes drifting once more to the entrance.

Every time the door opened, he looked up expectantly. Finally, after watching countless others enter and leave, Rebecca Miller walked in. She immediately smoothed her hair, disheveled from the autumn breeze, before spotting him. Her face brightened with a smile as she waved, gracefully weaving between tables to reach him. Antel stood, assuming it was customary on Earth to do so when someone joined your table.

"Hello, Andrew," Becky greeted warmly. "I hope I didn't keep you waiting long." She hung her backpack on the chair before sitting down.

"Hello, Rebecca. No, not long at all." He saw no reason to mention he'd arrived ridiculously early. She was a few minutes early herself. "Shall I order something for us?"

"Please call me Becky," she insisted with a gentle smile. Then, with a playful glint in her eye, she added, "Are you sure you want to pay? I don't want to be too expensive for you."

Antel smiled in return, recognizing the lighthearted joke.

The two went up to the counter to order. Antel let her order first. At first, she asked for a cappuccino, but when he ordered the hot chocolate he had his eye on for a while, she changed her mind and picked the hot chocolate as well. Antel paid using a bank card set up on the last expedition by the Rileean Government.

The previous expedition would, every so often, use the Black Cat to find a deposit of palladium or other precious metal in their solar system and bring some down to sell. They usually kept it to under a hundred kilograms to avoid inadvertently flooding the market. The account had amassed several million dollars by that point. The Rileean government could have just hacked their financial systems, but they didn't want to cheat their financial system through theft.

Initially, the money collected was saved in local banks under a fake identity, but when the previous missions discovered that a common place to store large sums of money anonymously was in a small country on the other side of the planet, Switzerland, they quickly made use of an account there.

"So Andrew," Becky said, settling back into her chair, "tell me more about your research. Dr. Carter mentioned you're studying modern political structures?"

"Yes, we want to make, if you will, a 'map' of international relationships, including forms of governments and other things," explained Antel.

"That sounds really exciting," she admitted. "Sorry, I'm a major history nerd."

Antel couldn't remember what 'nerd' meant. He assumed it meant someone who liked academic topics that were normally considered boring. He just smiled and picked up his cup to take his first sip.

When he took his first sip, he nearly sprayed it on the table. He struggled to swallow what he had in his mouth, and he felt it burn the entire way down. "Oh my Universe, that's hot!" He didn't expect it to feel like the surface of Thanderen. But the taste didn't disappoint him. It had that familiar chocolate taste he remembered.

Becky couldn't help but giggle. "I'm so sorry, I didn't mean to laugh at that."

"The heat took me by surprise. I think I'll be okay. But the flavor is amazing. I love it." Antel was sincere. He loved it, but he needed to be careful not to act like this was his first time drinking this beverage. He took slower sips from that point on until his drink cooled off a bit more. "But I think I lost the feeling in my tongue." Antel stuck his tongue out and touched it as if he were feeling for a pulse as he laughed.

Becky burst out laughing, then put her hand over her mouth when she realized everyone in the store heard that. "You have a good sense of humor," she managed to say while trying to control her laughter. "So, tell me what part you are personally working on."

"I'm doing a study on the various levels of technological development between the nations to see if there's a relationship between that and their political relationships." Antel must have rehearsed that a thousand times on Mars when he was preparing for the mission. He hoped it sounded plausible.

"Oh my God! That's super close to what I'm exploring in my thesis!" Becky's eyes lit up. "I'm studying how technological advancements have affected the path history has taken."

"I remember. Dr. Carter told me at her social gathering. Sounds like a very exciting topic." Antel was genuine. "I want to learn everything about your research. It would give me such a great perspective on mine."

"I would love to share details with you!" Becky's pitch raised just a bit. She was excited someone was taking such interest in her research.

"But first, tell me what got you into history and what made you think of combining it with technology?"

"Well, my dad's an attorney. He got me interested in social studies." She paused for a moment to take a sip, then continued. "My mom is a nurse. So the science part comes from her."

The door to the coffee shop chimed as a man in a dark blue military uniform entered. He was somewhat muscular and stood an inch or two taller than Antel, with broad shoulders and a rigid posture that commanded attention. His face wore a permanently sour expression, jaw tight with obvious tension.

Only Antel noticed him come in because Becky was facing away from the door. He might have paid no attention if not for the uniform —as a soldier himself, spotting other uniformed personnel was an ingrained habit, an automatic assessment of potential threats.

The man approached from the side, his shoes making deliberate steps across the floor. When Becky finally noticed him, her shoulders visibly tensed.

"Neil," she said, her voice flat and devoid of warmth. She deliberately avoided giving him the privilege of eye contact, staring instead at her cup. "What are you doing here?"

"I tried calling you," Neil said. "You aren't answering my calls or texts. Can we talk?"

"There's nothing to talk about." Becky wrapped both hands around her cup. Antel could see she was feeling a little rattled. "We've been over this. I have nothing more to say."

Antel remained quiet, assessing the situation. The man, Neil, was insistent.

Neil turned his gaze to Antel. "Who is this?" he demanded.

"I'm Andrew Rall," he said, keeping his voice calm. "I'm Rebecca's colleague from college."

"A colleague?" Neil's laugh was fake. "That's bullshit. Did you replace me already, Becks?"

"That's enough, Neil." Becky raised her head and looked sternly at him. "You don't get to tell me who I spend my time with."

"Come on, Becks." Neil put his palms on the table and leaned in. "Just give me five minutes…"

"The lady has made her position clear," Antel said as he slowly stood up. "This isn't the best time or place for this discussion."

Neil removed his hands from the table and stood upright, facing Antel directly. Neil's jaw tightened, and his fists clenched. For a moment, Antel thought this was about to get violent, and he would have to use force.

Neil looked around and saw that several of the other customers were watching, expecting a fight. "Fine," he said, stepping back. He turned to Becky and said, "We aren't finished, Becks. We'll need to talk eventually."

"No, Neil, we don't." Becky's voice trembled slightly. "Please just go. And stop calling me Becks. I hate that nickname."

Neil turned around and strode out. If the glass door wasn't intentionally slowed, he would have slammed it.

Becky's hands were shaking as she sank back into her chair.

Antel sat down and reached for her hands. "Are you okay?"

"Yeah," she said, nodding as she took a deep breath. "He likes showing up to places around campus, trying to 'bump' into me so he can try to talk me into getting back together with him."

"I'm sorry about that," she said, looking up at Antel. "Neil wasn't always like this."

"You don't need to explain," Antel replied gently.

"No, I want to." Becky's gaze drifted to the window, tracking Neil's uniformed figure as he marched stiffly toward the parking lot. She wrapped her hands around her cup, drawing comfort from its warmth. "We met through his sister at the start of summer. His family has three generations of Air Force officers, and he's absolutely devoted to his country—flag on his porch, hand over heart for the anthem, a big collection of guns. The whole patriotic package."

"For a while, things were good," she continued. "He was passionate about his job, dedicated. But whenever we'd hang out with his base buddies, he'd change, trying to fit in by making crude jokes or snide remarks. When I called him out on it, he'd just say, 'It's just locker room talk. Don't take it so seriously.'"

Antel nodded, listening intently.

"The real problems started when he began expecting me to play a certain role," Becky's voice softened. "He had this ideal image of what an officer's girlfriend should be—how I should dress at military functions, who I should talk to, what opinions I should express. Everything had to align with his career advancement."

She took a sip of her drink. "The sad thing is, underneath all that, there's still the guy who used to talk about flight mechanics with genuine passion. I just couldn't be with someone who wanted me to make myself smaller to fit his world."

"I understand," Antel said, finding himself recognizing certain aspects of Neil's attitude in some of his own colleagues back home. This type of Rileean was what they called a 'Hard-Line Nationalist.'

"Don't get me wrong," Becky added with a half-smile. "He's still being a complete jerk about this."

"But people are rarely just one thing," Antel finished.

Becky looked at him with appreciation. "Exactly."

"Incredible. Now I feel bad I didn't give him a beating." Antel was only trying to lighten the mood for her, but he felt a surprising sense of protectiveness within him.

She looked down at her nearly empty cup. "I'm sorry. This was probably more detail than you wanted to hear."

"I'm glad you told me." He wanted more than ever to be there for her. "He's never going to come near you if I have anything to say about it."

"He's a big guy, you know." She looked him in the eye. "Air Force trained."

"You let me worry about that. I'm not afraid of him." He couldn't tell her about his combat experience fighting many adversaries. Most of them weren't even human. He badly wanted to tell her about his experiences to show he wasn't afraid of another human who probably hadn't been anywhere near combat. "Someone as extraordinary as you deserves better."

She began to blush at his compliment. "You are too kind."

Antel saw that she didn't feel awkward being vulnerable with him in the slightest. This was getting to be rather perilous territory, he thought. He wasn't sure he wouldn't be emotionally compromised and risk undermining the team. He didn't anticipate developing feelings for her.

Becky picked up her cup and sipped the remainder of her drink. Then, using her tongue, she licked her lips clean from the hot chocolate that had wet her mouth. Antel couldn't take his eyes off such a tantalizing motion. If he didn't know better, he would have thought she did that on purpose.

"Thank you, by the way, for staying calm. I was worried it was going to escalate."

"Would you like to take a walk? The fresh air may help relax you."

"Sounds like a good idea."

They left the coffee shop and walked along the sidewalk. The road was somewhat busy with cars driving past, normal for this time of day. Becky's trembling subsided, and she began talking about her thesis research again. Antel listened carefully, occasionally offering insights. Antel had the advantage of being from a world approximately 200 years more advanced, based on past mission research data. It was almost like he was from the future. Some of those ideas she never would have considered unless she had his experience.

"So Andrew," she still didn't know his real name. "Tell me. What do you like to do when you're not at gatherings for the professors you visit?"

"Uh, I don't know." He was caught off guard by that question. "Maybe stargazing or visiting all kinds of museums."

"Museums?" Becky's eyes lit up. She put her hand on his shoulder, emphasizing her excitement. "We should visit the Denver Museum of Nature and Science. Have you ever been there?"

"No, I don't believe I ever have."

"Excellent! We should, for sure, go there. You'll love it." Becky took her hand off to pull out her phone as she momentarily stood on her toes and smiled. "Let me text you the address. We can meet up this weekend."

Antel hesitated. Did she just ask me out on a date? Antel's face began to blush. Personal entanglements weren't part of the mission plan. "Sure, I would love that. I'll see you then."

His pocket vibrated. Three short pulses. Antel pulled out his communicator and read the message on it. His face suddenly turned serious as he was reading. Sandun's message said he detected another subspace signal. This time it was during the day.

"Is everything okay?" Becky noticed the change in his expression.

"I'm so sorry," he apologized. "Something urgent has come up."

"Okay." Becky's face turned to disappointment. "I understand, of course. I hope no one is hurt."

"I'm sure no one was hurt. One of my classmates is probably running late and needs a ride." Antel didn't have the time to come up with a better excuse. He had to meet with Sandun quickly or they could lose the opportunity. "Let's plan for that museum visit soon."

After they parted ways, he waited until he turned the corner out of her sight, then sprinted to the car. Sandun was already waiting by the car.

"What have you found?" Antel asked Sandun.

"I have the signal. If we drive around a bit, we can triangulate an approximate location," Sandun replied as Antel entered the driver's side of the car.

"Are we able to decipher the signal yet?"

"No, but it's the same frequency as before." The signal needed three measurements to triangulate, but with an educated guess, it could be done with just two. One was a makeshift device Irina had installed in the car. The other was at the farmhouse. Sandun chose to drive due south since the farmhouse was to their east. It was the most efficient path, hopefully.

Only Sandun, Irina, and Antel knew about the subspace tracking equipment—Sandun for his experience as an intelligence officer, and Irina because she had the technical skills for assembling the makeshift equipment.

As they rushed to the suspected location, Antel's mind raced. If Terrans were responsible, it would shake the foundation of every estimate Arkonus had on their level of technology. If someone on the team was sending signals, who were they talking to and why?

His communicator buzzed again. Becky sent a message thanking him for being there for her when Neil confronted her. Antel stared at the screen. Guilt percolated within him. Was he getting too close to a Terran? Was her influence going to compromise his judgment? He brushed the thought away. Right now, he had bigger problems.

After a few minutes of driving, the digital readout displaying Arkonian numerals showed the signal strength beginning to drop. The source was probably behind them to the north. Antel turned the car around, but as soon as he started traveling north, the signal stopped.

"Curse the Liberator!" Sandun exclaimed. He was accustomed to a different expression due to the predominant faith in his home nation of Vora.

Was the signal coming from the campus or farther north of it? Antel cursed himself. If he hadn't been so occupied with Becky, they might have had a better chance of narrowing down the source.

The Earth's winds picked up. If Earth's weather was anything like Arkonus's, it meant rain was approaching. Somewhere behind them, in the city, Becky was going about her day, oblivious to his true origin. He needed to balance his duty with what was quickly becoming his personal life.

Missteps like this might cost him one day.

Chapter 5

The next morning, Antel woke up in a rather good mood. As he got dressed, all he could think about was Becky and the unexpected spark they started to feel for each other. He was able to make her feel safe and at ease. He didn't let failing to find the signal source bother him. He told himself, "At least we got some clues."

Antel pulled out his communicator and looked up Becky's contact information. He was tempted to call her that moment, but decided it was too early in the day. If she were sleeping in, he didn't want to wake her.

Antel then spent the rest of the day walking the property, checking on everything, and making sure everything was fine. Nothing really exciting, but it was his job to make sure the outpost was safe and functioning properly. If anything was a problem, he would need to send one of his subordinates to fix it. But since Ensign Falron was on top of things, Antel just felt like a useless "supervisor." He almost wished a dangerous wild Earth animal would jump out of the forest, forcing him to defend the outpost from it, but he knew that was highly unlikely.

Lunchtime eventually approached. Antel thought to himself, "With any luck, Becky should be up by now and I won't be waking her."

While standing outside, not far from the tree line, he scrolled to her contact information on his phone and put his finger over the call button. He froze for a second as his heart picked up speed. He'd been in combat situations where they fired nuclear missiles at his ship, saw companions shot at by Kentan shock troops on Rimlus, and other crazy moments.

But this was scary! He hadn't felt like this since he was in secondary school as a young teenager when he made his first call to a girl for a date. And he was politely rejected.

He moved his hand away, took a deep breath, and collected himself. "You're a soldier, Antel Ralnar. Act like one!" he thought, then pressed the call button.

It rang a few times before Becky answered, "Hello?" Her gentle voice nearly melted him.

"Uh, um..." No, stop this, Antel. Now isn't a good time to freeze up when talking to a woman. "Hi, Becky. This is Ant..." He almost said his real name. "Andrew. We had hot chocolates together yesterday." What an idiot. Of course, she would already know that. "How are you doing today?"

"Andrew! You called!" she said with a higher pitch. She was excited to hear from him. "I'm doing great."

"Glad to hear it," replied Antel.

"I had a wonderful time yesterday at the coffee shop. Except for... you know who. Um, so... Would you like to go to the Denver Museum of Nature and Science later today with a good friend of mine? They have some fantastic new exhibits."

"That sounds terrific. I would love to learn about all of that." Antel was sincere about that. Although his job wasn't to research the Earth and its knowledge of science, this was a great opportunity. He tried to convince himself this was why he was going out with her, but he knew that wasn't true. He just wanted to see her again. It didn't matter if all they did was watch traffic for hours. All of his attention was going to be on her anyway.

"Great! I'll text you the deets."

After settling on the plans for the afternoon, they said their goodbyes and disconnected.

As Antel hung up, he had that guilty feeling again. Part of him knew this was an unnecessary complication given his mission. But he was compelled to get to know her further. Going to a nature and science museum was a bonus.

"Hello, sir." Antel was so focused on his call that he didn't notice Sandun had walked up from behind him.

"Oh, my Universe! You startled me."

"Good thing you weren't armed or I'd be in trouble," joked Sandun.

"Very funny."

"I saw you just standing out here and wanted to check on you. But then I heard the last bit of your conversation. Sounds like you got yourself a date for this weekend."

"I'm making a huge mistake, aren't I?"

"No, my friend," Sandun put his hand on Antel's shoulder, "I say go for it. You need to move on from a certain someone. Everyone on the team agrees."

"Seriously? Is there a newsletter I'm missing?"

"You think the team wasn't going to notice?" Sandun laughed.

"I see. I might have to talk with them. By the way, what are 'deets' and what is a text?"

"Deets is slang for details." Just as Sandun was talking, Antel's phone made a ding sound. "And that's probably your text message. Good luck, sir. I need to make a routine check that the power levels on the generator are still under 5%. More than that, and we'd be an explosion waiting to happen."

Antel was surprised at how little he was thinking of Nela. It was as if she were completely erased from his mind. Of course, that was until Sandun brought her name up again. But it didn't bother him. There was something different about Becky.

No matter how hard he tried, Antel struggled to focus on his duties for the day. Yet he had a job to do. He couldn't let the outpost lower its guard. A lapse in security would compromise the secrecy of the outpost. The Empire had invested decades into running a smooth monitoring operation, and he didn't want everything falling apart because he was too distracted by personal matters.

It was time for the daily personnel briefing. The team usually had these meetings in the kitchen during lunch to make use of the large table. Antel took his seat at the far end so that he could have a clear view of everyone. Instead of a large monitor, everyone had tablets. The speaker would cast the view on his tablet to the others to share any visual items that needed to be shared by the team.

Sandun, a well-experienced veteran and his second in command, usually did most of the presenting. Antel only needed to sit back and ask questions. Usual topics included the day's activities for the scientists and any items that the team needed to be aware of for the upcoming few days. Usually nothing too exciting. For a while, Antel didn't realize he was tuning out Sandun because of the routine nature of the topics. But his attention snapped back when Sandun brought up something about a drone.

"Sorry, did you say drone?" Antel tried to act like he was listening the whole time, but Sandun knew better.

"Yes, sir." Sandun flipped the image on the tablet back to an image he had passed by a second ago. "This is satellite footage of a local military drone circling the area."

"Assessment?"

"I believe they are probably training pilots. But flight patterns suggest they might be looking for something."

"Could they be looking for us?" Antel asked him a hypothetical question.

"Doubtful. If they knew we were in the area, chances are they'd already know exactly where," said Sandun.

Serviceman 1st Class Trandenn spoke up. She offered her theory, "If I may, sir, it's always possible they spotted the Black Cat departing and are investigating."

Antel looked down at his tablet and pondered for a minute. "Hopefully, it's routine for them. But if it isn't, keep an eye on their drone activity, and if things change, let me know."

"Yes, Lieutenant." The serviceman replied.

When the meeting broke, Antel dismissed the group. As they began to disperse, Antel put his hand on Sandun's shoulder to have him stay back.

Sandun turned around to face Antel. "Yes, sir?"

"Can I get your opinion on something?" Antel spoke softly. "On a personal matter."

"Certainly." Sandun smiled, happy at the thought that Antel viewed him as a friend he could confide in. "What's on your mind, my friend?"

Antel felt self-conscious. "It's about the Terran woman."

"The one you called this morning?"

"Yeah, Rebecca." He paused for a moment to consider how to ask his question. "Do you think I'm making a huge mistake? Getting entangled with a native? I can't deny a strong connection with her."

"I think you're fine, my friend. If this young lady brings you happiness, I say embrace it. I'm sure you'll be able to balance the Standard Protocol with your time with her."

"And Nela? Do you think it's too soon?"

Sandun put a hand on each of Antel's shoulders. "Have you been thinking of Nela since you met this new lady?"

"Honestly, no. Not really. Maybe our relationship wasn't as serious as I thought it was."

"Then, my friend, it's not too soon. I hope you bring this Becky over soon so I can meet her. I want to see, for myself, how she has your heart in such a tangled mess."

"You know it's an expectation in Rileean culture that if a man invites a girl to his place, he plans to...uh...you know."

"You Rileeans are so silly. In my Vora, we don't worry about these things as long as we treat our ladies with respect and kindness." Then a devious smile crept over Sandun's face as he poked Antel in the arm with his elbow. "However, in this case, would that be so bad?" Sandun walked away to manage his duties, laughing on his way out.

"Very funny." Antel was a little embarrassed at Sandun's suggestion.

Later that evening, Antel entered the address of the museum Becky had messaged him into the GPS of his electric vehicle.

As Antel drove around the parking lot looking for a decent space to park, he could see Becky standing by the museum's elaborate entrance. Her beautiful black hair and those captivating brown eyes were unmistakable. He doubted she saw him drive up. He'd forgotten to tell her what his vehicle looked like, so she didn't know what to be on the lookout for.

The museum was enormous—bigger than even the one back in his home city of Sillence, in Rilee's Granilest province. However, the one in the capital city of Intallia might have given this one a run for its money.

It didn't take long for Becky to spot him walking through the parking lot toward her. Her smile brightened immediately as her hand shot up in an enthusiastic wave to get his attention. He had to remind himself to breathe. Her light jacket, a dark shade of pink, was worn over a casual light blue blouse. He felt underdressed for the occasion. The best he had was what he'd brought from Mars.

"You came!" Becky said as he walked close enough. "I was worried you would change your mind."

"Not a chance," Antel grinned, following beside her as they headed inside. "I've been looking forward to this for hours."

"Let me introduce you. Andrew, this is Sarah. Sarah, this is Andrew."

"Nice to see you again." Andrew shook Sarah's hand.

"Hello, Andrew," Sarah greeted him. "Nice to see you again, too."

"Oh, you two already met?" Becky was pleasantly surprised.

"Yeah," Sarah answered. "I gave him a campus tour not too long ago. I even mentioned you to him."

"Wow, small world. She's my best friend and... um," Becky turned to make mutual eye contact with Sarah.

"She's trying to say I'm Neil's little sister," Sarah finished Becky's sentence for her.

Antel wasn't sure what "small world" meant, but from the context, it sounded like it was an expression that explained away why people would randomly already know each other.

"She's the one that hooked me up with her brother," Becky added, then put up a joking smile. "But I don't hold that against her."

"Hey!" Sarah gave Becky a playful slap on the arm. Antel could tell they held each other in high regard despite the complication of Neil.

They spent the next few hours walking through all of the exhibits. Becky enthusiastically explained each exhibit to them in more detail than the museum literature. Her degree was in history, after all. She was especially passionate about showing Antel all about the era of early man. She was able to get into the finer points of how technology had affected the course of human history—exactly what she was writing her dissertation about.

As they walked through the wildlife sections, Becky put her hand on the side of his upper arm to get his attention. "Look at that!" He didn't notice her other hand pointing at a display of a large bird tending a nest of eggs. "Isn't she gorgeous?"

He was staring at Becky at the time when he said, "Yes, very." Then he suddenly realized he wasn't looking at what she was pointing at. He was embarrassed and hoped she didn't catch him staring at her instead of the display. He had to remind himself they were only friends at the moment. Antel didn't realize it, but Sarah noticed.

"Well, that's unusual." It was a bird he had never seen before. They didn't exist on Arkonus, or at least not in the part of the planet he was from. "Its head is white while the rest of the body is brown."

"What? Haven't you ever seen a bald eagle before?" She was curious how he wouldn't be familiar with the national bird.

"Uh, no, no. I knew what it was. I just never saw one in person. Just pictures." He hoped that was a good save. He wasn't so sure.

"City boy?" Sarah asked.

"Yeah, I'm afraid so." Not entirely true, but close enough. Did a suburban area count as part of a city?

Becky turned back to the eagle. "So majestic. It's easy to see why the bald eagle was chosen as our national bird."

"She does inspire patriotism." He quickly remembered this species of bird was a symbol of pride in this country.

Becky turned to Sarah and Antel. "I'm boring you two, aren't I?"

"You are absolutely not boring. You've been an excellent guide," said Antel. Sarah nodded in agreement.

At that very moment, Antel's stomach gave an audible grumble. "How embarrassing," he said to the girls.

The girls giggled together. "Sounds like someone is hungry. We'll just have to take care of that."

"The museum has a cafeteria," Sarah said, pointing to it at the other end of the hallway. "We can grab a bite there."

After purchasing lunch, the three of them settled at a table in the small museum cafeteria. Becky went on about the details of her thesis. Sarah, a junior in History herself, added a few suggestions that she thought Becky should include. Antel, unfortunately, knew almost nothing of Earth's history. The best he could do was offer the perspective of what Earth's future might be like, assuming their trajectory stayed on track—progress that would be damaged should the Standard Protocol be violated.

"See that machine over there?" Becky pointed at a replica of Voyager I. "It's out there just outside the Solar System, broadcasting messages about who we are. Do you think anyone will ever hear our messages?"

Antel thought about the irony. Arkonus had first discovered Earth through its radio and television broadcasts. That satellite's message was probably drowned out by Earth's own noise washing over its signal.

"Who knows?" Antel thought this was an interesting opportunity to ask first-contact questions. "If you were an alien civilization that heard the message, what do you think Earth would do? How would they—uh, I mean, we—handle it?"

Antel genuinely wanted to know her answer. The Empire could use the perspective of an expert from Earth on the subject.

"Can you imagine if it were discovered and aliens came down to visit?"

He had to fight the impulse to just tell her the truth—that the aliens were already here. Although to him, Earth was the alien planet. Antel wasn't sure what to say next. His pause felt like an eternity.

"How much do you know about who or what is out there?" he asked, pointing up, referring to space.

"Aside from conspiracy theories," Becky said as she stuffed a French fry in her mouth, "we're probably alone in the galaxy."

"The nearest alien is probably a whole galaxy away," Sarah added.

Antel's mind was in turmoil. He felt determined to tell her, but he knew he was risking everything he had worked hard for. The lies were killing him. He felt he had to confess. He didn't care that Sarah would hear the truth as well.

"Becky..." he attempted to begin, but paused for a moment. If he revealed the truth, would she understand? Would she forgive him for lying? His mind grappled with the enormity of what he was about to say.

At the last moment, he changed his mind. "Stay disciplined, soldier," he thought to himself. "I think I'm going to steal one of these," he said as he took the last French fry from her plate. He felt like an idiot. It probably sounded like that French fry was a big deal to him.

Becky shared a look with Sarah. Both of them smiled. Maybe taking an item from another person's plate implied something he wasn't aware of.

Chapter 6

Monday morning came too soon for Antel. He was still tired from working for hours studying the data Irina had recorded of the signals. So far, all he had learned was that there were two different signals. One was weaker than the other.

The weaker one was most likely between points on Earth, which made sense. Every time the weaker signal started, there was always the presence of an "echo" somewhere else on Earth. The device needed for this signal strength could easily be disguised as a typical Terran smartphone. But as far as Antel knew, he was the only one with such a device. There was another one back at the farmhouse, but it was locked away for emergencies. They rarely needed it. Normally, they used cellular calls to keep the risk of discovery low.

The stronger signal, on the other hand, was far more baffling. A signal that strong probably meant someone was communicating with someone farther away from Earth. Were they talking to someone on Mars? Such a device would need to be larger and much harder to hide. But where? They still couldn't find either source.

Antel and Sandun walked between the academic buildings, trying to give the impression that they were discussing their studies. In reality, they were monitoring for signs of any subspace signals.

Irina had modified the second subspace-enabled communicator the day before to be able to detect signal strength, and Sandun was using it to watch for the next time the signal appeared and to alert

Antel.

After Saturday's museum visit with Becky and her friend Sarah, Antel felt even more determined to solve this mystery.

"Any activity yet?" Antel asked quietly as they passed a group of students.

"Nothing yet, sir." Sandun's gaze never left the communicator. Ironically, no one noticed because staring at a smartphone while walking seemed to be a common occurrence on Earth. "But if the pattern appears, I should detect it right away."

Antel walked alongside Sandun with his hands in his pockets, pretending to casually enjoy the scenery. In truth, he didn't have to pretend. He did enjoy the view of the trees and watching small colorful birds chirping on the branches.

With everyone dressed casually as students normally did, Antel's attention was immediately caught when a uniformed person emerged from the History building. It was Neil. He was with his sister Sarah.

Sarah saw Antel in the distance and waved hello to him. Antel waved back. Meanwhile, Neil tried to hide the scowl forming on his face. Though Neil and Sarah continued walking, his gaze lingered a moment too long.

"Is that him?" Sandun asked. "Miss Miller's ex-boyfriend?"

"Yes, that's him. He is making Miss Miller's life... complicated."

"Yours too, it would seem, my friend," Sandun said. "Would you like me to vaporize him with my sidearm?"

"What? No!" Antel turned to look at Sandun, wondering if he was serious. Sandun, of course, was smiling widely. He was only joking to pester Antel. "You know, if you weren't also my friend, I'd make you run laps around this campus."

"I can tell from his body language that he is more than just jealous," Sandun's intelligence training showed through. "He looks like he wants to get into a serious altercation with you."

"I'm sure he does," agreed Antel. "I'm not afraid of him."

"Be careful with this one. Military men develop instincts about other military men. Even if they can't explain why." Sandun kept his voice low. "He may suspect we're not who we claim to be."

Sandun had a point. That observation made Antel uneasy. He never considered that Neil's military training might make him more perceptive to their cover stories' flaws. "Should we be concerned?"

"Worth monitoring, but I think the threat is minimal for now." Sandun gave a quick assessment.

"Unless he becomes more aggressive towards Miss Miller." Antel took a deep breath. "I won't let that happen."

"Speaking of Miss Miller..." Sandun nodded toward the building entrance where Becky had just appeared, her dark hair softly moved by the breeze.

Becky smiled when she noticed Antel, but when she saw Neil walking Sarah to her next class, her expression turned uncertain.

"Andrew! I didn't expect you today." Becky looked like she was about to kiss him on the cheek, but stopped herself. She turned to Sandun and spoke to him. "Hello, are you one of Andrew's friends?"

Sandun reached out to shake her hand. As an intelligence officer, he was well-versed in the local traditions. It was a critical skill for him to do his job and blend in. "Yes, I'm Sam. It's a pleasure to meet you. Andrew has told me a lot about you."

Antel's heart almost sank. Was Sandun trying to embarrass him on purpose? It wasn't too late to make him do those laps.

"I was just giving Sam a tour of the campus," Antel said. That was partially true. Sam hadn't spent a lot of time on the campus. She didn't need to know the real reason why.

Sandun took the next opportunity to show his phone to Antel as he pointed to it when Becky faced Antel for a moment. Antel understood that Sandun was trying to communicate that he had just detected the signal.

Antel's pulse quickened, but he kept his expression neutral. The signal was near, and it was active.

"I was just headed to my next class," Becky pointed in the direction of another building off in the distance. "Would you like to walk me to my class?"

He was torn. Antel wanted to, but he had a duty to find that source. "I wish I could, but I'm waiting for Dr. Solomon. He's talking with Dr. Carter now."

"Oh, Carter's not there," Becky said. "She's the one teaching my next class over there."

"Oh? Then I wonder what's taking him so long." Antel made a

note to ask Dahnt when he returned.

"Are you okay?" Becky asked. "You seem distracted."

"It's just our coursework stuff," Sandun answered for Antel. Lying came easier for the intelligence officer.

"I saw Neil just a moment ago," Antel wanted to change the subject quickly. "Is he bothering you again?"

"Today, no," her eyes rolled. "But he just happens to show up wherever I am often. It's bordering on creepy."

"If he makes you uncomfortable, let me know." Antel couldn't believe he was offering her protection. Somehow, it came naturally to him. He gently put his hand on her shoulder. "I mean it."

"That's very sweet of you, thank you," Becky blushed at the thought that Antel's hand touched her shoulder. "But I got it covered. Anyway, Dr. Carter's class will be starting soon. I better get going. I'll see you later."

As Becky walked away, Sandun said, "Damn, the signal just ended."

"Any idea where it came from?" Antel asked.

"It has to be one of these buildings." Sandun pointed at the History building and the Engineering building.

At that moment, Dahnt came out the main door of the History building, adjusting his jacket. He approached Antel and Sandun. "Hello, gentlemen. Any progress with the signal?"

"We got close," Antel told him. "It was coming from one of these buildings. You didn't happen to see anything suspicious, did you?"

"I'm afraid not," Dahnt looked over at the other nearby building and pointed. "But that's the engineering building right there. You think they could be getting close to figuring out subspace?"

"I hope not. The Council wouldn't be happy hearing that their experts' estimates were so off."

"I would make it a point to investigate that building when you get a chance."

"By the way, I heard Dr. Carter wasn't in the building. Why did it take so long in there?" Sandun didn't want to forget the question.

"I had to ask the secretary of the History department where Dr. Carter's next class was. I'm planning to attend today's lecture."

"I see," Antel replied. That did make sense. "Enjoy the class.

Sandun and I will be canvassing the campus. Maybe make plans to look at the engineering building when it's safe to do so."

Dahnt parted ways with the two soldiers. Antel and Sandun spent another hour wandering the campus, but they never detected the signal again. All they knew was the general location and that it was the weaker signal, meaning someone might have a subspace communicator.

As they ended the day, Antel and Sandun walked back to the car to wait for Dahnt. Antel's thoughts drifted to Becky. His feelings for her were growing. But Neil made matters complicated with him always on guard to win her back. If anyone was going to suspect him of lying, it would be him.

"I know you are thinking of her," Sandun observed.

"How can you tell?"

"You don't have to be a spy like me to notice, my friend. It's clear to me she's on your mind."

"Doesn't matter," Antel said, with a hint of disappointment. "It would never work out. I would be compromising the mission."

"You know, my friend, caring for someone doesn't mean the mission is compromised."

"It kills me that I have to lie to her every day," Antel confessed.

"I admit, I don't know how I would handle that. Maybe just tell her the truth."

"The truth? Are you kidding?" That wasn't an option for him. "That would be a violation of the..."

"If her professor, Dr. Carter, can know, it would make sense that her student should be told. I'm sure the senior lieutenant would understand that it would be less complicated to be straightforward with her."

"You make a good point, but..."

Sandun stopped walking. His hand grabbed Antel's shoulder to stop him as well. "I heard an expression here on Earth—Rules were meant to be broken."

"There's no such expression," Antel didn't believe him.

"Believe me. I overheard someone saying it the other day." Sandun started to walk to the car again. "You know, if Miss Miller knew the truth, you could have asked her if such an expression really does exist."

Antel considered it. Maybe Sandun was right. He did nearly tell her on multiple occasions. He still wanted to. The only thing keeping him from telling her was the Standard Protocol. His duty was very important to him.

He'd been viewing his feelings for Becky as a liability, but if Neil's behavior escalated, Becky could be vulnerable. His presence in her life, despite the deception, might be the very thing that kept her safe.

Antel decided that he would abide by the Standard Protocol and not tell her, but remain by her side to keep her safe. The balance was going to be a challenge, but he owed it to her to keep her safe.

"Should we inform Senior Lieutenant Ranston about our progress?" Sandun asked as he unlocked the car and entered.

"Not yet. I don't want to risk the message getting intercepted." Antel entered the car as well. "For now, let's watch and wait."

After they waited in the car for Dahnt to join them, Sandun drove them back to the farmhouse. The ride was quiet as no one spoke much. Antel's mind wandered back to Becky and her safety. It probably helped that Sarah, Neil's sister, was good friends with her. Neil would think twice about upsetting his sister. At least that's what he hoped.

The irony wasn't lost on him that she was passionately questioning alien life finding Earth's signals when an alien sat right next to her, who was there because of exactly that reason.

Antel thought about her questions. Would she understand if he told her the truth? Would she even believe him? Oh Universe! He so badly wanted to tell her, but his duty made that impossible. The turmoil in his stomach felt like a thunderstorm.

His mind went back and forth. Should he tell her or should he keep the secret?

As hard as it was to make the choice, he had to make the mission his priority.

Chapter 7

Antel sat at the kitchen table in the farmhouse, flanked by Sandun and Irina. They were studying the campus map displayed on their datapad, obtained from the secret Rileean satellite in orbit around the Earth. The Rileean satellite had scanned the interior of buildings as well as mapped the area using its quantum scanner. Quantum scanners took hours to generate results and weren't reliable for detecting people or other moving objects or smaller details, but they did a good job of obtaining a fuzzy layout of the walls, which made a decent blueprint draft.

The three of them carefully reviewed the scan results of the engineering building, looking for the least conspicuous approach.

"How about right here?" Sandun said, leaning over Antel's shoulder to point at the map. "It has the least foot traffic, if we go late at night."

Antel turned to face Irina. "How long do you think it will take to unlock the door?"

Irina pulled her dark hair back into a practical ponytail. "I think it will take a few minutes to disable the electronic locks. But I won't be able to do anything about the system logs. If they track when the doors are unlocked, we may have to be fast."

"And the cameras?" Sandun was thorough. He was well-experienced in covert actions like this.

"I can disable those with a targeted EMP right here." She pointed at a small closet in the corner of the building. "This looks like the surveillance server room. One of these will erase everything on the hard drives as well as render the equipment inoperable." She placed a small cylindrical object on the table. "They aren't going to be happy we fried their servers."

"Great work," Antel said, sitting back in his chair. "We should easily get in and out in a matter of minutes. With any luck, we'll find a subspace radio experiment running. In its early stages, subspace technology produced weak signals and necessitated bulky equipment. If it turns out to be Terran, we'll leave it there and report how advanced it is. If it's one of ours, we'll confiscate it and determine who's making unauthorized calls if we can."

Dahnt Sallain walked into the kitchen and grabbed the coffee pot for a refill. "Looks like you all are deep in thought. What are you working on?"

"We're going to check out the engineering building that you recommended." Antel had no reason not to tell him. Dahnt already knew about the mysterious signals. Besides, this action was his idea.

"Is that happening tonight?" He leaned against the kitchen counter and took a sip of his coffee. Sandun's spy skills told him something was suspicious about Dahnt's momentary interest, but he dismissed it as his imagination.

"Yes." Antel turned to Sandun and Irina. "We should plan for 2 AM local time."

"I see." Dahnt stopped leaning on the counter and walked slowly toward the living room. "I will obviously be back from the faculty dinner with Dr. Carter by that time."

While planning out floor-by-floor search plans, Antel's communicator buzzed. It was a message from Becky: "Coffee shop tomorrow morning before class?"

Antel couldn't help but smile. Sandun noticed and smirked. "Miss Miller, sir?"

"Yeah. Give me a minute." Antel began typing a reply. "Love to. 9 AM at the campus coffee shop?"

Her response came quickly: "Sweet! Can't wait to see you." The message included a symbol in the shape of a yellow circle with a smile in it.

Antel suppressed the guilt that always accompanied him when

they spent time together. Right now, he needed to keep his head straight. This covert mission needed precision, even if he didn't expect much to come of it.

He turned off the datapad and stood up. "I would recommend we get a good rest before the mission. We will still have a regular day ahead of us in the morning."

The alarm clock in Antel's communicator woke him from his nap. He looked at the time. "We have a few hours. Time to go," he said to himself as he got out of bed and began to change into his black and gray uniform. The uniform's design was nearly identical to his ordinary red and black uniform, except it was colored with a black and gray camouflage pattern.

When he entered the living room to meet up with Irina and Sandun, he saw they had already gathered the necessary gear for the mission: positronic energy pistols, kinetic energy personal shields, helmets with night vision, and a small pack of gadgets Irina, the technology expert, was going to need.

The first thing they did when they arrived at the campus was trigger a power outage for the side of the campus where the engineering building was located. The lights and cameras were all taken out. The security feeds in the building, if they were still running, were likely powered by backup power sources.

Everything was eerily quiet. The team was accustomed to the light hum of students' voices. The only thing they could hear was insects chirping. The three proceeded single file with Sandun in front and Irina in back. Antel was in the middle because Sandun insisted on keeping the highest-ranking officer in a safer position. Antel didn't want to take advantage of his rank, but he didn't have a good reason to question Sandun's suggestion.

They reached the side entrance they had agreed to use when the plan was established the night before. All three dropped to their knees to remain low.

Irina moved to the front and opened her bag. She pulled out a datapad and a small object the size of her palm. To a Terran, it looked like a high-tech hockey puck. It was a password cracking device that connected to any system's wiring and hacked it. The device attached to the door using a magnet. She turned on the datapad and connected to the device. The datapad displayed scrolling numbers using the Arkonian numeral system. After almost a minute, the scrolling stopped. The code was cracked, and the door clicked open. Sandun pulled it open and entered the building first. Antel and Irina followed.

The entrance they had selected was near the server room where the surveillance footage was saved. They chose that entrance for that reason. Irina pulled out another device that looked similar to the first, only a bit larger. She had to hold it in place against the door because the door wasn't made of metal.

The door used a normal physical lock that they didn't want to damage. Breaking down the door was out of the question. The team hoped that knocking out the server without unlocking the door would make it look like an ordinary mechanical failure.

It only took seconds. "Done," whispered Irina. "Surveillance server and its data are disabled."

The three stood up now that the cameras weren't watching them anymore and proceeded to each door on that floor along the main hallway. The doors had glass windows for looking inside without opening them. They took scans and visually searched each room from the hallway.

When they finished the first floor, they went up the stairs and started on the second floor.

They moved swiftly from door to door, looking into each room through the glass. The hallway was dark, and the only sounds heard were their footsteps.

"Contact ahead," Sandun called out in a low voice so that only Antel and Irina could hear. "Movement detected at the end of the hallway."

Antel peeked around the corner and quickly returned. He saw a distinctive light blue glow. That was no security guard's flashlight. That was a Rileean scanner!

"We're not alone," Antel whispered. "They look Arkonian, not local security."

Before anyone could ask questions, a blue particle beam that looked like lightning flashed past the team, hitting the wall and scorching it. The three took cover by some of the doors. Fortunately for them, the doors were inset into the wall a few feet, giving them decent cover.

Several more shots were fired, making more marks on the wall at the end of the hallway.

"Particle beam weapons!" Irina couldn't help but yell out. "Those are definitely Arkonians. Maybe Rileean."

"Pull back," Antel ordered.

The three of them, with their pistols facing toward the corner where Antel had peered, moved backward one doorway at a time.

When they reached the last few doors along their path right before the stairwell, the assailants—two of them—aimed their rifles and fired several rapid shots in succession.

The team had little choice but to return fire to keep the assailants from advancing further. Instead, they took cover in the inset doorways at their end of the hallway.

"They're trying to pin us down," Sandun said as the assailants took turns firing while the other took cover.

These are not basic combat tactics, Antel thought. He recognized their pattern as Rileean Imperial Forces.

When Antel got a better look at them, he saw that they wore exactly the same black and gray uniform as he did. Even the dull-colored flags on their shoulders were Rileean.

With his back to the wall, staying out of the line of fire, Antel yelled out in Intallan, "Hold your fire! We are Rileean!"

There was a moment of pause. Antel considered peeking around and looking, but a streak of blue shot past him at Irina. She fired back, but her shot shattered the glass window behind the assailants.

"Ah!" Irina screamed in pain. "I'm hit!"

Antel had expected that if there was going to be trouble, it would have been from local authorities. That's why the team had brought their kinetic shields to protect against bullets. These energy weapons sliced through those shields as if they weren't even there.

"Kossdra!" Antel wanted to kick himself. "If I'd known we were going to face our own, I would have brought the energy shields instead."

Sandun was stronger than Antel, so Antel ordered him to get Irina out of there while he laid down suppression fire.

"Are you sure, sir?" Sandun didn't want to leave his lieutenant behind.

"Go! Now!" Antel poked his arm around the doorway's corner and began taking multiple random shots. The goal wasn't to hit them but to keep them from shooting at Sandun and Irina.

Irina was able to keep her pistol steady in her right hand. Her left arm was charred and in pain. Fortunately, it was just a graze. A more solid hit would certainly have killed her.

"Let's go, Ensign." Sandun grabbed her shirt by the shoulders and dragged her into the stairwell. She was able to take shots back at the assailants. She hit one, but he was wearing an energy shield, keeping him from getting injured. Energy shields don't block one hundred percent of the energy, so the assailant took some damage, but it was minor. The ensign kept targeting him. She knew each hit drained the shield's batteries, so it was only a matter of time before the shield would fail.

She didn't get that far before Sandun was able to close the stairwell doors. He helped her get up and stay on her feet while they ran out of the building.

Antel was still in the hallway. Alone. He had a chance and fired his pistol at what appeared to be some sort of fuse box on the wall. The positrons, also known as anti-electrons, sparked a surge of electricity, causing the lights in the hall to light up brighter than they normally did and explode into bright sparks. The shooting temporarily stopped as the shooters, who were caught by surprise, tore off the eye-gear from their faces. Antel knew the night vision gear they had was going to be susceptible to that flash.

This allowed Antel to make a run for the stairs. He closed the door behind him and, with a low setting on the pistol, fired at the handle, melting it shut. He made a dash down the stairs and out of the building. He lost sight of Sandun and Irina, but he was hopeful they had made it to safety.

Antel ran back to the car but used a different route to hide his position from the assailants. When he was about halfway to the car, he saw it drive up and stop. Sandun had brought the car to him.

Irina was in the backseat, clutching her left arm. Her face was wrinkled in pain.

Sandun drove them for about ten minutes until they reached a neighborhood park where they could stop. Antel got out of the car and reentered it in the back.

"Let me see." Antel gently peeled back a flap of cloth that was torn from the shot that had wounded her. "Looks bad. You need medical attention."

"I'm sure Dalan can patch me up," she said through clenched teeth.

"Those were Rileean weapons and tactics," Sandun said, keeping watch. "Why would our own people attack us?"

"Good question." Antel's mind raced through all the possibilities he could think of. None made sense. "They knew we were coming. It was a trap."

"Are we being watched?" Irina strained to add to the conversation.

"It's possible," Sandun surmised. "I'll have to check our spy satellite when we get home. I think it's time this is reported to Senior Lieutenant Ranston."

"I agree," Antel said, "but not through a subspace message. This must be related to those mystery signals, and I don't want them to intercept our report. Subspace communications aren't secure anymore. I may have to go back to Mars in person."

Sandun rushed back to the farmhouse. A local hospital was out of the question. There was no way they would know how to treat an antimatter burn. Antel called ahead to have Dalan Myros, the medical officer, get ready.

When the car drove up to the house, Dalan was already standing outside waiting. He rushed to the backseat door and opened it. Antel and Dalan helped Irina into the farmhouse and into her room, where Dalan could examine her wound.

"This looks serious," Dalan said, with a disappointed look on his face. "I'm afraid I won't be able to treat her with what I have here. We'll need to get her to Mars. They have the necessary equipment for this."

"Will she be able to make the trip?" Antel was concerned about his ensign.

"Sure," Dalan said. "I'm going to give her a relaxant to ease the pain. She'll be a mindless mess during the whole trip, but she'll be fine."

"That's good news." Antel was glad that she had options. "I'll have Zhon land the Black Cat tomorrow night, and we'll take her back to Mars."

"We?" Dalan looked confused.

"Zhon will take me and Irina to Mars. I have to speak to Ranston, and I can't do it over subspace."

"I see." Dalan's confused look disappeared. "I'll keep her sedated and give you enough for the trip."

"Kossdra." Antel just remembered Becky. "I made plans to see her tomorrow. I'll need to cancel."

"That isn't necessary." It was no secret to the team that Antel and Becky were growing closer. "You go meet up with her. We have Irina's wounds under control. I have her stabilized for now."

"I suppose I should use it as a pretense to check out what chaos might be stirring in the engineering building due to last night's mission," Antel said.

Dalan only rolled his eyes. "Whatever works. Now get out. I have a patient to attend to."

The next morning, Antel waited at the campus coffee shop. He always ordered hot chocolate because he didn't like the taste of coffee, but today he might make an exception. He'd tried to sleep during the remaining hours after the mission, but he couldn't fall asleep. His mind was on Irina's injuries. The caffeine might help. He was exhausted.

When Becky walked in, her smile brightened his mood. She was wearing a blue sweater that accentuated her figure, making Antel feel that guilt between his duty and his growing attraction to her.

"You look so tired," she commented, sliding into the seat next to him. "Did you spend the whole night studying?"

"Not exactly." He didn't want to lie to her, but figured it would be easier to tell her a close enough story. "Irene got a serious injury to her arm last night." Irene was Irina's Terran name. "Now I need to help get her back home to a specialist because of some rare infection she picked up."

"Oh my, it sounds serious," Becky said, genuinely concerned. "Will she be okay?"

"Yeah. The doctor here is giving her painkillers so she can make the trip."

"Did you say you had to leave too?" Becky didn't seem to like that idea. "Are you and her…"

"Me and her?" He wasn't sure what she meant at first. "Oh, me and her! No! No! She's like a sister to me. We're not in a relationship."

Becky's smile returned. She put her hand on his and squeezed. "That's good to know." She didn't let go of his hand for a long time.

"I'm going to need to go out of town for a week or two," Antel told her. "She won't be able to make it home by herself. She needs my help."

"You are so kind and helpful. She's lucky to have you as a friend."

"Thank you."

"Just promise you'll hurry back," she said with a playful smile. "I know this really good Italian restaurant. I might have to invite someone else in your place."

Antel knew he should pull his hand away and maintain professional distance, but he couldn't. Instead, he took his free hand and placed it on hers. Now he was holding her hand with both of his. "We can't have that. I promise to get back as quickly as I can."

She blushed at that comment. Antel felt an ache in his heart. He was getting too deep, but he had to keep focused on who tried to kill him in last night's mission.

"What's going on over there?" Antel needed to change the subject before his heart made him make a mistake with his cover story. "It looks like an intense investigation."

"Yeah, last night there was a break-in," she said, looking at the engineering building as she spoke. "I heard there was a lot of damage inside."

"Wow. Do they know who did it?" He wanted to know if anyone was able to identify them.

"No, I don't think so." She turned back to face him. "The news is saying that the security cameras were damaged in the break-in. They might never find out."

"Interesting." Sounds like his team's identity was safe for now.

"I hate to leave you, but I have a class to get to soon," Becky said reluctantly.

Antel stood up as she stood up. Before he could react, she stretched up on her toes and kissed his cheek. "Have a safe flight," she whispered in his ear.

Antel froze. His heart rate felt like it doubled, and his face turned red.

Becky noticed and smiled at him. Her face was still within inches of his.

Antel watched her leave the coffee shop. He thought about the kiss on the cheek, but the activity at the engineering building, visible from the coffee shop window, reminded him of the mission and his near-fatal encounter.

Chapter 8

The Black Cat lifted off from Earth in the dead of night. After reaching space, Zhon guided the ship into low Earth orbit before setting a Mars rendezvous trajectory. The autopilot maintained acceleration at ninety percent of Earth gravity to minimize strain on Irina, who lay sedated in a bed in one of the quarters.

Zhon came down from the bridge deck to check on Irina. Antel was standing in Irina's room, already keeping an eye on her. "Course set for Mars. Should take four and a half days to arrive."

"Good to know." Antel barely registered the trajectory information, his gaze fixed on Irina's pale face. No officer was immune from feeling responsible for their subordinates' safety. Antel was no exception.

"How's she doing?" Zhon asked.

"The medic stabilized her. For now, she's fine as long as she stays sedated."

"Can you tell me anything about what happened down there?" Zhon was curious.

"Not yet," Antel said, keeping his voice neutral. "I want to brief Senior Lieutenant Ranston first." Zhon was a good friend to Antel, but as an officer, he couldn't justify telling people who didn't already know until the situation could be figured out. Antel was completely certain Zhon had nothing to do with the mysterious signals, but to be fair, he couldn't make an exception just because of that friendship.

Zhon nodded. "Understood. How long has it been since you've slept?"

"Not sure," Antel had lost track. "Day or two, maybe."

"You should get some rest. I'll wake you if anything changes with Irina's condition."

Antel wasn't sure he would be able to sleep with everything stirring around in his mind—Irina, the subspace signals, Becky, the list went on—but exhaustion claimed him almost immediately.

The next morning, Antel spent most of his time either checking on Irina or drafting and redrafting his mission report for Ranston. The skirmish in the engineering building suggested a serious breach of the Standard Protocol. Was there a competing Rileean operation on Earth? If so, why? And why attack their fellow people?

Antel spent the next four days organizing his thoughts. He wanted his report to be perfect before reaching Mars. He struggled to find a way to explain his relationship with Becky without getting himself into trouble.

As the Black Cat approached Mars orbit, Zhon made several adjustments to the trajectory to put the ship into a stable orbit. The usual plan was to make several orbits until a landing was made, but because of Irina, the plan was rushed. They were only going to make one orbit and land as soon as possible. Each orbit would take only a few hours, demanding Zhon's complete focus on navigation until touchdown.

Antel made sure Irina was properly strapped down to her bed to prevent injury, then strapped himself into his seat in the common deck. Because Irina was no longer in his view, his mind turned to Mars. It reminded him that Nela was going to be there, and that made his stomach tighten. Inevitably he would have to face her again.

Antel hadn't thought of Nela since meeting Becky. He was going to have to make an extra effort to avoid her. After their breakup, he had welcomed the Earth assignment as an escape. But now thoughts of Becky's smile intruded whenever memories of Nela surfaced.

The Black Cat touched down next to the base on the landing pad. The base's access tunnel stretched out and connected to the external hatch of the ship. The edges of the hatch gave a quick hiss as it opened. The pressure didn't need to be equalized, as both sides were already at normal pressure.

A medical team was already waiting to transfer Irina to the infirmary. Antel watched them carry her away on a stretcher before heading to Ranston's office.

The passageways of the base felt strange after so much time on Earth. The subtle red tint of Martian sunlight filtering through the passageway windows, the slight spring in his step from the lower gravity, the familiar hum of life support systems—it all seemed both foreign and yet achingly familiar.

Senior Lieutenant Ranston was waiting behind his desk when Antel entered. The office was spartanly furnished, with only a few personal items: a digital picture of Ranston's home city on Rilee, and an archaic gunpowder-powered rifle mounted on the wall.

"Lieutenant Ralnar." Ranston gestured to a chair. He didn't look happy. "I understand bringing Ensign Irina Falron back to Mars. What I don't understand is why you felt the need to return, too."

Antel took a deep breath. "Sir, just before returning, my team detected more of those subspace signals originating from the engineering building at the university. We investigated, following planned protocols for covert operations on Earth. We weren't sure whether we would find Earth-based technology or our own, if anything at all."

"Then?" Ranston asked as he reclined into his seat.

"Instead of finding any technology, we were ambushed by armed opposition. Rileean opposition."

Ranston leaned forward with his palms flat on his desk and took a sharp breath. "What? Are you telling me the truth, Lieutenant?"

"Yes, sir." Antel remained still in his chair.

Ranston's expression hardened. "Explain."

"They wore the same uniforms as we were wearing. Same gear too. They moved according to regular Rileean tactics. And..."

"And?"

"They fired on us with beam weapons—positronic rifles. We were outgunned with only our pistols. Ensign Falron was wounded by a positron burn as we fell back."

"How are you sure they're Rileean?"

"I called out for a cease-fire in Intallan. I could tell they understood me because they took a second to look at each other as if to get permission to continue. They knew we were going to be there and planned an ambush."

Ranston stood and walked to the window, staring out at the dusty Martian landscape. "Tell me about these subspace signals. Were you able to intercept the messages?"

"Not entirely, sir. We took recordings whenever we could, but they were encrypted with an algorithm we don't have in our database."

"Maybe it's time to abort the mission and bring everyone else still down there back."

Antel froze. He had promised Becky he would be right back. If Ranston ordered the Black Cat to retrieve the others, he wouldn't even get the chance to say goodbye.

He had to think fast. "Sir, I think aborting would be a bad idea. The Terrans will question our disappearance and may start investigating. The farmhouse would be in jeopardy."

"We can have Dr. Sallain tell the Terran professor we're aborting."

"True, but there are others." Antel knew he couldn't confess to Ranston about Becky. "The professor has students and colleagues who won't know the truth. One of them is bound to get suspicious." Antel wasn't sure he was convincing the senior lieutenant. He barely would have believed it himself.

Ranston crossed his arms and looked down at the floor. "On the other hand, we may need to find out who these unauthorized personnel are and what they are up to. If we leave, they won't have us interfering with their plans, whatever those plans are."

Antel exhaled. It appeared that Ranston had changed his mind on his own. "This means we should continue the mission, then?"

"We might as well," Ranston said, sitting back down and looking at Antel directly. "You have a second objective. Find out what they are doing, and who they are, and report back to me."

"But the subspace channels may be compromised. They might get alerted to our plans."

"Use your best judgment. If I don't hear from you, I'll assume you're in radio silence."

"Understood, sir." Antel stood up in anticipation of being dismissed shortly.

"And Ralnar," Ranston said. "Finding and dealing with the unauthorized personnel is your priority. The research is secondary. Let Sallain handle the research on his own."

"Understood," Antel said again.

"Be careful. Someone was willing to kill to protect whatever they are doing."

"Will you be reporting this up the chain?" Antel was curious.

"No. Like you said, they might intercept those messages. I won't be able to switch the encryption method without them finding out what we switch it to."

"Very true, sir."

"How is Falron doing?" Ranston changed the subject.

"The medic was able to stabilize her. He believes the base will be able to heal her." Antel informed him. "I was going to check on her later once the medical staff had a chance to evaluate her."

"Good. When she's better, I'll let her return with you. You will still need a technology expert. I wouldn't use her for combat, though. Dismissed."

As Antel left Ranston's office, a storm of thoughts swirled in his mind. The senior lieutenant's reluctance to report up the chain suggested he shared Antel's concerns about high-level involvement. But before he could ponder the situation further, a familiar voice stopped him in his tracks.

"Antel?"

Turning to see who had called out for him, Antel saw Nela standing in the passageway. Her sharp blond hair flowed freely instead of in her usual bun that she would put her hair in to keep it out of her work. Her expression was a mix of hope and uncertainty.

"Nela," Antel acknowledged her but said nothing else. He didn't feel like actually saying the word 'hello' and let her assume it was implied. He kept his voice professional, despite the tightness developing in his chest.

He was going to continue walking past her, but she stepped into his path. "I heard you were back. Can we talk?"

"Not now, Nela." Another short reply.

"Let's meet over dinner," Nela suggested.

"The Terrans have an expression. Tell your new guy that I don't want to be a third wheel." He tried stepping to the side, but she stepped to the side again to keep him from leaving.

"I have no idea what that even means. Please, just one conversation," Nela pleaded.

Antel thought of Becky's smile, of their conversations in the coffee shop, of the way she had kissed his cheek. But he couldn't tell Nela about any of that. "I'm sorry, I have a lot of work to do before heading back to Earth."

Nela's voice softened. "I made a mistake, Antel, giving you up for Syandos. I've regretted it every day since, and I am so sorry."

"Nela..." Antel sighed. "This was what you wanted. We both need to live with it."

"But things are different now. I've changed. That grad student... I don't think it's going to work out. I realized what really matters." She reached for his hand, but he pulled away.

"I need to go to the infirmary to check on Ensign Falron." It wasn't entirely a lie, but it was an escape. "Take care of yourself, Nela."

He walked away with a quick and intentional pace. Before he left for Earth, hearing those words from her would have meant the universe to him. Now they just made him feel empty. His heart was four days away on another planet, probably grading papers for her professor in a coffee shop and wondering when he would return.

In the infirmary, Irina was awake and alert. The medical staff had applied artificial flesh to the injury from the particle beam, though she would need several days of therapy before returning to duty and several more before she would be combat-ready.

"How are you feeling, Ensign?" Antel asked, resting a hand briefly on her uninjured shoulder to show he genuinely cared about her health.

"Much better, sir." She attempted to sit up, but the pain kept her from doing so. "Did you speak to Senior Lieutenant Ranston? I am so ready to go back and kick some ass."

"At ease, soldier," Antel smiled, pleased that her spirits were still good. "I did speak with him. He nearly aborted the mission, but he decided we need to get to the bottom of whatever conspiracy those assailants are up to."

"That's terrific. I'm ready. When do we head back?"

"But…" he added, "you aren't going to do any fighting. You're just my tech expert."

"I understand," she said with a disappointed tone.

"Get some rest. I'll need you in better shape when we return." Antel squeezed her good hand. "We're dealing with something bigger than we thought, and I need people I can count on."

"Thank you, sir. I won't disappoint you."

"You haven't yet." Antel smiled and then left Irina to get her rest.

That evening, alone in his quarters, Antel composed a message to Becky: "Medical specialist very optimistic about Irene's recovery. Missing our coffee shop conversations. Save me a seat?"

This message would have been beamed via subspace to the spy satellite around Earth and then sent to the cellphone provider as a text message.

He stared at the words for a long time before deleting them. Every subspace message was a risk. Not to mention, if anyone intercepted that message, it would put Becky in danger, and that was unacceptable to him.

As he thought about Nela's plea, he realized something had changed in him during his time on Earth. He was no longer just an observer of Terran life—he had become part of it. And somewhere between maintaining his cover and investigating mysterious signals, he had found something real with Becky.

The question was, could he protect her while uncovering whatever conspiracy had nearly gotten them killed in that engineering building? As he drifted off to sleep, Antel couldn't shake the feeling that those two challenges were somehow going to clash. He just had to figure out how to balance his feelings and his mission before everything fell apart.

Chapter 9

Antel adjusted his coat as he waited outside Becky's parents' home. The breeze was chilly, but his anxiety stemmed from more than just the wind. The skirmish in the engineering building last week occupied his thoughts.

When Becky emerged wearing a dark blue dress, his problems momentarily vanished. Her smile warmed him.

"Ready for the best Italian food in Denver?" she asked.

"Lead the way." He offered his arm, recalling his research on Earth's dating protocols. Not much differed from Arkonus customs.

As they walked to his car, he noticed her glancing at his face. "Something wrong?" she asked. "You seem distracted."

"Sorry. Just processing some unexpected developments in my research." That was only half true. The signals and the skirmish were both unexpected, and both were affecting the team's research. Still, each lie burned another scar in his heart.

The restaurant occupied a converted mansion from the Silver Boom period, built during Denver's mining prime. Original brick walls, lavish wooden trim, and high-ceilinged rooms now served the city's Italian food scene. The smell of garlic and herbs filled the restaurant, warm light glimmering off the restored brass fixtures.

After they were seated in a corner booth beneath an original bay window, Becky leaned forward. "So, how's Irene doing? Is she going to be okay?"

"She's doing much better," Antel replied. "As a matter of fact, her doctor let her return to Denver as long as she takes it easy."

"That's great news. I'm happy for her." Becky paused as their waiter brought water and took their orders. Once he left, she continued in a lower voice. "Have you heard about what they found at the engineering building?"

Antel's pulse quickened, but he did his best to keep calm. "Not much. What are people saying?"

"Strange stuff. The police initially investigated, but the military took over almost immediately. They've been super secretive about it." She took a sip of water. "And Neil's involved somehow."

"Neil?" Antel set down his glass carefully. "Are you sure?"

"Yeah. I've seen him spending a lot of time at the engineering building, talking with other officers. He looks... intense. More than usual. And no one else has been allowed in."

The waiter returned with their appetizer, a plate of homemade meatballs. Antel used the interruption to gather his thoughts. "Have they released any details?"

"Nothing official. But Neil's sister, Sarah, overheard him saying some of the surveillance footage survived."

Antel nearly choked on his food. "What?"

"They couldn't identify anyone, though. The intruders wore some kind of uniform, but no one recognized it." Becky studied his reaction. "You okay?"

"Just went down the wrong way." He took a sip of water to help clear his throat. The footage would show Rileean combat uniforms. Even if they couldn't identify individuals, those uniforms would raise questions.

His communicator vibrated in his pocket. Probably Sandun with an update. He ignored it, but he could tell Becky still heard it.

"The strangest part," Becky continued, "was the weapons they used. Sarah said the investigators were baffled by the damage patterns. Like nothing they'd seen before."

The weapons she was referring to were particle beam weapons. Of course, they wouldn't recognize the effects. Antel's communicator buzzed again.

"Sorry," he said, checking the display under the table. Multiple urgent messages from Sandun. "I need to take this. Would you mind?"

Becky's face fell slightly, but she nodded. "No problem, go ahead."

In the restaurant's quiet hallway near the restrooms, Antel opened his communicator and put it to his ear. "What is it?"

"Sir, we've detected the signal again," Sandun's voice came through clearly. "A new encryption pattern from before. This is the stronger signal. I think they're talking to someone off-world."

Antel glanced toward their table, where Becky sat alone with their appetizer. "Do we have a location?"

"I'm afraid not. I just detected it when I arrived home. I will need to leave to begin triangulating. If we meet now..."

"I can't. Not right now." The words felt heavy. "You got this. Take Emira if you need her."

"But..."

"Do what you can. I'll be there as soon as I can." Antel ended the call and returned to the table just as their main courses arrived.

"Everything okay?" Becky asked as he sat down.

"Minor issue. Irene needed to know where her medicine was." He maintained a neutral expression.

While they ate, Becky shared stories about her graduate research. Antel nodded at appropriate moments, but his attention drifted to the mission's mounting problems: mystery subspace signals, rogue Rileean soldiers, and possibly an off-world threat—perhaps on Mars itself.

He should be with Sandun, tracking the hostile Rileean forces personally. Yet leaving now would raise questions with Becky. He told himself he was staying with her because he didn't want to compromise his cover further, but Antel knew that wasn't true.

Becky could see Antel's mind was wandering and suspected it had something to do with the incident that occurred in the engineering building, so she changed the subject back to it. "By the way, about the investigation..." She paused to pull in a strand of spaghetti into her mouth. "Neil's been asking questions about you."

Antel set down his fork. "Me? Why me?"

"He cornered me after class yesterday. This time, he had the help of some of his subordinates."

"Did he harm you or try to frighten you?" Antel interrupted her.

"No. He wouldn't dare with his subordinates watching," she assured him. "He asked stuff like what you majored in, how we met."

"Questions that sound more about our relationship than about the incident in the engineering building."

"I know, right!" She tapped her fork on the table as if she were lightly stabbing it. "But he did ask some stuff about the engineering building. He seemed... suspicious."

"What did you tell him about me?"

"At first, when he started asking questions about us, I told him it was none of his business," she said. "But then he threw 'this is official business' at me."

"And?"

"The truth. You're a visiting graduate student working under Dr. Solomon." She tilted her head. "Was there something else I was supposed to tell him?"

"No. Sounds like you got it right." Antel made a conscious effort to keep his voice steady. Now that the Terran military... not the Terran military, the American military. Now that they were involved, things were going to get harder to balance. The fact that somehow Neil was put in charge added an extra level of complexity.

His communicator vibrated again. This time, he couldn't ignore it. The message was from Ensign Emira Khen. "Having trouble triangulating signal. Appears to be randomly jumping from location to location."

"Damn the Universe!" Antel thought to himself. He wondered if his decision not to be with them was making it harder for them. "Becky, I'm so sorry, but..."

"You have to go, don't you?" she finished his sentence with a hint of disappointment. "I understand. Really."

The waiter took Antel's payment and packed up the remainder of their order for them to take home.

As before, Antel opened the car door for her. This time, she surprised him by taking his hand.

"Whatever's going on," she said quietly, "be careful, okay?"

"Why do you say that?" Antel looked at her, wondering if she was seeing through his cover story.

"The timing of Irene's accident, the break-in at the engineering building, Neil's line of questioning, and now these urgent calls." She squeezed his hand to show she wasn't upset with him. "I'm not a fool, Andrew. I know something is going on. Something you can't tell me."

The urge to tell her everything returned. He wanted to say, "I'm not who you think I am. I come from another planet." But any breach of the Standard Protocol could end the mission and his career.

"It's complicated," he tried to remain vague.

She studied his face, wondering what lay behind his eyes, then rose on her tiptoes and softly touched his lips with hers and kissed him. "When you can tell me, I'll listen."

That kiss nearly stopped his heart. That kiss was now the only thing on his mind. He clasped her arms gently, met her gaze, then drew her close and returned her kiss.

After dropping Becky off, Antel drove back to the farmhouse. A storm brewed in his head. Unauthorized Rileean forces on Earth meant serious implications. Neil's involvement complicated an already precarious situation. Worse still, Becky might end up caught in the crossfire. The mission was slipping from his control, and his growing feelings for her only made it harder.

Sandun met him at the door. "Sir, we lost the signal a few minutes ago. We weren't able to locate it. We weren't even close."

"Show me what you have." Antel headed for the work shed. Sandun followed him.

Irina was already in the work shed, monitoring for more signals. Her arm was wrapped in a protective fabric to help it heal. When Antel walked in, she instinctively stood up. "Sir, we lost the..."

"Yes, I know," Antel said. "Please sit back down. You're still healing."

"Yes, sir. Thank you." She sat back down and turned towards the computer monitor. "You can see from the triangulation data that Junior Lieutenant Kandos took that the signal strength was all over the board. There was no way to pinpoint the real location."

"You tried." Antel wasn't disappointed in them. He felt more guilty for not assisting. "I should have been here to help."

"There wasn't much you could have done," Sandun tried to reassure Antel.

"Hack into the American military's network systems. Find out what you can about someone named Captain Neil Morris and his investigation of the engineering building skirmish."

"On it." Irina already began to work on it. With Rileean artificial intelligence technology, hacking the system wasn't going to be hard, only time-consuming.

"Oh, and place a monitoring program to keep us informed on their progress," Antel added.

Sandun spoke up, "Should we notify Mars?"

"No," Antel said. "Subspace communications aren't secure."

"Understood," Sandun said.

Antel walked back to the farmhouse. He walked at a slow pace, thinking. He thought to himself, "What does Captain Morris already know about the mission? We need to know what he's learned."

As for the unauthorized Rileean soldiers, Antel vowed that the next time he encountered them, he would be ready.

Later that night, alone in his room, Antel reviewed his personal logs one last time before going to bed. The mission was getting harder by the day. He needed to regain control of the situation before it spiraled further out of control.

His communicator buzzed. Becky sent a message. "Thanks for dinner and a wonderful time. We still have that dessert to finish."

Despite having to end their date early, she was remarkably flexible. It was clear to Antel that she was falling for him as much as he was falling for her.

Antel smiled. The happy feeling didn't last long. He couldn't forget that he had to protect her. Keeping her at arm's length was going to prove hard. As he typed his response, he wondered if he was protecting her or just protecting himself.

Chapter 10

Antel adjusted his seat in the campus coffee shop to put his back to the wall, ensuring he had a clear view of the entrance as Becky sat down across from him and pulled out her laptop.

"Check this out," Becky said as she brought up something on her laptop and swiveled it around for him to see. "This chapter is going to be about the technologies that shaped international relations during the Cold War. Pretty neat, huh?"

Antel scanned through it, not reading carefully since English characters didn't come naturally to him. Still, he grasped the general idea. Earth's Cold War wasn't all that different from Arkonus's. If anything, Earth showed better restraint. Arkonus was guilty of using a few nuclear bombs here and there, though they kept it to a minimum. They weren't stupid. They knew the effects it would have on the planet.

"Very fascinating," Antel commented. "It is so true that technology will have a powerful effect on the course of history. No matter the species."

Becky paused. "Species? The way you say that makes it sound like you're observing Earth from the outside." She smiled. "Like Earth was a test case." She laughed, but her gaze lingered a bit out of curiosity.

Antel immediately regretted the way he had worded that. Something they call here, 'lost in translation.' He meant to say no matter the culture, but habit made him say species. At least he didn't say planet. He almost said that.

Before Antel could fix his mistake by clarifying what he meant to say, the coffee shop's door opened, and in strode Neil. He looked like a man accustomed to having authority. He scanned the store and eventually found Becky. He approached their table with a smile that faltered when he noticed Antel was there with her.

"Becks!" Neil said, attempting to sound warm. His gaze briefly turned to Antel before returning to Becky. "What a coincidence running into you here."

Becky didn't believe it was a coincidence. "Hello, Neil," she greeted him coldly. It didn't matter how many times she told him, he never seemed to get it through his head that she disliked the nickname 'Becks.'

Antel sat back and observed Neil's body language. Neil was attempting to sound friendly, but the tension in his shoulders and his sharp gaze suggested an underlying agenda. Antel simply crossed his arms in his chair, waiting to see if he would need to intervene.

"I didn't expect you two were... uh... studying together," Neil continued. "Let me join you," he said, not waiting for an invitation. He pulled a chair from the adjacent table and turned it backwards. He sat in it with his chest pressed to the back of the chair and his arms resting along the top of the seat's back.

Becky was visibly getting more annoyed. Antel remained quiet, still assessing if and how he would need to intervene.

"So..." Neil looked over at Antel. "Andrew, right? My sister has mentioned you a few times. You're a grad student, too, I take it?"

"That is correct," Antel offered little in his answer.

"Also studying history?"

"Also correct," replied Antel with another minimal reply.

"I heard you're just a visiting student," Neil's tone sounded a little condescending. "What brings you out to Denver?"

"Our advisors are collaborating on a project," Antel said. "Dr. Carter has been an invaluable resource for Dr. Solomon."

Becky was getting uncomfortable with Neil's probing. She shifted in her seat and said, "Neil, was there a reason you stopped by?"

Neil dropped his smile for a moment. "I was just in the area and thought I'd check in with you." He then turned back to Antel. "So, what's the focus of your research? My sister says it's really similar to Becks' research topic."

Becky, growing frustrated with Neil, cut in, "Neil, what's your problem? Is this an interrogation?"

Neil raised his hands to pretend he was giving in. "Just trying to get to know your new," he paused for a moment, "friend."

"If you don't mind, we were in the middle of something." Becky was clearly irritated at the way Neil paused to say 'friend.' "Now that you've met him, can you please leave us be?"

Neil stood up. His jaw tightened. "Fine, I'll let you two get back to your work." He turned to look in Antel's direction to look him in the eyes. "Have a nice day."

"Likewise," Antel replied. It served no purpose to escalate the situation. His training taught him to be as diplomatic as possible, regardless of how hostile the other person's intentions were.

Becky watched Neil as he left the coffee shop. Once gone, she turned back to face the table. "I'm so sorry about him. He's been persistent about getting back together with me."

"Don't worry about it," Antel said gently. "He seems jealous, but I can handle it."

"Do you think this was coincidental?" She asked Antel to confirm her belief that it wasn't.

"No," Antel took a quick sip of his drink. "He left the store without buying anything."

"Wow, I didn't notice that," she said. "I'm impressed. You would make a great detective."

He merely smiled back. To Antel, this was second nature. His military training taught him how to identify potential Asentan terrorist threats.

Becky's tense breathing softened. "Still, it's not fair to you. I'll talk to him, let him know he needs to back off."

Antel didn't like that idea. "Becky, just let it pass. People like him only get worse when you approach them about issues like this. If the situation escalates, I can deal with him."

"Fine," she frowned, but nodded. "I'll take your advice. Thank you, Andrew, for being so understanding."

"Anything for you," he smiled at her and put his hand gently on hers.

Emira had just walked through the coffee shop door and, after finding Antel, headed straight to their table and joined them.

"Was that...?" Emira's thumb pointed over her shoulder.

It was clear who she was asking about. "Yes, it was him being a pest as usual," Becky answered.

Becky checked the time on her cellphone. "Looks like I have to go and meet up with Dr. Carter to review the latest progress with my thesis." She stood up and gathered her belongings.

"I should walk with you," Antel offered, starting to rise from his chair.

"No, no," Becky declined as she leaned in closer. "You catch up with Emma. I'll be okay."

"But..." Before Antel could say anything, she interrupted him with a long kiss on his lips.

"Text me later?" she added.

Antel was left speechless and breathless for a moment. All he could do was nod. He watched her leave the store, looking back at him once, then disappearing as she turned the corner. When Antel turned his attention back to the table, he saw Emira studying him with a smile. "What?" Antel asked rhetorically.

"That looked pretty serious," Emira whispered, maintaining English despite no one overhearing them.

"It's complicated," Antel replied. Without realizing it, he softly touched his lips where Becky had kissed him.

"I don't need to be an expert linguist to see that she's falling for you, sir," observed Emira. "The way she looks at you and how her body language changes whenever you are near."

Antel sighed. "I know I shouldn't let it continue, but..."

"But you're falling for her too," Emira finished his sentence. "Did you know my parents met the same way when they were in college, both studying xenolinguistics?"

"Only I'm not really a student," Antel countered. Taking the opportunity to change the subject, he added, "I didn't know your parents were xenolinguists."

"Yes, sir," Emira nodded. "Born and raised in Riland. Growing up,

I learned a lot about linguistic theory from them... which included body language."

Damn, Antel thought. She found a way to bring the conversation back. "I hear you did very well in the Academy Linguistics Program." Antel made another attempt to divert the conversation.

"Top of my class," Emira confirmed with a sense of pride. "We may want to put those skills into helping you strengthen your cover story before Neil trips you up about your background."

Antel leaned forward, lowering his voice. "Do you have any suggestions, Ensign?"

"We should probably fill in some details for your time at the University of Chicago. Photos, documentation, social media posts, etc. Irina can assist with generating some photographs and other documentation using the artificial intelligence systems at the farmhouse. We can make it very convincing."

"Won't they detect the digital manipulation?" Antel asked, thinking of what resources Neil may have with his military.

"Nah," said Emira confidently. "We're not editing existing photos. The AI will generate them seamlessly for us. We can ask Irina if she thinks they have the technology to detect that."

Dahnt and Liora arrived, interrupting Antel's and Emira's conversation.

"You two look tired," observed Antel.

"Yes, sir. Quite tired," replied Liora. "A whole day of discussing the historical context of relations between this country and another called Russia. Such a complicated past. Allies for a world-spanning war, followed by being rivals that fought via proxy wars. Sprinkle in cooperation on a few space missions. It makes me dizzy thinking about it." Liora fell into the empty chair that Neil had sat in only minutes ago.

Dahnt smiled at Liora's comment, a rare moment of emotion from a normally rigid professor, but remained standing.

"We should start heading back to the farmhouse," said Antel. "I'm going to need to discuss some cover story ideas with the help of Irina."

Liora and Emira whispered back, "Yes, sir."

Dahnt, never one for small talk, only said, "Let's go."

As they walked out of the store, Antel noticed a middle-aged man with black hair and olive-colored skin wearing a nice suit and tie discreetly watching Antel walk toward the store exit. The man stood out among the other younger students who made up the majority of customers.

How did I not notice this man until now? Antel thought to himself. I must have been distracted by Neil's sudden appearance.

The man was enjoying a cup of coffee while reading a small paperback book. His casual act reminded him of his surveillance of suspected Asentan terrorists. This man was most likely a law enforcement officer. Antel only hoped that this was just the man taking a break from his daily routine and not trailing him.

If that is indeed law enforcement and somehow catches on to what the team is up to, I'm going to have a hard time convincing him that I'm not a spy, Antel thought. *How does Sandun do it?*

Irina was sitting on the couch, working on her datapad, when the team filed into the farmhouse. She had her feet up and was doing her best to relax while still getting work done.

"I got your message about expanding your digital profile for your cover, sir," Irina said without looking up, her fingers scrolling through her notes on the datapad. "We may be introducing potential vulnerabilities with this."

Antel approached, taking off his jacket. "What vulnerabilities are you thinking we may have?"

Irina rotated the datapad to show him some of the AI-generated photos of him on the University of Chicago campus. "As good as these are, I can't be certain the Terrans don't have the technology to at least detect that they're fabricated."

"They seem like good enough pictures," Antel commented.

"Yes, but because I have little to go on for the university there, those buildings may have subtleties that someone with access to military-grade technology might detect. AI is becoming commonplace in the civilian community. It's not too much to expect their military to have better and top-secret algorithms."

Liora, leaning against a nearby wall and listening to the exchange, added, "I doubt they have that technology yet."

"With all due respect to the serviceman first class," Irina said, annoyed at the cultural expert making technology assessments, rolling her eyes, "it is my expert opinion that we should not fabricate more than one or two, if any at all."

Sandun chimed in, "I'm afraid, from a spy's point of view, I may have to agree. Too many fake pictures may make it harder to keep our cover story consistent."

Antel turned to Dahnt. "Doctor, what do you think?"

Dahnt said, "I heard from Dr. Carter that the US government has been developing more sophisticated tools for background verification. There's growing xenophobia against people from neighboring countries. I can only imagine how those people would react to people from an entirely different planet."

"Almost makes me wonder if this planet is even worth the effort," mumbled Irina.

"Calm down, Ensign," Antel said, sensing Irina's agitation growing and wanting to keep the discussion calm. "What the Rileean Council decides to do with the Earth is up to them. It's our job to make sure we give them unbiased data to work with."

The room fell silent from the tension that was stirring.

"My apologies, Lieutenant," Irina broke the awkward silence. "I didn't mean to say that. I'm just upset that my injuries are keeping me from going into the city with the team. It's hampering my ability to assess their technological progress."

"I understand your frustration. We need to stay focused and not let things like this distract us," Antel reassured her, but was concerned that her opinion could compromise the mission. "Those were Rileeans that shot at us, not Terrans."

"Understood, sir," Irina replied.

"If you think our cover would be at greater risk, then we'll drop the idea," Antel said. "It was only an idea."

Later, after the rest of the team retired for the night, Antel slumped into the living room couch, hoping for a moment of peace.

That moment was quickly interrupted when he heard Dahnt approaching from behind him. "Ralnar, can we talk?"

Antel assumed this was going to be serious. Dahnt hardly ever entered into conversation for conversation's sake with him. "Sure, take a seat."

"Lieutenant," Dahnt began, "I suspect that Irina might be compromising the mission."

"Over these fake photos?" Antel considered the discussion resolved.

"No," Dahnt said. "I have a feeling that when no one is watching, she is making subspace calls."

Antel sat up. "Go on. What makes you think that?"

"Have you noticed that every time you detect the signal, she's never around?" Dahnt observed.

"That's circumstantial," Antel countered. "Besides, neither are you."

"True, but each time, I've been with Dr. Carter. I've been too busy to make subspace calls. What's her excuse?"

"You make a good point." Dahnt got Antel thinking about whether he should be watchful of Ensign Irina Falron.

"Let's not forget, she's got the technical expertise to recalibrate our subspace radio."

"True, but I doubt she'll find the parts while stuck in the farmhouse due to her injury."

"Also, have you noticed that there weren't any mysterious signals while she was back on Mars?"

Antel was about to counter that, but he couldn't think of any plausible excuses. "Maybe I will have Junior Lieutenant Kandos look into this. Sandun's a better spy than I will ever be."

"That's all I ask," Dahnt said. His lips curved into a smug smirk that announced 'I rest my case,' then he walked to his room to call it a night.

The implication that Irina was the source sent a chill down his spine. Antel asked himself, "Could she have been deceiving me the whole time? Is she trying to compromise the mission?"

Chapter 11

It took a lot of effort to keep her mind focused on her dissertation research. All Becky could think about was Antel and the recent events surrounding him. The library was nearly empty that afternoon, so Becky was able to claim an entire table to herself. She had a stack of history books spread across the table.

There was something off about Antel. Between his sudden dashes out the door whenever his phone buzzed, Irene's "injury," a string of convenient emergencies, and the practiced way he delivered vague explanations, Rebecca couldn't help but question if his feelings for her were as genuine as hers were becoming for him. Every indication told her he liked her, yet she couldn't shake the feeling that he was torn about something.

Rebecca's train of thought was broken when she heard a voice call out to her. "Hey, girl. You look like you could use a break." Sarah Morris put her backpack on an empty spot on the table and slipped into a chair next to Becky.

"Hi, Sarah," Becky replied with barely any enthusiasm. "How's it going?"

"You look like something's bugging you." Sarah put her hand on Becky's shoulder. "Talk to your best friend."

Becky felt good knowing Sarah was always there for her, even if her brother Neil complicated matters.

"Um, I dunno," Becky put her hand over the hand Sarah had on her shoulder and gave it a friendly pat. "I really like Andrew, but something in my gut tells me something is going on that he's not telling me." She referred to Antel as Andrew, the Earth name he used, since she wasn't yet aware of his true identity.

"Like what?" Sarah asked. "He's not married, is he?"

"Oh God, no. I certainly hope not! He better not be married."

"Is he secretly seeing that girl Irene?" Sarah wasn't sure she should have put that suggestion in Becky's mind.

Becky shrugged, then said, "No, that can't be it. Irene knows about us and seems genuinely happy for us."

"I hate to say this, but Neil might agree with you that something isn't adding up," Sarah said.

Becky turned to Sarah, eyebrows raised. "Oh, really?" she asked. Then a sigh barely escaped her lips, and the corners of her mouth tightened. "What's Neil's problem this time?"

"He won't tell me why exactly, but he's been asking a lot of questions about Andrew."

"What sorts of questions?" Becky asked.

"Like where he gets his money, what's his background, stuff like that." Sarah then paused.

"What is it?" Now Becky was getting concerned.

"I heard Neil on the phone the other day." Sarah's voice, already low because of being in the library, lowered further. "He was talking to some guy, a special agent for Homeland Security."

"I thought he was looking into the engineering building break-in," Becky said. "He probably has to coordinate with Homeland Security, but what's that got to do with Andrew and his group?"

"Neil made it obvious that he wanted the special agent to look into Andrew and his finances," Sarah told her.

"Oh my God." Becky's face wrinkled in disgust. "Neil can be such a jealous jerk. Sorry to talk badly about your brother, but...." She ended that sentence with a growl of frustration.

"No, I get it." Sarah knew her brother was the obsessive type. "But have you noticed how little anyone actually knows about Dr. Solomon and his research?" Solomon was Sallain's Earth name, but neither Sarah nor Becky knew that.

Becky's eyes gazed down at the table at an empty spot. She had to admit to herself that she had noticed that only Dr. Carter seemed to know much about Dr. Sallain's research, but every time she asked her about it, Dr. Carter brushed off the subject, claiming it was classified.

"I trust Andrew," Becky said, but she was starting to wonder how sure she was about that trust.

"I do, too," Sarah said, "but something's off and Neil has people digging around."

"He's been trying to sabotage my relationship since we broke up," Becky said. "Dammit, Neil. This is low, even for him."

"I'm so sorry my brother is being such a dick. I feel terrible about this."

"It's not your fault, Sarah." Becky gently gripped Sarah's arm. "You've always been there for me. I appreciate that so much."

"Enough to pay for my next coffee?" Sarah tried to lighten the mood by joking with her.

"Very funny." Becky smiled and reached over for a friendly hug. "Speaking of coffee, I think I might just go to the coffee shop and get some. Wanna come?"

"Can't," Sarah said apologetically. "I got a paper due."

"Maybe next time."

Outside, the afternoon was crisp and clear. She was sure Antel had a good explanation that he couldn't tell her, but she wished she could get rid of the doubt she was feeling.

Becky walked into the coffee shop, ordered her coffee, and sat down at an empty table. The coffee shop was just as empty as the library. She pulled out her tablet and flipped through a document with her right hand while holding the coffee in the other.

Within a minute of opening the document, her mind drifted right back to her conversation with Sarah and all of the swirling mysteries surrounding Antel. Becky gave up reading her document and simply stared at the street just outside the window.

"Hello there, Miss Miller. You look like you're a million miles away." Dr. Evelyn Carter's familiar voice brought her attention back to the present.

"Sorry." Becky glanced at the tablet and realized it had gone dark from the screensaver long ago. "I was just exploring some ideas."

Evelyn set her stack of research journals on the table and sat down.

"How's that research going?" Evelyn asked.

"It's going well." Becky paused and decided to ask about Antel's group again. "I know those meetings with Dr. Solomon and his group are classified, but are you sure you can't at least tell me the topic? I mean, what could be so top secret about stuff the history department does? Is it a national security thing?"

"You're right, I still can't tell you." Dr. Carter didn't look like she enjoyed keeping this secret from her favorite student. "But it's not exactly national security per se. It might become one in the next few years, though."

"Vague, but I suppose that kinda explains why Andrew acts like he's hiding something." Becky exhaled slowly and waved a hand in surrender.

"My dear," Evelyn put her hands on Becky's, "I've seen the way the two of you are when you're together. Trust me when I say, the secrets he's keeping have no bearing on how he feels about you. Don't give up on him."

At that moment, her phone buzzed. Neil sent her a text: "We need to talk."

Becky's eyes rolled as she put the phone down on the table and tried to ignore the message.

"Everything okay?" Evelyn could sense the message was a new source of tension for Becky.

"It's fine," Becky responded. "Just some ex-boyfriend drama."

"I wish there was something I could do to help with that," Evelyn said.

Before she could say anything, the phone buzzed again. Neil's message read: "This is important."

"I'll let you deal with this," Evelyn said. She stood up and gathered her journals. "I wish you the best of luck."

Becky typed her reply to Neil: "Is this about Andrew?"

"Meet me. There's something suspicious about his background."

Becky stared at her phone, irritation battling curiosity. "Fine. Library in fifteen," she texted back, her thumb jabbing the send button.

As she grabbed her bag to head back to the library, she thought, "If I'm going to deal with Neil's drama, I'm bringing Sarah as my backup."

Becky returned to the library and sat down at the table she had previously occupied. Sarah's focus was on her textbook when she noticed Becky returning. Happy to see she had returned, a smile formed on her face.

"You're back!" Sarah cheered.

"Yeah," groaned Becky. "Neil wants to talk to me about Andrew, and I was hoping that with you here, he won't go full jerk-mode on me."

Sarah laughed at Becky's comment. "Speaking of Neil, here he comes."

Neil pulled out the empty seat next to Becky and sat. "We need to talk about Andrew."

Becky glared up at Neil, her lips pressed into a thin line. "There's nothing more to talk about."

"A guy shows up out of nowhere, you start dating him, and you think there's nothing to talk about?"

"Neil, you're acting childishly," Sarah jumped in with a low whisper. "Why can't you accept that Becky has moved on?"

Neil scowled at Sarah. "Neither of you knows much about this asshole. Where is he really from? Where are his thesis notes?"

"He's a graduate student from Chicago studying under Dr. Solomon," Becky reminded him. "What's so hard to understand about that?"

"And stop calling him asshole," Sarah butted in. "He's actually very kind."

"Yeah, but when I dug into Dr. Solomon and Andrew's online profiles, they seem rather light on details," Neil countered.

"So?" Becky crossed her arms and leaned back. She didn't want to show it, but a small part of her considered what he was saying. "You're just being obsessive, Neil."

"Becks, listen to me," Neil said, his voice growing frustrated.

"Are you done?" she asked Neil, her tone calm but dismissive.

Neil wasn't finished. "My gut tells me he's hiding something."

"Your feelings aren't proof," Becky responded. "You're just jealous."

Sarah nodded. "Big brother, this is about you not being able to accept that she is happy with someone else."

"You're not listening." The frustration in Neil's voice was growing.

"Go away, Neil," Becky demanded, her voice growing a bit louder. "I'm not in the mood for this right now."

Defeated, Neil stood from his chair and said, "Just be careful with this asshole. Something is fishy with him." He then marched out of the library.

Sarah waited until her brother passed through the library's doors, then turned to Becky. "Don't let my brother get to you."

"I wish he would mind his own business and move on." Becky maintained her composure, but internally, she had questions. Just as Dr. Carter made her feel better, Neil had to shake her trust in Andrew again.

"I think I'll take a break and go home, right after I drop off my latest draft of my thesis with Dr. Carter. See you tomorrow, Sarah." Becky got up and walked out of the library.

Becky unlocked the door to Dr. Carter's office with the key she'd been given in case she ever needed to enter when her professor wasn't there. The evening sun had started to cast long shadows in Dr. Carter's office. Becky was using a corner of the desk to sort her research notes to have them ready for her meeting with her professor. Becky pushed a stack of books a few inches over, but accidentally pushed a manila envelope off the opposite edge.

Becky reached to pick up the folder and the pages scattered on the floor. As she gathered them, one of the pages caught her attention. The letterhead was Dr. Carter's, but the text was written by hand. What caught Becky's eye were the strange symbols. They definitely weren't English or any other alphabet she had ever seen before.

"What the hell language is this?" Becky whispered. She studied the symbols almost as if she were trying to memorize them.

The sound of footsteps made Becky's heart jump. Dr. Carter walked in and saw that Becky was examining the page.

Becky's hand flew to her chest as she caught her breath. "I'm sorry," she said, composing herself and gesturing to the floor. "This packet fell off the table."

"That's okay," Carter said.

"Can I ask what this writing says?" Becky held up the unusual page to Carter.

"That's Dr. Solomon's," Carter said. "I have no idea what it says."

"What language is it?" Becky turned the page back to take one more glance.

"I'm afraid that's one of the things I can't tell you yet," Carter shrugged. "Those are just Dr. Solomon's notes. He must have left them by mistake."

"I didn't mean to pry," Becky said, stuffing the page back in the envelope. "I just noticed the strange writing."

"Let's not tell Solomon's group we have it." Carter put a finger to her lips. "I would like to keep this page to examine the writing, and if he finds out I still have it, he'll want it back."

Becky couldn't shake the nagging questions that kept surfacing. So many questions were swirling in her head that she wished her professor could answer.

Dr. Carter placed her book on the desk and paused, studying Becky. "Still troubled about Andrew, aren't you?"

Becky replied, "Something is telling me to at least ask questions."

Her advisor softened her expression. "My dear, I know you have a lot of questions, but trust me, there's a very good reason for the confidentiality."

"I do trust Andrew," Becky said. "I just wish I understood what was really going on."

"Why don't you take a break and go home," Dr. Carter said, placing a gentle hand on Becky's shoulder.

"I think I will."

Walking to her car, Becky's mind wandered back to those strange symbols. She couldn't figure out where they were from or whether they were an ancient script or not. Come to think of it, it looked like there was a table of data on the page. The text in the first column all had four characters. They had to be historical years, but why not use Arabic numerals? Aren't Arabic numerals practically universal?

Once she returned home, Becky headed straight to her bedroom and opened her laptop. Sitting at her desk, she searched for Andrew's academic profile and studied it. She'd looked at it before, but now she examined every detail with new scrutiny. His credentials from the University of Chicago seemed perfect—too perfect, perhaps.

She opened a new tab and began searching the archives of the university's history department. Daniel Solomon wasn't listed anywhere. The University of Chicago's website seemed to deliberately exclude mention of Solomon. Becky thought that was odd. Maybe he was kept off intentionally for classified purposes.

"This doesn't make sense," she muttered, opening another search window. "There should at least be some mention of him."

Hours passed, and it was getting late. Her eyes were getting tired. Despite all her efforts, she couldn't find any personal pictures of Andrew with family and friends. His social media presence was indeed practically non-existent.

"I got an idea!" Becky said. "Andrew isn't gonna like it, but I just have to know what's going on."

Becky's fingers hesitated over the "buy now" button as she considered ordering luggage trackers online. "I'm so sorry, Andrew. I feel horrible doing this," she said with a wavering voice as she clicked the button.

Instinctively, her eyes glanced at the clock on her laptop. "Ugh, it's late," Becky mumbled. "I was supposed to be relaxing."

Becky changed into a nightgown, turned off the lights, and slipped into bed. "I'm going to have to ask him directly what he's hiding. No more mysteries."

Chapter 12

Antel sat in the living room flipping channels on the television. Nothing was interesting to watch this morning, and he was bored and restless. It was a Saturday, and the team was taking the day off, as was the usual tradition for the Terrans.

Not finding anything worth watching, he eventually gave up and turned off the television. He stared at the wall clock for a moment and watched the seconds tick by. The tension among the team members had been growing since the engineering building skirmish and the mysterious signals. But until he had more to go on, this day promised to be rather slow. His thoughts kept returning to Becky.

As if the Universe heard him, Antel's thoughts were interrupted by the sound of crunching gravel outside. Antel began to worry. No one was expected to visit this secluded farmhouse out in the middle of nowhere. He sprang to his feet, drawing his particle beam pistol in one fluid motion.

The doorbell's chime hit Antel like a warning beacon, but when he looked through the curtain, he relaxed. Becky stood on the porch in front of the door. He didn't expect her today. Earlier, she had told him she wanted to focus on her studies today.

Antel opened the door and stepped aside to let her enter. "Becky! This is a nice surprise. I thought you needed to study today."

"I do need to study," she said, giving him a guilty smile as she patted the strap of her backpack that was over her shoulder as she stepped into the house. "I thought I'd bring my books and study here. Plus, I wanted to see how Irene was doing. I haven't seen her in a while. You don't mind, do you?"

"I don't mind at all." Antel directed her to sit on the couch next to him. "I'm always happy to see you."

"Don't you need to study too? It would be fun to study together," she said.

"Um." Antel had to think fast. He never expected to be watched as he studied. He had no textbooks and wasn't even actually taking courses. "I do, but I thought I was going to take a break today."

Becky didn't look convinced, but she shook it off as procrastination and let it pass. She sat down, opened her backpack, and pulled out a tablet.

"Would you like something to drink? Coffee, maybe?" Antel offered.

"Coffee would be nice, thank you."

"While I'm up, I'll also let Irene know you came to say hello." Antel got up from the couch, walked down the hall, and told Irina that Becky wished to say hello and see how she was feeling. Then he went to the kitchen to make Becky a cup of coffee.

Antel could overhear Irina and Becky having a warm talk while he worked on the coffee. It didn't take long for their conversation to shift to a new topic.

Antel heard Becky say, "I have noticed Andrew's been acting, uh, strange lately."

Antel's heart began to beat harder. "Is she on to me?" he thought to himself.

"Strange?" Irina asked. "How so?"

"He gets pulled away at odd times, and he's always evasive when I ask questions," Becky commented.

Antel could tell Irina was hesitating. He hurried up, finished making Becky's cup of coffee, and re-entered the living room. He was hoping his presence would make that line of conversation end because maybe Becky was confiding privately with Irina.

Becky looked at Antel as he approached the couch with her warm cup. He could tell she knew he had heard the conversation and decided not to try changing the subject. "Dear, I was just telling Irene..."

"Yeah, I heard," Antel said. There was no point in pretending that he didn't overhear her comments to Irina. "I'm very sorry if I've seemed distant. My project includes, um, some classified information. I don't mean to make you feel left out."

Yet another heart-crushing moment. Antel couldn't tell her the truth without violating the Standard Protocol, but her suspicions were only growing.

Becky took the cup but didn't take a sip. She gave him a piercing gaze. "Sensitive information?"

Irina took the opportunity to sneak away, sensing the moment was about to get awkward.

"Andrew, you're making it sound as if you're on a secret government mission," she said, her voice growing sharper. Her blood was beginning to simmer. "Tell me what is going on."

The irony was that her statement about being on a secret government project was exactly what he was up to. Just not for this country, and not the secret she was probably imagining. That irony made him hesitate a little too long.

"It's not like that." He wasn't sure what to say.

She sighed, setting the cup down untouched. "I do want to believe you. But every time we're together, you are either called away or your mind is somewhere else. I know something is going on. And don't tell me I'm imagining all this."

Antel opened his mouth to respond, but the Universe decided to take the cue, and an alert pinged on his communicator. Sandun had pretty bad timing.

Becky's gaze shifted to his pocket, where his communicator was.

"Sorry. It's nothing important." Antel avoided eye contact as he said that.

Becky crossed her arms. "Do you think I'm an idiot? I can tell there's something you're hiding from me."

Tension filled the air between them. Antel considered telling her everything, but he knew he couldn't.

"I can't explain it right now," he confessed. "But I assure you, it's nothing diabolical."

"Nothing diabolical?" Becky's eyes narrowed. "Andrew, the way you stumble at common stuff and that tiny hint of an accent makes it seem as if you're a spy or something."

Really? A tiny hint of an accent? Was he being overconfident about his accent?

"Even the way you curse. In moments where goddammit is the expected curse, you mention the Universe. What the heck? You're lying to me."

Antel's chest tightened. "Becky..."

"Stop it," her voice cracked. "Don't lie to me."

The guilt made his stomach twist into a tighter knot. "It's not what you think."

"I'm listening," she pressed. "Spit it out."

Antel's throat went dry as words failed him. He was at a loss for what to say. But the Universe decided to offer Antel a break. The front door creaked open, and Sandun stepped inside.

"Oh," Sandun said, nearly addressing Antel with a 'sir'. "I didn't know we had company. Hello, Becky."

"Hello," she replied, her tone still wary. "Are you able to tell me what Andrew is hiding from me?"

Before Sandun could say anything, Antel interrupted, "Becky, this isn't a good time."

"Why not?" she demanded. She looked at Sandun, hoping to pull some answers out of him. "Maybe it's because he's cheating on me with another woman?"

Sandun looked to Antel for a hint of what to say. "He is, most definitely, not cheating on you, my friend. I can assure you of that."

"But you can't tell me anything either?"

Antel struggled to think of something to say.

"Fine! Keep your secrets. But don't expect me to trust you if you can't trust me."

She pushed herself off the couch and headed for the door, her face turned deliberately away as she swallowed hard. Her eyes glistened in the light. Antel and Sandun were stunned into silence.

"I believe they use the term 'real smooth,'" Sandun said sarcastically.

Antel groaned, slumping back onto the couch. "I'm not sure how much longer I can keep this up."

"Are you sure we can't tell her? I think we should trust her. Her professor already knows anyway." Sandun was trying to be helpful.

"I can't violate the Standard Protocol." The weight of Becky's words hit him hard. He needed to find a way to balance his mission with his feelings for her or risk losing her trust forever.

Sandun watched Antel stand in the living room with his hand rubbing his forehead.

"Well, that could have gone worse, my friend," Sandun said. He wasn't sure if he should stay with Antel or give him some space to reflect.

"I'm not so sure it could have," Antel muttered. He stopped rubbing his forehead, bowed his head, and placed his hands on his hips.

"I believe we are lucky she isn't heading straight to that ex-boyfriend or to the authorities." Sandun was peering out the window, seeing Becky sitting in her car with the engine idling but not leaving. Tears streaked down her face.

"She's very smart. It's only a matter of time before she figures everything out on her own. My friend, I think you should just tell her before that day comes."

"You know I can't do that." Antel didn't look up. "The Standard Protocol...."

"Oh, stop that! You're just using that stupid law to avoid telling her," Sandun said boldly, not caring that Antel was his superior officer.

Antel slumped back onto the couch. "I hear what you're saying. And I've been on the verge of doing just that, but telling her could put her at risk. We still don't know what's in those unauthorized signals, only that they're probably from those rogue Rileean officers." Antel paused for a moment. "I've gone over it in my head hundreds of times."

"And?" Sandun asked.

"And I just don't know what to do," Antel admitted. "If I tell her, I might be putting her at risk. If I don't, she'll lose trust in me forever, and I may as well let her go. Also, not good, considering that she works directly with Dr. Carter. There would be no way to avoid her. Either way, the mission could be jeopardized."

"Not that you want to let her go," Sandun said. "You know what you want to do, but your sense of duty is powerful."

Antel was about to respond when they heard the door slowly creak open. Antel's heart jumped into his throat. Becky had returned.

"I think I will let you handle it from here," Sandun whispered as he walked away to disappear from the scene.

Becky stood at the doorway, still holding the doorknob. She looked shaken. Her face clearly showed she had been crying, but the tears were wiped away before she returned.

"Can I come back in?" she asked in a soft, low voice.

"Please." Antel patted the space next to him on the couch, asking her to sit with him.

Taking a deep breath, Becky closed the door, walked up to the couch, and sat by him. The tense moment earlier still weighed heavily on them, but she had a moment to collect herself and didn't want to leave things the way they ended.

"I'm sorry for storming out," she said, her voice still soft. "I just don't understand what's going on, Andrew."

Becky kept her eyes on him. "You don't have to tell me every detail. I get the feeling it's something big you need to keep from me. But I'm willing to meet you halfway. Is there anything you can tell me? Anything so I know I'm not insane for trusting you?"

Antel looked down to think. He couldn't break Standard Protocol, not fully, but maybe he could stretch it and tell her just enough without crossing the line.

"You're not crazy," he finally said as he looked back up at her. "And I don't blame you for feeling this way. I confess there is something that I...we can't talk about. It's confidential not just to you but to everyone else, too."

"My professor knows, doesn't she?" Becky was indeed smart and very observant. "Your group meets with Dr. Carter nearly every day, and each time she asks me to leave. I can tell it's all hush-hush stuff."

"It is. But I promise it's not spy stuff," Antel confirmed. "We're not trying to steal secrets of any kind."

Becky tilted her head. She was still feeling some skepticism mixed with some hope. "Then what is it? Is it a classified government project?"

"Um," Antel was determined to tell at least something. "Close, but it's not exactly like that. And that's the part I really can't tell you. I'd be breaking the law."

"The law?" Her eyebrow arched as she leaned back. "Okay, I think I get it. A little bit anyway. It's something sensitive but not exactly for the government, whatever that means, and not only is it not illegal, but you're bound legally to keep things secret. Did I get that right?"

Antel wasn't sure if what he was doing was illegal in the eyes of the American government, but he wasn't American. If they considered this as some form of espionage, then so be it. As far as he was concerned, he was following his government's laws, which had the best interest of both countries in mind.

Unsure of what he could correct from her statement, he simply said, "Close enough. Let's just say my colleagues and I are just observing cultural and political topics and writing a report on them. Opening up with the whole truth would adversely affect that research. This is why we're so secretive."

"Culture and politics?" Becky frowned. "Sounds rather vague."

"That's as much as I can tell you," Antel said, his eyes wide and vulnerable, holding her gaze with an intensity that betrayed his desperation. His shoulders tensed forward, hands slightly outstretched on his knees, as if physically reaching for her trust.

Becky sighed, leaning back into the couch. "Okay. I don't like the secrecy, but I'll try to be more understanding. You better be telling me the truth, or all bets are off."

"That's fair," Antel said. Relief finally washed over him like a cool wave, his shoulders dropping as tension drained from his body. "I assure you, I'll be as honest as I can. If there's something I can't tell you, I'll let you know."

"Will you ever be able to tell me?"

"Trust me, when this report gets out and the people in charge make their decisions, the whole world will know. And you'll know it was us."

Becky gave him a small, witty smile and gently poked a finger on his chest. "You are so lucky that I like you, Andrew."

Antel couldn't help but return with a smile of his own. "I'm lucky just having you in my life." He put his hands on her arms and pulled her in closer for a kiss.

The tension in his chest eased slightly. For the first time, he could finally focus on the mission without offending Becky. But this wasn't the end of the conversation. At some point, when the Council voted on how to proceed, whether in the next few years or the next few decades, he could finally tell her everything. But that could be a long time from now.

Antel shuddered to think that, depending on what the Council decided, it might be never.

Antel held Becky gently in his arms, trying to process their recent argument. It had been a tense conversation. Antel had done his best to be as honest with her as possible without giving away anything confidential, but there was only so far he could go.

After they took a moment to cool down, Becky lifted her head from his shoulder, her arms still wrapped around him.

"I think we both need a break. How about we go out for lunch?" Becky whispered. Her eyes were no longer wet, the redness around them beginning to fade as her composure returned.

"That sounds like a good idea," Antel agreed. "Did you have anywhere in mind? There isn't much in the area. The closest place is at least thirty minutes away."

"Anywhere is fine. I just need a change of scenery."

As they walked toward the cars, Becky suggested, "Would you mind driving? I'm still a bit drained from earlier." She glanced at him with a small smile. "I just want to sit back and enjoy the view."

"Absolutely," Antel nodded. They both got into his SUV, and Antel drove off.

The sun hung high as they followed the country road, warm light flooding the car as a gentle breeze flowed through the cracked windows. Becky's posture softened, their earlier conflict dissolving with each mile. Antel drove half an hour to the nearest small town, giving them a peaceful stretch of easy conversation and comfortable silences.

They found a Mexican restaurant in the nearby town and enjoyed their lunch. Between bites, Antel leaned forward in his seat, eyes brightening as he asked pointed questions about the Cold War she had mentioned to him before. He genuinely wanted to learn more about it, especially how they had managed to avoid using nuclear weapons.

Becky sat up straighter, her fork pausing midway to her mouth as her smile widened. She set down her utensils and gestured animatedly while explaining the events of the Cold War. Each time Antel posed another specific question, she'd lean closer across the table, her voice gaining enthusiasm. Not only did she explain the broad strokes, but Antel also pressed for increasingly minute details. Becky assumed he was challenging her by asking for specifics that no one had ever considered. Little did she know that his questions were meant to compare the events that had occurred on his world.

"How do you suppose events would have been different if even a small number of nuclear weapons hadn't been considered off-limits? What situation would have started it, and which side would have used them first?" Antel asked.

"Wow, that's an interesting question," Becky said. The question made her stop and think. "I think this might be a great chapter for my thesis. Dr. Carter would love this idea." Becky grabbed his right hand, interlaced her fingers with his, and gripped it tightly. She appreciated that he wasn't only listening but participating.

The conversation continued as Becky explained what was called the Cuban Missile Crisis to him.

Even as they sat there, enjoying each other's company, Antel felt an undercurrent beneath Becky's attentiveness. Her smile remained warm, but he noticed how she occasionally studied his reactions when discussing certain topics, her fingertip tracing the rim of her water glass as she listened with unusual focus. Something in her carefully maintained eye contact made him wonder if their argument had planted seeds of suspicion beneath her composure.

After the topic was thoroughly discussed, Becky said, "I think we should return home so I can get some studying done."

The drive back was pleasant. The rugged foothills stretched alongside them, scattered with hardy pine trees and scrubby vegetation clinging to rocky outcrops. The occasional ranch dotted the semi-arid landscape, where prairie grasses bent in the breeze beneath Colorado's vast blue sky. Much nicer than the barren sands of Mars, Antel thought.

After they arrived back at the farmhouse, Antel walked Becky inside. Just as Antel was about to close the front door, Becky remembered something. "Andrew, I think I dropped something in your car." Antel still had the keys dangling from his hand when she grabbed them. "Would you mind if I made a quick check?"

"I don't mind at all," Antel said. "Would you like me to get it for you?"

"No, no. Let me check, please," she insisted.

What Antel didn't know was that Becky detached one of the luggage GPS tracking devices from her keychain and stuffed it into the back seat.

"I love you, but I gotta know," Becky whispered to herself.

Chapter 13

Later that night, long after Becky had returned home for the day, Antel received a text message from her.

Antel stared at his communicator, rereading for the third time Becky's invitation to something called 'Blossoms of Light' at the Denver Botanical Gardens.

He debated his reply. They had been seeing each other for a little over a month now, but recent situations made him question whether this was a good idea. He feared for her safety. Every day, his feelings grew, but at the same time, the dangers had been accelerating, too.

"You look like you're defusing an antimatter bomb," Sandun joked, entering the kitchen to put a small dish in the sink to be washed later. "What are you focusing so hard on, my friend?"

"Rebecca invited me to an evening event tomorrow night." Antel turned the communicator toward his junior lieutenant. "Do you know what this event is about?"

Sandun walked up to get a closer look. "Looks like they decorated the city gardens with lots of small colorful lights." With a smirk, he then said, "Sounds romantic."

Antel turned the communicator back to himself and resumed staring at it. "The more time I spend with her..." He stopped, rubbing his thumb across his lower lip, his gaze drifting away from the screen.

"The harder it gets to keep up the secrecy?" Sandun finished for him. "Listen, my friend. I understand it's complicated, but you can't put your life on hold forever. The Universe may never give you another opportunity. Besides, she's more understanding about it now."

"Still," Antel said, "it makes me feel selfish for not focusing on the mission. But I also don't want to push it with Becky."

"Public events are great for our mission. You have managed to collect excellent cultural knowledge. I'd say better than Sallain's data."

"I don't know about it being that good, but thanks." Antel appreciated Sandun's compliment about the value of his experiences of Terran daily life. "Every time I'm with her, I feel like I'm betraying her trust. She deserves someone who can be honest with her about everything."

"Your feelings for each other seem strong enough," Sandun countered.

Antel didn't respond immediately. His thoughts drifted to their time together. Her enthusiasm for her dissertation topic was contagious. He loved that about her.

"That's the problem," Antel finally said. "I really do care about her."

His communicator chimed. Zhon on the Black Cat was making his usual check-in, a regular reminder of his duty to the mission.

"You should accept the young lady's invitation, my friend." Sandun started walking to the living room. Just as he reached the exit, he added, "Don't make me order you to accept."

"Order me?" Antel chuckled at Sandun's joke. "You're worse than Zhon. Both of you think you outrank me."

Antel replied to the message: "I would love to join you."

Her reply was almost immediate: "Yay!" followed by a yellow smiling face, something Terrans referred to as an emoji.

Antel tried to focus on reviewing Zhon's report from the Black Cat, but thoughts of the evening ahead kept intruding. The Standard Protocol was clear about maintaining cover. Though Antel hadn't violated it yet, the line had grown dangerously thin. At some point, a difficult choice would be inevitable: continue the deception or risk everything for honesty.

Antel arrived early at the Denver Botanical Gardens to make sure the area was safe. Unnecessary perhaps, but recent events had made caution his standard practice.

Once he was satisfied there was no danger, he strolled just outside the entrance as he waited for Becky to arrive. From outside, he could see thousands of lights twinkling across the gardens. Trees and sculptures were all wrapped in strings of lights.

During a moment staring at one of the lighted trees, Antel felt a tap on the shoulder. "Hey, mister. Don't I know you?"

Antel turned and saw Becky smiling back at him. Without warning, she moved in and gave him a quick kiss. He immediately caught the scent of her perfume. He could tell she was trying to make a good impression on him.

"Did you have a hard time finding a place to park?" she asked.

"Not at all. I arrived early to secure a good spot." This was true. Arriving ahead of time meant he could sweep for potential threats. Antel suppressed a smile, wondering how many couples used advanced satellite technology for parking reconnaissance. "Shall we?" He offered his arm to her, and they strolled into the gardens together.

A few hundred visitors streamed toward the annual event. They merged into the flow of families and couples entering the park. Becky used her cell phone to present their admission tickets to the attendant as they passed through the front gates.

Once inside, the crowd's movement was scattered and random, with people looking for their family and friends and then moving to different areas in the gardens to see all the lights on display.

Someone darted through the crowd. Antel tensed, his hand instinctively shifting toward his concealed sidearm before he realized it was only a child running to join his parents. His shoulders relaxed, but his eyes continued scanning the perimeter. Becky would pull his attention back each time she pointed out a unique arrangement of colors and lights.

"Are you okay?" Becky asked as they strolled by a pond. "You seem tense."

"I'm so sorry," Antel apologized, forcing himself to relax. "Work stuff. The past few days have been hectic."

"You want to tell me about it?"

"I don't want to burden you with my troubles," Antel tried to brush off the question. "Besides, this is a date, and my job right now is to make sure you have a great time tonight."

"Like I told you before, whenever you're ready, I'm here to listen." Becky was eager to help ease Antel's tension.

If only he could tell her his true identity. That would go a long way toward relieving his tension. "I prefer listening to your stories," he said, looking into her eyes. "Tell me more about what little Becky was like growing up here."

She let him change the subject, but her expression suggested she knew he was dodging details. They continued walking through the gardens, enjoying the endless displays of lights.

One particular tree in the center of a small pond caught her attention. She tugged Antel's arm, drawing him closer as she gazed at the tree's blinking lights alternating in colors. "I think this one is my favorite."

Antel stood by her side. He was struck by how naturally she expressed joy. He found himself relaxing, just a little, allowing him to enjoy the moment.

Then the spell was broken. A familiar voice came from behind them. "Well, what do we have here?"

Neil stood a few feet behind them, his sister Sarah at his side. She looked uncomfortable. Neil's arms were crossed. "This is a surprise."

"Neil," Becky said. The joy in her voice disappeared. "What are you doing here?"

"Just enjoying the light displays with my sister." Neil uncrossed his arms to gesture toward Sarah with an open palm, fingers slightly curved as if presenting her. "I wasn't expecting to bump into you here tonight. With him." His voice grew more tense with the last sentence.

Sarah tugged at her brother's sleeve. "Let's go, Neil. Can't you see they're on a date?"

That last statement made Neil's jaw clench. He shrugged off Sarah's grasp.

"In a minute, sis," Neil said. He took a step closer to Antel and looked him in the eyes. "You know, I've been doing some checking up on you, asshole. Your online presence is rather light on details."

Antel's pulse quickened, but he kept calm. "Is there something in particular you want to ask me?"

"Yeah." Neil's voice hardened. "Who the hell are you? What are you hiding?"

Becky stepped up. "Neil, stop harassing us. You and I are not together anymore."

"This guy is hiding something, and I'm going to find out what it is," Neil said as he pointed at Antel with a hand shaped like a pistol.

Normally, Antel would have taken that as an idle threat, but Neil had military connections. Antel wasn't sure if this country allowed its military to conduct legal investigations. It wasn't legal in Rilee. The only countries on Arkonus that allowed it tended to not be democracies and not friends of the Empire.

"You're just acting jealous and making a scene," Becky said, getting angry.

"You call that a scene?" Neil turned his body parallel to Antel and clenched his right fist. "This is a scene."

Neil swung with military precision, but Antel deflected it with a quick block. Neil's punching arm moved past Antel's face, missing it entirely.

As Neil pivoted for a left hook, Antel responded with the fluid efficiency of Imperial combat training. His hand struck Neil's neck with off-world precision, a technique no Terran martial art had ever witnessed, and the airman crumpled.

Neil lost his breath for a moment. Stumbling back, he put his hand on his neck, gagging as he tried to regain his breath.

Neil looked up and was about to try again, but Sarah stepped in the way. "Stop it right now!" She yelled, drawing the attention of some of the other visitors to the gardens.

Neil was about to push Sarah to the side, but he noticed the small crowd gathering when he heard the murmurs.

"This isn't over, asshole," he growled through clenched teeth. Straightening his jacket, he backed away. His pride was severely wounded.

Sarah gave Becky an apologetic look before leaving. Becky responded with a nod, letting her know she understood her quandary and didn't hold it against her. Sarah pulled Neil away, and they disappeared into the crowd.

Antel, unfazed by the confrontation, walked Becky to the nearest stylish concrete bench. He asked her to sit and sat beside her. He put his hand on hers to help calm her.

"I keep having to apologize for Neil," Becky said. "He's taking our breakup hard."

"If I'd lost someone like you, I'd be pretty upset too."

She looked at him with a smile. "That's so sweet."

Antel only responded by patting her hand softly.

"How did you pull off that move? Did you study karate or something?"

"I think it was just a lucky hit." Antel wondered if that might have been true. In a fair fight, he wasn't sure he could beat Neil. Years of Imperial military doctrine echoed in his mind. Rileean tactics prioritized taking every advantage they could. It was why the Empire had maintained technological superiority across Arkonus for generations.

"Neil did have a point though," she told him. "There's something mysterious about you. Something more than just your secret research project."

Before Antel could respond, his communicator buzzed in his pants pocket. Antel didn't know how to check it without being disrespectful to Becky.

"Go ahead." Becky felt this was part of his mystery. "I don't mind."

Antel wasn't sure if she was just trying to be patient or if she truly didn't mind. "I'll just quickly read it." He pulled it out and read the message. It was a priority alert from the Black Cat. Zhon detected unusual activity in orbit and was investigating further.

He should probably reply to acknowledge Zhon's message, but decided there was no need. His pilot would investigate regardless of explicit orders. It was just how Zhon operated.

"I know you're hiding something," she said, her expression softening slightly. "And I'm trying to be patient about it. I just... I want you to know you can trust me. Remember your promise to tell me whenever you can." She hesitated, then met his eyes directly. "But I need to know —are you at least being honest about your feelings for me?"

He stayed quiet for a moment, looking into her eyes. He put his hands on her cheeks, leaned in, and gave her a long kiss. When the kiss was complete, he returned to looking into her eyes and told her, "More than you know."

Satisfied that he was being honest with her, she put her arm around him and laid her head on his shoulder. "I'm sure you probably work for the government, right?"

"Something like that, yes." He leaned his head closer to hers. Her hair was soft and comfortable to the touch.

"There's a lot of 'something like that' in your life, isn't there?" she teased him. Then she got serious again. "And you're certain it's classified?"

"Something like that," he said with a half-smile.

"Very funny." Becky, without lifting her head from his shoulder, softly smacked him on his back. "Shall we go see the rest of the lights?"

They strolled through the final display, where blue lights rippled across the dark pond surface while the scent of cinnamon and clove drifted from nearby vendors. Fallen leaves crunched beneath their feet as they followed the path toward the exit, the autumn air carrying just enough chill to make their closeness welcome. Antel's communicator buzzed twice more, but he forced himself to wait.

When they finished, he insisted on walking her to her car. He didn't say it, but it was clear it was in case Neil was still around.

"Thank you for coming, Andrew," she said, squeezing his hand. "I enjoy spending time with you so much."

"I'm glad I came too. Watching you navigate a botanical crisis was definitely worth it," Antel said humorously, referring to the incident with Neil.

She smiled at his gentle humor then kissed him softly. "Good night, Andrew." She entered her car, allowing Antel to close the door for her.

Watching her drive away, Antel felt that familiar feeling of conflict between duty and desire. The communicator buzzed again.

Antel read all of the missed messages. Zhon was reporting that he had shifted the Black Cat's orbit to avoid detection. After careful study, he determined that someone was moving satellites around in a possible attempt to find him. Zhon did the oldest trick in the book and parked the ship near an ordinary civilian satellite and matched its orbit. They would specifically have to zoom in and look to see him. At the distance he was at, a quick scan would have registered the satellite and the Black Cat as a single object.

Antel replied, "Excellent work. Keep me posted." If Earth's governments were looking for the Black Cat, it would mean someone might be informing them intentionally. Those rogue Rileean soldiers must be up to something big.

Then, as if thinking about the rogue soldiers had made them materialize, Antel saw Neil speaking with someone inside a gray car off in the distance. Or was it black? It was hard to tell the difference in a poorly lit section of the parking lot, but he was fairly certain it was gray.

It didn't take long for Neil to notice that Antel saw him and say what Antel assumed was a goodbye to the driver. Neil turned and headed to his vehicle, watching Antel the entire way.

The gray vehicle turned its headlights on, pulled out of the parking space, and began to depart.

Without wasting a moment, Antel jumped into his SUV and pulled out of his parking space to follow the gray car.

Antel watched the gray car exit the parking lot and enter the street heading northbound.

As soon as Antel drove onto the street, the gray car immediately accelerated. Antel sped up to keep from losing them. His attempt at following without them knowing was over before it started. He wasn't surprised. The chase had commenced.

The gray car picked up speed and began recklessly passing cars along the way. Antel had no choice but to do the same to keep up. The fact that they started driving so fast once he saw them meant these might be those rogue soldiers or someone working with them.

The gray car took an unexpected right turn into a suburban neighborhood. Street lights poorly lit the street, but it was enough for Antel to still see them. After another turn, someone aimed something from the rear driver-side seat and fired. The blue energy pulse sizzled past Antel's vehicle. Every alert system in his mind fired at once. Imperial weapons. This just got serious.

A vacant car parked on the side of the street was hit instead, sending it into the air and rolling onto the yard it was parked in front of.

"That's surely going to attract attention," Antel muttered. Antel had little choice but to use his left hand to return fire from his driver-side window. Because he was right-handed, his shots were terrible.

Their next shot hit the street ahead of Antel, scattering pieces of the pavement in all directions, leaving behind a small crater.

Antel had to act fast. He pulled his left arm back into the vehicle, but that caused him to accidentally drop the weapon onto the floor in front of the passenger-side seat.

With two hands, he swerved to avoid the crater, nearly causing his SUV to spin. Luckily, his vehicle was an electric vehicle, and all the weight was evenly distributed along the bottom. Had it been a gas-powered car like the car he was pursuing, the front-heavy engine would certainly have put the car in an uncontrollable spin.

Antel hit the accelerator hard and closed the distance between them. He got within inches and would have had an excellent shot, but his pistol was still sliding around the floor out of reach. "Kossdra!" Antel cursed himself. He had no hope of reaching it while the vehicle was moving.

Then the shooter put his arm out again. This time, he was holding a different weapon. Antel strained in the darkness to identify it, but it was too late. As soon as he could see it was an EMP gun, he hit the brakes hard.

Antel's vehicle's brakes locked up, and all of the power in his car shut down. The SUV came to a screeching halt in the middle of an intersection. The gray car took another turn at an intersection up ahead and disappeared from his sight.

People started to turn on their front porch lights and peek out of their home windows to see what the chaos was about. It didn't take long for Antel to hear the sound of sirens in the distance. Antel slammed the accelerator, grateful that Irina had retrofitted his vehicle to include EMP-resistant shielding and only needed a few seconds to reboot.

The car surged forward with inhuman precision. He left the neighborhood as quickly as he could before he was identified by the residents. After getting back on the main highway, he slowed down to move at the same speed as the flow of traffic.

Once he was on the highway and was able to relax, he wondered who was in the gray car. He clenched his fist and slammed the steering wheel in frustration. They may have gotten away, but now he knew they had spoken with Neil.

Maybe it was time to have a chat with Neil. Find out what that conversation at the parking lot was about.

The game was far from over.

Chapter 14

Antel kept replaying the car chase over and over in his mind. He marched up the library steps toward the glass doors. He needed to talk to Neil about those men in the gray car, but first, he had to find a way to contact him without alerting Becky or Sarah. If they learned he was trying to meet with Neil, they would have questions he couldn't answer.

Through the library's lobby windows, he spotted Becky and Sarah at their favorite table in the history section. As usual, the table was covered with open books and a couple of laptops. It was their routine to study there every Monday morning before their classes.

Before he could approach the table, his communicator pinged. It was Sandun trying to reach him. Antel stepped back outside and answered the call.

"Status report?" Antel spoke first.

"Nothing yet. Still scanning for anomalous power sources," Sandun replied. They hoped to detect an energy source not native to Earth as a clue to where those men went.

"Keep looking," Antel ordered. "I'm going to see how to get Captain Morris's phone number without raising suspicion."

"Just be careful. Don't..."

Antel cut him off. "I know. I'll be careful." He disconnected the call and put the communicator back in his pocket. He then went back into the library and walked up to Becky and Sarah.

"Hello, ladies," Antel said with a smile as he walked up from behind Becky and put his hands on her shoulders to give her a gentle massage.

"Andrew!" Becky turned her head over her shoulder to look at him.

Antel took the opportunity to give her a quick kiss before she could continue speaking.

"You really know how to melt her heart, don't you?" Sarah commented.

Becky blushed at the comment. "I thought you were going to work on your project from the farmhouse today."

"I changed my mind." Antel pulled out the chair next to Becky and sat down.

"I'm glad you did," Becky said with a cheerful voice.

"Hey," Sarah had a huge grin on her face and joked, "where's my kiss?"

"You're going to have to wait until Becky isn't watching us," Antel returned with a joke of his own.

The three laughed.

Antel had a thought. He made a show of looking at the bookshelves. "Since I'm here, I need to look up a book on cyberwarfare. How can I look up the library's catalog?"

"You gotta use the library app," Becky said.

"He can't," Sarah jumped in. "He has to be a student here to access the app."

"Oh, that's right," Becky replied. "Here, use mine. Let me show you how it works."

Becky unlocked her phone and activated the library app, then put her phone in his hand and held his hand steady with hers so she could point out the app's features. The gentle pressure of her hand against his sent a warmth through his chest that caught him off guard. He pretended to learn the features, but in reality, he already knew how to use the app. His phone had the app installed with credentials that Dr. Carter had arranged for the team.

Antel gave her hand a grateful squeeze and proceeded to explore the app's book listings. He found a few candidates and jotted them down on a scrap sheet of paper, making sure to keep his notes in

English and not Intallan.

When Becky's attention became engrossed in her studies, he waited until she turned to flip a page in her textbook, then casually angled her phone away from her line of sight. He quickly switched to her address book and found Neil's phone number under the entry "Sarah's Brother." Antel jotted the number but slipped in a few letters to make it appear as just another book's catalog number.

"I found a few options," Antel said, closing the app with a casual tap before sliding the phone back to Becky with a friendly smile.

"Want some help?" Becky offered.

"No, I got this," Antel said, feeling guilty about the covert act he had just performed with her phone. He didn't want to betray her trust, but after last night's chase, he needed answers. He rationalized it by telling himself that there was a possibility she would be in danger too if he didn't investigate.

When he was out of Becky and Sarah's view, Antel slipped out of the library through the front glass doors. He turned the corner so they wouldn't accidentally spot him.

He stared at his communicator's numeric touchscreen. He wasn't thrilled to have to confront Neil. Meeting him alone ran the risk of a physical confrontation. He took a deep breath and mustered the courage to dial the number.

The phone rang a few times, then a sharp, deep voice answered, "Captain Morris."

"Neil Morris, this is Andrew Rall. We spoke…"

"Yeah, I know who you are," Neil swiftly interrupted. "How the fuck did you get this number?"

"That's not important right now," Antel answered. "We need to talk. In person."

"I'll bet Becky gave you this number," Neil guessed. "Why should I talk to you? The only thing I have to say to you is stay away from Becky so she can come back to me."

"Even if I let her go, it wouldn't be up to me if she returned to you," Antel said bluntly. "Even you have to admit that reality."

Neil was silent for a moment. He may have been possessive and jealous, but he was no idiot.

Changing the subject, Neil asked, "Fine, what do we need to talk about?"

"It's about the passengers of the gray car I saw you speaking with last night."

"You still haven't convinced me to talk to you. I don't owe you shit," Neil blurted. "Besides, I'm busy investigating the engineering building break-in."

"I can meet you at your work," Antel said.

"I'm on base right now. Buckley Space Force Base," Neil declared. "You seriously want to come on the base?"

"Sure, why not?" Antel thought that was a great opportunity. Neil probably thought the base would give him something Terrans called home-field advantage. It might, but it was a great opportunity to observe Terran military protocols. Senior Lieutenant Ranston would kill for a chance like this.

Another pause. "Okay, I'll arrange access for you. Get your ass to the south gate and ask the guard for me. One hour. Bring ID."

"I'll be there."

After hanging up, Antel contacted Sandun again. "He agreed to meet. On his military base."

"That's risky," Sandun replied. "Are you sure about this?"

"I'll be fine," Antel said confidently. "He's probably less likely to get into a physical fight while among his peers. If I did that, Ranston would court-martial me."

"Well, good luck then." Sandun's voice wasn't as confident. "I wish I could come along."

"Just monitor my location with the satellite."

"Yes, sir."

Antel stealthily re-entered the library and went back to the bookshelves. Since he never really looked for the books he said he was going to get, he simply returned empty-handed to the table.

Remaining on his feet, Antel glanced at his watch. "I need to run," he said as he reached down to give Becky a goodbye kiss. "Dr. Solomon needs me to go fetch some things for him."

"Everything okay?" Her concern was genuine, making his deception feel even worse.

"It's fine. He's asking for a couple of stupid books he forgot to bring with him." Antel tried to conceal the hard swallow as he continued to lie.

"Okay, but if he asks you to do his laundry, I would draw a line," Becky joked.

Antel pulled up to the south gate's checkpoint and pressed the button to lower his window. He had to remind himself that the pistol was still in the locked glove compartment. Opening the glove compartment would require knowing the passcode—a passcode that was written in Intallan characters. Scanning the glove compartment wasn't going to be a problem, as the material it was made of kept it safe from scanners.

However, none of that would prevent a crowbar from forcing its way in.

The security checkpoint at Buckley Space Force Base was remarkably similar to Rileean military checkpoints. Armed soldiers stood in the entrance's path, their weapons visible but not drawn. Surveillance cameras tracked his every move.

One of the guards approached his car. His skin color made him look like a Voran, just like Sandun, but something about his smaller nose made it clear he wasn't from Vora.

"ID and purpose of visit," the guard barked. He rested his right hand on his service weapon, but he didn't look like he was going to draw it—probably only a precaution in case Antel got violent.

Antel handed over his fabricated credentials. The guard took them into the guardhouse and examined them with an electronic device of some kind.

"I guess we're about to put Falron's handiwork to the test," Antel thought to himself.

The guard half-stepped out of the guardhouse and asked, "Who are you here to see?"

"I'm here to see Captain Morris."

The guard stepped back in and consulted a computer terminal. He then picked up something that Antel assumed was a radio instead of a phone and spoke into it. "Andrew Rall here to see you."

The guard paused to listen, then said, "Yes, sir." He put the radio away and walked back to Antel's car.

The guard handed Antel's credentials back to him and said, "Head up this road until you see the building labeled Leadership Development Center. Captain Morris is in the very next building after that one. Park in any space marked 'Visitor.'"

The barrier raised, and the guard who was blocking the path stepped out of the way to allow Antel to drive through. As the car rolled through, the car sensors detected multiple scanning systems inspecting the vehicle. Nothing sophisticated enough to detect his Rileean technology.

Antel found the Leadership Development Center on the left side of the road and parked the car in a visitor's space in the parking lot by the next building over.

When Antel entered the building, there were two attendants, both in military uniforms, sitting at the reception desk.

The female attendant looked up and asked, "Purpose of visit?"

"Meeting with Captain Morris," Antel said. This felt exactly like the bases back home. Antel was rather enjoying the moment.

"Please clear your pockets of anything metal and walk through the metal detector," the attendant said.

Antel removed everything from his pockets and placed them into a small plastic bin. Then he walked through the detector. The detector beeped. "Kossdra! What did I forget?" he thought to himself, worried he may have forgotten a piece of advanced tech.

The guard approached Antel with something that appeared like a battery-powered disciplinary paddle. "Arms out, feet apart." He ran a handheld scanner over Antel's body. The device chirped as it passed Antel's belt.

Antel let out a sigh of relief. "Just the belt buckle, thank the Universe!" he said in his mind.

The guard then handed the plastic bin back, but not before pulling out the phone. "You will need to leave this here at the front desk. No pictures or recordings of any kind are allowed beyond this point."

"Understood," Antel replied formally.

"Down the hall, office 106." The guard stretched out her arm, directing Antel to enter.

When Antel found room 106, the door was left open. Neil was sitting at his desk, examining a folder full of photos and assorted documents. The office reminded Antel of the bare-minimum offices on the Mars Outpost. The only things that differed were the large map of the Colorado region on the wall and a picture of Becky and him at some amusement park. Neil's optimism that Becky would return to him was misplaced.

"Close the door," Neil said as he shoved all of the documents into the folder and closed it, revealing the text "Confidential" stamped diagonally on the cover.

Antel closed the door and then waited for a second to be offered a seat. Hearing none, he took the seat anyway.

Neil's expression was hard. "Let's be clear, asshole. You're on my turf, so we're doing this my way."

"Fair enough," Antel responded.

"Okay." Neil leaned back in his desk chair and crossed his arms. "So what the fuck do you want from me?"

"I want to ask who was in that gray car last night," Antel was direct. "And what was said?"

"What do you think we said?"

"If I knew that, I wouldn't have come here to ask." Antel knew that question was meant to be confrontational. There's an expression in Rilee: "If someone asked a question they already knew the answer to, it meant they were up to something."

"What makes this any of your business?" Neil wasn't willing to be cooperative.

"I have reason to believe..." Antel hadn't thought this far ahead. He had to think of something fast. "I think those passengers pose a danger to my colleagues. Maybe Becky, too." He threw in Becky's name to entice him into helping.

Neil uncrossed his arms and leaned forward again. "They wanted to know about your group. What you were studying, background stuff, etc."

Antel wasn't sure he was telling the truth. "Background checks don't usually involve parking lot meetings."

"Maybe you're not as clean as you pretend to be." Neil gave a sly smile. "Are they a crime organization that's looking for you?"

"What exactly are you implying?"

"That's my line." Neil lightly slammed a fist on the desk. "Who are you really, Mr. Rall? Because your background check raised some interesting flags."

Antel was determined to maintain his cover story. "We're just a visiting research group from Chicago working with Dr. Carter. Nothing more."

"That's the thing." Neil opened the folder, pulled out a sheet, then quickly closed it again. "Your credentials check out perfectly. Too perfectly. Like they were fabricated all at once, six months ago."

"Are you going somewhere with this?"

"The men I spoke to had theories about you and your team. They think you might be foreign agents. Chinese maybe. Or maybe Russian."

Antel almost laughed at how wrong that was, but kept his face neutral. "And you believed them? Random men in a parking lot?"

"I'm not sure what to believe, Mr. Rall."

Clearly, Neil had no idea the men in the car were from another planet. There was an excellent chance Neil was unaware he, too, was from another planet. From what Antel gathered, those men were probably just learning what they could about his team and their weaknesses. They probably didn't want to break Standard Protocol either.

"Well, I can promise you that I am neither Chinese nor Russian." Antel took some joy in knowing that statement was indeed true.

Neil studied him for a long moment. "You're good, asshole. Really good. But I know you're hiding something."

"Aren't we all?" Antel stood. "If you're done with the accusations, I have work to do. I'm obviously not going to get much out of you."

"One more thing." Neil held up his phone. "My sister Sarah—she's been telling me stuff about your team. She's noticed some interesting patterns in your behavior. The way you pause at doorways and quickly check the corners, exits, and faces before stepping inside. How you always position yourself with clear sightlines to exits. Do you have military training?"

"I am no danger to anyone."

"Yeah, right." Neil's tone made it clear he didn't believe him. "I got my eye on you."

"Is that a threat?"

"Call it a friendly warning. And stay away from Becky. She deserves better than being used as part of your operation."

Antel wasn't sure how to respond without provoking a fight. He decided to keep his temper under control and marched out of the office and off the base.

"Neil may be clueless about my true origins," Antel said through gritted teeth, his knuckles whitening as he gripped the steering wheel tighter, "but he could still be a threat nonetheless."

Chapter 15

Lieutenant Antel Ralnar leaned forward in his chair, studying the waveform patterns scrolling across the subspace radio's screens from the recorded logs. The hum of the workshop's equipment reminded him of his time in training when they taught him and other cadets how to review subspace signals to monitor for Kentan activity. He never thought he would be monitoring for his fellow citizens.

The subspace transmissions were increasingly difficult to trace, even with Irina's enhanced monitoring equipment. Antel suspected the senders knew they were being tracked and were cleverly bouncing signals through the city's wireless network, a technique even someone as skilled as Irina hadn't anticipated.

"Lieutenant, take a look at this," Sandun's voice broke Antel's train of thought. "I think I've narrowed the source down."

Irina, determined to win this hide-and-seek game of technological skills, had devised algorithms for filtering out the subspace noise.

"What do you have, Kandos?" Antel asked Sandun as he rolled his chair to his station. While Antel was studying the recorded logs, Sandun was monitoring for real-time signals.

"I think I found something," Sandun said, excitement evident in his voice.

Irina stopped her algorithm monitoring and rushed over to Sandun's station to take a look at what he'd found.

"It's coming from the west side of the city," Irina pointed at one of the monitors beside the one Sandun was watching. "It's coming from the mountain range!"

"Give me a satellite image," Antel said, pointing at the satellite monitoring station. "Quick!"

Irina jumped into action. She accessed the satellite's controls and panned the view to the location in question. "Looks like a small town. But..." Irina frowned at the viewscreen. "This is strange."

"What is it, Ensign?" Antel asked as he got out of his seat to stand behind her. Sandun walked up to see as well.

"The infrared readings are rather low. It's as if the population of this town were merely a handful of people," Irina said, looking up. "It's as if the town were abandoned."

"Abandoned?" Sandun asked.

"Yes, sir," Irina put her finger on the monitor and pointed out the pink cloud on the infrared scanner. "Everyone in that town is limited to this area, but something is obscuring the readings."

"I don't know why, but it seems that town was probably completely abandoned, and our people are using it as a staging ground for something. They must be using an infrared mask to attempt to hide."

"No power infrastructure, no cell towers, minimal traffic nearby. It's the perfect place to set up operations while staying out of Terran view," Antel commented.

Irina zoomed in for a closer look at the parts of the town not obscured by the infrared masks. "These buildings all look weathered and deteriorating."

Why the Terrans would build then abandon a perfectly fine town was beyond them, but that was a question for another time. They needed to get to the bottom of this.

Antel studied the terrain surrounding the abandoned town. It sat nestled between forested hills, making it well hidden from random witnesses. The exits and escape routes were limited. The only efficient way to escape would be by air. He didn't see any cars on the satellite view.

"We need to check it out. Whatever they're doing, this could be our chance to catch them in the act," Antel said.

"Shall I prepare the reconnaissance gear, sir?" Sandun asked.

"Throw in the particle beam weapons," Antel replied. "I'm not planning to get outgunned again." The memory of the firefight in the engineering building was still fresh in his mind.

"Permission to join the team, sir," Irina pleaded. "I'm feeling much better now."

"I don't know," Antel responded.

"Please, sir, I need to find the bastards that shot me and kick some ass," Irina continued to plead her case.

"Fine. If Dr. Myros says it's okay, then you can come." Antel didn't have to be pushed too hard to be convinced. He appreciated her dedication. A good soldier perseveres even when injured, and she was doing exactly that.

Irina's grin grew wide. "Thank you, sir. I won't let you down."

"Doubt never crossed my mind, Ensign Falron," Antel said.

Just as Antel was getting a good feeling about the team's progress, his communicator chimed with an incoming message. Antel's stomach tightened when he saw it was from Becky. She was asking to make plans with him for the evening. He stared at her message for a long time, guilt gnawing at him, and he considered his reply.

"Sorry. Something came up with the research group. We need to do something by the end of the night. Secret stuff." Antel replied, adding 'secret stuff' to ensure she knew he was being honest this time. "Maybe tomorrow?"

He hit send before he could second-guess himself, trying to ignore the hollow feeling in his chest. The mission had to come first. It was always supposed to be the priority.

"Everything okay, my friend?" Sandun asked, returning with their gear bags. He knew the look on Antel's face wasn't mission-related.

"Everything is fine," Antel replied, but Sandun knew it wasn't. Sandun knew he had to decline something with Becky, and it was eating Antel up inside. "Let's run through the abandoned town's layout again. I want to know every approach vector and every escape route possible before we move in."

They had an hour to study the detailed maps and establish their infiltration plan as they waited for night to come. Another check of the subspace signals confirmed they were still there, completely unaware their attempts to mask their signals had been circumvented.

The team met by their red SUV. They packed up the trunk with their gear as they checked the weapons charges one final time.

"Ready?" Antel asked as he scanned the team for questions.

Everyone responded they were ready. Dalan Myros was coming along for medical support. He had also cleared Irina Falron for combat. Sandun and Antel made four. Perfect to not get outnumbered. Liora Trandenn stayed behind, and Dahnt wasn't a soldier so he didn't need to come either. He was out with Dr. Carter anyway.

Dressed in their dark tactical gear, the four of them entered the vehicle. Antel asked Sandun to drive so he could be free to make last-minute adjustments to the plan if necessary.

Antel took one last look at his communicator. Becky's reply only said, "I understand. Talk tomorrow. Good luck." It was almost as if she knew he was going into danger.

For over two hours, Irina monitored the signal from a handheld device she'd built, ensuring it didn't change or disappear while Sandun focused on the road. Dalan Myros cherished his rare opportunity away from the farmhouse, taking in the changing landscape as they traversed country roads, then city streets, and finally mountain passes.

Antel was supposed to focus on the mission, but with a two-hour wait, there wasn't much he could do. The plan was already arranged, and the gear was already packed. There was nothing to do but wait. Antel let his mind drift to thoughts of Becky. She would most definitely protest if she knew the danger he was headed toward. Despite their recent tensions, their connection remained undeniable. It was that bond that would make her insist he not put himself in this dangerous situation. But like every soldier in history on every planet, he knew this was his job and his duty.

"Latest satellite pass confirms at least four human heat signatures in the target area," Irina said from the front passenger seat, where she sat to have access to the SUV's computer system. "They're concentrated around these two buildings. I believe they're using one of them as long-term temporary shelter."

Antel studied the satellite images once more, making sure the situation hadn't changed. "Zoom out a bit," he asked Irina.

After zooming out to see the surrounding area, Antel pointed at a spot on the map that was missing trees at the end of a short road. "That spot looks like a campground. We'll park there and pretend to be ordinary campers."

"Without any camping gear?" Sandun asked rhetorically.

"I didn't say smart campers," Antel joked. Everyone in the vehicle laughed. "We'll slip into the woods and proceed directly to the town from there. Do we know if they have any surveillance equipment monitoring the area?"

"I'm not detecting anything, but we can't be certain there isn't any," Irina said.

"Is the signal still active?" Antel asked.

Irina checked the makeshift subspace tracking device she had been progressively improving. "Yes, sir."

"Still encrypted, I'll bet," Sandun commented.

"It is," Irina said. "However, now that we're getting close, I'm detecting an incoming message as well. That signal is stronger, so they're talking to someone in space."

Antel frowned, leaning over Irina's shoulder to see the readings for himself. "Can you decode any of it?"

"Negative. The encryption's military-grade, definitely Rileean," Irina said. "The incoming signal is using the same encryption pattern as the outgoing signal. Probably talking to their mothership. The signal characteristics are wrong for deep space communication. This is shorter range, maybe lunar orbit or closer."

The implications were troubling. If the rogue soldiers had support assets in near-Earth space, then the situation was even more dangerous than they'd suspected. Antel checked his chronometer — less than an hour until full darkness.

"We should move soon," Antel said, securing the last of their equipment. "The longer we wait, the more likely they are to..."

His communicator buzzed again. Another message from Becky: "Hope your work goes well. Miss you."

Antel closed his eyes briefly, pushing down the wave of emotion that threatened to surface. The mission demanded his full attention. He couldn't afford distractions, not when they were so close to uncovering the truth.

"Lieutenant?" Sandun's voice held a note of concern.

"I'm fine," Antel replied, tucking the communicator away.

"Remember," Antel told the team as they made their final turn onto the dirt road leading to the public campground, "observation only unless we have no choice. We need intelligence more than we need a confrontation."

Everyone replied with an "Understood."

"Though something tells me our guests aren't going to make that easy," Antel commented.

Sandun cut the SUV's headlights and switched to night vision. He had to drive slowly and carefully since he had to use the night vision feed displayed on the dashboard viewscreen, making driving more challenging.

The campground appeared just ahead, sparse with only a few vehicles scattered about. Behind some, families huddled around flickering campfires. The team scanned the area quickly, knowing their window of opportunity was narrowing with every passing minute.

The night air carried a slight chill as Sandun guided their vehicle through the darkness, the car's night vision system illuminating the unpaved road in ghostlike black and white hues. He found a vacant spot in the campground and rolled into the space. Only the quiet hum of the car's electric motor and tires on dirt broke the silence.

Antel, Irina, and Dalan checked their gear quietly, each knowing what to do.

"Dalan," Antel whispered, "maintain position here. If anything goes wrong..."

The medic nodded. "I'll be ready. Communication channel three, encrypted."

As they exited the vehicle, Antel froze. A car drove up and parked in another vacant space nearby. It was dark and hard to tell, but it didn't look like the escaped gray car. However, its profile seemed hauntingly familiar. He tensed—it looked exactly like Becky's vehicle. But that was impossible. She had no way of knowing they were here.

"Lieutenant?" Sandun's voice cut through his thoughts.

"It's nothing," Antel replied, pushing the disturbing possibility aside. "Let's move." It had to be a similar make and model to Becky's car.

They activated their night vision goggles, and the world transformed into stark monochromatic contrasts just like the car's night vision device. The abandoned buildings of the ghost town loomed ahead, their weathered walls and broken windows casting jagged silhouettes against the clear night sky.

"Signal strength holding steady," Irina reported, consulting her handheld scanner. "I'm getting a few heat signatures. They're moving. Looks like they're setting up some kind of perimeter."

Through his night vision goggles, Antel caught glimpses of movement—quick flashes of heat disappearing behind various structures. The disciplined way the figures maintained their positions spoke of military training.

They paused behind a cluster of trees, studying the patrol pattern. The rogue soldiers had established an effective defensive position, but their focus seemed concentrated on the main approaches to the town. A natural gap existed in their coverage along the northern edge, where a steep embankment made conventional access difficult.

"Over there," Antel pointed toward a partially collapsed wooden structure near the embankment. "We can use that for cover, then move between those two larger buildings. The infrared blockers they're using should help mask our approach."

Sandun nodded. "Ready when you are, Lieutenant."

The team began their careful advance, moving from tree to tree with measured precision. Their practiced movements showed their military discipline, each step placed deliberately to avoid loose rocks or dry branches that might betray their presence. The abandoned town's ancient wooden buildings creaked and settled around them, the sound mixing with the hum of wind through empty doorways and windows.

Halfway to their first objective, Antel's tactical computer detected an irregular energy reading. He froze, signaling the others to hold their positions.

"It's coming from a scanning system," Sandun murmured, consulting his instruments.

"Can they detect us?" Antel asked.

"Not if we time it right. The scan pattern has a three-second gap between sweeps."

They waited, watching the energy signature pulse across their displays. When the moment came, they darted forward in perfect synchronization. They cleared the sensor's range just as it cycled back to life. Antel's pulse quickened as he scanned for any sign they'd been detected.

As they reached the large wooden building, they pressed themselves against its weathered walls. Two figures emerged from another structure about thirty meters away, speaking in low voices that carried clearly in the still night air.

Antel caught part of the conversation: "...admiral wants us to secure access through the local asset immediately."

"Confirmed," the other replied, speaking in Intallan. "He's working on getting access as we speak. As soon as he can..."

A sudden crack broke the silence. Antel's boot stepped on a weak board. The conversation stopped instantly. In the fraction of a second before the shooting erupted, Antel caught a glimpse of the shuttle pod resting on the town's wide main street, clearly showing the Rileean flag and the ship's registration numbers, written in Arkonian numerals, along the rear side of the hull.

Then the night exploded with blue flashes of light from everyone's particle beam weapons, transforming the ghost town into a deadly crossfire of energy and chaos.

Chapter 16

Blue beams sliced through the darkness, casting eerie shadows before splintering the ancient wooden walls and nearby trees on impact. Antel dove behind a rusted water tank, feeling the ground rumble uncomfortably close to his position. The personal shields the team brought were for energy weapons and gave some level of protection, but those shields would only withstand so many hits before they stopped functioning.

"Contact! Four targets!" Sandun's voice crackled through Antel's earpiece. "The two you saw plus two more moving in to flank us."

Antel took a risk and carefully looked around the tank. These soldiers were definitely Rileean. They wore the same gear Antel's team was wearing, moved with the same practiced coordination that was standard training in the Imperial Forces, and most importantly of all, spoke in fluent Intallan, specifically the Rileean dialect.

"Spread out!" one of them shouted in Intallan. "Don't let them reach the equipment!"

Taking advantage of their repositioning to block Sandun's approach, Antel sprinted to better cover behind another old building. "Stand down!" he called out to the rogue soldiers, his voice echoing between the structures. "You're in violation of the Standard Protocol!"

The only response they gave him was another volley of particle beam fire. The walls of the building Antel was using as cover were scorched. He could smell the smoke coming from the blasted pieces of wood. If they weren't careful, the entire town could go up in flames and probably take out a large portion of the forest with it.

"Last warning," he tried again. "Stand down now!"

One of the rogue soldiers laughed. "You don't know who you're dealing with, Lieutenant!"

The use of his rank confirmed that these rogue soldiers knew exactly who they were fighting. These people weren't here by chance. They knew his mission was in progress and didn't care. Hell, they probably planned their shadow mission to coincide with his on purpose.

Antel's mind raced, trying to piece together the larger picture while simultaneously tracking enemy movements through his tactical display.

"Sandun, can you circle around to the opposite side? There's a shuttle pod back there," Antel ordered. "Keep them from escaping in it."

"On my way!" Sandun wanted to dart away to find a path to cut them off from accessing the shuttle pod, but he couldn't. Several shots were fired in Sandun's direction. "I can't move. I'm pinned down over here. These guys know what they're doing."

Antel checked his weapon's charge. Still at eighty percent—more than enough for a prolonged engagement if necessary. He took a deep breath, centering himself as his training kicked in. He needed to get this situation under control.

"Cover me," Antel ordered, then burst from his position, firing rapidly to force the rogues into cover. His first shot caught one of them in the shoulder, the particle beam partially penetrating their personal shields in a shower of sparks. The soldier stumbled but maintained his position, returning fire with impressive accuracy.

Sandun used the opportunity to launch a volley of precision shots that drove back the flanking team. The coordinated assault created a momentary pause in the rogue soldiers' weapon fire, and Antel pressed the advantage. He darted between buildings, closing the distance.

Out of the corner of his eye, Antel saw that to his right, one of the enemies had matched his advance and was trying to cut him off. He dropped and rolled as bolts of positrons crackled through the space where he had been standing. His return fire caught the soldier's leg, partially getting through his energy shield. The soldier went down with a scream of pain, his rifle crashing into the dirt.

"Man down!" another voice shouted. "Everyone, fall back!"

The firefight intensified as one of the rogues tried to reach their fallen colleague. Particle beams lit up the night, the barrage of energy weapons fire beginning to take its toll on the surrounding structures. A support beam in the processing plant cracked ominously, sending a smaller building crumbling to the ground.

"Don't let them reach that shuttle pod!" Antel commanded. He knew they were running out of options. The rogues were too well-trained, too prepared for this confrontation. Antel needed to make a choice—press the attack and risk catastrophic escalation, or capture and secure what intelligence they could from the fallen soldier and live to fight another day.

Before Antel could make that decision, the shuttle pod's engines whined to life, kicking up a cloud of dust. One of the rogues laid down covering fire while the craft powered up. The intensity of Antel and Sandun's barrage kept them from retrieving their fallen colleague, but Antel and his team were also pinned down, unable to prevent the evacuation. The rogue soldiers had little choice but to leave the downed soldier behind.

The craft's presence explained how they'd been moving undetected. That craft wasn't capable of interplanetary travel, much less interstellar travel, so it meant there was a larger vessel up there that it was a part of. This would also explain the subspace "reflection" they thought they had encountered on their first trip to Earth.

Antel, still clutching his rifle, knelt beside the wounded soldier. He was unconscious, but just to be sure, Antel checked for a pulse. Sandun and Irina stood around Antel, scanning the area for any signs of additional threats.

"We need to get him back to the farmhouse," Antel said. "Junior Lieutenant, restrain his wrists, then you and Ensign Falron get him back to the car. Have the medic check his injuries."

"On it," Sandun saluted, maintaining the formality required while on mission. He pointed at Irina. "Help me out, Ensign."

Sandun took out a plastic restraint strip and secured the soldier's wrists together. Then, with Irina's help, they carried him out of the town and back to the car.

As they trekked through the abandoned town, the silence was broken only by the sound of their boots against the dusty ground.

At the car, Dalan examined the soldier's injuries. "I've seen worse. He'll be in a lot of pain, but he'll survive," the medic said. Dalan then took out a syringe, prepared it with a pinkish-colored liquid, and injected it into the man's leg where he had sustained the worst injury.

They put the soldier in the back seat while Sandun and Irina stood on either side of him. Dalan sat up front to keep himself and the medical gear clear of the unconscious man in case he woke up and became violent. Sandun's hand hovered near his weapon, his gaze never leaving the soldier's face. Irina's fingers drummed silently against her thigh as she watched the rise and fall of the man's chest. Through the rearview mirror, Antel noticed Dalan repeatedly checking over his shoulder, the medical scanner gripped too tightly in his hand. They knew that this soldier could hold the keys to understanding the mysterious signals they had been detecting at random moments.

At the farmhouse, they quickly settled the soldier into a secure room and restrained him further by attaching his wrist restraints to the bed. Once secured, Dalan was able to address the injured leg under better conditions.

Antel's eyes never left the soldier, who was still unconscious. Thanks to Dalan, he was stabilized. "As soon as he's awake, we start. I want to know what he knows."

Hours passed. Dalan sat reading a paperback novel Sandun had purchased for him from a bookstore in the city a few days ago to help pass the time. Occasionally, he lifted his gaze to check for any movement from the restrained soldier.

Late into the night, the man's eyes slowly opened as he groaned in pain. The first thing he tried was to lift his arms in an attempt to retrieve the weapon he had dropped, only to find that he was no longer in the abandoned town and was instead strapped down on a bed.

"Cursed Universe!" exclaimed the man. "Get me out of these restraints."

Dalan stood up and walked into the hall, never letting the soldier out of his sight. "He's up," Dalan yelled down the hall, hoping they hadn't all gone to sleep yet.

Antel walked in first. The others didn't need to join him, but they were too invested in the conversation that was about to happen.

Standing over the man, Antel said, "You're Rileean." It wasn't a question. He simply stated it as a fact.

"Did the uniform give it away?" the soldier said sarcastically. A spark of defiance ignited in his eyes. The soldier tried to pull his hands against the restraints, but the attempt was fruitless. "You're eventually going to find out who I am. I am Lieutenant Ranon Ballnus. And obviously, I am Rileean."

"Whose orders are you following?" Antel pressed with a firm voice.

"What makes you think I'm not the one in charge?"

"Because they wouldn't have left your ass behind," Irina blurted, certain that Ranon and his companions were the ones who had shot and injured her in the engineering building.

"Who is your commander?" Antel demanded.

Ranon attempted to spit on Antel's boot but missed and hit the floor. "Drink my piss. I'm not telling you anything."

Antel leaned forward, his eyes locked intensely on Ranon's. "We'll find out eventually. But cooperating could mean the difference between a minimal security sentence and years in a maximum isolation facility."

Ranon sneered. "By the time you do, it will be too late to do anything about it."

"Why are you here? What is your mission?" Sandun walked up to Ranon's injured leg and gripped it hard. As an intelligence officer, Sandun was well-versed in interrogation techniques—using legal and not-so-legal methods.

Ranon screamed in pain but still refused to answer. As a soldier, he was trained to resist those same techniques.

"What ship did you come in on?" Antel tried again.

Ranon remained silent, his breathing heavy as he tried to put the pain of his leg's injury out of his mind.

The silence from Ranon was answer enough. Antel's eyes met Sandun's. Both understood they weren't going to get much out of him.

Chapter 17

Dark circles shadowed Rebecca Miller's eyes, and she stifled her third yawn in as many minutes. Her normally neat ponytail was hastily assembled, with stray strands escaping in all directions.

She sat at her favorite table in the university library, staring at her laptop but not focusing on it. The strange events from the campsite the night before kept playing in her mind. The blue flashes of lightning made no sense, and the way Antel and his colleagues had entered the forest with military precision. Something was not adding up.

She pulled out her phone and played the video she'd managed to capture. The vantage point was far, so the quality was poor. The low light didn't make it any easier. Each time a blue streak of lightning flashed, the silhouettes of people became easier to see. They looked like they were shooting at each other with lightning guns, no weapon she had ever seen or heard of before.

Then there was that aircraft. Toward the end of the battle, some kind of aircraft lifted off and shot into the sky. She might have thought it was a helicopter because it lifted into the air vertically, but then it turned its nose toward the sky and took off with impossible speed and barely any noise.

"Hey, girlfriend, you okay?" Sarah's voice startled her. Becky quickly ended the video and closed it. Sarah set down two cups of coffee and pulled up a chair. "You look like you've had a long night.

Did you even get any sleep?"

"I'm fine," Becky replied automatically with a mumble, but she knew she probably looked as exhausted as she felt. "Just got some stuff on my mind that I'm trying to sort out."

Sarah's face showed concern. "This is about Andrew, isn't it? Neil's been telling me..."

"Neil needs to mind his own business," Becky barked, perhaps more sharply than she'd intended. "I'm sorry, Sarah." Becky's tone softened. "I... I just saw something last night. Something I can't explain."

"I'm listening. Talk to me," Sarah spoke softly, putting a comforting hand on Becky's shoulder.

Becky hesitated. She wasn't sure where to begin. She was certain Sarah wouldn't believe her. "I think I witnessed some kind of confrontation."

"A confrontation?" Sarah's shoulders tensed as she leaned across the table, her coffee forgotten. Her eyes narrowed, scanning Becky's face intently. "Did someone assault you last night?"

"No, not me," Becky assured her. "I don't know what I saw. It was too dark to see much." Frustrated, Becky ran a hand through her hair. "First, I saw Andrew and his classmates dressed in hunting camouflage sneaking into the forest at a campground. At first, I thought they were doing one of those paintball games or something."

"I sense a 'but' coming."

"They were shooting at some other team with strange energy weapons from a sci-fi movie. Then, to top off the night, this aircraft took off and darted into the sky faster than I've ever seen before."

Sarah's expression turned skeptical. "Are you sure about what you saw? It was dark, and campgrounds are usually pretty far from any streetlights."

"I know it's hard to believe." Becky pulled up the video again. "Look at this."

They watched the grainy footage together. Even though the quality was poor, the blue flashes were unmistakable. The unusual nature of the lights was evident. Sarah's skepticism wavered. "Whoa. That's... strange. Have you asked Andrew about it?"

"No." Becky put her phone back down on the table. Her stomach churned with uncertainty. "How do I even start that conversation? 'Hey Andrew, I followed you into a forest to a ghost town and saw you in what looked like a laser tag game?'"

"How did you know he was at a campground?" Sarah asked.

Becky pulled out her car keys and planted them on the table.

"What am I looking at?"

Becky pointed to the luggage tracking tags. "I tossed one of these in his SUV and followed him on GPS."

"Are you serious?" Sarah's eyes widened in surprise. Then she sighed. "You gotta stop sneaking around and just have a heart-to-heart with him."

"We already did," Becky confessed. "He told me there was some confidential stuff that he couldn't tell me."

"And you didn't buy that?" Sarah asked.

"No. I took his word for it. But more stuff came up that made me want to find out for myself what was going on." Becky said. "I mean, if I find out by myself, he won't get into trouble for disclosing confidential information, right?"

"I'm not sure it works that way." Sarah sat back, processing what Becky had just shown her.

"Ever since Irine's injury, things have been different. He's hiding something big, something that goes beyond just classified research."

Becky pulled out her phone, showing Sarah the GPS tracking app. The signal from the tracker she'd planted on Andrew's car showed it was still at the farmhouse. "I need to know the truth."

"And what if the truth is something you're not supposed to know?" Sarah asked quietly. "What if there's a reason he can't tell you? There have been a lot of times when Neil couldn't tell me stuff because it was classified."

Becky stared at the tracking app, watching the small dot that represented Andrew's vehicle. "The mystery is eating me up inside."

Becky's phone buzzed. It was from Antel. "Missed you all day. Breakfast tomorrow?"

Becky stared at Antel's text message. Her chest tightened as she traced his words with her fingertip, a lump forming in her throat that she couldn't quite swallow away. She finally had to admit to herself that she was madly in love with him. So much so that she wasn't sure there was anything he could do to change that. Despite the mystery and secrets, he was still good for her.

She typed a reply. She was going to just ask about last night's events, but she quickly deleted it and typed something else. "Sure, my place around 7:00 AM. You haven't met my parents yet."

"Maybe I'll get some answers in the morning after I show him this video," she said.

His response came quickly. "On my way."

"See you there," she sent back.

Curious about what the back-and-forth texting was about, Sarah asked, "Is something up?"

"That was Andrew," Becky said as she slipped the phone into her pocket. "We're meeting at my place for breakfast in the morning."

"Well, that sounds really nice. Maybe you should ask him about the video during breakfast."

"Yeah, I plan to," Becky said as she stood up and shouldered her bag. "It's time for my class. Thanks for the coffee. I really needed it today."

"Anything for my best friend."

As she walked across campus, Becky tried to rationalize what she'd seen. Military testing seemed the most logical explanation, but that didn't account for the incredible technology she'd witnessed. And why would Andrew, supposedly a graduate student, be involved in something like that? The pieces of this puzzle were there, just waiting to be assembled. She just needed to figure out how they fit together.

Later, Becky sat cross-legged on her bed in her room, the glow of her laptop casting harsh shadows across her furrowed brow. Her dissertation notes lay scattered and forgotten around her, abandoned hours ago when a different, more urgent puzzle had captured her attention.

Instead of focusing on her dissertation, Becky's fingers flew across the keyboard as she documented each inconsistency: Andrew's occasional slip-ups with common idioms and the way his colleagues stiffened when she asked about their hometown. She scrolled back through her list, adding timestamps and locations to each observation, looking for patterns that might explain who these people really were.

"Honey?" Her father's voice called from downstairs. "Are you joining us for dinner tonight?"

"In a minute, Dad," Becky yelled back. Her eyes were fixed on the screen as she added bullet point after bullet point to her list.

She watched the video a dozen of times. The blue flashes weren't like any weapon she had ever heard of. And that aircraft defied explanation. If she were a conspiracy theorist, she would have thought it was a UFO sighting.

"None of this is making any sense," she whispered to herself.

Her father walked up to her room's doorway with concern on his face. "Rebecca, you've been hiding in your room all day. Something troubling you?"

How was she going to explain what she had witnessed to her parents? That her boyfriend might not be who he says he is? Her throat tightened at the thought. And what was her father going to say when he learned that she had used GPS trackers to monitor Andrew's movements? He was an attorney, so he would be very disappointed.

Becky saved and closed her document. "Just stressed about my dissertation, Dad."

"Something tells me that's not the only thing bugging you today," he observed. "You've seemed distracted about something for a while now. Is it that boy? What's his name again... Andrew?"

The only thing she could manage to say was "It's complicated."

"Relationships usually are," her father said. "Is he worth it?"

She lifted her gaze from her laptop to her father. "He is. I can't explain why I think so, but he is definitely worth it."

"In the end, that's all that matters," he advised her. "Well, dinner is ready. Mom made lasagna."

After her father left, Becky hesitated getting up and heading to the dinner table. Instead, she reopened her document and stared at her notes, trying to decipher the puzzle. Every rational explanation was accompanied by a detail that would contradict it.

She couldn't resist opening her browser and searching for information about advanced military technology. Nothing came anywhere close to what she saw. Energy weapons of some kind? Even science fiction movies would have made it more believable. But she had it all recorded.

Her phone pinged. Sarah had sent a message: "Maybe you should let this go. I'm sure he'll tell you when the time is right."

Becky stared at Sarah's message for a long time before texting her back. "Can't. Not this time."

Becky got up from the bed and started pacing. She pulled out her phone and typed: "Andrew, I know something strange is going on. Please just be honest with me." Her thumb hovered over the send button before she shook her head and deleted it. She tried again: "If you're in some kind of trouble, maybe I can help?" Delete. "Whatever 'confidentiality' means, I deserve to know what I'm mixed up in." Delete. She could smell her mother's lasagna from downstairs, but she had no appetite.

"Are you coming?" her mother called out. "Food's getting cold."

"Coming, Mom," she replied. She kept staring at her phone's blank message screen. How do you ask someone what he knows about strange events such as these, especially when he assured her he wasn't dangerous but couldn't tell her anything yet due to confidentiality?

With a frustrated sigh, she tossed her phone onto the bed and returned to her laptop to close it before heading downstairs. Just as she reached for it, the device chimed with a new notification. Dr. Carter had sent her an email about revisions she was suggesting to her dissertation. Now she had images of that strange language in Dr. Solomon's handwriting competing with academic obligations in her mind.

She tried to put it all out of her mind and finally went downstairs, where her parents were already eating.

"There she is," her mother said with a smile as she pulled up Becky's plate to put some food on it. "Homework must be keeping you busy."

Becky managed a weak smile as she sat down at the table. "Sorry, I've just got things on my mind."

"About Andrew?" her mother asked. "When are we going to finally meet this boy?"

"I invited him over for breakfast in the morning," Becky said.

"So what's on your mind?" her mother asked, looking at her father, knowing he knew a little about what was on her mind.

Becky pushed her lasagna around the plate with her fork. "Have you ever felt like someone you care about isn't who they say they are?"

Her parents shared another look.

"What do you mean, honey?" her mother asked carefully. "Are there problems in your relationship with him?"

"No. He's perfect, but some things just aren't making sense." Becky set down her fork. "What if you saw something... impossible? Something you couldn't explain?"

"Like what?" Her father's brow furrowed. "Is he keeping secrets from you?"

"Well, sorta." Becky set her fork down on the plate. "He said there was some stuff he wasn't allowed to tell me yet, so it's not like he's lying to me. And I believe him when he tells me I will find out soon. Maybe. I don't know."

Her parents remained silent. They weren't sure what to say.

"Isn't that the same thing Neil told you when you were with him?" her mother asked.

"True, but it's not the same thing," Becky said. "Neil's got military secrets, and he's never going to tell me what they were. Andrew isn't military. He can't even tell me if he was working on a government project or not."

She opened her mouth, then closed it again. She wanted to tell them about the events of last night, but how could she explain it without sounding crazy?

"Never mind," she said finally. "I think I just need some air."

Becky returned to her room and called Sarah.

"I can't wait until the morning," said Becky. She didn't even give Sarah a chance to say hello. "I gotta get answers tonight."

"Rebecca Miller! Don't do anything stupid," Sarah warned.

"I have to know, Sarah. This mystery is killing me."

"It's getting late, and Andrew's probably asleep right now," Sarah added.

"He'll wake up for me. I'm going to Andrew's place right now. Andrew's car is still there. I can see it on the GPS."

"Becky..." Sarah's voice was heavy with concern. "I think you should wait until morning."

"I'll be careful," Becky promised. "But I have to do this."

Becky's hands gripped the steering wheel tightly as she drove toward the farmhouse. As she left the city limits, the clouds that had shrouded Denver gradually dispersed, revealing a canvas of stars impossible to see through the urban light pollution. The three-quarter moon hung suspended in the night sky, casting pale light across the empty highway. She had rehearsed what she would say dozens of times. She would show Andrew the video, present her evidence calmly, and demand honest answers.

As she approached the long driveway leading to the farmhouse, she turned off her headlights and rolled to a stop on the gravel path, far enough away to remain hidden from anyone inside the house.

The farmhouse was mostly dark, except for a few dim lights on the ground floor. Her heart pounded so loudly she could hear it even over the low rumble of her idling engine.

"What am I doing?" she whispered to herself. "This is insane."

As she sat in the car, trying to work up the courage to drive up to the farmhouse and knock on the door, movement caught her attention.

A figure emerged from the house. It was Antel, but not dressed in his typical casual jeans and button-ups she had grown accustomed to. Instead, he wore dark camouflage gear, a stark departure from his usual style, moving with the same precise military bearing she had observed in her video. Moonlight reflected off something holstered on his belt. It appeared to be a weapon, though not like any gun she had ever seen. This was longer and sleeker.

She watched his silhouette in the darkness circle the house while holding some sort of handheld device. After completing a loop around the house, he stopped and stared at the device while turning in different directions, as if the device he was using was a directional finder.

Barely breathing, Becky watched as Antel headed toward the tree line. His movements were purposeful and tactical, like a soldier on a mission.

Her phone vibrated again. Sarah: "Please tell me you're not doing anything stupid."

Becky's fingers shook as she replied: "I know what I'm doing. He's sneaking into the trees. I'm gonna follow."

"What? Becky, where are you? What's happening?"

She silenced her phone and slipped it into her pocket.

Andrew had disappeared into the forest, but she could still make out his path in the moonlight where broken twigs and flattened grass revealed his trail.

All her prepared speeches had evaporated. This wasn't going to be a simple conversation.

She had managed to catch him in the act of repeating last night's strange events.

"Come on, Rebecca," she whispered to herself as she quietly got out of her car. "You wanted answers. This is your best chance to get those answers."

The cool night air carried the scent of pine needles. Her shoes crunched softly on the gravel as she made her way toward the tree line. She froze, certain that Antel must have heard her footsteps. After a tense moment, she realized he was too far ahead and focused forward to have noticed the sound. There would be no going back now.

Her heart was pounding hard. She pulled her phone back out and started another video recording. If anything should happen to her, at least there would be evidence. Then she slipped into the shadows, following the path Andrew had taken into the darkness.

Behind her, the farmhouse stood silent and mysterious against the starlit sky, its secrets still untold. But not for long, she thought. One way or another, she would have her answers tonight.

"Please forgive me for this, Andrew, but I just have to know what's going on," she muttered quietly to herself.

Chapter 18

It was fairly late. Sandun was taking the first shift watching the prisoner, Lieutenant Ranon Ballnus. Everyone else had already gone to bed for the night.

Antel was about to doze off to sleep himself after a hard day of dealing with the search for the mothership to which the shuttle pod belonged when he got the alert of another subspace signal. And this time it was nearby!

Antel turned on the makeshift directional finder Irina had built earlier. It was crudely put together, but it was all he needed. The digital readout pinged. The display indicated the signal strength was strong. It had to be very close to the farmhouse.

Antel took a slow lap around the house to measure the signal at various locations. The strongest point would give him a clue to the direction he needed to take.

"Must be that way," he whispered as he attempted to peer through the trees toward the direction the indicator told him.

Antel patted his sidearm to make sure he brought it with him. He decided the particle beam pistol was good enough and left the rifles locked in the weapons closet. If things escalated, he could call for backup.

Antel felt better knowing he didn't need an excuse to sneak off this time. He considered waking one of the other team members for backup, but something told him he should keep them near the farmhouse in case those rogue soldiers were attempting to rescue Lieutenant Ballnus.

As he pushed deeper into the forest and farther away from the farmhouse, Antel was completely unaware of the figure trailing him from behind. If there was going to be trouble, he only expected it to be in front of him.

Becky Miller saw Antel was wearing some sort of hunter's outfit, but he was only carrying a pistol instead of a hunter's rifle. She was curious why Antel was behaving oddly. He was clearly looking for something. She suspected it would lead to more strange events like those from the previous night.

Becky enjoyed hiking, so the long trek through the forest wasn't too difficult for her. She tried to get closer without being seen.

Then he stopped and muttered something. Becky wasn't sure if he was muttering too softly for her to make out what he was saying or if it wasn't in English.

"Where are you hiding?" Antel said in Intallan.

Becky heard Antel mutter something, but she couldn't hear him well enough to make out what he said. She wasn't sure, but it might have been another language.

He pulled out his makeshift device and checked the signal strength. Still speaking in Intallan, he said, "I'm getting closer for sure. It has to be right here somewhere."

He put the device away and then turned on his night vision goggles. Antel adjusted his goggles to scan for metallic objects instead of heat sources.

"Ah. There you are," Antel said quietly as he pointed in the direction of a strange piece of equipment in a clearing up ahead. He didn't realize Becky was watching him.

The piece of equipment was a metallic box with a satellite dish on the top. The box was held up by a sturdy tripod, its feet firmly staked into the ground. Clearly, it was meant to stay here unattended. It was for remote access. The dish on the top was a subspace dish. He found his source. But this transmitter told him nothing about who was operating it. All he could surmise was that it was recently placed here.

"Let's see what you're hiding inside," Antel said, again in Intallan, but he didn't think he needed to be as quiet, assuming whoever put the transmitter here was probably not around. He approached it and opened the access panel to view the inside control panel.

This time Becky heard him clearly. "That was definitely not English!" she thought. She leaned forward, straining to see and hear better.

She was gripping a branch that protruded from the tree in front of her, using it to steady herself for a better view. With a sudden crack, it snapped under her weight. She dropped to her knees behind the trunk of the tree, heart racing. Antel turned sharply, scanning the area for the source of the noise, but seeing nothing, he dismissed it as local wildlife and resumed accessing the transmitter.

From the display panel, he could see the signal was getting encrypted with a non-standard algorithm. He plugged in a small chip he pulled from one of his pockets into the panel and pressed a few keys to get it to give him a copy of the encryption keys. Instead of bringing back the whole transmitter, Antel decided it would be better to try to listen in on the messages without alerting the operators. Moving the transmitter would alert them and make them switch to another encryption algorithm.

He put the chip back in his pocket and closed the access panel. Then he started walking back to the farmhouse. Antel got no more than a few feet before he heard a noise behind him. His training kicked in, and he instinctively pulled his pistol out, swung back in the direction of the sound, and aimed toward the noise.

A ball of blue light crackled through the trees toward him. The shot sailed wide to the right, leading him to believe the shooter was not trained with weapons.

"Who's there? Show yourself!" Antel yelled in Intallan, assuming the shooter was another rogue Rileean soldier. He scanned the trees for signs of an assailant but saw nothing. His night vision wasn't going to pick up anything if the shooter was hiding behind a tree.

The assailant fired another shot. This time, too far to the left. Antel saw the figure jump behind a tree and took his shot. The assailant was a rather poor marksman, but dangerous nonetheless. The tree that was hit exploded into pieces. That was when he heard a yelp from behind him. He didn't know it was Becky.

"Kossdra!" Antel cursed. "Am I surrounded? This could be bad."

Spinning around, Antel bolted toward the source of the yelp, weapon raised and ready to fire at whoever might be lying in wait.

"Becky?" Antel was shocked. "What are you doing out here?"

Becky looked at him with fear in her eyes. Her body was paralyzed in terror. Antel realized he was still pointing his pistol at her and pointed it down to the ground. He reached out to her with his left hand to help her up. "I'm not going to hurt you, but we have to move. Let's go."

Before she could say anything, another blast ripped through the trees, cutting through leaves and branches. Had it not been for some of those branches, this one would probably have hit him. Antel jumped on top of Becky, doing his best to cover her body from the blasts.

The impact knocked them down onto the ground. Antel quickly got back up and pulled her by her hand. "Please, Becky, let's move!" He didn't give her a choice. He pulled her until she had no choice but to run ahead of him. He stayed behind her as her cover from the blasts coming from the assailant.

"What's going on? What kind of weapons are those?" she demanded with a trembling voice.

"Later, I promise," Antel whispered to her. "Follow me." He pivoted sharply and led them at a sprint away from the assailant, weaving through the densest part of the forest.

After a few minutes, he could hear the shots getting farther and farther away. Odd, the shooter didn't appear to be following them. The shooter apparently valued anonymity over capturing Antel.

"Stop here. Lie down on the ground," Antel ordered, as he took off his backpack and pulled out a large, lightweight blanket. The blanket wasn't for keeping warm. It was for more camouflage.

Becky wasn't sure what to do. She hesitated getting down on the ground and stayed on her knees.

"Trust me, lie down. Hurry," he said.

Becky gave in and laid down on her stomach. Antel threw the blanket over the two of them and he laid on his stomach next to her. He pulled out his pistol again and kept it ready in case.

They lay flat under the camouflage blanket, barely daring to breathe.

Minutes stretched into what felt like hours. Becky was too frightened to break the silence, her eyes constantly scanning the darkening forest. Finally, Antel whispered, "I don't think he followed us. I think he was only trying to scare us away from the subspace transmitter. He probably didn't want an all-out shootout because he was such a terrible shot."

"The what?" Becky worked up the courage to speak. "Start talking, mister. What the hell is going on here? And this time, don't lie to me. I know you haven't been honest with me about everything. You've been acting very strangely for a while now. I want answers."

Antel looked at her face and could see a mix of fear and anger. He knew this moment would eventually come, but he hoped it wouldn't have been so traumatic for her.

"I think my chances of being able to abide by the Standard Protocol just dropped to zero," Antel thought to himself as he began.

"Becky," Antel said. "I need you to keep an open mind. What I'm about to tell you isn't going to sound believable, but it will be the truth. Once I tell you, I'm begging you not to let anyone else know. Can you do that for me?"

"Okay," Becky nodded, her gaze never leaving his. "I promise."

Becky could hear Antel take a deep breath. "First off, Andrew is only my English name. My real name is Antel Ralnar."

"Antel Ralnar?"

"Yes," he confirmed. "And I'm not from Earth."

Her eyes narrowed in disbelief. "You're right, I don't believe you. I said I wanted the truth. Don't give me this horseshit, Andrew... Antel... whatever."

"It's true. I'm from the Rileean Empire, a sovereign entity on the planet Arkonus. My team has been sent here on a research expedition to learn about Earth's political environment. Things like alliances and rivalries. Maybe some historical background for understanding things better."

She remained skeptical. "Wouldn't it have been easier to just register for one of Dr. Carter's history classes?"

"In a way, we did. She already knows about us."

"Is this the big secret Dr. Carter couldn't elaborate on with me?"

"We made a deal with her. She teaches Dr. Sallain and the team about Earth, and we'll teach her about our planet under the condition that she not publish any of it until we give her the okay."

"Dr. Sallain?" She didn't know that name.

"Oh, sorry. Dr. Solomon's real name is Dr. Sallain."

"Oh, this just gets deeper and deeper, doesn't it?" she commented. "So what was that weird box on a tripod back there?"

"That was a subspace transmitter. It's for communicating in space at large distances. It's technology your people shouldn't have yet for another one or two hundred years."

"And that?" Becky pointed at his pistol.

"This is a particle beam pistol. It fires balls of positrons, a type of antimatter. If set high enough, it can be very destructive." Antel paused for a moment before continuing. "Standard gear for a soldier. I'm a lieutenant."

"Soldier?" Becky's eyes widened again. "Are you studying us so you can conquer us?"

"No, no. We're not planning to conquer you." Antel hesitated. "Well, there is a small minority in my country that wants to, but they're in the minority. The consensus is just to assess if Earth is a threat or if we can safely open up relations, and which nations on Earth we can trust. Making the wrong friends here on Earth could be bad for future relations."

Becky said nothing, processing everything he'd told her and all she'd witnessed.

"Becky?" Antel was worried she didn't want anything to do with him anymore after this.

"I have to ask again, what about us? Are your feelings for me genuine, or is it just a spy trick?" She turned back to look at him. Antel could see she was doing her best to hold back tears.

"I'm breaking my oath to obey the Standard Protocol by telling you all of this, and risking the success of my team's mission, but I can't help the way I feel about you. This might be the biggest mistake of my career. The smartest thing would have been never to let my personal feelings risk the mission and stay clear of you, but..." Antel's eyes pointed down to the ground in embarrassment.

"But this alien soldier is not that smart," her face turned to a smile as she tapped her finger on his chest. Now she was trying to hold back a laugh.

"When I'm with you, my judgment just gets tangled up. Did I get that expression right?"

Just before she leaned in for a gentle kiss, she whispered, "Close enough."

After waiting probably twenty minutes, Antel decided it was probably safe to head back to the farmhouse. The shooter must have been long gone and likely didn't head to the farmhouse, as Sandun would have started blasting away. Antel got up and then helped Becky to her feet. He kept her wrapped in the camouflage blanket as a precaution as they quietly made their way back to the farmhouse.

"The assailant is gone now," Antel said as they entered the house. "We're safe."

"Can I stay with you tonight?" She looked up at him, her voice still unsteady. "I'll feel safer with you. I don't want to be alone." Her pulse was finally beginning to slow.

"Um, okay, sure," he said, shifting nervously. "I can stay on the couch. That way, you can have the bed to yourself."

She studied his face, noticing his discomfort. "Is there a problem, soldier?"

"Well…" Antel hesitated. "I'm not sure I mentioned this before, but in my culture, inviting a girl over usually meant he was planning to… you know…"

"Is that why you've been so careful whenever I've asked to come over?" A small smile formed on her lips. "You've been quite the gentleman."

"My honor wouldn't allow me to presume," he said quietly. "I would never disrespect you that way."

She moved closer, her eyes searching his. "You know, after what we've been through today… I don't want to be alone, but it's more than that." She reached for his hand. "I trust you, Antel. More than I've trusted anyone in a long time."

"I trust you too," he said, his voice low.

The tension between them shifted, fear giving way to something else entirely. The day's danger had stripped away pretenses, leaving only what mattered. Their eyes locked, and in that moment, something unspoken passed between them. She smiled, the earlier fear replaced by a playful gleam in her eyes.

"So, my alien supersoldier can fight off attackers with laser guns, but gets nervous around a girl?"

Becky walked to his bedroom door and opened it. She leaned against the door frame and posed in a sensual way, beckoning with her finger. "Get in here and let's find out what my supersoldier's got."

The big grin on her face made his face turn red.

Chapter 19

Antel called the team meeting at the usual time. As the crew filed into the kitchen, Sandun froze momentarily in the doorway when he spotted Becky seated at the table. He shot Antel a questioning glance before taking his seat.

Dr. Sallain entered next, his datapad tucked under his arm. Upon seeing Becky, he deliberately slid the device into his jacket pocket with a subtle frown.

"Lieutenant?" Emira whispered to Antel, her eyes darting between him and Becky. "Are we breaking protocol?"

Irina was less subtle, placing her datapad face-down on the table with a sharp click before sliding into the chair opposite Becky. Dalan and Liora exchanged uncomfortable glances as they took the remaining seats, their datapads clutched a bit too tightly in their hands.

The unspoken question hung in the air: Why had an Earth civilian been invited to their classified briefing?

"Good morning, everyone." Antel paused for a moment. "You're probably wondering why Rebecca is sitting among us during our staff morning briefing."

Everyone looked at each other but said nothing. Finally, Sandun spoke up, uncertain whether to address him formally or not. Sandun had no choice but to switch to Intallan. "Sir? Are we to understand that Miss Miller has been told about our true identity?"

"Yes, she now knows everything." Antel announced, pinching the bridge of his nose as he exhaled heavily. "This wasn't planned, but circumstances last night forced my hand." He switched back to English for Becky's sake, his shoulders visibly tense as he glanced around the table at his team. "Becky, dear, I think it's time I tell you what their real names are and what their real duties are."

Becky put her hand on his, her eyes wide with a mixture of wonder and apprehension as she nodded silently.

"Going around the table." Antel began, pointing at each person, calling out their real names and ranks. "This is Junior Lieutenant Sandun Kandos, the team's intelligence officer."

"I prefer the term spy." Sandun smirked. His joke made Becky smile.

Antel pointed to the next two. "Ensign Emira Khen, our linguist and communications officer. Ensign Irina Falron, our technical specialist."

Becky straightened in her chair, meeting each pair of eyes with newfound intensity. She offered a small, tentative wave, her historian's mind visibly cataloging their true identities against the cover stories she'd been told before.

Antel continued. "This is Dr. Dalan Myros, our medical officer."

Antel pointed at Dahnt and was about to introduce him, but Dahnt leaned forward abruptly, cutting Antel off with a dismissive wave of his hand.

"I am Dr. Dahnt Sallain, Professor of Exo-Political Science." He announced, chin lifted. "I'm not military like the rest of them." His tone carried an unmistakable note of arrogant pride, his smile thin and condescending as he regarded Becky with the air of someone examining a specimen from a primitive civilization.

"Exo-Political?" The term confused Becky.

"Alien politics." Dahnt explained, annoyed that he had to clarify. "To us, you are the aliens. We're here to study your world's political environment. To get a better understanding of the natives of Earth."

"I see." Becky said. The odd questions they'd asked about American elections, their stilted reactions to local customs, the strange technology she'd glimpsed: puzzle pieces that had never quite fit now snapped into place in her historian's mind.

"And this is Serviceman First Class Liora Trandenn, our cultural and socio-political analyst." Antel introduced the final person at the table.

"Now that you're in our club, I would love to pick your mind on a few things." Liora attempted to use Terran vernacular. "Did I say that right? Pick your mind? I'm still getting my toes wet with Earth expressions."

"Pick your brain." Becky corrected her. "And it's 'getting my feet wet,' not toes."

"And of course, I told you last night, I'm Lieutenant Antel Ralnar. I am the ranking officer of this expedition."

"Okay, now that's out of the way, let's get to work." Antel said. "Last night I detected another subspace signal, this time right here in our trees."

Emira's eyes widened with surprise, while Dr. Sallain raised his eyebrows so high they nearly disappeared into his hairline. Dalan blinked rapidly, processing this unexpected information. Only Sandun maintained his composure, having already been privy to this particular development.

"Ensign Falron, take Serviceman Trandenn and go into the forest and retrieve a subspace transmitter. I was hoping to leave it undisturbed, but they found out I was there, so pretending we don't know is out."

Becky just sat quietly in awe. She had always sensed Antel was a confident person, but watching him give commands with quiet authority revealed a new dimension to him that made Becky reassess everything she thought she knew about the man she'd been dating. He impressed her with his leadership skills. He didn't need to hold back anymore.

"Last night, as I was investigating the transmitter, someone shot at me."

"At us." Becky corrected him, straightening her shoulders with a pointed look. She wasn't about to let him minimize her involvement in what had happened.

"At us." Antel resumed. "He was a poor marksman, so I have my doubts he was one of the rogue soldiers. Junior Lieutenant Kandos, see if you can figure out which way the assailant went. Or any other clues as to who he or she was."

"Yes, sir." Sandun acknowledged.

Then Antel turned to Dalan. "Dr. Myros, how is our prisoner doing?"

"Wait! What?" Becky jerked backward, her fingers instinctively curling against the edge of the table as she leaned forward. "Did you say you have a prisoner?"

"Yes, long story." Antel told her.

"He's knocked out. The medication I gave him this morning is going to make him drowsy for hours." Dalan reported.

"What's this about a prisoner?" Becky wasn't going to let this pass.

"Night before last, we had a major skirmish at some abandoned small town. We managed to capture one, but the others got away."

"You mean at the ghost town." She said. "This explains a lot."

"That reminds me." Antel said. "I gave this some thought last night, and I will need to travel up to Mars to deliver Lieutenant Ballnus. Khen, can you contact Rell and arrange a pickup tonight?"

Emira nodded. "Yes, sir."

Becky leaned closer to Antel, her voice dropping to a conspiratorial whisper as she arched an eyebrow. "When exactly did you find time to 'think' about this last night? As I recall, your mind was otherwise occupied." A hint of mischief played at the corners of her mouth as her eyes held his.

She didn't mean for anyone else to hear that, but it was clear to everyone at the table what she said. Sandun abruptly coughed into his fist while Emira pressed her lips together, shoulders shaking with suppressed laughter. Irina suddenly found her datapad fascinating, though her ears had turned pink. When Antel caught Dalan's widening grin, he leveled a stern look across the table, and the team's amusement quickly settled into barely contained smiles.

"Um, does this mean you'll be gone for a few months?" Becky had to ask. She wasn't thrilled with the idea of him going on a long space voyage just as she was learning his true identity.

"No, it's only going to be for a week or two." He told her. "And, uh, since you're already in on our secret, I think it might be best I bring you along. My superior officer will probably have questions for you when he finds out I had to let you in on our secret."

"Wow. Mars? Me?"

"Hell yeah! I wanna go!" Becky practically bounced in her seat, eyes alight with excitement as she leaned forward eagerly. "What's on Mars?"

"We have an outpost there. Not much else." Antel said, trying not to oversell it. To Antel, life in the outpost was fairly routine. He didn't consider the unique opportunity that Becky considered this trip to be.

"Does this mean I'll be the first from Earth to set foot on Mars?"

"I'm afraid not, Miss Miller. There have been a few others. Dr. Carter, for one." Dahnt cut in.

"Makes sense." Becky mumbled to herself. "All this must be what Dr. Carter's been keeping from me."

"Does everyone understand their tasks?" Antel asked the team.

The team all responded, "Yes, sir."

Antel finished with "Very good, then. Dismissed."

Just as everyone got up to begin their tasks, Sandun put one hand on Antel's shoulder and the other on Becky's shoulder. "I'm so glad you finally know about our mission, my friends. I've been telling Antel here to loosen up and that you would understand."

"Thank you, Sam, uh, what was it? Sandun." Becky felt welcomed by Sandun's comments.

"Excellent memory, my friend." Sandun replied. Then, before leaving to work on his tasks for the day, he turned to Antel. "And you. You better not drop this in the sewer. This young lady is perfect for you."

"Was that expression your version of 'don't fuck this up?'" Becky asked Antel.

"Something like that, yeah." Antel stood up. "I'd better go pack. Tonight we are leaving for Mars."

"I'm gonna need to pack too, right?"

"Yeah, we can do that after dinner with your parents. This will give you all day to think of an excuse for leaving town. We still can't tell them yet."

"Sir, yes, sir." Becky joked as she flashed him a standard Terran salute.

Antel only smiled. He decided he would show her the correct salute another time.

Antel turned on his datapad and began reviewing signal data while Becky gathered her backpack and worked on her dissertation. Dahnt lingered behind, methodically gathering his papers.

"Lieutenant," Dahnt said, his voice carrying across the kitchen. "A moment of your time?"

Antel glanced up, noting how Dahnt remained standing at the far end of the table. His posture was stiff and formal. The scientist's fingers drummed a controlled pattern on his datapad, a subtle sign of impatience that Antel had come to recognize from their previous disagreements.

"Of course." Seeing that Dahnt wasn't getting any closer, Antel assumed he needed to hear what Dahnt had to say with some distance from Becky.

"Regarding our signal analysis," Dahnt continued in Intallan, his eyes briefly flicking toward Becky before returning to Antel. Antel caught the pointed glance and felt a twinge of irritation at Dahnt's obvious discomfort with her presence.

"The frequency patterns we're tracking show signs of intentional misdirection. The shifts are too predictable."

"Explain."

"They could be broadcasting their actual communications on entirely different bands while we waste resources on decoys." Dahnt's fingers tightened around his datapad, his knuckles whitening slightly as he maintained his rigid posture. "And I find it... interesting... that these signals consistently appear when Ensign Falron isn't around."

Becky briefly glanced up at the unfamiliar language before returning to her work, but Antel noticed Dahnt's posture tighten further at her presence.

"Dahnt, you've raised concerns about Irina before," Antel replied, keeping his tone neutral. "You may have a point about her absence each time there's a signal, but nothing in her behavior indicates she's involved."

"I merely present observable patterns, Lieutenant." Dahnt straightened, adjusting his collar. "Also, on a separate note, Earth's technological advancements, such as their quantum encryption capabilities and weapons development, are all progressing faster than our models predicted."

"I haven't seen that," Antel disagreed, annoyed that Dahnt managed to abruptly change the subject to yet another settled matter. "But even if that were true, that's not our primary concern right now. Our mission is to study their national and international political structures. Alliances, forms of government, hostilities, that sort of thing."

"We shouldn't ignore the implications just because it isn't our direct mission. All of this warrants consideration."

"If you have solid evidence, bring it to me and we can include it in our report." Antel was getting annoyed. "Otherwise, stick to the mission parameters."

"Is that an order?"

"You know I can't give civilians orders unless it's in an emergency. But I'm sure your grant could be affected if you don't bring back a helpful report."

"Don't let your opinions become clouded," Dahnt said, his voice lowering with a cautionary bite, his gaze flicking toward Becky before returning to Antel. "Don't let personal factors influence operational decisions."

Antel could see Becky pause in her writing, glancing between them with a questioning look at the foreign speech before giving a small shrug and turning back to her notebook.

Antel's jaw tightened. "Dr. Sallain, I assure you my judgment isn't compromised."

"Of course not." Dahnt's tone remained carefully measured. "I would be negligent if I didn't point out potential variables to you." He paused, then added, "I'd like to speak with our prisoner. Since I'm not military, I might yield better results."

Antel studied him. Something in Dahnt's carefully neutral expression made Antel hesitate, but the request itself was reasonable. "Fine. If he tells you anything helpful, I want to know about it right away."

"Naturally." Dahnt gathered his remaining papers. "And, Lieutenant? The Standard Protocol exists for valid reasons. All of them." His gaze flickered once more to Becky before he turned and left the kitchen.

Antel's throat tightened as he considered how far he'd already bent the rules. He watched Dahnt go. He knew that Dahnt didn't like him, but he did make valid points, especially with his precisely chosen words about the Standard Protocol.

"What was that about?" Becky asked quietly.

"Just mission details," Antel replied, but Dahnt left him wondering how much trouble he should expect to find himself in when he met with Senior Lieutenant Ranston on Mars.

Antel decided not to let any of that distract him. As far as he was concerned, capturing the transmitter, finally not having to keep secrets from Becky, and the progress into uncovering the rogue soldiers all meant he was finally winning. He pushed Dahnt's warnings from his mind. The doctor's concerns were noted, but Antel had kept everything under control so far. For the first time in weeks, he could sit across from Becky without the weight of deception between them. Meeting her parents tonight would be another step forward. Antel allowed himself a small smile as he watched Becky organize her notes, determined to enjoy this evening without the shadow of protocol and duty hanging over him.

Later in the day, Becky drove home to prepare for her Mars trip. Antel accompanied her to finally meet her parents. Becky sat at her parents' dining room table, watching Antel charm them with idle conversation. After the events of last night, his presence in such a normal setting felt surreal.

Her father, Robert, was a middle-aged man with a round face and thinning gray hair and the habit of leaning forward intently when something caught his interest. Despite being an attorney, he was a science buff and was fascinated with Antel's "theories" about the future. Antel made confident predictions about what he thought Earth's future would look like, explaining how "antimatter power cells will make current battery technology obsolete within the century." Becky couldn't help but think that Antel was sort of cheating because he was using his own planet, Arkonus, as a guide.

"I'm so glad you could join us for dinner after all," her mother, Elaine, a slender woman in her early fifties with long brown hair and a warm smile, said as she passed the garlic bread. "When you had to cancel breakfast this morning, I was disappointed, but dinner turned out to be a much better way to first meet you, Andrew."

"I apologize for the change in plans," Antel said, pausing his meal entirely. "There was an urgent situation at the house that required immediate attention."

Becky's father studied Antel over his glass of wine. "I understand you are also a history graduate student. Becky tells me your project is classified. Is there anything you could say about it? Like maybe at least why the secrecy over something related to the subject of history?"

"Dad," Becky interjected, "remember I told you he can't talk about it? He's consulting on a government project."

Her father nodded slowly, the understanding clear in his eyes even as disappointment flickered across his features. "Right. I was only asking because Becky here was very concerned about it recently."

"Actually, Dad," Becky said, meeting her parents' eyes, "Andrew explained everything to me last night. I can't share the details because he wasn't supposed to tell me, but I understand now why there had to be so much secrecy." She reached for Antel's hand under the table, her fingers intertwining with his in a firm, reassuring grip. "I trust him completely."

Her mother's worried expression softened. "Well, I'm so relieved. You've seemed so troubled lately, dear."

"Which reminds me," Becky said, glancing at Antel before turning back to her parents. "I need to tell you both something. Andrew invited me on a short trip. We'll only be gone for a few days."

Her father set down his fork. "Where to?"

Becky hesitated, knowing she couldn't tell them about Mars. "It's related to his work. I can't say more than that. Let's just say it's in the desert." The words felt heavy on her tongue, each one a small betrayal of the openness she'd always shared with her parents. Her stomach twisted as she watched their faces. The same faces that had comforted her through every scraped knee and broken heart now looked at her with a mixture of concern and confusion she was powerless to ease. The weight of the secret pressed against her chest like a physical thing, making it hard to breathe normally. She put her hand gently on Antel's wrist and gave him an apologetic look that told him she finally understood how much his deception must have broken his heart each time.

"Rebecca," her father started, but her mother touched his arm gently, a subtle signal to let it go. "She's a grown woman, dear," her mother said. "And if she trusts Andrew, we should too."

Antel sat up straight in his chair, his military bearing evident as he prepared to make a solemn promise. "Mr. and Mrs. Miller, I give you my word that I'll keep Becky safe. This trip is important for both of us."

Her father studied them both for a long moment before nodding. "Okay, keep in touch when you can."

"We'll try," Becky promised, squeezing Antel's hand. She knew her parents didn't realize the true significance of this dinner. They didn't know it, but they were sending their daughter not just across the country, but across the void of space to another world entirely. Seeing the trust in their eyes, the way they'd chosen to believe in her judgment and in Antel despite their obvious concerns, filled her with a warmth that had nothing to do with the cozy dining room. Their acceptance didn't just mean everything to her; it felt like a blessing for the impossible journey ahead.

Chapter 20

The Black Cat's hull gently vibrated as Junior Lieutenant Zhon Rell eased power to the engines. Becky was seated in one of the seats on the crew deck, the deck just below the bridge. Standing over her, Antel was connecting and adjusting her safety straps.

"You are all snug and tight now," Antel declared as he yanked one last strap. "This is going to feel like the most intense roller coaster ride you've ever been on."

Before he could step away, Becky's fingers dug into Antel's arm. "This is going to be safe, right? I mean, there's no chance the rockets will blow up in the middle of liftoff, right?" Her stomach knotted with that familiar mix of fear and excitement, like those seconds before a roller coaster's first plunge.

"Dear, that's not going to happen. You have nothing to fear." Antel saw her hands trembling. He took her hands and squeezed. "I'll be right here by your side. Junior Lieutenant Rell promised me to keep it under three g-forces. The worst that can happen is that you'll pass out."

"Okay, I trust you, Antel," Becky said just before she realized what he said. "Wait, did you say pass out?"

"The three times normal gravity is only for a few minutes as we take off," he reassured her. "Once we're en route to Mars, we'll be at a comfortable one-g for the rest of the trip."

Antel strapped himself in and took her hand to comfort her. With

160

his other hand, he pressed the comm button on the armrest, then spoke in Intallan. "Rell, we are all strapped. You may lift off when ready."

"Understood, the trip should take us 3.8 days, in case you'd like to let our guest know."

Antel let go of the comm button and turned to speak to Becky in English. "We're about to take off. Rell says the trip should take 3.8 days."

"Three? I thought you said it was a little over four days." Becky's memory was excellent.

"The planets have moved closer since the last trip. If we waited for the right moment when Earth and Mars are at their closest, we might get it down to two days!" Antel was showing off. "Faster at a higher acceleration in case of emergencies."

"Wow, Mars in two days." Becky's eyes widened, and her jaw dropped slightly. "NASA would be so jealous if they ever find out. So no warp speed?"

"You mean hyperspace," Antel said as a matter of fact. "That's reserved for interstellar travel. Planets are too close together to navigate in hyperspace accurately. The Sun's gravity well would throw our trajectory off."

Becky had so many questions swirling in her head, but before she could ask the next question, the Black Cat's soft vibration changed to a hard rattle as the weight of gravity gradually increased.

The Black Cat lifted off the ground and shot into the sky. Becky expected to hear the roar of flames, but instead, she heard a loud whine coming from the ship's four thrusters.

All of Becky's questions suddenly disappeared, replaced with the thrill of the takeoff. She squeezed Antel's hand as hard as she could as she yelled in slow motion, "OH MY GOD!"

Antel looked over to check on her. She had her eyes closed, and her other hand was clamped hard on the armrest. This reminded him of his first time launching into space, when he was a young boy. His family went on a trip to Arkonus's larger moon, Turek, for a vacation. He remembered his first liftoff was exhilarating.

To her credit, Becky didn't pass out. But her heart was pounding so hard it could have helped power the ship.

Once the ship reached space, Zhon shut down the thrusters and only used short gravitational wave bursts to enter a circular orbit, a necessary step before charting the path to Mars. Then, after thirty minutes, not even a third of the way around its orbit around the Earth, Zhon aimed the ship in the proper direction and turned the thruster back on, but this time at a comfortable acceleration.

Antel unstrapped himself after Zhon gave word that he was done. He then moved to Becky and began unstrapping her restraints.

"That was..." Becky put her hands on her chest and paused to catch her breath. "That was exciting!"

Antel reached into a storage space inset into the wall behind her and pulled out a small white paper bag.

"Here." Antel handed the bag to her as he began unstrapping her restraints.

"What's this for..." Becky said, then she felt a surge in her stomach. It felt like a volcano erupting. She immediately realized what the bag was for and threw up in it.

Antel took the bag and sealed it as he smiled at her. "I'm impressed, you took that rather well. Normal commercial flights usually take off much slower than that, but we couldn't risk staying in the sky for too long, or we would get discovered."

The next three days blurred together. To Becky, the trip felt about the same as an ordinary plane ride. Cruise was probably more accurate since they didn't have to remain seated.

Up until the last moment before their final approach, the most exciting moment was when Zhon had to shut off the engines, turn the ship to face the opposite direction, and begin the deceleration portion of the trip. That gave her plenty of time to enjoy the zero gravity.

But when Zhon told her that Mars was approaching and would be visible through the windows soon, she was excited to marvel at the sight of a new planet. She bounced from window to window looking for the red planet.

"I can't see it." She was beginning to get disappointed.

"Look down," Antel told her. He was sitting at the common room's table, finishing a nutrient-rich but tasteless drink. They had just had dinner.

Her brow furrowed. "I thought there was no 'down' in space," she stammered, her voice uncertain.

"The Black Cat is decelerating at the moment. The ship is most likely pointing away from the planet." He pointed toward the floor. "Mars is probably that way."

Becky's eyes lit up again as she ran over to one of the windows and looked in the direction Antel called "down."

"Oh wow, Antel, it's so beautiful," she said, without taking her eyes off the slowly growing red sphere. "Am I seriously going to be one of only a few first Americans to set foot on Mars?"

"Yeah, I suppose that's true," Antel replied. "Did I just mess up future Terran history books?"

"Add this to the list of things NASA won't be happy about." She turned to look at Antel. "Don't tell me you beat Neil Armstrong to the moon, too, did you?"

"The Moon? Nah. He probably landed there before we discovered Earth." Antel got up and walked to the window to share the view of Mars. "We rarely ever set foot on the Moon. We considered it too close to the Earth to set up a base. The risk of discovery would have been much higher there."

Becky felt that was an odd reason not to land on the Moon. Antel made it sound like the Moon was nothing more than some tiny uninhabited island a cruise ship would skip right past without thinking about it.

Antel moved behind her and wrapped his arms around her as they watched Mars approach. They wanted this moment to last forever, but eventually, Zhon called out from the ship's communications system, letting Antel know to strap in as he was about to prepare for landing.

The landing was smoother than Becky expected. The ship didn't have to decelerate as hard on Mars as it had to on Earth since there was no rush to avoid detection. Zhon was able to make the descent as gently as he could.

"Welcome to Mars," Zhon's voice crackled over the ship's intercom. "You are officially one of a select few Terrans to ever visit Mars."

"Time to play the music with my superior officer," Antel sighed, knowing this was going to be a difficult conversation.

163

"Face the music," Becky chuckled. "It's face the music."

"I knew the way I was saying that expression couldn't have been correct," Antel said as he finished unstrapping her seat belts. "But it still makes no sense."

"I can't wait to see inside this base." Becky's excitement was contagious.

"Stay close to me," he told her. "There's going to be a lot to take in, and most everyone there can't speak English."

"Aye, aye, Captain!" Trying to be silly, she gave him a salute in the traditional Terran salute with her hand over her brow.

As they stepped from the ship into the docking bay, Becky was amazed at the efficiency of the base. The walls looked like they were made of steel, but she was sure it was advanced alloy. Next to every door was some kind of panel, presumably for controlling the door. Maybe an intercom to boot.

The base was bustling with activity. Uniformed personnel moved back and forth, conducting their daily routines. Most of the uniforms looked the same as Antel's red tunic and black pants. The biggest difference was the markings on the shoulders, which had to be their ranks.

A couple of them, as they passed by Antel, saluted him. The first thing she noticed was that their salute was different from Earth's. The flat palm was placed diagonally across the heart instead of over the eyes.

"Lieutenant Ralnar, welcome back to Mars," said one of the men in Intallan. "The senior lieutenant asked us to take care of your luggage for you and your companion."

"Thank you, serviceman," Antel replied in Intallan. Then he turned to Becky. "These servicemen are here to take our stuff to my quarters."

"Servicemen?" The term confused her because they didn't look like mechanics or the sort.

"Those are their ranks, Serviceman 2nd Class and Serviceman 3rd Class. They're not officers. They're what you might call enlisted," Antel clarified.

"Ah, gotcha."

"But he's an officer," Antel said, seeing the senior lieutenant approaching. Antel stood at attention and saluted him. Becky just watched. Antel's sudden formality meant this one probably outranked him.

"Welcome back, Ralnar," Ranston snapped a quick salute, allowing Antel to end his. "Who is our new guest?" The only word Becky understood was Ralnar.

"Sir, this is Rebecca Miller," Antel replied in Intallan. This time was easier to understand. She immediately knew Antel was introducing her to his boss.

"Nice to meet you," she extended her hand to shake his. "You can call me Becky for short."

Ranston hesitated. He didn't understand what the outstretched hand meant, but when Antel translated what she said and explained the meaning of the handshake, he stretched out his hand to meet hers.

"Hello, me is Kalos Ranston," he did his best to say in very broken English. "Welcome on Mars you be."

"Thank you," she smiled back at him because she assumed he might not understand what she said. A smile was hopefully universal.

Ranston turned to tell Antel, "We will discuss the details of her presence in my office later. For now, feel free to give her a tour. Just keep her away from sensitive areas."

"Yes, sir," Antel replied.

After showing her around, Antel took her to the base's mess hall. The large room hummed with the activity of personnel in conversations with each other. To Becky, it looked no different than a small high school cafeteria: food trays, long tables, even the line for the slop cafeterias like to call food.

Antel and Becky sat in a quiet spot away from the crowd. It was then she realized that many of them were taking glances at her. For many of them, this was probably their first time seeing someone from Earth up close. A few would say something in their language and point in her direction. They weren't being impolite. Anyone she saw pointing her way made it a point to wave hello to her with a welcoming smile. As strange as it felt being looked at as someone important, she still liked it there.

A graduate student shuffled forward, wringing his hands, and spoke rapidly in Intallan with his eyes darting between Antel and Rebecca. "He wants to know if Earth's musical scales evolved independently or if Terrans use a mathematical basis for harmony," Antel translated, and Rebecca shook her head with a laugh, saying she was a history student, not a music theorist, which made the student's face fall slightly before he launched into another animated stream of words. "Now he's asking if you know whether they at least write music in some kind of written notation," Antel said, and Rebecca perked up, explaining the little she knew of musical scales.

She was about to talk about some of Earth's famous composers from the past but was interrupted when another crew member edged closer, then another, until a small crowd had formed, all speaking at once in overlapping questions that made Rebecca feel like she was facing an impromptu press conference. "One at a time," Antel said in Intallan before turning to Rebecca. "They want to know about Earth food, Earth weather, Earth customs, basically everything." A woman pushed through the group, speaking slowly in heavily accented English: "Is... is true that Terran people remove shoes before entering homes?" When Rebecca explained that it varied by culture and family, the woman's eyes widened as she turned to the others and spoke rapidly as if Rebecca had settled a disputed theory.

Antel was scrolling through something on a datapad. He said mostly they were just messages from his parents or siblings from home. A few here and there were bills. She thought it was funny. "I guess even in the future, you still have to pay your taxes," she told him.

She watched the room intently. It felt like a vacation abroad. Antel would look up at Becky every few minutes to make sure she knew he wasn't ignoring her. She didn't mind him catching up on his messages. She was busy marveling at the experience.

Then Becky saw a young woman with blond hair, blue eyes, and a slender build approaching them. Very pretty. Someone approaching to talk with this Terran was normal, but this time seemed different. Becky immediately noticed that Antel saw the woman approaching and appeared tense. He sighed and mumbled in English with a sarcastic tone, "Kossdra. Perfect timing."

"Something wrong, dear?" she asked as softly as she could, touching his arm to try to relax the tension in his shoulders.

Before Antel could say anything, Nela was already at the table and sat across from them. Actually, instead of across the table from Becky, as everyone else who wanted to meet her did, this woman sat across from Antel.

Becky whispered to Antel, "This feels awkward."

"Antel!" Nela said in a high-pitched, excited voice. "It's so good to see you back."

Antel only said one word, "Nela," in a low tone that advertised his annoyed feeling. Antel turned to Becky and summarized the what Nela said, "This is Nela. She's basically saying hello to us."

"She is your ex, isn't she?" Becky asked him. She could sense the annoyed tone in his voice.

"Yes," he answered Becky's question. "I'm sorry about this." He didn't bother to translate back to Nela.

Becky, sensing that the atmosphere had changed, extended her hand. "Hi, I'm Rebecca Miller."

Antel had to explain to Nela the meaning of the handshake as he translated Becky's greeting.

Nela shook Becky's hand after Antel explained what it meant and only said her name as she pointed to herself with her left hand, "Nela Molain."

The awkwardness was palpable. Antel had meticulously maintained an emotional distance from Nela since their breakup, but proximity had a way of reopening old emotional pathways. He could see Becky observing, watching his every subtle shift in body language.

Nela turned to Antel, "We need to talk about us, Antel. I don't think we should ruin a great friendship just because, uh..." Nela glanced at Becky for a moment, "...just because we moved on. You look happy now, and I'm happy for you. But please."

Antel leaned back, crossing his arms, his face unreadable. "You're right. Miss Miller makes me very happy," he said as he uncrossed his arms, leaned forward, and grabbed Becky's hand and held it.

Becky didn't know what they were saying, but she could tell she probably should let it play out without interrupting them.

"So why not go back to being friends?" Nela asked in Intallan.

"We're not going back to being friends," Antel said, his voice low. A muscle twitched near his jaw.

Nela's fingers curled around her datapad. "I thought maybe..."

"No," he cut her off, glancing at Becky. "That's our past. It's time for me to create a new future."

"I understand." Nela was disappointed. "In that case, would Miss Miller be interested in discussing Terran political systems for my thesis research?"

Antel hesitated. "Our time here on Mars will be short. Miss Miller would need to agree." He hadn't translated to Becky yet.

"Could you ask her?" Nela fought back a tear. "It would be very helpful."

Antel took a deep breath and exhaled in a puff. "Fine." Antel turned to Becky and switched to English. "She's asking if you would be open to talking with her about Earth's political systems."

"Sure, why not?" Becky said.

"Feel free to decline if you don't want to," Antel added.

"No, it's fine. Besides, I'm curious about anyone foolish enough to let you go."

"You're not going to ask her about me, are you?" Antel rolled his eyes.

"No promises," Becky gave him a guilty smile.

A sharp ping interrupted them. Antel's datapad displayed a terse message: "Ralnar. My office. Now."

He exhaled, tension visible in the set of his shoulders. "My commanding officer wants to speak with me," he told Becky, leaning in for a quick kiss.

"Good luck," Becky said, her eyes tracking his movement. "I'm sure she can find a translator while you're gone."

Antel stood up and headed out of the mess hall.

He had to meet with the Senior Lieutenant anyway to discuss events on Earth, but the tone in the message felt like he was going to be in... how do the Terrans say it? In deep shit.

Chapter 21

Senior Lieutenant Ranston's office felt cold, not in temperature but in atmosphere. His steel-blue eyes bore into Antel like a high-powered proton beam. Antel could see him drumming his fingers on the metallic table surface. A datapad lay on the table with Antel's report displayed on the screen.

"Lieutenant," Ranston said, his voice terse and clipped, "take a seat."

Antel took the seat on the opposite side of the desk from Ranston.

"Let's start with this vehicle chase through the middle of the city." Ranston was referring to the car chase after his date with Becky.

"When I exited the park and proceeded to my vehicle, I saw suspicious activity in the parking lot," Antel began to recount the events starting from the moment he saw the car. "I saw someone I knew standing by the vehicle and speaking with an unknown person or persons sitting inside the vehicle. At first, I didn't think much of it until they abruptly ended their conversation as soon as they saw me looking in their direction. I then decided…"

"Who was that person?" Ranston cut him off.

"Sorry?" Antel acted confused, but he knew who Ranston meant.

"The 'person you knew.'"

"Oh, his name was Neil Morris, an officer in the Terran military."

"How do you know this Terran, and why were you at this," Ranston paused to look it up on his datapad, "Botanical Garden? Did you develop a new hobby with flowers?" Ranston's voice sounded both upset and sarcastic at the same time.

"Um...no, sir, I was..." Antel tried to respond carefully.

Ranston cut him off again. "I presume it was a date. A date with Miss Miller."

"Yes, sir," Antel admitted.

"Did it occur to you that forming a relationship with a Terran was a risk to the mission?" Ranston leaned back with his arms crossed.

"I did consider that," Antel said, "but Miss Miller is Dr. Carter's graduate student. Honestly, it was only a matter of time before she learned about us anyway. At least she agrees to keep the secret."

"That's just luck," Ranston blurted. "But you're right. Given how close Carter and Miller are, this might make it easier to keep your cover. You just make sure it stays a secret."

"Understood." Antel's heart finally began to relax. That could have been worse.

"So, according to your report, you feel the mysterious signal, the rogue soldiers, and this car chase were all related?"

"It would be too much of a coincidence otherwise."

"I agree. It's clear the passengers of that car were some of the rogue soldiers. But there's something I don't get."

"Sir?"

"Everyone with the ability to speak English is either accounted for back on Arkonus, here on Mars, or on your team. How, in the Universe, could they speak with a Terran without a translator?"

"That's a good question." Antel's brow furrowed in curiosity. He looked down and put his hand on his chin to think. "The only thing I can think of is that more people have learned English who aren't in our records, or maybe Morris learned Intallan."

"I seriously doubt he learned Intallan," Ranston said. "We're missing something."

"Another possibility is that someone on the team is violating Standard Protocol and is coordinating with these rogue soldiers."

Antel considered telling him that Dahnt suspected Irina, but perhaps out of bias, Antel couldn't imagine how that would be the case.

"And where did these rogue soldiers come from?" Ranston

wondered out loud.

"Rilee?"

"Not what I meant," Ranston said. "I mean, how did they land on Earth? My guess is they're the ones behind the unidentified subspace messages."

"They must be communicating with a ship somewhere in the system," Antel theorized. "That's the only explanation I can think of."

"We need to keep to radio silence," Ranston ordered. "We don't want them to listen in on our conversations."

"Yes, sir."

"Keep it to scheduled check-ins. Take a subspace jamming unit with you back to Earth. See if you can make use of it to somehow catch them. Lethal force is approved."

"Understood." Antel was excited. The thought of possible combat was his expertise.

"Is that long-range subspace transmitter still in the forest on the farmhouse's grounds?"

"No, sir," Antel said. "I had the team bring it into the farmhouse."

"This Morris person, military officer, you say?"

"Yes, senior lieutenant, I think." Antel's heart nearly dropped. "Wait. Are you thinking that these rogue soldiers are sharing technology with the Terran military?"

"If they are, this would be serious." Ranston clenched a fist. "I need you to get to the bottom of this. We may as well make good use of Miss Miller. She would make a good asset for this."

"An asset?" Antel was confused. Just a few minutes ago, his relationship with Becky was a liability. Now she's an asset?

"Don't get me wrong. I'm still not happy about this, but the Standard Protocol only requires that we keep our presence from becoming common knowledge on Earth. Making a few exceptions here and there is okay as long as they don't spread it," Ranston explained.

"Understood." Antel felt a wave of relief. He knew he was getting close to crossing the line, but the Senior Lieutenant's interpretation of the Standard Protocol Law made sense. Antel couldn't help being hard on himself. Something Sandun was trying to explain to him.

"You will need to balance your personal feelings with the mission. She will need to understand that. Meanwhile, her knowledge of

Earth's infrastructure could make her invaluable in apprehending those rogue soldiers while navigating local authorities and military carefully."

Ranston reached over to a set of buttons on his desk and pressed one. "Serviceman, please find Miss Miller and escort her to my office."

"Yes, sir," crackled the serviceman's voice over the desk speaker.

The door buzzed. Ranston pressed the button on his desk. "Yes?"

"Miss Miller is here, sir."

"Send her in," ordered Ranston.

Becky entered, her gaze darting between Antel and Ranston. The military office made her feel even more out of place, alien technology humming in the walls, officers in crisp uniforms speaking a language she couldn't understand.

Ranston gestured to a chair. She recognized the invitation despite the language barrier.

As Becky sat, she looked at Antel, wondering if they were in some kind of trouble. Antel covered her hand with his, giving a reassuring squeeze.

Ranston spoke to Antel directly. "Lieutenant, brief her on the incidents she doesn't know about."

"Yes, sir." Antel turned to Becky, switching to English. "Senior Lieutenant Ranston wants me to update you on what's happened on Earth."

Her brow furrowed. "I thought you told me everything."

"I told you what I could. Some details that, as an officer, I needed to keep confidential."

"From me?"

"From everyone. As a military officer, there will be things I can't share."

She exhaled through her nose. "Fine. I get it."

Antel laid out the facts. He told her about the mystery signal that first alerted them to the rogue presence, the shootout at the engineering building where Irina was injured, the grey car he followed after their date at the city gardens, and finally the forest attack where he found the subspace transmitter.

She was speechless. She knew things were serious when that

crazy weapon in the forest shot at her, but this was bigger than she expected. Much bigger. She never could have imagined how much was going on.

"That's everything," Antel said.

Ranston's next words were clipped, professional. Antel translated: "He's asking if you have questions."

Silence stretched. "Do you think Neil might be involved? How convenient that they'd approach him of all people."

"They likely observed our altercation. He was an obvious choice—someone with a grudge against me." Antel repeated his answer in Intallan for Ranston.

"You're certain he doesn't know the truth?"

"Fairly certain. He isn't acting like he knows anything."

"Then they've been watching you." Her voice sharpened. "That's the only way they'd know to approach him."

"Agreed."

Her eyes widened. "Wait, you guys wouldn't tell me all this unless you needed my help."

Antel translated Ranston's next statement: "We believe the rogue soldiers contacted your ex-boyfriend. We need to know what they talked about. He wasn't that forthcoming with me. Since I've already confronted him once, another approach would raise suspicions."

"Okay." The word came out uncertain.

"You can refuse. I'd prefer you weren't in danger." His jaw tightened. "Especially involving Neil."

"Why not Dr. Carter?" she asked.

"Carter doesn't know Neil. He wouldn't trust her. As his ex, you have a reason to contact him without suspicion."

"And Ranston trusts me?"

Heat crept up his neck.

She covered her mouth, stifling a laugh. "Because your commanding officer knows I have incentive to help."

"Something like that."

"I'm just a history student. Are you sure I can do this?"

Ranston's response was firm. Antel translated: "We need to know their plans before they can use him against us or Earth."

Fear shifted to determination in her expression. "So I'm actually helping? Not just observing?"

"Helping, yes." Antel kept his voice level despite Ranston's presence. "But you stay away from danger. These operatives have already killed. They won't hesitate."

"I'm in." No hesitation. "I want to help."

After translating, she gave Ranston a thumbs-up and a nervous smile.

As they left Ranston's office, Becky took his hand.

"She is now more involved in the mission, and it was all my fault," Antel thought.

Antel sat in his quarters, facing the monitor. Becky sat on the bed and waited as he flipped through his messages until he reached the one he was looking for. It was a recorded incoming message from his parents back home in Sillence, Rilee.

The message was a reply to a message that Antel had sent them the last time he was on Mars. In that message, he had mentioned, among other things, his growing connection with Becky.

He tapped the keyboard, and his father's image appeared on the screen. Aral Ralnar, a fifty-year-old man with a stern yet kind face, had dark blond hair just like Antel's but beginning to gray.

Beside him was Rina Andolf, a forty-five-year-old woman with a slender build, brown hair, and fair skin. She was wearing a nice light-colored blouse with a modest V-neckline. Her face had a gentle smile. In his culture, wives didn't take their husbands' surnames. Instead, daughters took their mothers' surnames.

His father spoke first. "We are so glad to hear from you, Antel," said Aral in Intallan. "You looked healthy and well in your message."

Rina leaned closer to the camera. "You seem well, but you spoke of challenges that worry us. Are the documentaries about the Terrans accurate? They make it sound like the people are kind, but everyone there is armed and shooting each other is commonplace."

"I'm sure that's not accurate," Aral cut in. "But if it is true, you should be careful there."

Antel made a mental note to tell them Earth was nowhere near as dangerous as the documentaries portrayed it. Ironically, Antel thought, the most dangerous people he had encountered on Earth were other Rileeans.

"Speaking of Terrans," Antel's mother said, "who is this Rebecca you mentioned?"

And there it was. It didn't take long for Becky's name to come up. Leave it to his mother to get excited about her boy's love life.

"She must be very special to have won your heart," Rina continued, her voice warm with motherly affection.

Becky saw Antel's face begin to flush. "Everything okay, dear? I thought I heard my name."

"Yeah, they're just asking about you." Antel paused the playback of the message. "I may have mentioned you in my last message to them."

Becky sat up, crossed her arms, and put on a big smile. "May have mentioned me?"

Antel just returned a smile, then resumed the playback.

"I hope she doesn't compromise your mission," Antel's father said. Leave it to his father to bring him back to reality. "If you two get serious, you may have to figure out if you could bring her here or if you may have to stay there on Earth. Remember, bringing her here could become a future diplomatic incident."

"Staying on Earth would mean you would have to resign your position in the Imperial Forces. That would make you a nameless resident with no real proof of documented existence," Rina added. "You would have to live in hiding."

"Kossdra," Antel muttered in Intallan. Becky remembered Antel had told her it meant "curse," which was short for "Curse the Universe," the Rileean version of "Oh shit."

That was not something he had thought about. Antel wasn't sure he should worry Becky about the logistics of their long-term future today. He simply said, "It's nothing to worry about," and decided to figure it out later.

Rina put her hand on Aral's shoulder. "Of course, if she makes you happy, Antel, we would love to get to know her."

The message continued. It covered other family topics, such as Antel's sister and her current projects for her graduate studies. The message ended with his parents expressing their love and reminding him to stay safe.

Antel exhaled slowly. His parents' words were gentle yet clear. While they trusted him, they still worried.

Antel switched from playback to recording. He straightened his posture and centered the monitor on him. Speaking in Intallan, he began his reply.

"Mom, Dad, it's always great to hear your voices," he said.

Seeing a son recording a message to his parents warmed her heart. Although she understood none of what he was saying to them, she could still hear the caring in his voice.

Antel continued speaking in Intallan for a little while. Becky's mind was starting to tune out the conversation when she heard her name—the only words she understood. Her attention was quickly pulled back.

Antel paused and looked over to Becky. "Becky, come closer. I would like to introduce you to my parents."

"Me?" she asked.

Antel scooted in the chair to give her half of the seat so she could sit by his side.

Antel resumed in Intallan. "This is Rebecca Miller. She goes by Becky." Then he turned to Becky. "Say hello."

"Um." She was feeling a bit awkward, but gave a genuine smile and waved her hand. "Hello. It's so nice to meet you."

Antel translated her greeting into the camera for his parents. Antel finished by telling his parents, "Well, until our next message. Love you both."

Antel thought to himself, "My parents are bound to have an endless barrage of questions for me on their next call. For now, I'll just need to balance the mission and Becky, all while keeping her out of danger."

Chapter 22

Antel sat on the living room couch and sifted through the data on his datapad. His feet were propped up on the coffee table. He was so engrossed in his work that he didn't hear Becky walking up from behind. She was holding a plate with a grilled cheese sandwich cut in half in one hand and a hand towel in the other.

Becky surprised him with a light tap on the shoulder with the towel and said, "Hey! Feet off the table."

"Huh?" Antel said, his attention returning to the real world.

"You heard me. Feet off the table," she repeated.

He pulled his feet off and put them on the floor, then cracked a joke. "I think you would get along with my mother very well."

She only smiled as she sat next to him. "Here, try one of these."

He picked up half of the sandwich while glancing back at his datapad. He took a bite. He put the datapad down on his lap, and his eyes shifted to the sandwich. "Mmm. I like this. What is it?" he said with his mouth full.

Just as Becky was going to answer, Antel's datapad made an audible beep. Antel's expression shifted to a concerned frown as he picked it back up to see what the warning message was for.

"What's the matter?" She saw his face change.

Antel squinted his eyes at the datapad. "I got an alert. Someone's exploring our background and financial information." Antel stood up and called out for Sandun. "Junior Lieutenant, you need to see this."

Sandun entered the living room from the kitchen with a glass of water in his hand. "Yes, sir?"

"I just received a notification." Antel handed Sandun the datapad. "Do you know anything about someone accessing our background and financial records?"

"No, sir." Sandun put his cup down on the coffee table and grabbed the datapad. He reviewed the data carefully.

"Thoughts?" Antel asked.

"These queries aren't random. They are all from the same origin point," replied Sandun. "Someone might be investigating us. I'm going to have to conduct a reverse search. Investigate the investigator."

"We need to brief the rest of the team," Antel said. He was about to call out for the rest of the expedition members, but as if on cue, there was the sound of a vehicle driving up and parking in front of the farmhouse.

"Are we expecting someone?" Becky was peeking through the window blinds to see who drove up. "He's probably FBI. He's dressed in a black suit and tie."

Antel's heart sank. He didn't need this right now. "Let me get the door. That way, he has to talk to me first." Antel walked up to the door and stood outside waiting for the man to approach him. He took a deep breath as he prepared himself for what was to come.

"You must be Andrew Rall." The man had a faint accent Antel didn't recognize. The man walked up to Antel, pulled out a badge from his inner suit pocket, and displayed it for Antel to see. "My name is Special Agent Rafael Navarro. I'm with the Department of Homeland Security. Can I have a moment of your time? I'll need to speak to the other residents too." It took Antel a moment, but he realized this was the same man he had seen watching his movements at the coffee shop days ago.

"Yes, Special Agent, I am Andrew Rall." Antel turned sideways and gestured to the farmhouse's front door. "Please come in."

As Navarro entered the house, he scanned the room, quickly studying it for details. Since the Arkonian technology was all in the work shed, there was little risk of being discovered. But then Antel realized the datapads weren't in English.

Antel picked up the datapad and handed it to Becky as if cleaning up for a guest. "Dear, you don't want to lose this again. You should put it in your backpack."

Becky got the hint. She took the datapad. "Thank you for finding it, dear." She took it and left the room to hide it somewhere in Antel's room.

Antel gestured his hand toward the couch, offering Navarro a seat in the living room. He asked, "Would you like anything to drink?"

"No, thank you." Navarro sat. "I'm okay."

Antel sat down and asked him, "So, how can I help you today?"

"Well." Navarro pulled out a document from the manila folder he brought with him. "My information tells me this home is shared with several people, one of which is Dr. Solomon. Can I assume he's in charge of this place?"

Antel figured Navarro probably assumed that, since Dahnt was the professor and he was only a graduate student, Dahnt was in charge. That was a good sign. It meant the agent wasn't aware of their true identities. Not yet, anyway.

"Um, he's not home right now. I'm his graduate student. Would that make me second in charge?" Antel smiled to make it sound like a joke. Navarro didn't need to know that he was in charge in moments like this.

"Sure, I can talk with you, I guess." Navarro scanned the page one more time. "I'm probably going to need to speak with everyone in the home anyway."

"Are we in trouble for something?" Antel wasn't aware of any laws they may have broken, except for perhaps being in the country without a visitor's permit.

"No. No trouble," Navarro stated. "Unless there's something you need to tell me."

"Nothing that I'm aware of." Antel couldn't help but compare this law enforcement officer to those in his country. Just like Navarro, they liked opening up conversations with small banter meant to make those they were questioning relax and make opening up easier.

"Quite a place you have here." Navarro commented as he looked around the room again. "This is more of a temporary living situation while you conduct research?"

"Yes, that's correct." Antel nodded. "We're analyzing historical records, demographic information, and political trends. Boring unless you are a political science enthusiast."

Navarro turned to face Antel directly. "Mr. Rall, I've been looking into you and your co-residents. I've been finding some inconsistencies. Your backgrounds are rather minimal, and your funding sources appear unusual."

"Oh? How so?" This was it. The expedition team had practiced for a moment like this. His only concern was Becky. He didn't expect to get confronted by local authorities while she was here. She might make a mistake that would tip the agent off. It wouldn't be her fault, of course. She didn't practice with the team. Also, he was never supposed to get involved with a Terran in the first place. A problem he would need to solve another day.

"Our funding comes from academic grants," Antel explained.

"Yes, but those academic sources have been challenging to track," Navarro remarked.

"Did the money come from an illegal source?" Antel knew the truth. He didn't want to tell him that they regularly found large deposits of palladium in the asteroid belt and brought them down to Earth to sell to a local precious metal company. They limited it to a hundred kilograms at a time so as not to flood the economy by mistake. In reality, they had amassed millions of dollars so far. The Rileean government could have just hacked their financial systems, but they didn't want to steal the money through fraud.

"Your backgrounds all feel made up." Navarro leaned forward and made strong eye contact with Antel. "If I didn't know better, I might think you're foreign agents. Mr. Rall, are you a spy?"

Antel felt a chill down his spine. He did his best to keep his composure and maintain eye contact. "No, of course not." Antel didn't think that was convincing enough.

"Special Agent Navarro." Antel began. "Those are serious accusations. I assure you, we are not spies." That wasn't entirely true. The technicality amused him; they weren't working for any rival nation, after all. "If there are any discrepancies, I would love to clarify any questions you have."

At that moment, Dahnt walked in. "Whose car is that out..." He was interrupted when he saw Navarro sitting on the couch. "Um, hello."

Antel stood up. "This is Special Agent Navarro. He has a few questions he would like to ask us."

"Certainly," Dahnt said.

Navarro stood up himself. "If it's okay, can I speak with each resident individually somewhere private? Kitchen, maybe?"

Dahnt led Navarro to the kitchen and volunteered to get questioned first.

Becky returned from Antel's room and heard the trailing end of their conversation. "Not sure you know this, but if you need to, you are allowed to stay silent. All you need to do is ask to speak to your lawyer."

"Good to know. Thank you," Antel whispered. "It might be a good idea for you to leave so he doesn't ask you any questions."

"Are you sure?" she asked.

"Yes, go ahead and go home. If he asks, I'll tell him we assumed he didn't need you since you aren't a resident here."

"Okay." She planted a goodbye kiss, grabbed her backpack, and left before the agent could notice.

While Dahnt kept Navarro busy, Antel went down the hall and asked Sandun to summon everyone else to the living room. Without speaking, Sandun gestured to his hip where his sidearm would be.

Antel waved it off. The last thing they needed was a shootout with law enforcement. The officer had a valid reason for his suspicions. With so many of them getting questioned, Antel was getting a little worried the Standard Protocol would be violated by mistake. One small mistake and this mission could all come crashing down.

His mind drifted to Becky. She knew their secret. Antel hoped that knowledge didn't put her at risk. He wasn't sure what he would or could do if she got entangled in this agent's investigation.

The sound of footsteps brought his mind back to the moment. Navarro stepped out of the kitchen for a moment. He faced Antel and said, "Mr. Rall, can we speak now?"

Antel nodded and followed Navarro back to the kitchen. He sat at the kitchen table across from the agent.

Navarro pointed at what Antel assumed was a recording device that was lying on the table between them. "This is just for my records," he stated. "You don't mind, do you?"

Antel did mind, but didn't think it was wise to decline. "Not a problem."

"Andrew Rall." Navarro took a moment and paused for effect. "Please state your full name and occupation."

"Andrew Rall," he answered, trying to remain calm. "I am Dr. Solomon's graduate assistant."

"Mm-hmm." Navarro made a note on a blank page titled Andrew Rall. "Mr. Rall, can you explain to me the nature of the research you are conducting with Dr. Solomon here? In detail, please."

Antel wasn't sure Dahnt's response was going to match his perfectly, so he hedged his bets and disclaimed, "Well, Dr. Solomon could explain it better than I can. My studies are just a part of the bigger research project."

"I understand, Mr. Rall. Just describe your part for me."

"Well, we're here to get a detailed picture of the relationships between contemporary nations and correlate that against their forms of government."

"I see." Navarro's tone sounded a little skeptical. "Does any of this research require access to sensitive government data?"

Antel felt an alarm going off in his chest. Remaining calm, he said, "No, it doesn't. Everything we need is either publicly accessible or part of Dr. Carter's notes. Are you suggesting we've been accessing confidential national secrets?"

"No, I'm not suggesting that." Navarro felt a bit defensive, but he had to remember that he was doing the questioning, not Antel.

"Given that Dr. Solomon is the only professor here, I would assume that he was basically in charge here."

"That's right."

"Then why do I get the feeling you're the one actually in charge?" Navarro put his pen down flat on his stack of documents.

"What would make you think that?"

"When I questioned the others," Navarro thought for a moment about how to state his observations. "I got the feeling that most of the residents here consider you to be just as important, if not more important, than Solomon."

"That might be because I have seniority among my fellow students." Antel had to think of something fast. This special agent was no idiot. He must have had a lot of training in how to question suspects.

Navarro seemed to consider Antel's explanation carefully. "Okay, Mr. Rall, I appreciate you taking the time to speak with me. My investigation is not over. I'll be keeping an eye on your group here. Especially you. If I suspect a national security threat, I'll have no choice but to bring you in."

"I understand." Antel was worried that this was going to make his job of protecting the team while keeping the Standard Protocol safe from breaches much harder. "I assure you, Special Agent Navarro, we are no threat to..." He almost said "your nation's security." "... national security."

The two stood up and shook hands. Navarro gathered his belongings and left the farmhouse. Antel felt some relief that the questioning was over. But he knew this wouldn't be the end of it. If the expedition wasn't careful, it would be only a matter of time before Navarro got what he was looking for.

Once Navarro had left, the team, still gathered in the living room, stood in a loose circle. Dahnt's arms were crossed tight against his chest, Emira was biting her lower lip, Sandun's hand was hovering near where his sidearm would be. Only Irina met his eyes directly, her chin raised slightly.

Antel addressed the group that was still assembled in the living room. "We need to operate with more attention to detail. The agent is very good at his job, and if we make any errors, our mission will unravel."

"Understood." Sandun, Irina, and Emira said in unison.

"What caused him to begin this investigation in the first place, sir?" Irina raised her hand as she asked Antel.

"I don't know for certain, but I believe it had to be Neil Morris who called the authorities to have us looked into as part of his investigation into the engineering building firefight," Antel hypothesized. "After doing his initial digging, this agent came to believe there might be something going on after all."

Emira spoke up, with worry in her voice. "Are they monitoring our communications? If they intercept..."

"We'll need to be extra careful," Antel interrupted. "We need to minimize our subspace communications. We can't be sure whether they can intercept those messages or not."

"Irina, I need you to sweep everything for any monitoring devices that might be lurking around in the farmhouse. And, in the name of the Universe, hold off on accessing secure Terran servers."

"Yes, sir." Irina saluted.

"Sandun." Antel turned to him. "I need you to check for any suspicious Terrans that may be watching us."

"On it," confirmed Sandun.

As the team dispersed, Antel walked up to the window and looked out at the forest that surrounded the farmhouse. The peaceful greenery reminded him of the Rileean province of Granilest. It was a sharp contrast to the tension he was feeling in his gut. Their mission kept getting harder and the stakes continued rising.

He reminded himself that he was going to need to talk with Becky and Dr. Carter. It was only a matter of time before they got asked questions. He needed to make sure they got their stories straight.

Antel allowed himself a small smile. This was going to be a challenge, but he felt up for it.

Chapter 23

Becky sat at the kitchen table, surrounded by stacks of books and papers, as she worked on her dissertation. The sunlight streaming through the window highlighted the dust particles floating in the air. Influenced by her recent experiences in space, she imagined the three-dimensional pattern of particles as a miniature starfield. Each particle became a distant sun, suspended and illuminated in the golden light.

She was so engrossed in thought that she didn't notice the car pulling up to the house until her mother called out from the living room.

"Becky, there's someone here to see you," her mother said, a hint of concern in her voice.

Becky looked up to see her mother standing at the front door speaking with a tall, imposing, well-dressed Hispanic man with a stern expression.

"Hello, I am Special Agent Navarro of Homeland Security," said the man as he displayed his identification badge as proof.

As he stepped into the light, Becky's heart skipped a beat. It was the same man who had come to the farmhouse to question Antel and his colleagues. Her breath caught in her throat as their eyes met.

"Agent Navarro, what brings you here?" her father asked, extending a hand in greeting.

Navarro's handshake was firm, but his gaze never left Becky's face. "I'm just following up on some leads, Mr. and Mrs. Miller," he said, his voice deep and commanding. "May I have a word with your daughter?"

Becky's parents exchanged a concerned glance, then her mother nodded and said, "Of course, Agent. Please, come in."

Yesterday, following Antel's suggestion, she'd left the farmhouse quickly to avoid the agent's questions. But now, as Navarro's eyes seemed locked on her, she realized that her attempt at evasion had not gone unnoticed.

"Becky, could you take a break from your studies and join us in the living room, please?" her father requested, his tone steady and measured.

Becky nodded, trying to appear calm, and joined her parents and Navarro in the living room. As they sat down, Navarro's gaze never wavered from hers, and she felt like a suspect heading to the witness stand.

"So, Rebecca Miller," Navarro began, "I understand you're quite close to Andrew Rall. Is that correct?"

Becky nodded, fighting to keep her face from betraying her panic. "Yes, that's right. We've been friends for a while now. Since the beginning of the semester, I think."

Navarro's eyes narrowed slightly. "I see. Well, I've been looking into Mr. Rall's background, and I have to say, there are some holes in his background check."

Becky's heart began to race, but she tried to keep her composure. "What kind of holes?" she asked, attempting to sound nonchalant. "Is he a suspect in a crime?"

Navarro leaned forward, his elbows on his knees. "Let's just say that Mr. Rall's story doesn't quite add up. And I've been wondering if you might know something about it."

Becky felt a surge of panic rising within her. She forced her breathing to remain steady. She knew that he was fishing for information, and she needed to be careful not to reveal too much.

"I'm not sure what you're asking me, Agent," she said, trying to appear ignorant of the facts. "He's a student from Chicago."

Navarro's gaze intensified. Becky felt like he was seeing through her bluff.

"Is that all you can tell me?" he asked. "You must know more about him."

She felt her parents' eyes on her. Apparently, they thought that was a good question. "Anything specific about him you need to know? You could always just ask him after all."

"I did, Miss Miller," Navarro said. "I'm just cross-checking his answers with yours. Does your dissertation research intersect with his? Are you two collaborating on your efforts?"

"No, not really," Becky said. "We haven't needed to collaborate much. Our projects focus on different areas."

"Anything else you can tell me about him?" Navarro pressed.

Becky sat back and crossed her arms. "You wanna know if he's good in bed or something?"

Her father groaned. He didn't like her comment, but Robert understood she was only being sarcastic.

"I'm not sure that's relevant, but I think you might be more involved in this than you're letting on." Navarro softened his tone, knowing that he needed to keep his cool if he wanted straight answers. "Miss Miller, it didn't go unnoticed that when I came to the farmhouse to question Mr. Rall and his roommates, you left rather quickly. Almost as if you were trying to avoid me."

Becky's pulse quickened, but she tried to keep her cool. "I just didn't want to get in the way," she said, as she held out her hands to either side with her palms up, attempting to appear innocent.

Navarro's expression was skeptical. "I see. Well, I did want to speak with you, too, but I decided I could always just meet with you later. But it got me wondering if maybe you were trying to protect Mr. Rall... or yourself."

Becky felt a cold sweat break out on her forehead, but she struggled to maintain her composure. Navarro was pressing hard. He was no idiot. She needed to be careful not to reveal too much. But as she looked into his piercing eyes, she couldn't shake the feeling that he already knew more than he was letting on.

Robert Miller felt the tone of Navarro's questions growing increasingly probing. His expression turned from curious to concerned. He leaned forward in his chair, his eyes locked onto Navarro's.

"Agent Navarro, I think it's time for us to take a step back here,"

Robert said, sensing the questions becoming more probing. His voice was firm but polite. "These questions are beginning to feel pretty pointed, and I'm not sure I'm entirely comfortable with this line of inquiry."

Navarro's gaze switched to Robert, a hint of annoyance flashing across his face. "I assure you, my goal is only to get to the bottom of some discrepancies with Mr. Rall and his colleagues." Navarro switched back to Becky. "Miss Miller, there could be consequences if you're holding back important information."

"Unless you have a warrant, she has no obligation at this moment to speak with you," Robert advised him.

"Cooperating would help her boyfriend's case, Mr. Miller. Unless she's hiding something," Navarro attempted to intimidate Robert.

Robert nodded, his eyes never leaving Navarro's face. "I appreciate your efforts to keep our nation safe from possible terrorism, but as an attorney, I have to advise my daughter on her rights and interests. And I think it's time for us to clarify what's going on here."

Becky felt a surge of relief and a sense of gratitude towards her father, who was using his knowledge of the law to protect her rights.

"Agent Navarro," Robert continued, "could you please tell us what specific discrepancies you've found in Andrew Rall's background? And what exactly do you hope to achieve by questioning my daughter about him?"

Navarro paused for a moment as his expression turned guarded. "I'm not at liberty to disclose all the details just yet, Mr. Miller. I did some checking on Andrew's background, and I'm finding some inconsistencies. We're trying to determine if they're indicative of anything more... serious."

"Who is 'we'?" Robert was determined to protect his daughter. "Is there a specific crime under investigation?"

"I was asked the member of the Air Force investigating a possible espionage incident that occurred on campus," Navarro admitted, referring to the engineering building.

Robert opened his mouth to speak, but Becky jumped in. "Agent Navarro, this is just Neil Morris's attempt to interfere in my relationship with Andrew."

"Maybe Neil should be investigated," said Becky's mother, who had been quiet for most of the interview.

"I did consider that maybe Captain Morris was using his position to apply pressure on you and Andrew, but when I dug deeper, I did find some inconsistencies that warranted further investigation," countered Navarro.

Robert's eyes narrowed. "Inconsistencies? That's a pretty vague term, Agent. Can you give us something more concrete to work with?"

Navarro sighed, his shoulders relaxing slightly as he seemed to concede the point. "Counselor, let's just say that we've found some gaps in Mr. Rall's employment and educational history. I can't even locate his parents or other relatives. And to make matters more suspicious, I dug into the rest of his colleagues and found the same gaps."

Becky felt her heart skip a beat, wondering if Navarro was getting close to the truth about Antel's true identity and mission.

Robert nodded thoughtfully, his expression unreadable. "I see. Well, Agent Navarro, Andrew and his colleagues' backgrounds notwithstanding, I think it's time for us to consider whether this line of questioning is entirely relevant to your investigation. And perhaps we should discuss what rights my daughter has in this situation."

Navarro remained silent for a moment as an understanding passed between them. Becky sensed that her father was drawing a line in the sand, marking the limits of how far Navarro could push his questions. She felt good knowing her father would do whatever it took to keep his daughter safe, but she also knew that when the agent left, she was going to have questions to answer from him, and lying to him was not in the cards, especially if he was ever going to need to represent her in court.

Navarro knew that pushing further would just make it harder to get any new information. He didn't expect Becky's father to be an attorney. If she wanted, she could stop cooperating and "lawyer up."

Special Agent Navarro thanked the Millers for their time, shook their hands, and took his leave.

As soon as Agent Navarro left, Becky's father turned to her with a concerned expression. "Okay, Becky, spill it. What's going on? Whatever Andrew is up to, it sounds like there's more to it than a classified project."

Becky hesitated, feeling the weight of her promise to keep Antel's secret. She'd promised Antel secrecy, but now must choose between that promise and honesty with her father.

"Nothing, Dad," she said finally, trying to sound casual. "I don't know what that agent is talking about."

Robert raised an eyebrow. "Young lady, I can tell when you're lying. What's going on with Andrew? What kind of trouble is he in?"

Becky sighed, feeling trapped. She knew she couldn't keep lying to her father, but she also couldn't break her promise to Antel without his permission.

"I need to talk to Andrew about this," she said finally. "Can I call him?"

Robert nodded. "Sure, but then I want the whole truth. Clear?"

"Yes, of course, Dad."

Becky nodded. Feeling a sense of hope, she quickly grabbed her phone. She dialed Antel's number, praying he would answer.

Becky paced back and forth in the living room as the phone rang. When Antel finally answered, she felt a surge of relief.

"Hello, love," Antel said, his voice low and smooth, unaware of her situation. "I wasn't expecting your call tonight."

"It's my dad," Becky whispered, glancing over her shoulder. "That agent who came to the farmhouse and questioned everyone was just here. He just left, and now my dad is asking me questions. I don't know what to tell him."

There was a pause on the other end of the line. For a moment, Becky wondered if Antel was going to hang up on her.

"Sure," Antel said. "I just finished on campus, so I'm nearby. I'll come over. Let me talk to your parents."

Becky felt the tension in her shoulders soften. She knew that with Antel by her side, she could get through this.

"This means a lot," she said, feeling grateful.

Becky disconnected the call and put the phone back in her pocket. She turned to her father and said, "Andrew is coming over. He has all the answers."

Robert nodded, his expression understanding. "Okay, sweetie. Let me and your mom know when he gets here so we can all talk about this together."

Becky nodded, her stomach still knotted with anxiety. She knew that the next conversation was going to be difficult, but she also knew that it was necessary, and Antel would be there to help her.

As they waited for Antel to arrive, Becky couldn't help but think about how much her life had changed since she met him. She had fallen in love with an alien, and her life had never been the same. But as she thought about Antel, she knew that it was all worth it.

When the doorbell rang, Becky shot up and sprang to the door. She opened the door to find Antel standing on the porch waiting patiently.

She threw her arms around him, her body trembling as he pulled her close. Antel did his best to comfort her and get her to relax.

Antel greeted her parents politely, then turned to Becky. Taking her hands and looking into her eyes, he whispered, "Relax, I've got this."

As they all sat down on the couch, Antel took a deep breath and began to explain. "I come from a planet we call Arkonus. I'm not really a student. That's only a cover story. My team and I have been sent to Earth as part of a mission to research and learn."

Becky's parents looked at each other with shock written all over their faces.

"Thank goodness," Becky said with relief. "The truth is finally coming out." Becky could feel the pressure beginning to subside, but she knew the conversation wasn't over. They still had to be convinced it was true.

"Okay, let's say we believe you. Why are you here?" Robert asked, his voice firm but controlled. "What aspect of the Earth are you studying?"

Antel explained the expedition's mission. He told them how they came to learn about Earth's national and international political environment. He told them about how he had met Becky and how they had fallen in love.

As Antel spoke, he saw Becky's mother's polite smile falter, a fleeting shadow of disbelief in her eyes. Becky's father remained unmoved, arms crossed and a skeptical frown etched on his face, his gaze fixed on Antel.

"Okay, Andrew," Robert, ever the cross-examiner, tried to throw Antel off, "if you're not from Earth, how did you get an ordinary

English name?"

"Oh! Can I?" Becky asked Antel. She could tell this speech was getting annoying for him.

"Please." Antel smiled, hoping she remembered all of it.

"Mom, Dad, may I present to you Lieutenant Antel Ralnar of the Empire of, uh…" She forgot the official name of the Empire.

"Of the Federal Empire of the Imperial Republic of Rilee on the planet of Arkonus," Antel finished for her.

Her parents sat in stunned silence, her mother's hand frozen halfway to her mouth.

"You still don't look convinced," Antel observed. He took out his cell phone. First, he showed it to them so they could see that it appeared as a normal smartphone. Then he entered a passcode, and the screens all changed from English to Intallan. The features were different, but since no one there but him could read Intallan, they didn't know that.

"What language is that?" Robert was fascinated.

"That's my language. It's called Intallan, the predominant language of my home country of Rilee."

"How do I know this isn't bullshit?" Robert was getting annoyed.

Becky pulled out her phone and searched through her videos. Once she found it, she sat on the couch between her parents and played back the video she had taken of the battle at the ghost town.

"This just looks like a B-rated sci-fi movie," Robert muttered.

"Are these photos and videos for real?" Elaine asked.

"Yes, ma'am," Antel confirmed.

"And here," Becky wanted to reinforce her proof, so she opened the pictures she took when she was on Mars. The pictures included some of Antel's friends and clearly showed the Martian landscape visible through the windows. There were even some pictures of her floating in zero-g while Zhon was preparing to make maneuvers to head to Mars.

The winner was a short video she took as a group selfie. A few of Antel's friends crammed into the camera's view and said hello and other greetings in Intallan.

"Oh my God, this must be all true," Robert said, looking at Elaine, who was also shocked.

One or two pictures he could disregard as fake, but there were so many pictures and videos that it looked like a vacation trip. The videos showed people in red and black uniforms speaking an alien language. He was sure footage like that could not have been fabricated.

"How does Agent Navarro fit into all this?" Robert asked, his voice still firm.

Antel explained how his involvement started when the skirmish occurred in the engineering building. He confessed that it was indeed his team, but the only reason the agent was able to get this far in his investigation was because of Neil. Neil's plan was only to break up Antel and Becky's relationship out of jealousy. The fact that he accidentally pointed Navarro in the right direction was exactly that, an unfortunate accident.

Her parents couldn't speak for what felt like an eternity. Becky was finally able to let go of all of the tension in her muscles. The only remaining hurdle was that Homeland Security agent. But her father could help her with that.

Chapter 24

Antel and Becky held hands as they walked, enjoying the breezy October wind. They entered the campus coffee shop, fingers intertwined. The store was bustling with students chatting and laughing over cups of coffee. As they entered, Antel's eyes scanned the room out of habit. That's when he spotted Neil at a small table by the window, sipping coffee with his sister Sarah.

Becky noticed Neil too, her pace quickening. Antel sensed the coming confrontation.

As they approached the table, Neil looked up, his eyes meeting Becky's. Neil closed his paperback book and set it on the table.

Becky marched straight to the table. "Neil, we need to talk."

Antel followed closely behind, his eyes never leaving Neil's face, monitoring for trouble.

Sarah, sensing the unease, stood up. "I think I should give you all some space," she said as she excused herself to grab a refill on her drink.

Neil leaned back in his chair and crossed his arms. "This is the first time you've come to me. What's on your mind, Becks?"

Becky put her hands on her hips, her eyes blazing with anger. "You know exactly why I'm here, Neil. And I keep telling you not to call me Becks."

"Whatever." Neil rolled his eyes. "What am I supposed to know already?"

"You had to get Navarro to do your dirty work," she growled. "You got him to investigate Andrew and his group just to get to me. And now he's coming to my house and interrogating me. Was that also part of your plan?"

"That wasn't my intention," Neil said defensively. "I'm only looking out for you. This guy is trouble, and he's going to drag you in."

That was probably true, Antel thought. If it weren't for his presence, Becky would be focused on her studies and not chasing him around as he dealt with dangerous situations.

Becky's voice rose, her temper continuing to climb. "You're the asshole who pushed Navarro to start investigating them in the first place. And you're just encouraging him to push ahead. He questioned me right in front of my parents!"

Antel could feel her anger and frustration, and he placed a reassuring hand on her shoulder.

Neil shrugged. "Like I said, I was just looking out for your best interests. You're involved with someone who's clearly hiding something." But his next statement caught both Becky and Antel off guard. "To be perfectly honest, I did call Homeland Security to have them look into this guy and his buddies, but I have since asked Navarro to close the investigation."

Surprised, Antel and Becky exchanged perplexed glances. They did not expect that. "Why?" Antel jumped in and asked. "Earlier, you were determined to see me brought down."

Neil's expression turned guarded, his gaze settling on Becky after a quick glance at Antel. "Let's just say I realized it wasn't a good idea to pursue it further." His voice was flat and unconvincing. Antel sensed there was more to the story than Neil was letting on.

"What? Why?" Becky persisted, brow furrowed. "Neil, you're leaving something out. Tell us why you really asked him to stop. What changed your mind?"

Neil pressed his lips together, refusing to elaborate.

The silence stretched uncomfortably between them. Becky glanced at Antel, eyebrows raised in silent question. He gave her shoulder a gentle squeeze, conveying that they would figure this out together.

Neil broke the silence. "I've said all I'm going to say about this. I have somewhere to be." He stood up, grabbed his bag, and nodded to Sarah as she returned with her refill.

As Neil walked away, Becky turned to Antel, her forehead creased with confusion. "What the hell just happened? Why would he ask Navarro to stop the investigation?"

Antel shook his head, equally perplexed.

Becky glanced over to Sarah, who didn't leave with Neil. "Do you know something?" Becky asked her.

Sarah just shrugged. "Sorry, I have no idea why. Something about needing to close the engineering building break-in case as soon as possible."

"I don't think I'm in the mood for a coffee this morning," Becky told both Sarah and Antel. Becky then turned and walked out of the coffee shop.

Antel gestured goodbye to Sarah and walked quickly to catch up with her.

Antel couldn't help but wonder what Neil's true reasons were for trying to call off the investigation. It seemed that Neil's primary intention was to cause chaos in his life, but he never intended it to spill over to Becky's life. His motives were based on jealousy, but he was not going to be a direct threat to the mission as long as he never learned about his team's alien origins.

Becky's voice broke the silence. "Do you think Neil knows anything about your, um, secret?"

"I doubt it," Antel replied. "He's just a desperate ex doing stupid things in an attempt at breaking us up, and most likely has no idea about me."

"But if he finds out…"

"Then he may become a bigger problem," Antel admitted, "but I think we're safe from him for now."

They walked in silence for a few more blocks, traffic noise and distant conversations filling the quiet between them. Finally, Becky stopped abruptly, realizing she had no real destination.

"I don't understand him," she muttered, shaking her head. "Why would Neil suddenly tell Navarro to back off, only for Navarro to keep digging? It doesn't make any sense."

Antel stepped closer and wrapped his arms around her for comfort. "It just means we should focus on Navarro instead of Neil's childish behavior."

Becky rested her head on his shoulder. "I'm scared. Not scared of Neil or Navarro, but scared of whatever trouble this investigation could lead to. I've seen too many movies where the Army kidnaps someone once they discover he's an..." Becky lifted her head and looked around, then put it back on his shoulder. "...an alien, then they do experiments and such on him."

"Really?" Antel didn't expect such an aggressive action from any alien species, much less from other humans. "Would they really do that?"

"Wouldn't they be tempted to do that on your planet?"

"Um, no. I don't think so."

Becky pulled back slightly to look him in the face. She raised an eyebrow, unconvinced.

"Okay, I suppose if our first experience with alien life had been on our planet, maybe. But we first encountered aliens in space, and they were hostile. The species from Kentus," he admitted. "That encounter happened about 130 years ago."

"Oh, you're gonna love this story as a student of history," he said, smiling as he thought of how exciting this historical event was going to be for her. "Remind me to tell you about it later."

She lightly smacked Antel in the chest as she smiled. "No fair! You can't tease me like that and get away with it."

Antel laughed and pulled her into a tight hug.

"What do we do about Navarro?" Becky changed the subject back to their issue.

"I have no idea," Antel said. "I wish I knew what our options were."

Becky's eyes lit up. "My Dad might have some ideas. Maybe he can figure out what we can do."

"Senior Lieutenant Ranston was right, you are an invaluable asset to the mission."

Becky melted against him, giving him a soft kiss. "That's so sweet that you remembered he said that. I want to help however I can."

Antel kissed her back. "Then let's go talk to your father."

Becky pulled out her phone and tapped a quick text message to her father. "I'll tell him we're on our way," she said, tucking the phone back into her pocket.

As they continued walking, Becky glanced sideways at Antel. "Do you ever regret getting involved with me?" She grabbed his hand to hold it as they walked.

The question was unexpected, but Antel's response was immediate. "No," he said firmly. "It was against my better judgment, but I was so drawn to you. There was no way I could have stopped myself. But I do regret putting you in danger."

Becky had a large smile and tightened her grip on his hand. "Well, I'd rather be in danger with you than safe than missing out on having you in my life."

Antel lifted his hand, bringing hers up to his lips. He gave it a gentle kiss. "Let's hope your father has some answers."

Robert leaned back in his office chair, fingers interlaced. He listened as Becky and Antel explained what they'd learned from Neil.

Robert raised his eyebrows. "I feel like he asked for the investigation out of haste, and now he regrets it because it's backfiring on its intended purpose of breaking you two apart."

"I understand keeping your identity secret," Robert continued, "alien dissections and all."

"There's that 'dissection' theory again," Antel thought to himself. "Is everyone here more interested in our organs than our advanced technology?" Antel seriously doubted Terrans' first instinct would be to capture and cut up an alien. He was certain that if Earth's first alien encounter was with beings who looked human, like himself, reactions would be different.

"It's only a matter of time before Navarro uncovers Antel's secret," Becky told her father.

"That's right," Antel said, his voice measured but laced with tension. "Navarro has already flagged inconsistencies in my background. If he keeps digging, he will eventually find out where we're really from, and that would mean the team allowed the Standard Protocol to be violated."

Robert raised an eyebrow. "This 'Standard Protocol' of yours... what happens if it's broken?"

Antel hesitated, his gaze flickering to Becky. "Depends on how it plays out. If Navarro keeps the secret from going public, we might be fine."

"And if not?" Robert asked.

"If our existence becomes public knowledge, lots of things might happen." Antel turned his face down for a moment, not looking forward to having this conversation with Becky here and giving her more to worry about. "First of all, my team and I, probably just me, would be court-martialed and sent to prison."

"Oh my God," Becky tried not to panic. "I can't let that happen."

"Second, and more important to you, it opens up the dialogue in Rilee about possible options. One, supported only by a minority but still an option, is to preemptively set your civilization back to prevent it from becoming a future threat."

"They would really do that?" Robert asked.

"The chances of that would be very low unless something serious accompanied the Standard Protocol violation. Something like taking hostages or executing any of the expedition members."

"Oh, this just gets better, doesn't it?" Becky said sarcastically.

"You mean like an alien dissection," Robert added.

"Somehow, from my planet's experience, no civilization less advanced would ever dare that. I think we might be okay on that point. Just don't shoot at us."

Robert quietly thought for a moment. Then he looked back at them. "I'm not sure what options we have unless he formally charges you with something."

"Just thinking out loud here," Robert said. "What if we ask him to meet us here and explain to him what you just told me? He might just understand. Especially since you didn't actually break any laws. Not on purpose anyway."

"Out of the question," Antel objected to the idea. "That would be a huge risk to the Standard Protocol. If he feels obligated to inform his superiors, this would spiral out of control."

"True. It was just a thought." Robert didn't press the idea further.

"Not even as a last resort?" Becky wasn't willing to give up on the idea.

"Still can't take the risk," Antel said with determination.

"But that would mean you could be arrested for not cooperating,"

Becky's voice sounded as if she were begging him to consider it.

"As an officer of the Imperial Forces, that's a risk I signed up for."

"You can be so hardheaded," Becky's disappointment was clear. She leaned back in her chair, uncertain if she wanted to look at Antel.

"Can you generate fake documentation that may fill in the gaps in our cover?" Antel asked.

"As your attorney, I wouldn't be allowed to help you 'commit a crime,'" he explained. "The best I could do would be to tell you where your gaps are and let your team handle it. Of course, you can't tell me or I'd be aiding a crime."

"That makes sense," Antel said. "Rilee has similar attorney provisions, too."

"Other than that, I could try to slow him down long enough for you to finish your mission," Robert offered.

"That sounds like a better plan of action," Antel agreed.

Robert Miller pulled out his wallet and took the card that Special Agent Navarro gave him. He placed it on the desk next to the phone and began to dial the number on his office phone.

"Let's see what Navarro has for us," Robert said as he was dialing.

"Department of Homeland Security, Special Agent Navarro speaking," a gruff voice answered.

"Navarro, this is Robert Miller," he said calmly and professionally. "I am Rebecca Miller and Andrew Rall's legal counsel. We spoke earlier." He made sure to use Antel's Earth alias.

"Yes, I remember you," the voice replied over speakerphone. "How can I help you, Mr. Miller?"

Robert leaned back in his chair. "Regarding the concerns you have about my clients, could you tell me the scope of your inquiry and whether there are any allegations against them?"

Navarro's response came swiftly and reflexively. "I'm afraid I can't share details about an ongoing investigation. But I can assure you that we're following credible leads."

Tapping a pen against the desk, Robert considered his words carefully. "That's a little vague, Agent Navarro. My clients have been cooperative. I'd like to know what grounds you have for continuing this investigation."

Navarro's voice hardened slightly. "I am looking into the missing gaps in Mr. Rall's, his professor's, and his classmates' backgrounds. Beyond that, I can't comment."

"Is there nothing you can tell me? Perhaps something specific could help clear my clients."

There was a moment of silence. Only faint background conversations audible from Navarro's end could be heard. "I'm not at liberty to discuss specifics, Mr. Miller. If your clients have nothing to hide, this will resolve itself in time."

Robert rubbed his temple. "Agent Navarro, I understand you have a job to do. I only want to ensure that this investigation isn't straying into harassment or baseless scrutiny. If there's an issue, my clients would like to address it directly."

Navarro's tone softened. "I understand your concern, Mr. Miller. I'll take your comments under advisement. If there's anything your clients need to know, I'll be sure to inform them. And I promise to give them fair treatment under the law."

"That's all I ask," Robert replied, his tone polite but firm. "Thank you for your time, Agent Navarro. Have a good rest of your day."

"Same," Navarro said before the call ended with a quiet click.

Robert pressed the disconnect button. He wasn't entirely satisfied with the conversation, but it hopefully put Navarro on notice that this wasn't going to be easy.

"Let's see how much time this bought us," Antel told Robert and Becky.

Chapter 25

As the evening sun set on the horizon, trees and the farmhouse cast long shadows. After a long day of navigating legal issues, Antel decided to take a break for the rest of the night and spend some quality time with Becky.

Becky walked out with a couple of mugs of hot chocolate to join Antel on the porch swing. As she sat down and handed Antel his mug, his communicator dinged. He pulled it out of his pocket to check the message.

"Who's that?" Becky asked.

"Dr. Sallain," Antel said, putting the phone back in his pocket and taking one of the mugs from Becky. "He says he's still with your advisor and will be out longer than expected. He told me not to worry about him."

"You sound like you don't believe him." Becky sensed skepticism from Antel.

"I don't know. He's been gone more than usual lately." Antel's mug felt warm in his hands. He took a slow sip, savoring the chocolate's aroma.

Becky looked up at the Moon in the night sky. "Does your homeworld... um... Arkonus have a moon like that one?"

"We have two," Antel said, looking up at the Moon as well. "Turek, the bigger one, looks a lot like yours, only a little darker in color and smaller."

"And the other one?" Becky asked.

"Kalina. It's the size of a big asteroid. A little brighter than your Moon." Antel turned to look at Becky, who was still staring at the Moon. "There's a story behind our moons about Turek and Kalina. In ancient mythology..."

"What's that?" Becky interrupted him and pointed to the sky. From a distance, a pair of lights could be seen flying low just above the trees. The lights were getting closer.

Antel had a bad feeling this wasn't going to be good. His military training took over, muscles tensing instantly.

"Becky," he said, trying to remain calm for her sake, "get in the house."

"What's wrong? Are we in danger?"

The humming grew louder. "Inside! Now!" Antel threw his mug down and grabbed her arm, making Becky drop her mug, shattering it on the ground.

"You're scaring me." Her voice quavered, heart hammering against her ribs.

Antel could feel her muscles tense as he pulled her into the house. The humming intensified to a roar. In Intallan, he yelled, "Everyone, incoming!"

The team scrambled into action. Irina unlocked a closet using a hidden panel in the wall by the closet door, and the team started tossing particle beam rifles to each other.

Antel didn't have time to get one for himself. He was too focused on Becky's safety. He pulled her under the kitchen table. The table was heavy and very sturdy, and Antel hoped it would protect them.

The team had no chance.

A missile fired from the drone tore through the house, causing the roof to come crashing down around Becky and Antel. Two legs splintered, but the sturdy surface still kept the roof from crushing them.

Antel had to dig the two of them out of the rubble that crashed down around and on top of them. When they finally emerged to see the damage, debris and flames were all that remained of the farmhouse. Antel instinctively looked around for the others, calling out in Intallan, "Sound off."

Only the crackle of flames answered him.

"Where are the others?" Becky's voice was shaking.

"I..." He wasn't sure how to tell her. "I don't think they made it," he said quietly, his voice heavy with the weight of what he couldn't bring himself to say directly. He began digging around to see if he could find survivors. Becky helped.

Out of the corner of his eye, Antel saw blue beams of light coming out of the forest. The beams seemed to be scanning around for targets.

Becky saw the lights. "What are those lights from?" she said, the panic in her voice clear. "Those are Arkonian weapons, aren't they?"

Antel saw what was left of the armory closet and pulled a pistol out of the rubble. "Let's go," Antel tried not to speak too loudly. "We have to get out of here before they get here."

Antel pointed into the forest in the opposite direction from the source of the blue beams of light. "That way. Go."

Becky ran into the forest. She ran as fast as she could. Antel, a fast runner himself, stayed just behind her, providing cover against potential gunfire.

The loud blast lit up the sky for a short moment. The ground and trees rumbled. The shockwave knocked Antel and Becky to the ground. The explosion startled Becky, and through the ringing in his ears, Antel heard her scream. Their pursuers now knew there was at least one survivor. Antel's mind raced as he processed what had happened. The drone must have hit the power generator. Rileean soldiers wouldn't have been stupid enough to shoot at an antimatter generator standing so close to it intentionally. The drone must be Terran.

Antel rose back up, pulling Becky up with him. They continued running. As they ran, Antel looked back and saw their pursuers were still getting up themselves.

They ran for a few minutes before Antel needed the two of them to stop moving for a moment. By remaining motionless, he hoped to make it harder to get spotted. He wasn't sure Becky would be able to hear him. Her ears were probably ringing too. He dropped to the ground and pulled her down with him. He put a finger on her lips to let her know to remain quiet.

Minutes felt like hours as they huddled in the dark, listening for approaching soldiers. When Antel was satisfied their pursuers had headed in the wrong direction, he got back up and had the two of them move to a new hiding place.

The sound of the drone's hum started to get closer as it came for another pass. Are the Rileean soldiers coordinating with a Terran military? This couldn't be a coincidence. Antel looked towards the sound but he couldn't see the drone in the dark sky. Thoughts of those alien dissections she and her father had told him about started to run through his head. He shook them off, still not believing Terrans would be that cruel.

The branch of the tree Antel was standing next to exploded into pieces. Several shots of particle beams crackled past them, destroying other trees. He wasted little time. He aimed the particle beam pistol he was carrying where the shots came from and fired back.

Antel was sure he didn't hit the pursuer, but he caused enough destruction of the trees around him to make the shooter stop.

"Stay here and watch me..." Antel whispered to Becky.

"You're not going to leave me, are you?" Becky was about to panic.

He put his hand on her shoulder. "I'm not leaving you. Trust me. Stay here and watch me. When I give you a thumbs up, you pretend to be scared and scream, okay?"

"Oh, I won't be pretending," she said. Her heart was beating so hard it felt like it was going to break out of her chest.

Antel kept low and dashed around to make the angle wider for the shooter. When he felt he was in a good position, he raised his thumb to Becky.

At first, Becky tried to scream, but fear robbed her of her voice. "Keep calm, Rebecca. You can do this," she told herself. Once she gathered her courage, she screamed as loud as she could with the highest pitch possible. "AH!"

The shooter couldn't see Becky, so his next few shots in her direction all missed. Becky screamed some more. Her heart felt like it was going to bust out of her chest. It took all her willpower not to panic.

Antel was watching. When he pinpointed the soldier's position in the dark, Antel, a rather good marksman, fired one blast. The soldier's body exploded into pieces, painting the nearby trees red. Antel got up and ran at full speed to the target to make sure he had killed him. Satisfied he was dead, Antel removed the night vision goggles and backpack of gear from what was left of the body.

He then dashed back to Becky's position. She was in a ball, crying as she hid behind the tree. She nearly screamed again when she heard Antel approaching.

"You're safe. It's me." Antel tried to keep her calm, but he knew that was going to be impossible. He placed the night vision goggles he took from the body onto Becky's head and turned them on. "This should help you see in the dark. Let's go. We have to get far from here."

The drone eventually left. Antel knew the Rileeans, most likely those rogue soldiers again, had spread out and were conducting a search sweep, which is why the dead soldier was separated from the others. It was only a matter of time before his allies came to his aid and found that they were too late.

They moved quickly. After more than an hour, Antel and Becky put miles between what was left of the farmhouse and themselves.

Becky was breathing heavily from the running. "What do we do now?" Becky asked, wiping tears from her face. Her hands were trembling from the traumatic experience.

Antel looked back in the direction of the farmhouse. He couldn't see it through all of the trees, but he imagined what it looked like. A fire smoldering, smoke billowing up, and the bodies of his team scattered among the debris. The mission had failed and Terran authorities would be investigating soon.

"The situation just escalated in a hurry," said Antel, thinking out loud. "There must be something bigger going on. I need to find out and put a stop to it."

"Where do we start?" Becky took off the goggles from her head to take a look at them.

"We?" Antel's mind was on the farmhouse, but when she asked that, his focus returned and he turned to Becky. "I don't think so. There's no way I can put you in harm's way. Even if I didn't feel strongly about you, it would still be wrong of me to put a civilian in danger."

"Hey!" She got serious. "I'm helping whether you like it or not."

"I can't, in good conscience…"

Becky interrupted him with only a look. She balled up her fists and put them on her hips.

"Uh…" Antel tried to continue.

She tilted her head to the side, her eyes narrowing as her expression grew even more serious.

Antel sighed. "There's no point in arguing with you, is there?"

"Nope. You're stuck with me."

"Fine. First, we have to get away from this place. Local authorities will be arriving soon. If we're still here, they'll suspect us of foul play. Let me see what the Black Cat can tell us."

Antel reached into his pocket for his personal communicator, only to discover that it was missing. He must have lost it in the chaos.

"Curse the Universe," Antel said.

"What?" Becky whispered back.

"I lost my phone."

Antel opened the bag of gear he took from the dead soldier and dug through it.

"Excellent!" Antel pulled out a communicator. He spoke into it in Intallan. "Ralnar to Black Cat, do you read me, Black Cat?"

Only static could be heard. Antel repeated the message. When it still didn't work, he listened to the static carefully.

"What is it?" Becky was curious. To her, it just appeared as if he were staring at the device.

"I'm afraid someone is jamming our signal," Antel said as he closed the device and put it back in his pocket. "This communicator isn't strong enough to break through and reach my starship in orbit."

She instinctively looked up as if she were hoping to see the ship. "You sure it's still there?"

"I hope so. Let's go."

"Where are we going?" Becky put her arms down and started following alongside him.

"To the road. Once there, we'll need to figure out something. Walking back to Denver would take hours."

While walking through the trees, Antel tried to make a call from his communicator. Looking at his device, his face twisted in frustration. "Damn the Universe, subspace is being jammed. Someone was prepared."

As they got close to the road, wails of sirens rushed by. The authorities were just arriving on the scene to put out the fire. Becky's feet were aching. Her casual sneakers weren't meant for hiking in the wilderness.

"We need transportation," Antel told Becky as they came out of the tree line and reached the side of the road.

"I could call Sarah," Becky suggested.

"Sarah?" Antel heard her but was unsure about the idea. "Neil's sister, Sarah?"

"Yeah, she stays up late a lot doing homework. I'm sure she's not asleep yet."

"I wasn't worried about her being asleep."

"Relax." Becky pulled out her cell phone and dialed. "She's not going to arrest us. And Neil's not a policeman."

"Still. At least tell her not to let anyone know who she's picking up."

"Sarah?" Becky's voice cracked. "I really need your help. Can you come pick me up?" She left out Antel intentionally.

"Are you okay?" Sarah expressed worry in her voice.

"There's been an incident."

"Let me call the police. Where are you?"

"No wait! Don't call the police just yet. Besides, they're already on their way."

"You're scaring me, Becky. What sorta trouble are you in?"

"I can't explain right now," Becky said. "Let me text you my location. We're walking along the road."

"We? Are you with someone?"

"Um…" Becky slipped with her words. "Yeah, but don't ask any questions. Trust me." Becky was hoping to give Sarah plausible deniability.

"Okay, on my way."

"Thanks, and don't tell anyone, not even your brother."

"Got it." They disconnected the call.

"She's not going to tell anyone, is she?" Antel asked.

"Nah, she's good. I trust her," Becky reassured him.

They waited just inside the treeline to remain hidden. After waiting nearly an hour, a blue compact car slowed and pulled over near them.

"That must be her," Becky said, standing up. She raised her palm towards him. "You wait here just in case."

Becky walked up to the car's driver's side. Before making it to the door, a girl stepped out.

"Becky?" the girl asked.

"Sarah!" The two girls ran up to each other and gave each other a long hug.

"Becky, are you okay?" Sarah whispered into her ear. Neither wanted to let go of the other. "You're shaking."

"I'm okay. Just rattled."

Sarah loosened her hug to look at her directly. "What happened?"

At that moment, Antel came walking up, catching Sarah's attention. Sarah let go and pulled Becky behind her. "Who goes there?"

"It's just me, Andrew," Antel said as his dark figure slowly became easier for Sarah to see.

Chapter 26

"Is anyone going to tell me what's going on?" Sarah was getting impatient.

Antel took a deep breath, considering how to tell her without compromising the Standard Protocol. "Well... A drone from the sky attacked us while soldiers tried to clean up after the destruction." Becky noticed that he left out the fact that the soldiers were aliens.

"Are you serious?" Sarah was in disbelief. She looked at Becky to see if Antel was telling her the truth.

"It's true," she confirmed.

"Why? Are you dangerous or something?"

Becky was about to speak, but Antel stopped her. "I can't tell you everything because much of it is classified." He hoped he was being believable.

"Are you a spy?"

"I can't answer that question." Antel couldn't think of anything better to say. "But I can say that I'm not an enemy spy." That was technically true.

Sarah looked at Becky. "Is he for real?"

"I'm afraid so." Becky looked down at the ground. Lying didn't come easily for her, especially to her best friend. She finally understood why every time Antel lied to her, it burned in his heart.

Sarah alternated looking at the two of them until she finally rolled her eyes. "Fine. Let's get out of here." She turned to head back to the car, then saw the plume of smoke barely visible in the darkness of the night. "Oh my God, is that smoke from…"

"It is," Becky answered.

"I heard on the news over the car radio that there was an explosion," she commented. "I didn't know that it was at Andrew's place. They're calling it a potential domestic terrorist attack."

Antel got in the back seat, allowing Becky to sit up front next to her friend.

As Sarah slipped back into the driver's seat, she caught a glimpse of Antel's face in the rearview mirror. Usually, he was composed, but tonight he was filled with tension, scanning their surroundings for potential trouble. She turned the car around and headed away from the farmhouse back in the direction of the city.

"Thank you again for coming," Becky said with a shaky voice. "I know this is weird, but…"

"Weird doesn't even begin to describe it," Sarah interrupted.

Antel's jaw clenched. When they discover he's not dead, they're going to assume he's that terrorist. He hadn't killed them, but the broken promise to keep them safe now felt like a lead weight in his stomach. And now Sarah was tangled in this mess too, each passing moment adding to the crushing burden on his shoulders.

"Sarah," Becky began carefully, "I can't tell you everything, but Andrew and his colleagues… they're not terrorists. They were the targets. I was nearly killed, too."

Sarah's eyes darted to the rearview mirror again. "Then why don't we call the police?"

"Because the people after us must have connections," Antel spoke for the first time, his voice sounding scratchy. "We can't assume they haven't compromised local law enforcement channels."

A car appeared in the distance behind them, its high beams blazing. Antel's hand instinctively moved to his particle beam weapon.

"Sarah," he said quietly, "in case that car is following us, turn into a side road and shut off your lights."

Sarah guided her car into a dark side road, her breathing quick and shallow.

"Now what?" she asked.

They waited in tense silence as the other vehicle cruised past their hiding spot. After a few moments, Antel released a breath he hadn't realized he was holding.

"Probably my imagination, but I wanted to be sure," Antel said. "We need to keep moving. Sarah, do you have somewhere safe we can go? Somewhere not connected to Becky or me?"

"Well, my roommate is out of town," Sarah offered after a moment's hesitation. "My dorm room should be safe."

Becky reached forward and squeezed her friend's shoulder. "I feel terrible dragging you into this, Sarah. But thank you so much."

"How about thanking me by explaining what's really going on," Sarah replied, pulling back onto the main road. "I'm not stupid. This spy story isn't cutting it. Why is that Homeland Security guy so obsessed with investigating Andrew and his friends? Why did you feel the need to put GPS trackers in his car and follow Andrew the other night?"

"Wait, what?" Antel was caught off guard. "Is that how you were able to figure out where I was?"

"Um, Andrew, I feel awful about that, but..." Becky turned around just enough for him to see the guilt on her face.

"I suppose I deserved that," Antel said, in no mood to argue the point. Besides, he thought, if the roles were reversed, he wouldn't have lasted as long as she did before resorting to things like that.

"He must really love you," Sarah observed, "if that's as upset as he's gonna get over those luggage trackers."

Becky tried not to turn her head to allow only Sarah to see the expression on her face while not letting Antel see. Becky had a glint in her eyes that told Sarah how smitten she was with him.

The rest of the drive passed in tense silence, each lost in their own thoughts as they wound through the darkened streets of Denver, away from the smoldering ruins behind them.

Sarah's dorm room, only meant for two, felt small and cramped with three people inside. Thankfully, Sarah's roommate was not in town that week.

Antel sat by the window, occasionally peeking through the curtains at the campus below. It was late, so there weren't very many people outside other than students returning from late-night parties.

"You should get some rest," Antel told Becky, sitting on Sarah's roommate's vacant bed, still wearing clothes dirty with soot from the farmhouse destruction. "I think we're safe for the moment."

"Safe?" Sarah's voice cracked. She sat next to Becky, trying to be as supportive as possible. "You got Homeland Security agents crawling all over your place thinking you might be a terrorist." Sarah put a protective arm around Becky and stared straight at Antel. "What kind of trouble are you getting my Becky into? If anything happens to her…"

"It's okay," Becky whispered, still trying to recharge her energy. "He's the good guy in all this." Becky leaned her head onto Sarah's shoulder. "But I really appreciate how you're looking out for me."

"Still…" Sarah continued, "you better promise nothing bad happens to her."

"I promise."

Becky's head popped up. "Hey! Wasn't Sallain out late with Dr. Carter? Let's call him and see if he's okay."

"I can't," Antel said. "I lost my phone in the attack. I don't have his number."

"Then what's that?" Sarah pointed at his pocket. She saw him pull out something that looked like a cell phone earlier. "And who is Sallain?"

Antel realized she was referring to his subspace communicator, the one he took from the dead soldier. "Um, this isn't exactly a phone. It's uh…" He wasn't sure what to call it without giving away too much.

"It's an experimental device." Becky knew what it was and knew he was struggling to keep its true function a secret. "Oh, and Sallain is Dr. Solomon's real name."

"Real name?" Sarah asked.

"Long story," Becky said.

The room became uncomfortably silent for a moment until Antel broke the silence. "Dear, I think you should, for now, get as far away from me as you can. If they catch you, you can claim you don't know where I'm at and you have no idea about any terrorism stuff."

"Like hell," Becky said firmly. "We're staying together."

"Things are going to escalate for me," Antel pleaded. "You shouldn't be mired in it too."

"I can't..." Becky started to speak but wasn't sure what to say.

He turned to Sarah, who had been watching their exchange with growing confusion and fear. "I know you have questions, and you deserve answers. But right now, the less you know, the safer you are. I can't put you at risk either. As soon as it's safe, I must leave too."

"So what am I supposed to do? Just forget everything I've seen?" Sarah asked.

"No," Becky turned to her and said. "But you need to act normal. Go to classes. Stick with your normal routine. If anyone asks, even Neil, you haven't seen us."

An emergency alert popped up on Sarah's phone, making everyone jump. It was a short alert warning residents.

"Warning, be on the lookout for suspects Donald Solomon and Andrew Rall. Details to be given on the local news shortly," the alert read.

Sarah reached for the TV remote and aimed it at the small TV in the dorm room. It flickered with the image of Agent Navarro standing at a podium. His face was stern as camera flashes illuminated the local Denver police department seal behind him. The three of them watched with tense silence.

"At approximately 2300 hours tonight," Navarro began speaking, his voice sounding official and carrying the weight of authority, "a significant explosion occurred at a property approximately 45 miles east of the City of Denver in what, initially, appeared to be a tragic accident, has been revealed to be something far more disturbing."

The screen split to show images of Dahnt and Antel. Navarro continued to speak. "These individuals," Navarro continued, "posing as academic researchers, are persons of interest in this explosion."

Becky's hand found Antel's in the darkness of the room. He squeezed it gently, his mind racing through the implications. The news was making them look as suspicious as possible.

"Most concerning," Navarro's voice grew harder, "we have determined that their identities have been completely fabricated and may be domestic terrorists."

Sarah muted the TV as footage began playing of the destroyed farmhouse, smoke still rising from its ruins. "They're going to find me," she whispered. "They'll know I helped you."

"No," Antel said firmly, though his own heart was racing. "I think you are still in the clear. As long as you stick to your routine, there's no way to connect you to us." He turned to Becky and continued, "But this is all the more reason for you to go home. I will think of something and leave soon, too. I will have Sarah text you a coded message letting you know when and maybe where I went."

The news broadcast switched to a news anchor. The ticker along the bottom of the TV said that Dr. Carter was being taken in for questioning in connection with the alleged domestic terror plot.

Antel saw the news about Dr. Carter. He slammed his fist into the bed and cursed in Intallan. "Kossdra!"

Becky knew the word he spoke was in his native tongue. She knew it was a curse word because she'd heard it a few times before.

Sarah wasn't sure what he said. She was about to ask what it meant when Antel added, "She doesn't deserve this." Antel's jaw clenched. Dr. Carter had been their primary contact on Earth, vetted and approved by the Rileean government. Now she was paying the price for helping them, and he was powerless to intervene.

"We need to help her," Becky insisted.

"I want to, trust me, but we can't," Antel replied, the words tasting bitter in his mouth. "Any attempt to contact her would only make things worse. They're watching her, hoping she'll lead them to us." He ran a hand through his hair in frustration. "This situation is getting worse by the minute. Everyone who could help is either dead or detained."

Sarah's phone buzzed. She received a text from Neil. Her hand shook slightly as she read it. "He's asking if I've seen you. Says it's important."

"Don't respond," Antel said quickly. "Neil may not have wanted it to go this far, but I'm sure he would love to see me tossed to the wild animals."

"Thrown to the wolves," Becky corrected him.

"Right, wolves."

The exchange made Sarah wonder. Why does he always get these idioms wrong? And why does Becky always have to correct him? A question for another day, Sarah decided.

"Sarah, please take Becky home. I will stay here with the lights off."

"I told you..." Becky was going to insist.

"No! That's an order." Antel couldn't believe he just said that, but he refused to let anything happen to her. "You go home. Sarah will keep you informed about me."

Becky gave a sour face but stood up and decided Antel knew best. She hadn't forgotten that he was a soldier and had probably been in bad situations like this before. The fear in her made her first reach out and hold Antel as tightly as she could. She whispered, "You be careful, soldier. I can't lose you."

He hugged her back, kissing her hair as she lay her head on his shoulder. "I will do my best to get back to you no matter what."

After they left, Antel sat in the dark room and waited. In the hour he waited, all he could think about was how he failed to protect the expedition. It felt worse knowing that only he survived. Wait, that's not true. Dahnt should be alive, he thought. I need to at least bring him to safety. Dr. Carter, too.

Tired of the darkness and boredom of waiting around, Antel pulled out from the gear bag the subspace radio. Adjusting the channels and various other settings, he attempted to establish contact with the Black Cat.

"This is..." Antel reconsidered saying his name in case the channel was being monitored. It was possible that the rogue soldiers didn't know he survived. "Black Cat, can you read me, Black Cat?"

No answer. He tried again a few more times, each time adjusting the channels. Each time, there was no answer. The only thing he heard was static.

"Something's wrong." Antel's mood was worsening. He listened to the static carefully.

"It's white noise from a subspace jammer," he muttered. The ship the shuttle pod was from was probably the source of the jamming signal. This, of course, meant that if he couldn't send and receive signals, neither could they.

A police car cruised slowly past his hiding spot. He ducked behind the wall away from the window until it passed.

Then the dorm's doorknob began to turn. Someone was trying to enter. Quickly, Antel pulled out the particle beam pistol and aimed it at the door.

After what felt like an eternity, there was a click, the door swung open, and a hand slapped the wall next to the door and turned on the lights. Sarah finally returned.

"Holy shit!" Sarah jumped, dropping her keys to the floor and raising her hands as if she were being robbed.

Antel realized he had the pistol aimed straight at her, and that scared her. He lowered it. "So sorry, Sarah," he apologized. "I didn't know who was coming into the room."

"Dammit, Andrew." She was just catching her breath. "Who da fuck did you think it was?"

"You're right, but I couldn't assume it was you."

"Hey!" She pointed at his pistol. "What the hell kind of gun is that? Neil was always a big fan of showing off his collection of guns. I've never seen any that look anywhere near like that."

The best he could come up with was, "Long story."

"Not good enough." Sarah appeared to be drawing a line in the sand. "Now that Becky isn't here, I can say whatever I want to you. You better spill it, dude."

"I already told you that I can't tell you."

"If you don't start talking, I might have to call that Navarro agent," threatened Sarah.

"You wouldn't." Antel started to worry about Sarah. "You promised Becky, your friend."

"This is to protect her." Sarah crossed her arms and stared straight at him. "I don't want to break my promise to her, but if you're too dangerous for her, I have to think of her."

"You are a good friend to her," Antel said as he holstered his weapon and sat down on the bed. "I can see why she believes in you."

She said nothing.

"At least can you promise this stays between us? Not even Neil can find out?"

"Is this something Becky already knows about?"

"Yes, she is fully aware of everything I'm about to tell you."

"Okay, I'm listening. I won't tell anyone."

Hoping she was sincere about that, he explained his alien origins, violating Standard Protocol yet again.

"Wow, that's all so science fiction," she said skeptically. "Can you prove any of it?"

He thought for a moment, then remembered. "You recall me saying 'Kossdra' a little while ago?"

"Yeah, what does that mean? Is that in your planet's language?"

"Not the entire planet, but yeah, it's in my native tongue," he told her. "It's the equivalent of when you would say shit."

"Say more stuff in your language," she was curious if he could. "But wait." She took out her cellphone and set it to record.

"Um, okay." He said before switching to Intallan. He repeated his name, rank, and mission, giving her a decent amount to listen to.

"Okay, now say all that again a few words at a time." She let Antel say a handful of words, then she played the recording to see if he was saying the same words as the first time or making them up.

"Oh my God," she had to sit down on her roommate's bed across from Antel. "Either that's some European language or you really are from another planet."

"Tell no one."

"So I'll bet that thing that looks like a phone is really a space phone?"

Antel laughed at the term 'space phone'. "It's a subspace communicator."

"So, call your planet?"

"I tried to call my ship, but someone is jamming the signal."

"The bad guys that destroyed the farmhouse?"

"There's a very good probability that it was them, yes. But I just had an idea. Do you have any tools?"

"Sure, in the closet I have a small case of tiny assorted tools."

Antel took out the tools and began disassembling the subspace radio. It wasn't easy since the Terran tools didn't quite fit the Arkonian screws. He got it open and began tweaking the wiring using some aluminum foil scraps he found in her trash bin. He did his best to replicate Irina's work to get a makeshift subspace signal locator fabricated.

Sarah just watched, impressed that he was so capable at high-tech work. Then she remembered, he was never really a history student; he was a secret alien soldier the whole time.

It took half an hour to finish, and the end product looked like a dissected frog taped to a cardboard box. "Got it. This should help find the source of the jammer. If I'm lucky, it won't be in orbit."

The signal was strong, very strong. It had to be very close. They walked up and down the halls, hoping not to get spotted by another student, a risk he needed to take. By checking the signal at the end of each hallway, he was able to triangulate its source.

"Get me a campus map." He said as they returned to her dorm room. He took the map and a ruler he saw earlier in the closet and made measurements. He drew circles at the ends of each of the hallways. His eyes lit up.

"This is a good time to say, 'Kossdra!'" he said.

"Why, what did you come up with?"

"The engineering building of all places!" He remarked. "I need to infiltrate the engineering building and shut it down. This could get violent, so you stay here. Let Becky know with vague words so if the authorities are tapping your messages, they'll be thrown off."

He stood up, checked his weapon's charge, pulled out the night vision goggles, and handed the rest of the bag to Sarah. "See that Becky gets that and no one else."

"Roger that," she saluted him with the same Terran salute Becky kept using.

"If anything happens to me, tell Becky..."

"Don't finish that sentence!" Sarah pointed sternly at him. "You better make it through this. I don't want to see my best friend heartbroken."

Chapter 27

When Becky got home after Sarah dropped her off, she hoped her parents were still asleep. She was tired and needed a break so she could deal with them in the morning.

She wasn't that lucky.

"Oh my God!" her mother, Elaine, yelled as Becky tried to open the front door quietly. "You're okay!" Her mother ran up and gave her daughter an embrace. Naturally, as a mother, Elaine was fraught with worry that something horrible might have happened to her daughter.

"Yes, I'm fine, Mom," Becky said. Looking up from the embrace, she saw her father, who was just as worried. When Elaine let go of Becky, Becky walked up to Robert and hugged him too.

"I'm so glad you're safe," Robert said. "But we have to talk."

"Can't it wait until morning? I'm beat."

"Not for this," Robert said. He looked at her and noticed her clothes were covered in dirt. "From the looks of it, we almost didn't have this conversation."

The three of them took a seat at the kitchen table.

"I guess you heard about the explosion?" Becky asked rhetorically.

"What caused the explosion? Is Antel still..." Robert tried to be tactful. "Is he..."

"He's fine, Dad," she confirmed. "I'm probably the reason he wasn't killed in the attack."

"Oh?" Elaine asked.

"If it weren't for me, he probably would have been in the house when the drone blew it up. We were outside enjoying the stars. If it weren't for that, we wouldn't have seen the drone coming."

"Drone?" Robert jumped back in. "The news never said anything about a drone!"

"Well, at first it was a drone, then these Rileean soldiers came out of the forest in formation and attacked. I don't think they expected the drone to blow up the farmhouse. But it looked like they were working together."

"An alien drone?" Robert followed up with another question.

"Something tells me no," her brow furrowed as she thought about it. "If it were alien, it would have used those weird blue beams. No, I'm willing to bet it was American because it shot at us with a regular missile."

"Someone is covering up something!" Elaine exclaimed.

"Maybe, but hold on," Robert was trying to be open and logical about the situation. "It's possible the drone was after those alien soldiers."

"No, I'm pretty sure they were on the same team," Becky said with confidence. "The drone didn't stick around to deal with the soldiers. Come to think of it, I don't think the drone killed any of them. The only enemy soldier killed was the one Antel blew away while trying to get me to safety. I guess another thing that I did that saved him was keep his attention on my safety instead of holding his ground against those soldiers and getting himself killed."

Robert was about to ask another question but was interrupted when the house phone rang. At this late hour, he knew this wasn't going to be good news.

He picked up the phone. "Robert Miller speaking."

Robert was quiet for a moment as he listened.

"No, Agent Navarro," Robert said, his tone becoming firmer. "Any questioning of my daughter will happen with me present, and only after we've had time to review the situation. Can we meet in the morning?"

Another moment of silence as Navarro spoke.

"Very well, we understand the severity. Give us an hour." Robert hung up the phone and then told Elaine and Becky, "We've got an hour to talk about the details."

"Well," Becky started, "you already know most of what I know."

"Sweetheart, we're already in danger. There's a federal investigation centered on our house, and your boyfriend is being hunted by Homeland Security. At this point, I'm betting there is nothing you say now that can make this worse. Tell me what happened after the explosion."

"We ran into the forest in the opposite direction. Antel and one of them got into a shootout. Antel totally cleaned his clock." As she said that, a flicker of admiration crossed Becky's face. He was very skilled, she thought, a new sense of admiration dawning within her.

"Go on," Robert said.

"Um, then we got away and reached the main road. From there, I called Sarah to pick us up. We went back to her place and talked about the situation for a bit, then Antel decided it wasn't safe for me to be near him and made Sarah bring me home."

"Good for Antel!" Elaine said. "I'm glad he's making your safety a priority."

Robert ran a hand through his graying hair. "I was wrong. This does sound worse."

Becky's phone buzzed. A text from Sarah: "You know who just left. He went to drop off his engineering homework."

Becky replied, "Thx." She understood her 'code.' It meant he was going to do something in the engineering building. The same place where he encountered the enemy soldiers the first time around.

The phone buzzed again. Sarah added, "I know his secret now. I won't tell."

Looks like Antel had to tell her too. Becky really hoped when all this was over that he didn't get court-martialed over all of this.

"Becky." Her father's tone was gentle but firm. "Navarro will be here soon. We need to decide how to handle this."

A plan started forming in her mind. "Dad, what if I told you there's evidence that might help prove he's an alien if it comes down to needing to go that route? Something in Dr. Carter's office."

"Dr. Carter? Your advisor?" He frowned. "They took her into custody."

Becky nodded. "There's a document, something I saw in her office the other day. It had unusual writing on it. One of his teammates, Dr. Sallain, uh, Solomon, wrote notes in his native language, and Dr. Carter managed to keep them. If I could get to it..."

"Absolutely not," her mother interjected. "You're not breaking into anywhere."

"Mom, please. This is important. Besides, I got a key."

Robert held up a hand. "No one is going anywhere. We're going to handle this legally." He checked his watch. "Navarro will be here in forty-five minutes. We need to..."

A sharp knock at the door cut him off. Elaine walked up to the window and peered through. "It's him. He's early."

Robert stood up and headed to the front door. "Remember, let me do the talking. Don't volunteer any information."

Becky's heart raced as her father opened the door. She knew her father was good at his job, but she was still scared.

Agent Navarro stepped in, his suit impeccable despite the late hour.

"Mr. Miller. Mrs. Miller." Navarro nodded to each of them before fixing his gaze on Becky. "Miss Miller. Thank you for agreeing to speak with me."

"We haven't agreed to anything yet," Robert said. "You're here earlier than discussed."

"Time is critical in these situations." Navarro remained standing. "We have GPS data from your phone showing your movements. We know Andrew Rall's movements as well, and we know that both of you were there when the explosion occurred."

"Then you know where he is?" Becky kept her voice steady.

"No, we last saw his signal at the explosion site. An initial search uncovered several bodies inside the home and one outside in the forest. Interestingly, the trees near where the body was found in the forest were damaged with a similar weapon as the one that was used in the engineering building. Might you know anything about that?"

"Sorry, I'm no weapons expert," she told him. Robert was ready to stop her from answering any question that might hurt her case. So far, the questions weren't incriminating.

"How did you manage to get home without your car, Miss

Miller?" Navarro asked his next question.

Robert raised a hand, letting Becky know not to answer that question. "Just because you tracked her car and phone to that location does not guarantee that she was physically there at the time. This is circumstantial evidence."

"True," Navarro said. "But the fact that your car was there could mean you might be an accessory to a crime. I have every right to bring you in for questioning. However, I think we can help each other instead."

Robert stepped forward. "If you're proposing some kind of deal..."

"No deals yet. Just conversation." Navarro finally sat, his movements deliberately casual. "Becky, I know you care about Andrew, but I don't think he is who he says he is, and I think you know that too."

Becky didn't respond to that statement.

"By the way, our investigators found an awful lot of tracks, and the pieces of the farmhouse moved around as if the site was cleaned of any evidence. There was even a work shed that looked like it was gutted of whatever was in there. Care to tell me what you know about that? Is Mr. Rall working with another group and is with them at the moment?"

"I don't know anything about another group, but if there was one, he's probably not with them. Maybe that group you speak of was after him."

Robert jumped in. "Has your investigation considered that perhaps that other group is the real culprit, and Andrew may be a victim in all this?"

"The thought had crossed my mind," Navarro confessed. "But I have to explore all options on the table."

"Do you have any specific questions to ask?" Robert was getting tired.

Navarro stood up. "Let's get a good night's sleep and talk tomorrow."

After Navarro left, Becky was able to breathe again. "Why didn't he take me in?" she pondered out loud.

"Good question," Robert said, curious too.

"I've watched enough crime dramas to know he probably wants to keep an eye on you and hope you lead him to Antel," Elaine said. "For his sake, don't go anywhere near him or he'll get caught."

"I have to get to that document," she said quietly.

Robert sighed heavily. "Maybe that might be helpful. But you're not going alone. Get in the car and let's go together."

The campus was eerily quiet that night. Becky and her father parked several blocks away and walked, trying to look like any other late-night visitors.

Robert checked his watch. "You're sure you can get us in? They don't have alarms for this late at night?"

"Nah, we're fine," she brushed off the idea of an alarm. "I come here late at night from time to time to get work done. Dr. Carter gave me a key if I ever needed to borrow one of her books."

"The benefits of being a graduate student, I suppose," her father observed.

She nodded, pulling out her student ID. The card reader beeped green. Becky pulled open the door to the building and they walked in. The door locked behind them. The key was needed to exit the building.

They walked up to Dr. Carter's office. Becky pulled out her keys and picked out the correct one. She used it to unlock the door and gestured to her father to enter. "Welcome to my professor's office."

When Becky turned on the lights, she immediately saw that the office was ransacked. Books were displaced, papers scattered. It was searched before they got there. Nothing was damaged, but signs of a thorough search were evident.

Becky went straight to the filing cabinet where she'd last seen Dr. Carter with the document. The cabinet lock was broken. Looks like they had to break the lock to get access.

She looked through the folders. When she noticed a few were missing, she looked around the room and saw a stack on the desk. She picked up the stack and began flipping through the folders.

"Ah, here it is." She pulled out a folder that Dr. Carter labeled Aboriginal Languages. Smart, Becky thought. The investigators probably saw this sheet and assumed it was some ancient tribal language.

"Got it." She pulled the page and waved it in victory. Then she handed it to her father. "Check this out."

"Wow, this is really cool." The page wasn't typed. It was handwritten. "This is legit handwriting of an alien language. Does it say anything important, like who shot JFK?"

"Funny, Dad," she said. "It's just Dr. Solomon's scrap notes."

"So I'm looking at alien chicken scratch?"

Becky laughed. "Yeah, I guess so. You need to hold on to it just in case Antel needs it as evidence or something."

As Becky was locking the office back up, her phone buzzed.

"It's an unknown number," she told Robert. "Should I answer it?"

"Yeah, I think you should."

Becky pressed the accept button and put the phone to her ear. "Hello?"

"Hello?" the caller said. "Is this Rebecca Miller?"

"Um, it is. Who is this?" she replied, looking at her father as she shrugged her shoulders.

"This is Dr. Sallain. I tried calling Antel, but he isn't picking up. Is he okay? Did he survive the explosion?"

"It's Dr. Sallain," she quickly informed her father.

"He's fine. We managed to escape. How did they not catch you when you were with Dr. Carter?" Becky asked. "They took her in for questioning."

"I was on my way home at the time," Dahnt told her. "I saw the explosion and turned around. Do you know where Antel is?"

She was about to tell him that he was headed to the engineering building, but something inside her told her to wait before divulging that information. "Uh, not at the moment, no. Sorry."

"Why don't you come by the engineering building with me?" Dahnt suggested. "I'm hiding out here. Then, when you get in contact with Antel, you can have him join us."

"Let me find him first."

"Very well," his voice carried a note of disappointment that made Becky's suspicions sharpen. Something about his tone felt calculated, too practiced. "Have him get here as soon as he can so we can plan an escape from your planet."

"Sure thing, Professor," she played along, her mind already racing through his convenient absences during every crisis. "I'll let him know."

Dahnt simply said, "Thank you," before disconnecting the call.

Becky stared at the phone for a moment, pieces clicking into place. She turned to her father. "He wants me and Antel to meet him at the engineering building."

"You look like you don't trust him."

"My gut is screaming not to trust him anymore. Think about it. He's conveniently absent every time something terrible happens. The timing is too perfect."

Robert's expression darkened as he considered this. "Could be a trap."

"Oh my God, Antel could be walking straight into danger. I gotta warn him."

"How do you know this?"

"Sarah texted me and said he was headed there right now."

"How can we warn him? He doesn't have his phone," Robert said.

"I'm going to have to stop him. Keep that document safe." Becky pointed at the page he was holding and then sprinted away.

"Becky, no..." Robert almost yelled it but thought calling out her name was a bad idea. There was nothing he could do. She was determined to prevent Antel from falling into Dahnt's trap.

He prayed for both of them. He couldn't bear to lose his daughter, but he knew she would be devastated if anything happened to Antel. He wasn't sure which was worse.

Chapter 28

Antel made his way across the campus, being as discreet as possible in case anyone recognized him. His mind had time to think about the day's events. He felt terrible that he had let his team down and allowed them to die so tragically.

He would have surely died along with his team had it not been for Becky. She told him earlier that what he felt was called 'Survivor's Guilt.' Of course, as a soldier, he was well aware of the term even though his world called it 'Survivor's Remorse.'

The cool air flowed around him. Antel needed answers. Who was operating that subspace jammer from the engineering building, and why there, of all places?

He knew the attack was from a Terran drone. The initial destruction was from the drone missile, but the huge explosion occurred because the power generator was probably hit by the drone's weapon fire.

There was probably a small leak of antimatter, but it was a very tiny amount because the generator was only charged for enough energy for a single house and the surrounding sheds and structures. The explosion was the antimatter getting used up by interacting with the regular matter on the ground and in the air. Had this been a larger power station on Arkonus, the devastation could potentially be much greater, but the safety features minimize catastrophes.

Antel made it to the front door. He took a gamble that whoever was operating the jammer was probably paying more attention to the building's back door and assuming anyone coming in the front was supposed to be there anyway.

Antel took out the wireless digital systems decoder, the same device Irina first used to unlock this very same door, and attached it to the lock with the magnet. Using the datapad, he easily cracked the code despite the building personnel changing the code after the first time Irina hacked it.

When the door clicked open, he slipped right in and made his way to the floor where the skirmish took place. He assumed they would probably be using the same floor and maybe even the same room as before.

He hated making Becky worry. He pulled out his pistol. For Becky's sake, he planned to be as cautious as he could be.

The hallways were eerily quiet. As he walked down each hallway, the only sound he could hear was his footsteps. He couldn't shake the feeling that he was walking into danger.

As he neared the room in question, he raised his pistol and prepared to shoot anything that moved. The last time he was here, someone shot at him. He moved slowly toward the door. As he reached with his left hand for the doorknob and turned. Locked. That's when he noticed the digital panel of numbers. After the last incident, they must have decided to reinforce security with this panel. Antel thought, "This actually makes it easier. I can now use the decoder."

He had to reholster his firearm so he could manage the decoder and the datapad. Just as he was about to attach the decoder to the panel, he heard voices on the other side of the door. Quickly, he darted around to another inset doorway and hid. He put the decoder and the datapad back in the backpack that he borrowed from Sarah. Then he pulled the pistol back out and readied it once more.

The voices opened the door. They were speaking in Intallan. His heart raced.

"...timeline is progressing smoothly now that Ralnar and his team are no longer interfering," said one of the voices.

"Is that... That's Dr. Sallain's voice!" Antel was shocked to hear Dahnt's voice planning something with the enemy. Who is he talking to?

Dahnt continued, "The Earth Outpost has been destroyed and the entire team, aside from myself, has perished."

The other voice responded, "Excellent." Antel didn't recognize the second voice. "The admiral will alert High Command and blame the attack on the Terrans. His attack force is already in the system and should be here in a few days. By the time the Council figures out the truth, his attack force will already be done with their strike. The only thing holding us up is gaining access to the Terran satellite network. Once the uplink is in place, we can begin Operation Chaos."

Antel's heart dropped. Satellite network? Operation Chaos? This was serious.

"So tell me about this panel that you wanted to show me," Sallain said, returning the subject to the reason they stepped out of the room.

"This panel is fake," the other voice started talking. "The door still uses a physical lock that can't be hacked digitally. As soon as Antel tries to open it with a decoder, the plates under the floor tiles will electrify him."

"A trap! Good to know," Antel thought to himself.

He had heard of Operation Chaos before last year, when he returned home to visit his parents during his off time. Before returning to Mars, he had heard some of the other officers discussing options for Operation Chaos and asked him for his opinion. He told them he still needed to assess Earth's capabilities before giving them a good answer. He didn't tell them he was opposed to the idea, regardless. The Empire wasn't in the business of conquering regions that had the support of their people. Now, if Earth were having civil uprisings and not doing so well against more powerful oppressors, Rilee would step in, but he didn't get that impression of Earth.

This was far worse than he had imagined. They were planning, not just espionage or sabotage, but a full-scale invasion. Once his team had submitted their report, the Rileean Empire would have no desire to intervene militarily. But the death of the expedition team would certainly rally support.

This admiral, learning from the lessons of the occupation of Kentus, planned to render Earth's ability to wage a coordinated asymmetric war impossible. It would have been a genius idea if it weren't so reprehensible.

Who is this rogue admiral? Antel wondered.

"Any word on Lieutenant Ralnar?" the second voice asked.

"No sign of him," Dahnt answered. "He is likely hiding out somewhere with his girlfriend, Rebecca Miller. I was able to contact Miss Miller and request that she and Ralnar come here and join me." Antel felt a surge of panic in his throat.

The second voice laughed. "That's brilliant! We can accuse him of assisting the Terrans out of love for his new girlfriend."

Antel needed to know more about this uplink. He focused on their voices as hard as he could. The air-conditioning vents made listening a little challenging. But, to his disappointment, the two re-entered the room, locking the door behind them.

"Curse the Universe!" Antel thought. "If only they said more about this uplink."

At that moment, Antel heard footsteps coming down the hall from the direction he came, making his exit impossible. He prepared to duck around the wall of the inset doorway, aim his pistol at the sound, and fire if necessary. His heart was pounding.

No! It was Becky. If they discovered they both were already here, her life could be at risk. He re-holstered his pistol, then quietly and quickly moved to intercept her.

Antel grabbed Becky, putting his hand over her mouth to keep her from making noise, and pulled her into another one of the inset doorways.

"What are you doing here?" Antel whispered. "You're supposed to be at home."

Before she could say anything, she lunged to embrace him. "Thank God you're okay. Dr. Sallain called me."

"I heard," Antel replied.

"Really? How?"

"I just overheard him talking to another Rileean down there by that door," Antel pointed down the hall, not being accurate about which door he pointed at.

"When he called, I got suspicious and figured he was setting a trap for you." Her eyes began to show some tears.

Antel pulled her back in to repeat the embrace. "As dumb as coming here might have been, I can't help but feel a bit proud. Your instincts were right."

Wiping the tears that formed, she gave him a huge smile. "Hey, my super-soldier can't do it all on his own."

"Nope," Antel smiled back. "He can't do it alone."

"So now what?" she asked.

"How do your people say it?" Antel thought this was a good moment for a Terran expression. "Let's get the fuck out of here."

Becky nearly laughed, but she covered her mouth with her hand to stop herself.

With his pistol out, Antel kept his eyes periodically looking back as they left the building the same way they came in.

Once outside, Becky grabbed his free hand and pulled him toward the history department. "This way. My Dad is probably freaking out over there."

"Your Dad?" Antel got a little worried. "He's going to strangle me for all the danger I put you through."

"Nah, he won't kill you. He'll just beat the crap out of you," she joked.

"You're joking, right?" Antel knew his father would consider beating the 'crap' out of any man that put his daughter in any danger.

As they got closer, Robert could be seen standing where Becky left him when she darted off.

He didn't look happy, Antel observed.

"Daddy, we made it!" She was proud of herself. "It was indeed a trap, but Antel's safe."

"Thank God," Robert gave him a look. "Remember your promise not to let any harm come to Rebecca."

"I'll never let anything happen to her," he stated.

"Okay, so talk," Robert said. "What's going on? Becky tells me there was a drone involved. Are you sure it was an American drone?"

"It had to be," Antel said.

"I knew it," Becky felt vindicated again. "Because it used regular bullets and missiles instead of that blue lightning, right?"

"No, because if the plan was just to destroy the farmhouse, they could have shot at it from orbit."

"Oh shit!" Robert said. "How are we supposed to defend against that? Why use an American drone when they had a much easier option?"

"Because they want to accuse Terrans of striking first. They may have hacked access to the drone as part of their plan."

"How do you know this?" Becky asked him.

"In that conversation, I overheard Dr. Sallain and another Rileean," Antel explained, "they specifically said that was their intention. They're planning something called Operation Chaos."

"Dr. Sallain?" Both Becky and Robert said together in near unison.

"He's been deceiving us the entire time," Antel said.

"Holy fuck. I knew it! That asshole!" Becky blurted.

"Rebecca Miller!" Her Dad was not the cursing type.

"Sorry, Dad. It just came out," she apologized. "So, Antel, tell us more about this Operation Chaos."

"Dr. Sallain has been plotting with an admiral to prepare for an invasion."

"An invasion?" She leaned back and covered her mouth with her hand. "You mean like in the movies? An alien invasion? War of the Worlds kind of stuff?"

"Sort of, yes." He put his hands on her shoulders for reassurance. "He's planning to take control of Earth's satellite network and make your leaders believe there's a nuclear attack occurring. Then he's going to block satellite communications to keep them from figuring out it's all a trick. That's the chaos part."

"What is that supposed to accomplish?" She was afraid to hear the answer.

"Chances are, the major powers on Earth will launch their missiles for real in response to what they think is a first strike against them."

"Oh my God," she said. Becky's face turned pale. "They're talking about the end of the world! Why would he want to kill everything here? What does he get out of it?"

"First, you'd be surprised how resilient humans are. Earth will survive this."

"But?"

"But your civilization will be set so far back it will become easy pickings for a takeover."

"How can you be sure of that?" She was always under the impression that a nuclear war would just mean the end of the world.

"Arkonus has had its share of war, and we're no strangers to nuclear power." He knew nothing he said was going to reassure her. "Actually, our people are rather impressed how your planet managed to avoid using them for so long."

"But it will be bad, right?"

Antel didn't say anything. He just looked down at his feet. He didn't need to say anything. She understood by the silence.

"So what's the plan?" she asked.

"I wish I could call this in," Antel replied. "I wasn't able to disable that subspace jammer, so contacting the Black Cat isn't going to happen any time soon."

"How about calling Mars directly?" Robert suggested.

"The big subspace radio was destroyed in the farmhouse explosion," he sighed as he glanced at the subspace communicator he was using as a makeshift jammer detector. "And my small communicator won't reach Mars."

"Is it time to call the authorities? FBI? Homeland Security?" Robert made another suggestion.

"I seriously doubt they would believe this crazy story. Besides, since that drone was American, someone on the inside may be helping them. We can't trust anyone. We need to lock out Sallain and the admiral from accessing our Rileean satellite."

Antel considered his options. First, he needed to figure out how to connect to that satellite. Then, second, he needed to figure out how to lock Dahnt and the admiral out. This wasn't going to be easy, but at least he had a goal.

"That sounds like a good plan B," she said. "How can we help?" Becky was eager to do what she could to help. "Put me to work."

"I don't think so," protested Antel. "There's no way I'm going to let you get involved in something this dangerous. I would be derelict in my duties if I put a civilian in harm's way."

"Listen, mister!" Becky crossed her arms and gave him a stern look. "This civilian isn't planning to let you do this alone. Besides, this is my planet, not yours." Antel could tell she didn't like the term civilian from the way she emphasized it.

"Becky!" Robert was going to protest her involvement.

"Sorry, Dad, but not this time." She gave her father a stern look as well. "If Earth is in serious trouble, there's no way I'm going to sit back and let it happen."

"But I can't let anything happen to you. I would never forgive myself if..."

"Stop right there," Becky leaned forward and covered his mouth with her index finger. "I can help. I know someone who might be able to help."

"Really? Who?"

"Neil is in the Air Force..."

"That's an even worse idea. Once he's done laughing at us, he'll probably arrest us himself."

"Technically, he can't arrest anyone," Robert's inner lawyer spoke. "As military, he's barred from police activity on US soil."

"See, it's not such a bad idea," she pleaded. "I'm sure he can help. He might be an asshole but he's very patriotic about America."

"But..."

She interrupted him again. "His Air Force connections can get us access to that satellite. Maybe you can disable it or lock him out. Not to mention, he would still do anything to earn me back."

"Uh..." Antel couldn't think of a counterargument to that point. That actually sounded like a good idea. Or it would have been if it weren't Neil. "Okay, I have to admit that has potential. But..."

"No buts," she pulled out her phone. "I can call him right now and arrange a meeting."

"What about the Standard Protocol?" he reminded her.

"If Sallain and that admiral succeed, Earth will find out anyway."

"Good point," Antel wondered why she didn't follow in her father's footsteps and go into law. She was determined.

"Let me call him. We don't have to tell him everything," Becky added. "Just enough to get his help."

Antel put a hand on the back of his neck and thought about it. Everything in him told him this was a bad idea. But in the absence of a better idea or any idea, his options were dwindling.

"You trust him?"

"As a friend, no," she was honest. "But as someone who wants to serve his country, yes."

Antel paused. He brushed his fingers through his hair. "If we do this, and I mean if we do this, we only tell him what is absolutely required."

"Deal!" Becky felt giddy inside. "Dad, can you leave us here and go home? Let Mom know the plan."

"Becky, I can't. As your father…"

"Dad, I'm a big girl. I got Antel in case there's trouble."

"Why can't I at least stick around?" Robert argued.

"Because Neil would feel like we ganged up on him and won't be as willing to help," she said. "Oh, and maybe you should keep Antel's gear safe. If things go south, I don't think we want Neil to get his hands on any of it."

"Fine, you two be safe," Robert was not happy with the arrangement, but he trusted his daughter. "And you, keep your promise and make sure she isn't hurt."

"Yes, sir," Antel said.

"If we fail," Becky commented, "I won't be the only one getting hurt. We can't fail."

After Robert left them to return home, Antel turned to her and said, "Okay. We have to strike a balance between telling him everything and violating the Standard Protocol."

"Understood, sir," she snapped a salute, trying to be cute.

"I can't believe I'm letting you in on this," Antel sighed. "And that's the wrong salute."

She pulled out her phone and pointed at it.

"Fine." He gave in. "Call him and plan an in-person meeting."

She scrolled through her contacts and clicked on Neil's entry. She waited for a few moments. After a few rings, Neil answered.

"Hello?" the voice said. "Becks? What's going on? Did that asshole hurt you?"

"I'm fine, but… Listen, I… we need to meet. We need to talk about something of vital importance, and I think you can help." The name "Becks" still annoyed her, but this time she let it pass.

"We? Who's 'we'?"

"Andrew and I." She almost said Antel's real name.

"Andrew?" Neil said. "Fuck off. I'm not talking to that motherfucker."

"Neil!" She interrupted him. "This is important. Can't you put your feelings aside for one minute?"

There was a long pause on the phone.

"Neil? Are you still there?" asked Becky. She assumed he hung up on her.

"Yeah, I'm still here. Fine, but this is just for you. He'll be lucky I don't kick his ass. When and where?"

"We're on campus at the moment. Maybe at the courtyard in front of the history building in an hour?"

"In an hour?" Neil growled. "Fine, I'm on my way."

Antel and Becky headed back to the courtyard and waited. They sat on one of the benches and tried to relax. Neither of them spoke while they waited. Both of them were too focused on how they would approach this meeting with Neil.

Antel's doubt gnawed at him. His gut still told him this was a bad idea. To convince Neil, Antel would inevitably have to break the Standard Protocol again, and this person couldn't be trusted with this information. It didn't help that he was associated with the Air Force, but it's precisely for that reason that they needed Neil.

"The Universe hates me today," he thought to himself.

His thoughts shifted to his fallen expedition members. They came to observe and learn about Earth. The mission was supposed to be one of peace, but now Dahnt and this mystery admiral were using them to frame the Earth for a tragedy they didn't commit. They didn't sign up for this.

Antel wanted to clench his fists, but he didn't want to worry Becky. He failed to protect his team, but he promised he wasn't going to let tragedy fall on her or her planet. If people back home visited, they would see that Earth wasn't some random alien planet. It was just like home. The languages and cultures might be different from his, but there are countries on Arkonus that have less in common with each other than with these.

Was he really the right person for this? He was trained as a soldier, not a spy, not a politician. And how was he going to stop Dahnt and the admiral's plans and not break the Standard Protocol? If he warned the authorities, they would just arrest him as either a lunatic or a terrorist.

Antel decided that even though he didn't think trusting Neil was a good idea, he was going to trust Becky and see where this went.

Chapter 29

Antel attempted to dust off some of the dirt still on his clothes from the attack, but was unsuccessful. He glanced at Becky sitting beside him on the wooden bench in the history building's courtyard.

"How late is it?" he asked her.

Becky looked at her cellphone, which she was gripping for comfort as they waited for Neil's arrival. "It's almost 3 AM," she told him.

Antel could tell she was feeling chilly in the early morning air. The lampposts did nothing to keep them warm. He wanted to put his arm around her, but if Neil saw that when he arrived, it would only antagonize him further. Best to keep anything that might anger him to a minimum.

He wasn't looking forward to the meeting ahead.

"Are you sure about this?" he asked her, keeping his voice low but unable to mask his unease. "Neil's anger toward me is hardly a recipe for a productive discussion."

Becky placed a reassuring hand on his arm. "Neil's an asshole, but he loves his country, Antel. He hates you, sure, but he'll listen if we give him a chance. Besides, you need his help to stop Dr. Sallain. We have to try."

Antel gave her a mumbled "Okay," though his instincts screamed this was not going to be okay. The risk of further exposure, especially to someone as volatile as Neil, made his stomach churn.

A car rolled up to the curb and parked. A dark sedan bearing official government plates. Becky and Antel both stood up from the bench and walked to meet Neil halfway to his car.

Antel's body tensed as Neil stepped out, dressed in his Air Force uniform in an attempt to portray authority. He adjusted his cap as he walked toward them, his eyes fixed on Antel with thinly veiled disdain.

Neil stopped a few feet in front of them. "Becky," he greeted politely. Moving his gaze to Antel, a sneer tugged at the corners of his mouth. "So, what was so important you had to drag me out at 3 fucking AM? What do you want?"

"Neil, I need you to hear us out," Becky spoke first.

Antel took a deep breath, forcing himself to remain composed. "I need your help."

Neil's laugh was sharp and cold. "You? Need my help? That's rich. First, you steal my girlfriend, and now you want a favor?"

Antel resisted the urge to snap back. Instead, he replied calmly, "This isn't about Becky. It's bigger than us. Lives are at stake."

Neil folded his arms, his posture screaming skepticism. "This oughta be good. Convince me."

For a moment, Antel hesitated. Explaining the situation without revealing his identity was proving more difficult than he anticipated. "You've seen strange things recently, haven't you? Unexplainable events, advanced technology."

Neil's eyes narrowed. "Get to the point, asshole."

Antel couldn't think of how to say what he needed to say without admitting his secret. "Curse the Universe," he said, speaking momentarily in Intallan. Then, resuming in English, he began to tell Neil the truth. "Neil, I'm sure you won't believe me at first, but I am not from this planet. My entire team, uh, classmates, and professor, and I are part of an expedition to study Earth. But others from my world are here on Earth, and they are not here with good intentions."

Neil's expression shifted. Antel didn't know how to read what crossed his face before it hardened again. "You expect me to believe this bullshit?"

"I know it's a lot to take in," Becky interjected, "but during your investigation into the engineering building's break-in, you must have seen shit that doesn't add up."

"Do you remember when I asked you about the gray car a few days ago?" Antel asked him. He could see that Becky was surprised that he had already spoken to Neil without her knowledge recently. "The one at the Botanical Gardens parking lot?"

Neil's expression remained unchanged. "Keep talking."

"Those people you spoke to are the bad actors I was referring to," Antel told him. "After they drove off, I followed them. This led to a shootout before they got away."

"They missed their target," Neil said sarcastically as he pointed at Antel.

"Didn't you notice none of them spoke English except for perhaps one of them?" Antel questioned him. "I'll bet the one that did had a thick accent."

Neil's gaze turned to the ground as he weighed his options. His jaw worked silently, the tension evident in every line of his face. When he finally looked back up, there was something different in his eyes—a cold calculation that hadn't been there before.

"You're right about the accent," Neil said slowly, then his voice hardened.

"Sorry?" There were only a few people on Arkonus who could speak English without an accent, and he was confident he knew them all. "He didn't have an accent?"

"You're late to the party," he said bitterly. "I know your precious secret, Lieutenant Antel Ralnar."

Antel was shocked, but before he could say anything, Becky jumped in, "What the fuck? How did you already know his real name?"

Neil smirked humorlessly. "Dr. Sallain told me everything and told me not to let you know that I knew." Neil used Dahnt's real name, too. "He told me way before the botanical gardens incident. He caught up with me when he saw me drive up to the Museum of Nature and Science."

"Were you following me?" Becky demanded an answer.

"No," Neil said, "but who do you think dropped off Sarah?"

"So go on," Antel wanted the conversation to stay on topic.

"Well, Sallain and his buddies approached me in the parking lot.

They told me shit I didn't believe, so they had me meet with them and they showed me this super cool ship landing in the middle of a field. After that, we made a deal and I've been letting them use the engineering building's Air Force lab."

"This makes sense now," Antel said. "You got your Homeland Security to investigate me, hoping it would break Becky and my relationship. But when it started to hit too close to Dr. Sallain, he asked you to call it off."

"By then, it was too late, right?" Becky jumped in. Things were becoming clear to her as well. "Navarro had too much to go on to just quit because you said so."

"What's in it for you?" Antel knew there must have been a motive for him to prioritize Sallain over Becky.

"Sallain said he'd share some of his people's tech so we could defend ourselves from bad elements from his world. From people like you. He's going to make me the go-between to the U.S. Government. As a bonus, this should set me up financially for life."

"All I had to do was give them access to our drone systems and satellite uplinks. I didn't know they were planning to..." Neil trailed off, looking uncomfortable.

Becky gasped, covering her mouth with her hands. Antel's mind raced. Of course, Dahnt had already made his move, undermining everything.

"And you believed him?" Antel asked, his voice growing even more serious.

Neil's glare returned. "Why wouldn't I? He had proof. And if you think I'm just going to trust you over him, you're delusional."

Antel stepped forward, his tone urgent. "Sallain is lying to you. He has no intention of keeping those promises. He's using you to further his own agenda. He plans to cause massive devastation to your world, and he needs your help to gain access using a satellite uplink."

Neil laughed bitterly. "And I'm supposed to take your word for it? You're the liar here. He told me you would say all of this one day. But smart, figuring out about the uplink. That much is true. He needs it to mask his landings on Earth when he ships me all this cool gear."

"Goddammit, Neil. Stop it!" Becky yelled, stepping between them. "You have no idea what's going on. Antel's trying to save lives."

Neil's expression softened as he looked at her, but his resentment remained. "And you're just going to believe him? This alien? He isn't American. Fuck, as far as I'm concerned, he's an illegal alien."

Becky nodded firmly. "Yes, I do believe him. Because he's proven himself to me over and over again. And if you'd stop being so stubborn, you'd see it too."

Antel met Neil's gaze. "If you keep helping Sallain, he'll make you regret it. He's not interested in your wealth or your career. He's here to destabilize Earth, to make it vulnerable for his own purposes. I should have seen this before. He's a hard-line nationalist and doesn't give a damn about people other than his own."

Neil's jaw worked silently for a moment before he took a few steps back. "You don't know shit about me."

Neil's hand drifted slowly toward his back, where Antel caught the telltale bulge of a concealed weapon. Every instinct Antel possessed suddenly screamed danger.

"You think you have all the answers, don't you? Big fucking hero riding his white horse in to save the day. But you're nothing but a liar and the asshole who ruined my future with Becks."

Antel held his ground. His instincts screamed danger. "Neil, I don't want to fight with you. This isn't personal."

Neil's face twisted in rage. "It is to me."

In one fluid motion, Neil stepped back and drew his service weapon. "You think you have all the answers..." The rest of his words were lost in Becky's scream as the muzzle flash lit up the courtyard.

Antel felt the impact before he heard the bang. All he felt was the searing pain in his head as everything went black.

Through the ringing in his ears and the encroaching void, one sound cut through everything else—Becky's voice, raw and broken, screaming his real name: "ANTEL!"

Chapter 30

"ANTEL!!!" Becky's scream tore from her throat with such raw force that it probably woke up a few students still sleeping in the student residence building across the street. The same one Sarah's dorm was in. Becky didn't care if the world heard his true name. Becky dropped to her knees, her legs giving out beneath her as she lunged for Antel's body. Her hands shook violently as she reached for his face, the sight of his closed eyes making her stomach lurch. Blood roared in her ears as she screamed again, "GET UP! YOU CAN'T LEAVE ME!"

"We have to leave. Get up," Neil barked, his voice sharp and unyielding. Becky twisted her arm, trying to free herself, but his grip only tightened. "Stop struggling," he hissed, pulling her toward his car.

"Let go of me!" she screamed, thrashing against him. She put a palm on Neil's chest for leverage to pull her other arm free, but Neil's grip was strong.

When they reached his car, he yanked open the passenger door and shoved her inside with such force that her shoulder slammed against the opposite seat. She immediately grabbed for the door handle, but Neil had already pressed his key remote. The electronic locks clicked into place, trapping her inside while he circled to the driver's seat.

"You're a psychopath! What are you doing?" Becky shouted, twisting to reach for the door handle, but it wouldn't budge. The car was designed not to allow the doors to open once the shift was put into drive. Panic surged through her chest, mixing with the overwhelming grief that threatened to drown her.

"I'm saving you," Neil snapped, slamming the gas. The car sped off down the campus streets.

Becky didn't bother to put on her seatbelt. "Saving me? You just murdered Antel!" she cried. The image of his body flashed before her eyes, and her voice cracked. "Do you even realize what you've done?"

His eyes stayed fixed on the road, his jaw tight. "That thing was an alien. He was lying to you, Becky. Manipulating you."

"You don't know anything about him!" she shouted, her voice cracking with grief and rage. Hot tears streamed down her face, her vision blurring as she tried to focus on Neil's profile in the dashboard light. She fumbled in her pocket with trembling fingers, the cool surface of her phone slippery against her sweaty palms. Her heart hammered against her ribs as she tried to unlock it without drawing Neil's attention.

"He was a danger to America, to our way of life, our freedoms," Neil claimed. "His people are a threat, and Sallain is helping us defend ourselves by offering us advanced technology."

Becky's breath caught as she glanced at him. His face was pale in the glow of the dashboard, his eyes wild. He wasn't the Neil she'd once known. This man was a stranger. Unhinged.

"A danger?" she said, her voice shaking. "You believe that so strongly that you had to kidnap me? To kill someone I..." Her voice broke. "Someone I cared about?"

Neil's jaw clenched, and for a moment, the only sound was the hum of the tires on the asphalt. "You were never meant to be with him. I'm the only one who can take care of you. You're just too stubborn to admit you still want to be with me."

Her stomach churned at the mention of any desire for Neil. Neil repulsed her now more than ever. Becky glanced out the window, the world rushing past in a blur of headlights and shadows. She had to get out of this car. Now.

Her fingers trembled as she managed to type out a partial distress message on her phone. She tried to send it to Sarah, one of the recent contacts in her phone's history.

The car swerved sharply onto a dirt road, throwing her against the door and causing her to fumble the phone. Becky bit back a cry of pain, her heart pounding. The countryside stretched out in endless darkness, broken only by the faint outline of trees. She couldn't see where Neil was taking her, but she knew it wasn't anywhere good.

Neil saw the phone fall to the floor and hit the brakes hard. The hard stop forced her body to slam into the dashboard. While she was disoriented, he reached down and took the phone. Becky tried to pry it from his hand. He smacked the side of her face to make her stop struggling. The fact that he hit her made her freeze in shock. Neil was able to turn off the phone and put it in his pocket.

"Where are we going?" she demanded, her voice rising.

"Somewhere safe," Neil muttered. "Meeting up with Sallain."

Becky's blood ran cold. "You're crazy to be working with him. He's the reason all of this is happening!"

Neil's laugh was harsh, almost bitter. "You think you know everything, don't you? Sallain's offering me a way out. A way for America to defend itself from his empire." His grip on the wheel tightened. "He's going to share their technology with us. We'll be unstoppable."

Becky stared at him, horrified. "You're betraying Earth," she whispered. "For what? Money? Power?"

"This is for my country!" he asserted. "The money and power are just a bonus. You don't get it. This is about survival. About being on the winning side."

Neil made a final turn into the driveway of an abandoned military base. The guardhouse was unmanned, but the gate itself was open. He drove right in. None of the light posts were on. The area was dark. For a military base, there was a dearth of buildings.

The car jolted to a stop in front of what appeared to be a building. Becky didn't recognize the purpose of such a small building that looked nothing more than a large concrete outhouse.

Neil got out first, slamming the door and circling to her side. Becky's pulse raced as he opened the door and grabbed her arm, dragging her out. As he turned to close the door, she twisted her arm and got free. She ran as fast as she could back to the guardhouse to attempt to escape, but Neil was faster. He caught up and tackled her to the ground.

"You're going to regret this," she said as she tried to move her face off the grass that got in her eyes.

Neil ignored her, picking her up and pulling her toward the concrete structure. It was an entrance to stairs that led deeper into the ground.

He pushed her in and blocked her path back out by walking down the stairs from behind her.

"Start walking," he ordered.

"What is this place?" she wondered out loud.

"Decommissioned missile silo."

"Seriously? Are we gonna…"

"Relax, there's no radiation down here," he reassured her. "The nuke isn't even here anymore."

When they reached the end of the stairs, they were presented with a locked door with a numeric keypad, keeping it locked.

The air was thick with tension, every sound amplified in the oppressive silence. Becky's eyes darted around, searching for anything she could use to her advantage.

As he fumbled with the keypad entering the code, Becky's heart pounded as she realized this was her chance.

While Neil's attention was on the keypad, she sprang into action and bolted up the stairs, her sneakers rattling the old rusty metal steps along the way.

Again, Neil was still in better shape than she was. All she could hear was the thudding of his boots as he chased her up. As before, she didn't get far. Once he grabbed her arm, she stopped, fearing that getting tackled on the stairs would have probably broken bones.

"You're not thinking clearly," Neil said, his grip like a vice. "This is for our country, our planet."

Becky's chest heaved with sobs as she looked at him, her face a mixture of fury and despair. "You've lost it," she said, her voice cracking. "Antel was trying to protect us. He died protecting us."

Neil's face twisted with anger. "Stop saying his name! He's dead, Becky. He was never one of us."

Becky's body sagged in defeat as Neil dragged her through the door he managed to unlock. As they entered, Neil kicked the door behind him to shut it. The click of the lock was audible enough for Becky to hear. She was locked in now.

He pushed her to a chair and tied her wrists to it. She couldn't fight anymore. The fear and the grief were overwhelming.

She closed her eyes, a single thought echoing in her mind: I have to survive. For Antel.

Neil forced Becky into a small vacant office space and tied her to the chair. Becky's wrists felt raw where the ropes rubbed into her skin. The damp, suffocating air in the missile silo made her feel like she was locked in a large metal can.

She strained to hear the voices echoing from the adjacent room over her heart as it pounded loudly in her chest. She could barely make out Neil's angry voice.

She shifted and squirmed in her chair, but the ropes wouldn't budge. Neil had tied them well. Even if she managed to get free, where would she go? The exit was locked. Every time she imagined an escape, she could picture Neil's enraged eyes blocking her path.

From the other room, Neil's voice grew louder. "This had better be worth it, Sallain. I've stuck my neck out for you. Killed for you. You promised me I'd have the tech to change the game, and I'm not walking away empty-handed."

Becky leaned forward in her chair, straining against the ropes as she tried to breathe as quietly as possible. Every word might be crucial. She needed to understand what they were planning, what Antel's death had accomplished for them.

Dahnt's voice drifted through the thin wall, smooth and almost soothing. "Patience, Captain Morris. The rewards I've promised you are within reach. Once the satellite uplink is complete, the data we retrieve will solidify your nation's position as a powerful player on this planet."

"What's in this data?" Neil sounded suspicious. "I asked for weapons, high-tech gear, that sorta stuff."

"What good is getting a cache of cool gadgets if you can't make more?" Dahnt's voice said. "Trust me, Captain. With the data, you'll be able to make your own. And understand it too."

Another voice interrupted. She recognized it as Intallan but didn't know what it meant. Then Dahnt responded to the voice with a short, quick phrase. She assumed the person reported something, and Dahnt simply said "Thank you."

Neil's voice cut through the alien dialogue. "What's he saying? What's going on?"

Dahnt shifted back to English, his tone measured once more. "Lieutenant Noli Threnn's commanding officer is asking him to check on the timeline."

"Timeline for what?" Neil asked, a hint of unease creeping into his voice.

Becky's heart raced as she strained to hear Dahnt's response. His voice dropped, forcing her to hold her breath and focus.

Dahnt's chuckle was soft, condescending. "Nothing that concerns you, Captain. Your focus should remain on getting my satellite access to your satellite network. This will make it possible for us to then transfer the data directly into your data centers."

One of the rogue soldiers spoke again, and Dahnt responded curtly in Intallan. Becky's pulse quickened as fragments of the conspiracy began clicking into place. Satellite uplink. Timeline. Data retrieval. If she could just piece together their complete plan, maybe there was still a way to stop it, but the more she heard, the clearer it became that Dahnt was orchestrating something far beyond Neil's understanding or control.

"You're dodging the question," Neil snapped. "What's this about a timeline? I've done everything you asked," Neil said finally, his voice quieter but still defiant. "Don't forget that."

"And I have not forgotten," Dahnt replied smoothly. "Your assistance has been noted. Now, I suggest you focus on preparing for the uplink. The window of opportunity is small, and failure is not an option. If we delay too long, actors on my homeworld will have the opportunity to put our plan to a swift and abrupt end."

Becky's stomach churned. She had no idea what the uplink entailed, but it was clear it was the linchpin of Dahnt's plan. She had to find a way to warn someone, to stop whatever they were about to do. But first, she needed more information.

"What about the admiral?" Neil asked suddenly, his tone hesitant.

Becky's ears perked up. Admiral? Who was that?

Dahnt's voice turned colder, more formal. "Admiral Mallus has no concern for the details of this operation. His focus remains on the larger picture. Rest assured, Captain, his interests align with ours. This was all part of his plan."

Becky's mind raced. Admiral Mallus. Now she had a name and rank. She didn't know much, but it was more than she had before. Whoever this admiral was, he was the architect of this whole thing.

The door in the room she was tied up in swung open, and a soldier wearing the same black and gray camouflage uniform she saw Antel and his team wear stuck his head in and looked at her. Then he immediately closed the door. He was probably just checking up on her, she thought.

Soon after, one of the rogue soldiers barked something in Intallan. It was likely the soldier who just checked up on her. Dahnt's response was sharp, almost impatient. Becky's heart sank. Whatever they were planning, it was happening soon.

"He informed me that Miss Miller is still secured in the next room."

"What's the plan for Becks?"

Becky's breath hitched. She pressed herself against the back of the chair, her pulse hammering in her ears.

"She's a complication," Dahnt said flatly. "One that I would prefer to resolve sooner rather than later."

"No," Neil said quickly, his voice firm. "She's not part of this. I'll handle her."

Dahnt's chuckle was dark. "See that you do, Captain. I have little patience for sentimentality."

The sound of footsteps echoed through the silo, drawing closer. Becky's breath quickened as Neil and Dahnt's voices faded. She wanted to act now, but she was helpless to do anything. As the door creaked open, Neil's shadow loomed over her. Neil and the soldier who checked up on her had just walked in. She had a feeling she was out of time.

"Everything okay in here?" Neil asked, his tone casual but his eyes sharp.

Becky swallowed hard, forcing herself to meet his gaze. "You tell me," she said, her voice steady despite the tremor in her hands.

Neil's expression softened for a moment as he walked close to her to check on the rope. "Everything will be back to normal soon, Becks," he said quietly. "You'll see."

Becky's left leg kicked up as hard as she could, striking Neil between the legs with her foot. Neil bent over in pain for a moment, as the other soldier burst into laughter. "And stop calling me Becks."

Neil gave the soldier a dirty look, but the soldier didn't care. He was still chuckling as he said something in Intallan to him.

"I don't know what you just said," Neil responded as he composed himself from the embarrassing moment.

"He probably said, 'Serves you right,'" Becky guessed from the soldier's tone and continued chuckling. Neil and the soldier then left the room, leaving her by herself again.

Alone now, with nothing to distract her from the crushing reality, the full weight of the night's events crashed over her like a physical blow.

Antel was gone. She'd seen him fall, seen the life drain from his eyes. The memory hit her with a force that made her chest ache, her breath turned to sharp, shallow gasps. Tears welled in her eyes, spilling over as she clamped her teeth down on her bottom lip to keep from sobbing aloud. But it was no use. The sound escaped her, a broken, guttural cry that echoed through the empty room.

"I'm so sorry," she whispered, her voice cracking. Her words felt like they vanished into the void, unheard and meaningless. Guilt twisted in her stomach, a sharp, gnawing pain that wouldn't relent. Trying to get Neil's help was her idea. Antel put his full trust in her, and it got him killed. If she'd only come up with another plan, maybe he'd still be alive.

Her mind latched onto every memory she had of him. The way he seemed to carry the weight of the world on his shoulders without complaint. His gentle touch that made her heart flutter. And his promise that he would keep her safe. He did his best, and it cost him his life.

Becky closed her eyes, her tears falling freely. "Antel," she choked out, her voice trembling. The sound of his name only made the emptiness more unbearable. He had been so much more than she'd realized, and now he was gone. She would never get to tell him how much he meant to her, how much she loved him.

Chapter 31

Antel's consciousness returned in fragments, the world around him blurry and spinning. His memory of what happened was slowly returning to him. As his senses sharpened, he realized he was alive. He was shot! At a range of perhaps two or three arm lengths! It was a miracle of the Universe that he survived. Disoriented, Antel heard voices as he blinked against the morning sun beginning to rise.

He was fortunate that the kinetic energy shield was fully charged. Had it not been, it wouldn't have done its job. Of course, a hit like that probably drained its power to zero.

"There's no blood? How is that possible?" Navarro's voice was filled with disbelief. He examined Antel from head to toe, noticing no entry wounds. Anywhere! This just wasn't possible.

Antel mustered all the energy he could to sit up. Navarro moved closer to him and gripped his shoulder to steady him.

"Are you okay? Andrew, can you hear me?"

"Um..." Antel put a hand on his head and pressed hard as if it were a migraine. "That really hurt," he said, his voice shaking slightly. The memory of the bullet's impact against his forehead was still vivid like being struck by a sledgehammer.

"No puede ser!" ("It can't be!") Navarro exclaimed, his voice thick with disbelief. Antel didn't recognize the language he spoke. English probably wasn't the only language he spoke. That would explain the unusual slight accent Navarro had.

"Excuse me?" Antel looked up at Navarro with his eyes still squinting.

"You were shot point-blank. What are you?" Navarro's tone was sharp.

"Not here," Antel said weakly, his words barely audible. Loud noises were still hurting. Despite the ringing in his ears, he could hear someone running in his direction.

"Hold it right there, ma'am," Navarro's voice became professional. He asked the approaching person to stand back. "This is a police matter," he continued as he pulled out his Homeland Security badge to show the person.

"Sir, I know this man. He's my best friend's boyfriend." Antel recognized Sarah's panicked voice. She must have heard Becky's scream and come running down from her room.

"Becky!" Antel's heart sank. He remembered the scream before he blacked out. "Where is Becky?" Antel tried to get up but stumbled back to the ground.

"Take it easy, Mr. Rall." Navarro did his best to keep Antel steady while keeping him from getting up. "You've been shot."

"Where is Rebecca Miller?" Antel demanded to know.

"Neil took her," Sarah said. "He dragged her into his car and he drove off like a bat out of hell."

"We have to find them," Antel tried again to get up, but stumbled just as before. "Where did he take her?" his voice thick with guilt.

"I'm not sure where," Sarah said.

Navarro was just listening but decided to jump in. "Sarah?" he confirmed her name was indeed Sarah. "Sarah, did you witness the shooting?"

"I didn't see the shot fired, but when I heard Becky scream Antel's name, I jumped out of bed and looked out of the window." Sarah pointed up at one of the windows in the student residence building.

"Sorry, did you say Antel?"

"I mean, Andrew," she tried to correct herself, but it was too late.

"No, you said Antel," Navarro wasn't an idiot. "I heard Becky's scream too. She yelled 'Antel'. What I'm learning is that Antel is his name." Navarro turned to look at Antel and asked, "Care to explain?"

"Long story," Antel was in no mood to explain anything.

"Well, you'll have plenty of time on the way to the hospital. You need medical attention."

"No! We can't go there." Antel struggled one more time to get up and succeeded this time. Navarro helped him steady his balance for a moment until Antel was able to stand unassisted.

Navarro pulled out a pair of handcuffs and put them on Antel. "I'm going to need to put these on you in the meantime. Let me take you to the hospital in my car."

"I'll make you a deal," Antel tried to compromise. "You take me to Elaine Miller's home. She's a nurse. If we go there, I'll explain everything." Antel gave up trying to keep his secret from Navarro. But he wanted it as leverage for the moment.

"You were just shot! Do you think you can just walk this off? Besides, this isn't negotiable. You don't get to make demands."

"Let Mrs. Miller decide that," Antel said. "Plus, Mr. Miller is my legal counsel. We can make this all official. I'll even tell you things I'm not legally allowed to tell you. But not here. Deal?"

"Are you FBI or something?"

Antel didn't answer. He waited for a deal.

Navarro was silent for a moment as he thought about it. He looked at Sarah but didn't expect her to give any advice. "Fine. Against my better judgment, I'll take you there."

"Sarah, go get that bag of gear and meet us at Becky's house. Also, contact Dr. Carter to join us. Be quick."

Sarah nodded and sprinted toward the dorms. Antel leaned on Navarro as they made their way to Navarro's car, his thoughts racing. He couldn't afford to lose Becky. Or Earth.

"Gear?" Navarro's curiosity piqued. "What kind of gear are we talking about?"

"I'll show you at the Millers' house. You may need to call them to make sure they come home if they're currently at work."

"I'll handle that, don't worry," Navarro said.

As Special Agent Navarro walked Antel to his car, he secured him in the back seat. The rear doors were designed not to open from the inside, and a barrier separated the back and front seats.

Agent Navarro then got in the driver's seat, paused, and sighed.

Navarro said, just loud enough for Antel to hear, "I can't believe I'm doing this." Navarro took out his phone and made a call. He called Robert, the attorney, and asked him to contact his wife, Elaine, and request they meet at his home in fifteen minutes.

"Okay, everyone should be on their way," Navarro informed Antel. "This better be worth it, Mr. Rall. Because every minute we waste puts Rebecca Miller at risk."

"It will be, trust me," assured Antel. "What I'm about to tell you will be, um, let's just say unbelievable."

"Let me make another call and have a BOLO put out on Rebecca Miller." Navarro was about to dial another contact when Antel interrupted.

"Wait! What is a BOLO?" Antel asked first in case it was nothing critical.

"It's a 'be on the lookout' alert to every law enforcement officer in the area," he explained. "It's the best way to find her before anything bad happens to her."

"No! Don't!" Antel protested. "The people who have her have connections. You would be putting her at greater risk. We need to plan this out."

"What are you talking about?"

"Captain Morris is well-connected and will act irrationally if he finds out. He probably won't hurt her as long as he thinks he got away with it."

Navarro couldn't argue with that. Antel had a point. "Fine, but time isn't on our side."

Navarro started up the car's engine and drove to the Millers' home. When he arrived, Robert was already there because he was working from home that day.

"Elaine," Robert told him, "is still on her way."

Robert answered the door, "Gentlemen, come on in and make yourselves comfortable." Robert only saw Navarro and Antel, but not Becky. "Um, Andrew, I thought Becky was with you. Is she not with you today?"

Antel looked down at his handcuffs. "We need to talk. All of us. Together."

"You're making me worry," Robert said.

The three sat quietly as they waited for the others. Robert brought everyone a cup of coffee. Antel didn't want to tell him he didn't like the taste, so he took a cup and began to sip it.

Sarah and Dr. Carter arrived first. Sarah entered the house with the bag of gear in hand. She was on her way to campus when she received the call and changed her destination to their home.

Elaine Miller took a little longer. She had to finish up with a patient before she could excuse herself from the hospital.

When Elaine entered the house, she saw everyone gathered in the living room. She saw Antel in handcuffs and that agent pacing around, looking at the photographs of family milestones and vacations around the room.

"Okay, I took off from work," Elaine said. "What's the emergency?" She looked around the room and realized Becky was not among them. "Wait! Where is Becky?" She turned to Antel and asked again, "Where is my daughter?"

Navarro sensed Mrs. Miller was about to panic. "We believe she is okay for the moment, please could you attend to Mr. Rall's injuries as we discuss everything?"

"Injuries," Elaine walked up to Antel and checked him. "Are you okay, dear?"

"I have a stinging headache from my gunshot hit, but I'll be fine," Antel told her. "This is our compromise to avoid going into the hospital."

"Gunshot?!" Elaine scanned him again, but this time much more carefully. "Where is the bullet?"

Antel put a finger on his forehead, "Neil shot me here."

"Oh my God!" Elaine started to shake. "And my Rebecca?"

"I saw Neil pull her into his car and drive off with her," Sarah said. "I'm pretty sure my brother doesn't want to hurt her. He's too obsessed with getting back together with Becky."

"Okay, stop everything," Navarro called for everyone to stop talking. "Andrew Rall, as promised, everyone is here. Where's my explanation?"

"This is becoming a routine," Antel muttered, "If I say anything untrue, please, anyone jump in and say so. I want the agent to know I'm not lying."

Antel took a deep breath and began his speech. By now, he could recite it word for word the same way each time. "My real name, as you suspected, Agent Navarro, isn't Andrew Rall, it is Antel Ralnar. I am a lieutenant in the Imperial Forces of the Rileean Empire."

Antel continued the full story. Everyone, besides Navarro, knew fragments of the story but today they would learn it all. He began explaining his mission and the missions before his. How the previous mission built up their knowledge of Terran languages over many years. His expedition's mission was to build on that knowledge and study its political environment. They needed to know which Terran countries could be trusted and which were merely untrustworthy dictatorships. The Rileean Empire was determined not to side with the wrong nations. It was a mistake we've learn from our past mistakes.

As he continued the story, he recounted the infiltration into the engineering building to investigate a subspace signal that could not have possibly been Terran in origin, the night of the car chase, the shootout at a ghost town on the west side of Denver that the rogue soldier attempted to set up a base at, the drone strike, and ending on Neil's 'murder' of him.

The story took a couple of hours because Antel left out no details. He was coming clean, Standard Protocol be damned.

Dr. Carter decided to help Antel's case. "Agent Navarro, like Antel said, I was approached by the previous mission, they gained my trust, and arranged for me to help teach them about the Earth. The deal was that I had to keep it all a secret until they allowed me to go public. Until now, I kept that promise."

"And that's why Dr. Solomon, or Dr. Sallain, met with you so often?"

"Yes, sir," she said. "I'm not surprised you suspected me early on."

Navarro's expression was impossible to read. He heard them out. Then his expression darkened. "You expect me to believe this whole story?"

"Sarah," Antel looked at her, "Could you take out something that looks like a tube of toothpaste from the bag, please?" Then he turned to the Millers, "Can either of you bring me a knife? The sharpest you have?"

Everyone was confused by his request, but he had his reasons.

Sarah set the spray can on the living room coffee table. Mr. Miller brought out a steak knife and set it next to the tube.

Antel approached the table, but Navarro had concerns. "I'm not sure I want you to pick up that knife."

"Trust him," Robert said, "as his legal counsel, I can vouch for him." Robert looked to Antel to make sure that was true.

Antel nodded.

"Fine, but I'm watching you carefully," Navarro rested his hand on his sidearm, but didn't pull it out yet.

Antel knelt in front of the items, rolled up a pant leg, took the knife, and then stabbed himself in the leg. He yelled in anguish but did his best to keep control of his pain. Everyone in the room gasped and nearly jumped to stop him.

"Mrs. Miller, can you confirm this cut is indeed real for the group?"

"Um, obviously." Elaine knew it didn't take a genius to know that was real. She tossed him a small towel to deal with the bleeding.

Antel then picked up the tube. It looked like an ordinary tube of some sort of cream, but the labeling wasn't in English. He took off the cap and applied some to his wound. It was a soft pinkish material. It looked like a thick lotion that had to be properly smoothed over the wound, filling it and covering the surrounding area. After a few minutes, when the cream dried, the pinkish color turned to a lighter shade of pink.

"Mrs. Miller, can you examine it now?" Antel asked.

Everyone was in shock.

Elaine felt around the area of the wound. It was gone, covered by this pink soft 'clay'. "It looks healed except for this weird lump of flesh you just applied.

"Did you just paint skin on your wound?" Elaine looked up and asked Antel.

"It's called artificial-flesh. It's a cream that creates temporary 'skin' to heal injuries or burns. The 'fake' skin has an artificial DNA that slowly copies the real skin it is attached to, helping to transform real skin. After a few days, you won't even know it was there."

"Neat, but what does this prove?" Navarro was still skeptical.

"Agent Navarro," Elaine said, "This stuff is amazing! Trust me when I say we don't have anything like this in the hospital."

"As for the bullet to the head," Antel took off his overly thick belt. First, he verified it was out of charge from the strong hit in the head by the bullet, then handed it to Navarro. "Tell me you have one of these on your planet, too."

Navarro rubbed his temples as the weight of Antel's words sank in. "So you're saying Earth is on the brink of an alien invasion?"

"Yes," Antel said. "And I need your help to stop it."

"Oh, I just remembered something." Robert went to the kitchen where he had been working before they arrived and grabbed the document with Dahnt's handwriting on it. "If that cream didn't do the trick, here's more evidence." Robert handed the page to Navarro.

"After seeing that magic cream and how the gunshot to the head was blocked, I think I may be coming around." Navarro took the page and looked at it. "What language is this? Is this your planet's language?"

"My nation's language," Antel said. He didn't need to see what the document said. "It's just one of many languages on my planet."

"What does it say?" Navarro handed it to Antel to read.

Antel stood up and reached for the document. He examined it. The lettering and symbols were unmistakable. It was in Intallan script. Dahnt's handwriting.

Antel's eyes moved across the document, and the blood drained from his face. He sank into the nearest chair without realizing it.

"These aren't just operational orders," he said, his voice hollow. "They're Sallain's strategic notes." He forced himself to focus on the text, translating the critical sections aloud. "Operation Chaos... use Earth assets against the farmhouse to justify military action to the Council."

His voice caught as he continued reading. "But there's more. Phase Two involves hijacking Earth's early warning systems through the satellite network. They plan to simulate incoming nuclear strikes from each nation against the others."

"Oh my God," Elaine gasped, her hand flying to her mouth. "They're going to trick everyone into thinking they're under attack?"

"Nuclear powers will retaliate against phantom threats," Antel said, his hands beginning to shake. "While Earth tears itself apart fighting the wrong enemy, there won't be anyone left to mount a defense when the real invasion begins."

The document slipped from his trembling fingers as he read the final section. His face went pale.

"What is it?" Robert asked, alarmed by Antel's expression.

"There's a contingency plan," Antel whispered. "If I interfered with their operation..." He swallowed hard. "They planned to take Rebecca as leverage to force my cooperation."

The room fell silent except for Sarah's sharp intake of breath.

"You mean they were always planning to use Becky against you?" Dr. Carter asked quietly.

Antel nodded, staring at the fallen papers. "All this time, I thought I was protecting her by keeping her close. But I was making her a target."

"Wait," Sarah said urgently. "But they think you're dead now, right? Neil shot you. So maybe they don't need to hurt her anymore. Maybe Neil's just... being Neil. Trying to win her back."

Navarro leaned forward. "The girl's got a point. If they believe you're out of the picture, Becky might just be dealing with a jealous ex-boyfriend, not alien conspirators."

"But for how long?" Antel put his head in his hands. "When they realize I'm alive, she becomes a target again."

Robert tried to sound reassuring. "We'll find her, Antel. We'll..."

"You don't understand," Antel interrupted, his voice breaking. "Billions will die in a war against the wrong enemy. My team is dead because I failed to see the threat among us. And now the woman I love is in danger because of my bad choices."

He looked up, his eyes filled with despair. "I've endangered your world more than I've protected it. Every decision I've made has made things worse."

Dr. Carter reached out toward him. "That's not true. You've..."

"It is true," Antel said, his shoulders sagging under the weight of failure. "I can't do this. I'm not the right person to save anyone. I'll just make everything worse than it already is."

The weight of Earth's impending destruction, his team's deaths, and Becky's capture crashed over him like a crushing wave. For the first time since arriving on Earth, Lieutenant Antel Ralnar felt truly defeated.

Silence filled the room like a suffocating blanket. Antel's shoulders sagged under the weight of every failure. His team was dead, Becky was somewhere out there paying the price for trusting him, and billions of innocent people faced annihilation because he couldn't see the threat right under his nose.

"I can't do this," he whispered, his voice breaking. "Everyone who counted on me is dead or captured. I've endangered your world more than I've protected it. Maybe... maybe I should just turn myself in to the authorities. Let them handle this."

"Antel, no," Dr. Carter said softly. "You can't give up now."

"Give up?" Antel's voice wavered. "I never should have started. Look at the results of my leadership. My entire team is dead because I trusted the wrong person. Becky is kidnapped because I made her a target. I never should have fallen for her in the first place."

"Don't you dare," Sarah snapped. "Becky chose to be with you."

"And now she's paying for my stupidity," Antel shot back. "This isn't some small operation gone wrong. This is massive devastation that will set your civilization back to the Stone Age! And it's happening because I was too blind to see what Sallain was planning, too distracted by my feelings to do my job properly."

Navarro stepped forward, his expression unreadable. "You think you're the first to feel like that? I've had moments when I was drug busting in Texas when I wanted to give up. Operations went sideways, good people died because of calls I made. But I kept going and got the job done."

Antel looked up, meeting Navarro's determined gaze. "This is different. Every decision I've made has led to disaster. My presence makes everything worse."

"If you hadn't come here," Robert interrupted firmly, "we never would have known about the threat at all."

"Would that have been worse?" Antel's voice cracked. "Maybe

under another officer's leadership, Sallain's plan never would have gotten this far."

"Listen to me, Lieutenant," Navarro said, stepping closer, his voice intense but gentle. "I've seen soldiers break under pressure. I've seen good men give up when the odds were impossible. But you? You threw yourself into a firefight to save Becky. You risked everything to protect people you barely knew. That's not failure, that's what heroes do."

The words cut through Antel's despair like a blade. He looked up, something flickering in his eyes. It wasn't hope, but a stubborn refusal to let Sallain win.

"Sallain is counting on you giving up," Navarro continued. "Don't give him that satisfaction."

"Besides," Sarah added quietly, "Becky would kick your ass if she knew you were even thinking about quitting. She didn't follow you all this way because she thought you were perfect. She did it because she believed in you."

Antel closed his eyes, feeling the weight of their words. When he opened them again, there was steel in his gaze.

"You're right," he said quietly. "I may not be the right person for this. But I'm the only one here who can stop it." He straightened, resolve hardening like cooling metal. "Universe be cursed, if I let Sallain destroy everything I've come to care about."

The Universe may have been making his job difficult, but as long as he wasn't dead yet, he had to stop Dahnt and that admiral or die trying. For Becky's sake. For Earth's sake. He had promises to keep.

Chapter 32

Antel had a new team. If you had asked him only a few days ago if he believed this group of Terrans would all come together and support him, he would have brushed it off as nonsense. But here they were, determined to see this through.

Robert and Elaine Miller's involvement was straightforward. They wanted to save their daughter from Neil's grasp.

Sarah was complicated. She loved her brother but understood he was too arrogant for his own good. He got that from their father. But Becky was her best friend, the first friend she made when she started college. Although she didn't want harm to come to her brother, he brought this on himself, and she also didn't want harm to come to Becky.

Navarro was unexpected. This agent was first brought in to investigate Antel and the expedition members as a ploy by Neil to interfere with Becky's budding relationship with Antel. Now, Navarro was on a new team. He went from investigating Antel to helping him. And he was helping Antel at the risk of his own career.

None of this felt real to Antel, but here they were. All assembled around the Millers' kitchen table, brainstorming how to proceed.

"I estimate we have perhaps five days, maybe even less," Antel began, "before any of the admiral's forces reach Earth's orbit."

"And you're sure we can't call up any of my supervisors to help?" Navarro had to make sure that was still off the table.

"If they learn of this, they will act much slower than we can afford, and increase the probability that everything here becomes public knowledge," Antel said.

"If that's the price we pay..." Navarro still wanted to explore the idea before abandoning it for good.

"Sallain and the admiral can act faster than we can," Antel argued. "If they need to, they can skip the satellite access and just start hitting cities at random from orbit. There's a ship up there in orbit that can cause enough trouble to keep Earth busy until the attack force can arrive. It's not the best plan because they would lose Council approval, but it would still be too late."

"Don't you have a ship too?" Robert asked. "I mean, how did you get here, after all? You could call them up for support."

Antel pulled out what was left of the communicator. "I'm afraid I had to repurpose it as a signal detector," he said. "Besides, I'm sure the subspace jammer is still blocking signals."

"Mierda," Navarro cursed in his language. "So, how do we find them?"

"Can you put a trace on Rebecca's phone?" Elaine asked.

"Normally, yes," Navarro frowned, "but this would require a warrant from a judge."

"And that would raise all kinds of questions," Robert, the attorney, added.

"So we can't trace Neil's phone either?" Elaine was trying hard to find a solution.

"Can't for the same reason," Robert explained.

"I can try calling my brother," Sarah suggested as she pulled her cell phone out and waved it to the group. "If he's going to answer any calls, mine would have the best chance."

"Can't hurt," Antel said. "See if you can figure out where he is."

"But keep it casual. Don't let him suspect anything," Navarro recommended.

Sarah dialed her brother's number and waited. The line rang twice before he answered.

"What is it, Sarah?" Neil's voice was tense.

Sarah tried to keep calm. "Hey, Neil. I wanted to check on you. Where are you at?"

"I'm busy right now," he replied curtly. "What do you need?"

Sarah could tell Neil was inside a structure that made his voice sound like it was in an echo. "Doesn't sound like you're on the base. I hear an echo."

Neil's sigh crackled over the line. "Not now, Sarah. I've got too much going on. I'll call you later."

"Wait," she said quickly, her mind scrambling for something else to say. "At least tell me where you're at."

There was a pause before he replied, his voice clipped. "I'm fine. Listen, I've got to go. I'll check in soon."

The call ended before she could respond. Sarah stared at the phone, frustration and worry boiling beneath her calm exterior. She returned it to her pocket.

"He's not going to tell me anything," she said, sinking into her chair. "He's too busy and too careful. He practically rushed me off the phone."

"I'm calling Becky's phone." Elaine wasn't going to give in. She dialed, but it went straight to voicemail. "No answer. Maybe her phone is off."

"Or destroyed," Antel was being realistic. "He would be negligent if he didn't put kilodritts between himself and that phone."

"Kilodritts?" Navarro asked. "Never mind, not important."

"Wait a minute!" Antel's eyes widened. "Sarah, do you know anything about how she tracked my movements?"

"Yeah," Sarah looked away from making eye contact with Antel. "She felt really bad about that. Me too for not telling you."

"That's okay." Antel wasn't upset about it. "Tell me how she did it. Isn't there something on her keychain that connects to it?"

"Holy shit, that's right!" Sarah saw where Antel was going with this. "Yeah, when she bought those luggage trackers, it came in a pack. The extras are attached to her keychain."

"And what are the chances she would still have those keys?" Antel followed up.

"Pretty good," Elaine's voice sounded more optimistic. "Her house keys are on it. She would have that keychain even if she didn't drive that day."

"Excellent," Antel said, feeling like they were making progress.

"Sarah, I need you to get me access to whatever tracks those devices."

"We need her laptop," Sarah said.

"I got it," Elaine wasted no time. She dashed upstairs to get her daughter's laptop and brought it back. "Here."

Antel looked at it but was uncertain how to use it. "Sarah, could you...?"

Sarah swiveled it to herself. "Hmm. Can't. It needs her password. Shit!"

"Are we fucked?" Navarro asked.

"Maybe not," Antel brought out the decoder and the datapad. He set the decoder on the keyboard since he assumed the circuitry was contained there and not on the monitor itself. Using the datapad to operate the decoder, Antel was able to easily bypass the login screen within seconds.

"Daaaamnnnn," Navarro said in slow motion. "I want one of those! Your civilization's got some cool stuff."

Antel only smiled and swiveled the laptop back to Sarah. "Find our girl."

Sarah took a moment to figure out where the browser bookmark was for the website, but after finding it, finding the luggage trackers was easy.

When the screen displayed a blinking dot on a map, she caught her breath. "There! She's there!" Sarah said, pointing to the screen, her voice excited at their success.

Antel looked at the map. "What is that? It's far outside the city."

"Let me see," Navarro came around and took a look for himself. "She's at a decommissioned missile silo outside the city."

"Do you suppose they would be able to set up a satellite uplink from there?" Antel asked.

"Yeah, maybe. The equipment they need is probably all there," Navarro said. "My guess is Sallain's people would only need to interface their equipment with it."

"Then that's our target." Antel stood up. "This won't be easy, and we'll probably have to do this after nightfall. We need a plan."

"We're going to be outnumbered and outgunned," Antel warned. "We need to somehow even the odds."

"How many of them do you think we're dealing with?" asked Navarro.

"More than we'd like," Antel admitted. "Maybe four. Three, if the one I delivered to Mars put them a man short."

"You can't use any of your cool tech?" Robert asked.

"They're going to have the same, if not better tech," Antel said.

"We'll have to outsmart them, then," Navarro said. "Ideas?"

"Well," Antel scratched his chin as he thought about it. "Their shuttle pod should be parked nearby. Perhaps if you fire at it with your conventional weapons, they'll come out wearing their kinetic shields instead of their energy weapons shields."

"They can't wear both?" Robert asked, making sure every scenario was considered.

"The different kinds of shields interfere with each other," Antel explained. "Wearing both would drain the battery in minutes and leave you defenseless. You have to choose between protection from bullets or protection from energy weapons."

"And they think you're dead!" Elaine was excited. She saw a plan forming.

"Exactly," Antel pointed at her. "When they come out ready to shoot you, I'll be on the opposite side and take them out."

"Are you a good shot?" Navarro's brows furrowed with concern. "There might be four of them."

"I'm a decent shot," Antel didn't want to oversell his marksmanship, but he was an excellent marksman. "We'll have to do this at night. Anyone I miss will at least be lit up from the light of the antimatter blasts, and you'll be able to see them better."

"The perimeter here is densely forested, which will give us cover. I have fence cutters that will get us in undetected," Navarro offered. "I have some tactical gear in my car: vests, helmets, night vision, the works."

"Excellent," Antel was pleased.

"Let's say by some miracle, we get in," Navarro's pessimism was obvious. "What then?"

"Not sure," Antel admitted. "What can we expect inside? What's the silo's layout like?"

"It's essentially a hole in the ground," Navarro said. "The control room is probably at the bottom in an adjacent room."

Antel's expression darkened. "And Neil?"

Sarah's heart sank. She looked at Antel with a pleading look, afraid her brother would be killed.

"He'll probably be in that control room with Dr. Sallain," Navarro replied. "If they have equipment for creating an uplink, that's where they would set it up."

Antel looked at Sarah. "I'll do my best not to kill him."

"Thank you," her voice cracked.

Elaine's voice broke through the discussion, trembling but firm. "Just… promise me you'll bring her back. Please."

Antel took Elaine's hand and met her gaze, his expression serious. "I promise. She means a lot to me, too."

Chapter 33

Driving through the country roads in his Mercedes, Robert Miller felt out of place. He couldn't use Becky's car. Her car was destroyed in the drone attack. He drove to the end of the road they determined would get them the closest without using the front gate. As Robert approached the end of the road, he turned off his headlights and used only the moonlight to guide him the rest of the way. There were only two homes at the end of the road, but their lights were off. The residents were probably asleep.

Antel checked his particle beam pistol one final time while Navarro assembled his sniper rifle in the back seat. Both were dressed in tactical protective gear that Navarro had in his vehicle.

"Well, gentlemen, this is as far as I can take you," Robert said as the car rolled to a stop. They took one last look at the car's GPS map. "The silo should be in that direction about half a mile."

Antel nodded. "Thank you, Mr. Miller."

"Call me Robert," Robert requested. "I think you've earned it."

Antel put his hand on Robert's shoulder. "We will get Becky back safely."

"You better," Robert replied, his knuckles white on the steering wheel. "And Lieutenant? Make those bastards pay."

Antel and Navarro slipped out of the car and watched Robert drive away.

Navarro shouldered his rifle and checked his night vision goggles.

"Ready?"

"Ready," Antel confirmed.

They moved swiftly across the open field, keeping low to avoid detection. As they got close, a single light post was operating. The other light posts were all off. With their night vision, Navarro and Antel could make out the shuttle pod's sleek form near the entrance of the silo.

"Two soldiers," Antel whispered, scanning the area through his tactical visor. "They're standing around near the shuttle pod."

"I'll take up position here," Navarro whispered back. "You should get a good vantage point from there."

"Agreed," Antel concurred. "Are you a former soldier?"

"Army," Navarro said proudly.

Navarro took up position behind a small ridge, setting up his rifle.

"Remember, their personal shields will stop your bullets. Aim for the ground near them. The debris might disorient them enough for me to get a clean shot."

Antel moved into position, using the uneven ground for cover. Once in position, he quickly waved a hand. Navarro waved back to confirm he saw Antel's wave.

"Dios me guíe," ("God guide me") Navarro whispered to himself in Spanish as he tapped his forehead, stomach, left , and then right shoulder.

Navarro put his eye to the rifle's scope and aimed for one of the soldiers' feet. The hope was that the dirt kicked up would keep their attention on Navarro. Since they thought Antel was dead, they weren't going to expect the particle beam.

Navarro kept his breath steady and pulled the trigger. As planned, dirt was kicked up. Not enough to cloud their view, but that wasn't what they were trying to do.

The soldiers yelled in Intallan and lifted their particle beam rifles in Navarro's direction. Because of their confidence that the shields they were wearing would protect them, they made little effort to find cover. Instead, they adjusted their night vision headgear and scanned the area for the shooter.

Navarro got a second shot out, this time shattering a piece of concrete. As the two soldiers aimed their weapons at him, Navarro ducked below the ridge for cover.

Antel took the opportunity. He fired at the soldier on his left and hit him. Unprotected from energy weapons, the soldier exploded into pieces of flesh. The explosion launched the rifle the soldier was holding into the air, and it landed several feet away.

The other soldier began to panic, yelling something unintelligible in Intallan. He turned to face Antel as the more lethal threat. As he turned, his position shifted a bit, causing Antel's second shot to miss. The shot instead struck the shuttle pod's engine housing.

There was a moment of perfect silence before the fuel cells detonated. The explosion lit up the night like an artificial star. The remaining soldier disappeared in the fireball as the shuttle pod shattered into pieces. Burning debris rained down across the complex.

"So much for stealth," Navarro muttered, abandoning his sniper position. He sprinted toward Antel. He needed to move fast before they locked the whole place down.

Antel holstered his pistol and dashed toward the destroyed shuttle pod, retrieving two particle beam rifles from the fallen rogue soldiers. As Antel picked up the second rifle, Navarro arrived at Antel's side.

"There's no time for a full training session," Antel said as he adjusted the power setting to an appropriate level. "There, that setting should be fine. Just aim and pull the trigger, just like one of your weapons. Good luck."

"Got it," Navarro replied, his eyes showing that he was excited to get the opportunity to use such a unique and powerful alien weapon. Navarro then said to Antel, "If I die tonight, just being able to use this weapon might just be worth it."

Antel just smiled. He knew Navarro was going to enjoy this weapon.

"Of course, I'm not planning to die tonight!" Navarro clarified.

They reached the silo's main entrance, a small concrete building with a single door. Before opening the door, Antel noticed what he assumed was a power unit of some kind.

"Is that for the installation's power?" Antel asked Navarro.

"Yeah," Navarro confirmed. "It's a power transformer."

Antel raised his rifle and fired. The transformer exploded in a shower of sparks, hopefully plunging the complex into darkness.

"With any luck, the backup power systems are offline due to being decommissioned years ago," Navarro commented.

Navarro opened the door, allowing Antel to move in first. He was ready to shoot anything that tried to stop them. The installation was indeed in the dark. Shooting the transformer worked.

"Night vision," Antel commanded on instinct. He wasn't Navarro's commander, but they were both experienced soldiers, so no one really complained. Antel's was more advanced and lighter than Navarro's, but in this situation, both were adequate.

"That shuttle pod supported a capacity of four, so either there are another two down here, or, with some luck, they're short by one because of the one I captured earlier."

The entrance door led directly to a long set of metal stairs that showed years of neglect.

"Control room should be three levels down," Navarro whispered. "At the bottom of these stairs."

They descended carefully, checking down the center of the spiral to see if anyone was approaching from below.

They were nearly to the bottom when Antel could hear Neil's distinctive voice. "You keep working on that uplink, I'll hold them here!"

Antel froze mid-step, his hand shooting up to halt Navarro. "Neil," he breathed, barely audible over the distant sound of typing. His eyes locked with Navarro's. "He thinks I'm dead. We can use that."

Navarro's gaze swept the stairwell, landing on a stack of metal supply crates crowding the landing above. He jerked his chin toward them. "Get behind those. When he comes for me, take him."

Antel's boots whispered against the concrete as he slipped into position, the particle beam rifle cold in his grip. His heart hammered against his ribs. One wrong move and they'd lose their only advantage.

Navarro sucked in a breath, then began his ascent backward, each deliberate boot-strike ringing like a bell through the metal stairwell. CLANG. CLANG. CLANG.

"FEDERAL AGENT!" His voice boomed off the concrete walls.

"THROW DOWN YOUR WEAPONS AND COME OUT WITH YOUR HANDS WHERE I CAN SEE THEM!"

"GO TO HELL, NAVARRO!" Neil's roar exploded from below, followed immediately by the sharp crack of gunfire. Muzzle flashes strobed in the darkness as bullets screamed past Navarro's head, sparking off railings and punching into concrete with sharp pings and thuds.

Antel pressed himself deeper behind the supply stack, adrenaline flooding his system. The smell of gunpowder filled the stairwell.

Come on, Antel thought, muscles coiled. Take the bait.

Neil's tactical boots rang against the metal steps. He was cautious but determined. He was coming up, just as they'd hoped, weapon raised and focused entirely on the federal agent retreating above him.

Antel was ready. Neil never saw him coming. He struck Neil in the arm with the butt of his particle beam rifle, forcing him to drop his handgun. The gun fell back to the lowest level and completely out of Neil's reach.

Antel's second strike was to the back of the knee. Neil screamed in pain and fell onto the stairs. The only thing keeping him from rolling down was his quick grip on the railing.

Neil's eyes widened in shock as he recognized his attacker. "You... you're dead! I shot you in the head!"

Navarro heard that. "Noted. Thanks for the confession."

Antel was incredibly angry. Normally, he was calm and collected, but today, after what Neil put him and Becky through, his eyes flared red. He was prepared to end Neil right there. He wanted to set his energy rifle higher than necessary and splatter his blood and flesh.

Antel pressed his rifle against Neil's temple. "You killed me first," he said coldly. "I think it's only fair I return the favor. Don't you agree?" His arms lifted the rifle's aim to line it up better.

Neil was frightened. His face tensed, and he closed his eyes as hard as he could. His hands were up as a plea to Antel not to kill him.

For a long moment, the only sound was their ragged breathing in the darkness. Then Antel pulled the weapon back slightly. "No. You're not worth it." He slammed the rifle's butt into Neil's temple, knocking him unconscious. "But I at least owe you that."

Navarro joined Antel at Neil's body. "I got this, you check on

Sallain." Navarro took out standard-issue zip ties and restrained Neil's hands and feet.

Antel readied his rifle and walked toward the door. "Ready. Let's end this."

The door was locked. Neil had locked it behind him to buy Dahnt time. There was a numeric keypad by the door.

Navarro looked at the panel. "You didn't bring that decoder, did you?"

"No, but I got something better," Antel grinned. "Stand back." He adjusted the rifle's power setting and aimed at the door.

The shot shattered the door, and molten shrapnel burst into the stairwell. The power setting was strong enough to break away the pieces of concrete that the door was fastened to.

"Dios mío!" (Oh my God, in Spanish) Navarro was impressed. He lifted the rifle he was holding and glanced at it, admiring its elegant form yet powerful punch.

The pungent smell of melted metal lingered in the air as Antel and Navarro moved through the gap where the door once stood.

The room was filled with old Terran equipment with cables connecting them to a small, suitcase-sized machine of Rileean design. The LED light on the small machine displayed a bar with three-quarters colored red and the rest colored green. The green was increasing and would soon completely replace the red. Clearly, something was in the process of being transmitted.

Dahnt's fingers moved rapidly across the interface panel, inputting the final commands with urgency. He leaned over the console, his hands working with focused speed to complete the sequence. His face was illuminated by the dim blue glow of the emergency lighting. Without looking up, he continued typing frantically.

"Dr. Sallain, step away from the console," Antel ordered, targeting his particle beam rifle at his former colleague.

Dahnt's fingers hesitated for a moment. "Lieutenant, this is for the security of our people! You need to give me access to the spy satellite."

"I said, step away from the console. Now!" Antel pulled out the pistol he had holstered with his left hand. In a single motion he set it to the lowest setting and fired at the wall as a warning shot. The blast left a smoking crater in the concrete. "That was the lowest setting."

Dahnt stopped typing. He turned around to face Antel and raised his hands slowly. "Your codes were quite challenging to crack, Lieutenant Ralnar. I'll give you that."

"Get up out of the seat, turn, and face the wall," Antel barked.

Navarro didn't understand what they were saying, but he got the gist of it. Navarro pulled out a few more zip ties and restrained Dahnt's hands behind his back.

After Dahnt's hands were restrained, Antel flipped him around and got in his face. "Where is she?" Antel demanded in Intallan, his voice barely masking his anger.

Dahnt gestured to the adjacent room by looking in that direction. "She's in there. All this for a Terran. You're betraying your people and your empire."

"Navarro, I need to undo whatever he did quickly. There's no time. Please check on Becky for me." Antel told him as he holstered the pistol and placed his rifle on a vacant seat near the console. He wasn't sure how much time he had, so he had to work fast.

"You got it." Navarro, seeing that Antel needed to focus on blocking access to the satellite and that Dahnt was sufficiently restrained, rushed to the next room to check on Becky.

In the adjoining room, Becky's head snapped up at the sound of footsteps. Her wrists were raw from struggling against the ropes Neil had tied her to the chair with.

"Agent Navarro, I'm so glad you found me." Becky's voice was hoarse. "The lights went out, and I heard what sounded like a fight next door."

"It's okay, Miss Miller. We're getting you out of here," Navarro said, pulling out a small knife to cut through the rope.

"Agent Navarro?" "How did you find me?" Her voice caught in her throat as she remembered the sight of Antel getting shot in the head. "Agent, Neil... He shot him... He shot Andrew."

"There's someone next door that wants to see you," Navarro interrupted with a slight smile as he freed her hands.

Becky rubbed her wrists, confusion evident on her face. "What do you mean?"

"Go see for yourself."

On unsteady legs, Becky made her way to the doorway. She froze at the threshold, her hand flying to her mouth as she saw Antel, who was just finishing up on the console.

"Antel?" Becky gasped, her voice barely a whisper as she stared at him. Her mind couldn't process what her eyes were seeing. "No... you're not... I saw you..." Her hand trembled as she reached out, afraid he might vanish if she touched him.

He turned at the sound of her voice. "Becky..."

Her legs nearly gave out beneath her. The world seemed to tilt as she struggled to breathe, her heart hammering so wildly in her chest she thought it might break through her ribs. When she finally convinced herself he was real, she launched herself forward, nearly toppling him over as she ran into his arms.

"You were DEAD!" The words tore from her with a force that surprised even her, somewhere between a scream and a sob as she pounded her fist against his chest. "I SAW YOU DIE!" Tears streamed down her face as relief and anger collided inside her. "I thought I'd lost you forever..." Her voice broke on the last word as she collapsed against him, clinging to him as if afraid he might disappear again.

Antel caught her and held her tightly as she buried her face in his shoulder, her body shaking with sobs. Throughout his embrace, she couldn't bring herself to release her grip on him, her fingers digging into his tactical vest as if to reassure herself he was still there. Each breath he took, each beat of his heart against hers was a miracle she couldn't quite believe.

"How?" she finally managed, pulling back just enough to search his face, her hands still gripping his arms. "I saw the bullet hit you... I saw you fall... How are you here?"

"I may have left my sidearm with Sarah, but I made sure to wear a kinetic energy shield," he explained gently. "He only knocked me out for a minute. Navarro had been following you to get to me."

Navarro, standing at the doorway to the adjacent room, only shrugged with a guilty smile.

As Antel's words sank in, Becky's overwhelming grief transformed into something else: fierce determination. He was alive. They still had a chance. Whatever they faced now, they would face it together.

"Don't you ever do that to me again," she said, punctuating each word with a light finger poke to his chest, her voice still unsteady. "I thought I lost you."

Antel caught her hand and pressed it against his heart. "Never," he promised softly. "I'll always come back for you. Even if I have to come back from the dead."

With visible reluctance, Becky let him release her, though she stayed close as he turned back to the console. "Give me another minute." He stopped the system from successfully gaining access, but he still needed to make sure they could never access it again.

"The interface is crude, but it would have worked. A few more minutes and Sallain would have had full access to your satellite network."

Navarro asked him, "How far did he get?"

The interface between the Terran satellite network and the Rileean spy satellite was completed, but Dahnt was minutes away from getting control of the spy satellite.

He pressed a final sequence of commands, and a message in Intallan displayed on the monitor. "There. You're locked out permanently, Sallain. You'll never access our systems again."

"You can't stop what's coming, Lieutenant," Dahnt said, not caring that the Terrans in the room didn't understand Intallan. "The admiral's strike force is already in the star system and is on its way. All Mallus needs to do is access the satellite physically. Earth's defenses will fall, and the Rileean Empire will finally secure our safety from any future Terran threat."

"I keep telling you, Earth is nowhere near advanced enough to be a threat, even if they wanted to be," Antel countered.

Before leaving, Antel disassembled the uplink system and brought the most important parts with him. All of them ascended the stairs and exited the underground installation. Antel made Dr. Sallain and Captain Morris march ahead of them with their restraints, keeping them from considering escape.

Becky stayed close to Antel while Navarro kept his weapon trained on the prisoners. The gravel crunched beneath their feet as they made their way toward the perimeter fence back to the meeting point where Mr. Miller would be waiting.

Surprising everyone, bright lights flooded the area where they were standing. After their eyes adjusted to the bright light, they saw a car parked along their path.

"It's the gray car from the car chase!" Antel dropped the equipment, raised his rifle, and pulled Becky behind him. "Everyone down!"

A voice called out in Intallan from behind the headlights. "Lieutenant Ralnar! Stay where you are!"

Antel squinted against the glare, making out the silhouette of a figure standing beside the vehicle. The metallic glint of a rifle barrel caught the light.

The rifle remained steady. "Let's make a deal. Release Dr. Sallain. He'll walk to me slowly with the equipment you're carrying, and then we'll leave. No more deaths for tonight."

"And the Terran?" Antel asked about Neil.

"Keep him. He served his purpose," Dahnt said coldly in Intallan.

Navarro shifted his stance to get closer to Antel and whispered, "Antel, what's he saying?" Navarro gestured at his rifle, asking if he needed to use it.

"Don't," Antel whispered in English. Antel knew the smart thing would be to end this with a shootout. Some from both sides would likely die, but he would at least successfully eliminate the admiral's chances for success. But he couldn't bring himself to do it. Becky was right behind him, and he was not willing to take that chance with her life.

Becky gripped Antel's arm. "You can't let them go. Not after everything they've done."

"I can't let anything happen to you." Antel wasn't going to change his mind.

The rifle barrel shifted slightly. "I won't miss, Lieutenant. The Terran woman dies first if you refuse."

"Alright," Antel called out in Intallan. "But if you harm anyone, there won't be a place in the empire where you can hide."

"Just release them."

Antel turned to Navarro. "Let Dr. Sallain go."

"Hey, what about me?" Neil started to feel betrayed. He didn't know what was said about him and was just figuring out that they no longer needed him.

"Are you serious?" Navarro protested.

"Do it." Antel's voice left no room for argument. "I can't risk more lives tonight."

Navarro reluctantly cut the restraints. Dahnt rubbed his wrists, a smug smile crossing his face. "Wise choice, Lieutenant."

"Take this and move slowly," Antel ordered as he handed the equipment to Dahnt and watched them walk toward the car.

Neil yelled to Dahnt as he approached the gray car, "Why are you leaving me behind?"

Without turning around, Dahnt only turned his head slightly and said in English, "Captain Morris, you should have believed the Lieutenant. I was never going to give you any technology. Your people are a threat and we're going to fix that."

When they reached the car, the driver backed up, keeping his rifle trained on the group. Dahnt climbed into the back seat.

"This isn't over," Antel called out as the car door slammed shut.

"No," Dahnt replied through the open window. "It's just beginning. Locking us out of satellite access just means we'll have to access the satellite physically. Fortunately for us, I managed to turn on the beacon. It's only a matter of time before Admiral Mallus finds it. And now that Captain Morris has established the interface, we'll finally get what we want."

The car reversed quickly, spraying gravel, before turning and speeding away into the darkness. Its taillights soon disappeared around a bend in the access road.

Becky let out a shaky breath. "They're going to try again, aren't they?"

Antel nodded grimly. "Yes. We are going to need another plan."

Chapter 34

The group trekked back to the rural neighborhood where Robert Miller was waiting in his vehicle. The only source of light was the front porch lights of the houses and the moon.

As they approached the car, Robert saw that Neil was among them and stepped out of the car, his face tightening at the sight of him.

"You bastard." Robert advanced toward Neil, his attorney's composure gone. "You could have gotten my daughter killed."

Navarro moved to intercept Robert, but the older man was surprisingly quick. His fist connected with Neil's jaw before anyone could stop him. Neil stumbled backward, attempting to block further hits to his face with his hands.

"Mr. Miller." Navarro grabbed Robert's arm. "We need him to be cooperative right now."

"Cooperative?" Robert's voice dripped with contempt. "As an attorney, I can guarantee that the evidence against you is substantial. The drone attack alone carries severe penalties. Attempted murder, terrorism, conspiracy..."

"I get it." Neil wiped blood from his lip. "Everything I did was for my country."

"Sallain manipulated you," Antel cut in. "And now that he doesn't need you, he's discarded you while he implements his real plan."

Neil's shoulders slumped. "What are my options?"

"Option one," Navarro said, "we process you through official channels. The evidence includes unauthorized access to military systems. You'll face federal charges for treason and conspiracy."

"Can you spell Guantanamo, asshole?" Becky barked over her father's shoulder, slowly enunciating "asshole."

"Or?" Neil asked quietly.

"Or we document the drone incident as a training exercise gone wrong due to compromised systems. You'll face disciplinary action for unauthorized access, some time in prison, and be dishonorably discharged."

"And what do I have to do in return?" Neil asked.

Antel jumped in. "In exchange for you never letting anyone find out about the Arkonians' presence here."

"You're willing to downgrade the charges against me?" Neil sounded skeptical. "Just like that?"

"Captain Morris, we're both soldiers. As far as my people are concerned, we were both acting in our respective nation's best interest." Antel's calm, disciplined reasoning returned.

The others couldn't help but respect Antel's honor and his sense of duty to his homeland.

Before heading to the Millers' residence, Navarro took Neil to the local county police department and had him officially booked as per their deal.

By the time they reached the Millers' home, it was already past noon. Navarro and Robert entered the home and discussed the arrangement that was made.

As he walked in, Antel saw that Elaine had just finished holding her daughter and thanked Navarro. Elaine then, when she saw Antel enter, rushed to him and held him tightly. "Thank you so much for rescuing my Rebecca."

"*Tehr heisht rinkuvi*," Antel told her. You're welcome in his language. He didn't need to try so hard to keep everything strictly in English with his new allies.

Sarah was relieved her brother wasn't killed, but completely agreed with their deal. She gave him her word that she would make sure he kept his and gave Antel a gentle hug to thank him for not killing her older brother.

The Millers' kitchen had become an impromptu war room. Antel's datapad and other various notes covered the coffee table as Elaine Miller brought in another round of coffee. She paused to hug Becky, still processing how close she'd come to losing her daughter.

"We need to focus on stopping the admiral's strike force before it arrives," Antel said, loading a satellite map of the Denver area on the datapad.

"He is planning to physically access the satellite and use the interface Neil was tricked into establishing," Antel continued. "He is planning to then use the connection to deceive the Earth's network of satellites into believing there is an ongoing nuclear missile war beginning."

"Why didn't this admiral do this from the start? Why waste time with an uplink?" Navarro asked.

"Without the uplink, the only way to control the satellite is a direct connection," Antel explained. "The satellite has built-in features that keep it from getting detected by sensors, and should that fail, it has thrusters to adjust its orbit to evade capture."

"And?" Robert asked, sensing there was more.

"And Sallain managed to at least disable the sensor blocks. It's only a matter of time before the Hammer finds it amongst all of the Terran satellites."

"And catching it?" Navarro beat Robert to the question.

"Catching it won't be that hard for a Rileean ship. The satellite was only designed to evade Terran attempts to catch it," Antel said. "Besides, the satellite's technology is perhaps decades old by now."

Robert's analytical mind questioned the details. "OK, so the satellite is now detectable. But if the uplink is stopped, how can he access Earth's satellite system?"

"The uplink was terminated, but Neil was able to reprogram the interface between our satellite and Earth's," Antel answered. "Once he can connect to one Terran satellite, gaining access to the rest will be very easy."

"What about the Black Cat?" Becky asked. "Can't they help?"

"That's probably our only option, but I can't contact them with that subspace jammer... Wait!" Antel stopped mid-sentence, his eyes widening. "The subspace transmitter. The one I seized from the forest.

If it survived the drone attack..."

"At the farmhouse?" Navarro leaned forward. "The place is probably crawling with police and federal agents by now."

"Not to mention media," Robert added. "The drone attack made national news."

"We don't have a choice," Antel said. "If that transmitter is our only way to contact the Black Cat, we need to retrieve it. We need that transmitter."

"I guess it's you and me again," Navarro said. "Let's take my SUV."

Navarro's SUV crept along the dark country road near the farmhouse driveway. Antel stepped out of the vehicle dressed in the tactical gear Navarro loaned him. It fit a little loose on him, but not enough to worry about.

"I'll handle the deputy," Navarro said, parking behind a stand of trees. "You have twenty minutes to find that transmitter while I keep the officer on duty distracted."

Once Antel was out and dashed into the forest, Navarro drove up to the deputy and began conversing with him about possible leads or evidence the deputy may know about, and if others had been seen casing the area. Antel couldn't hear any of the conversation, but that's what he assumed it was about.

Antel moved silently through the undergrowth. What was left of the farmhouse loomed ahead.

He scanned the debris carefully, thankful for the cloud cover hiding the moon. He found the transmitter beneath a fallen support beam, the main unit dented but intact.

As planned, approximately twenty minutes later, Navarro drove back up to the same spot where he dropped Antel off. Antel stuffed the transmitter and its tripod into the backseat and then got in the front.

"Got it," Antel declared. "Hopefully, it isn't too damaged to use."

"Curse the Universe!" Antel grumbled, examining the transmitter under the Millers' back porch light. "The encryption chip is damaged."

"Is it still usable?" Robert asked.

Antel said, "The main unit is functional. I can modify it to send a message using the Standard Pulse Protocol."

"What is the Standard Pulse Protocol?" Navarro asked.

"A sequence of pulses made up of quick pulses, long pulses, and double pulses," Antel explained.

"All that technology and we're resorting to the alien version of Morse code?" Robert joked. Navarro chuckled at the joke as well.

Antel didn't understand what Morse code meant, but he was too occupied to care. He worked quickly, rewiring components and adjusting the power output. The device hummed to life, its indicator lights blinking steadily.

"Will the Black Cat detect it and recognize it?" Becky asked.

"I really hope so," Antel was trying to stay optimistic. "The pattern is a standard emergency code. If Junior Lieutenant is monitoring subspace, trying to get through the white noise, he might just hear the pulses. If he detects our signal, he'll know we'll be waiting for him at the extraction point."

"Where's that?" Becky asked.

"It's on the west side of the city. Far up in the mountains," Antel pointed towards the direction he thought was west but got it wrong. The others understood what he meant.

"I'll drive," Becky said, holding up her father's car keys. "You look like you're going to fall over." Becky slept for a few hours while Antel was retrieving and repairing the transmitter, so she felt a bit refreshed.

The extraction point lay deep within the mountains. First, they'd have to navigate to one of the scattered campgrounds, then push onward along a rutted dirt road that would eventually dissolve into the rough, rocky landscape.

Becky made Antel take a nap during the two-hour drive. When she reached the end of the road, she looked over at Antel. He looked like he was finally getting some well-deserved peace, and she was reluctant to wake him. He was doing so much for her and Earth. He could have just sided with Dahnt and gone home free. His people weren't going to be at any risk. But his honor told him this was wrong to do to an indigenous population. That's the phrase she heard him say once. To him and his civilization, we're the Native Americans to his Spanish Empire.

"Antel," she lightly tugged at a strap on his shirt. She tugged so gently that he didn't feel it. She felt guilty for ending his sleep. She tugged a little harder.

"Are we there yet?" Antel asked.

She giggled. She wondered if that was a common expression on his planet among their impatient children, too. "Yep. End of the road."

"Then I walk from here," Antel said.

"Don't you mean 'we'?" she said as they exited her father's car.

"No, you need to go home. This could get dangerous if we get into a ship-to-ship battle with the Admiral's ship, and there's no telling how big it is. The fact that it had a shuttle pod already tells me they're bigger than we are for sure."

"I don't care," she insisted. "I'm not leaving your side."

"This time I mean it," he placed a hand on her cheek. "This might be a losing fight, and I'm keeping my promise to ensure your safety."

"But…"

"That's my final say on the matter," Antel's heart ached, but he had to put his foot down.

"Can I at least walk you to the landing site?"

He thought about it for a moment. "I suppose that's fair." He took her by the hand and they hiked through the trees until they reached a large enough clearing for the Black Cat to land.

It wasn't there yet. Antel prayed Zhon could hear the emergency beacon he left running at the Millers' residence.

They waited for an hour or two and finally saw the Black Cat descending from the sky. Antel was about to give up when Becky spotted the black object in the dark sky. They watched it drop from the sky quickly to avoid detection and slowed its descent with a hard thrust.

As the Black Cat came to rest in the clearing, Antel turned to Becky. They gazed into each other's eyes for a moment, then held each other tightly.

"You be careful up there," Becky pleaded.

"I will."

Antel leaned toward Becky for what might be their final kiss when movement flickered in his peripheral vision, a shadow detaching itself from the treeline.

"GET DOWN!" he roared, tackling Becky to the ground just as a searing blue bolt of energy split the air where her head had been. The particle beam scorched the earth beside them, sending up a shower of sparks and molten soil.

The rogue soldier burst from the forest, his weapon raised but trembling with restraint. "SURRENDER THE SHIP!" he bellowed in Intallan, advancing with predatory precision. "Step away from the Black Cat and you live!"

"That's never going to happen," Antel snarled, rolling behind a fallen log and drawing his pistol in one fluid motion. He squeezed off three rapid shots, blue energy bolts screaming through the night.

The soldier dove sideways, but his return fire deliberately struck the ground near Antel's position, close enough to spray dirt and stones, but carefully avoiding the ship behind them. "I don't want to kill you, Lieutenant, but I need that ship!"

Antel grabbed Becky's arm, realizing their advantage. "He can't risk damaging the Black Cat. It's his only way off Earth! Move!"

They burst from cover, zigzagging across the clearing. The rogue soldier's shots peppered the ground around their feet, each bolt precisely placed to herd them away from the ship rather than kill them.

"The ramp!" Becky gasped, her lungs burning.

Behind them, the soldier broke into a desperate sprint, attempting to reach the ramp before they could. His boots pounded against the forest floor, closing the distance with terrifying speed.

Antel spun and fired backwards without breaking stride, forcing their pursuer to stumble and dodge. "He's trying to board with us!"

The ramp touched down just as they reached it. Antel practically threw Becky onto the metal surface, then leaped after her as the soldier made a flying leap for the ascending ramp.

"ZHON!" Antel slammed his fist on the comm panel. "EMERGENCY TAKEOFF! There's a hostile trying to commandeer the ship!"

As the engines spooled, Antel quickly strapped Becky into a seat and then strapped himself to the seat next to her. The Black Cat's engines erupted to life and shot up toward the stars, leaving the stranded soldier screaming in fury below.

Zhon didn't know Becky was on board, or he wouldn't have accelerated at full power. She passed out less than a minute into the liftoff.

Through the viewport, Antel could see the curvature of Earth below, knowing somewhere up here, the Admiral was preparing to implement his plan.

It only took Becky a few minutes to regain consciousness. She was disoriented and confused. "What just happened?"

"We took off with a hard acceleration," Antel said as he checked her vital signs and administered an oxygen mask to help her feel better.

"Oh Lord." She put a palm on her forehead. "I got a headache."

"That will pass."

Not realizing the straps were still securing her, she attempted to get up. "I feel so weak, too."

"That will also pass," Antel smiled at her to reassure her as he monitored her recovery closely.

"Where are we?" Becky saw the blue and white sphere she recognized to be the Earth. "Are we in space? Again?"

"Yes, ma'am. Looks like you got your wish after all and joined me on the Black Cat."

"Those shootouts never get easier to get used to, do they?" she commented.

"Nope."

"Lieutenant Ralnar," Zhon's voice boomed through the cargo deck's speakers. "I have located the satellite and I have a missile lock on it."

"Any sign of another Rileean starship out there?"

"For a moment, I picked up the transponder of the Hammer near the Moon," Zhon replied. "I think I lost it because it went around behind the Moon and should be back on my radar in a few minutes."

"Classification?"

"Corvette class starship."

"Well, that helps," Antel was grateful it was at least not the Battleship Rilus. A corvette-class starship was one step up from the

Black Cat, a scout-class starship.

Of course, that doesn't mean it isn't on its way as part of the strike force. "I'm on my way up. And I have a guest with me."

Chapter 35

Antel and Zhon watched their monitors as the missile accelerated toward the satellite. Seconds felt like hours. All Antel could hear was his breathing inside his spacesuit's helmet.

It was standard procedure for crews to put on their spacesuits, connect their air feeds to the ship's systems, and then evacuate all of the air from the ship back into storage. The idea was that if the ship's hull were to take damage during combat, at least the crew would be safe from losing all of their air to open space.

At the last moment, as it approached, the missile missed by mere feet and continued past it.

"Kossdra!" Antel slammed his fist against the armrest of his chair. "It was on target. How could it have missed?" His heart hammered in his chest as the consequences flooded his mind. Earth remained vulnerable, Becky's world still in danger.

"I'm detecting signal interference," Zhon's voice crackled over the spacesuit's speakers. "Mallus is jamming the missile's targeting systems with a focused subspace jammer."

"Damn it!" Antel hit the same spot on the wall again. The memories of the farmhouse attack, his fallen team members, all of it threatened to overwhelm him. He'd come too far to fail now. The people of Earth were counting on him, even if they didn't know it.

"Can't we shoot another missile at it?" Becky asked. Antel glanced over at her, noticing how she gripped her seat restraints, knuckles white inside her gloves. Despite the fear evident in her rigid posture, her voice remained steady.

"The Black Cat only carries two missiles at a time," Antel said. "We just wasted one." He kept his voice calm for her sake, though every instinct screamed at him to act faster.

"So we only have one left?" Becky rolled her eyes. "Great!" She was adapting to the situation faster than he would have expected, channeling her fear into determination, a trait he'd come to admire in her.

"Yes, so we better use it wisely," said Antel. His training from countless simulations kicked in, but the stakes had never been this high before. This wasn't just another mission. Becky's entire planet hung in the balance.

"What about blasting it with that big gun you're controlling?"

"The satellite is shielded," Antel explained, his fingers dancing over the targeting controls. "It would take several direct hits to break through. Not to mention, we would have to get dangerously close to manually target it since the turret's targeting system is also being jammed."

"And there's no way to override their jammer?"

Antel shook his head, his mind racing through tactical options. "I'm afraid not." A year ago, his only concern would have been completing the mission and returning to Nela. Now, he kept glancing at Becky, acutely aware that his decisions determined not just her survival, but the fate of her entire world. His whole life had changed because of Becky.

"Zhon...," Antel called through his spacesuit's intercom, but was interrupted when the Black Cat shook violently.

"We've been hit!" Zhon called out. "Shields held, but they're down to sixty percent and recharging slowly."

Antel was about to order Zhon to make a run for the satellite, but now he needed to deal with the immediate threat. The Hammer must be closer than he thought. That same jamming signal was probably affecting the Hammer's targeting systems too, which explained why their shot hadn't been perfect.

"Evasive maneuvers!" ordered Antel. The tremor in his voice betrayed what he tried to hide—not fear for himself, but for Becky. He'd promised to keep her safe, and now she was in the middle of a space battle.

Zhon was an excellent combat pilot. He rolled the Black Cat into a spiraling dive, the ship's hull groaning under the G-forces. The stars wheeled past the viewscreen as another particle beam shot seared past their starboard side. Despite his training, Antel still felt his stomach lurch as Zhon pulled them through impossible maneuvers.

He glanced over at Becky to check on her. To his surprise, instead of panicking, she was watching the tactical display with intense concentration, her lips moving slightly as if calculating trajectories. Despite having no training for this, she was analyzing the battle, adapting to the chaos around her. When she caught him looking, she gave a tight smile that seemed to say, "I'm still here. Keep going."

Antel swung the turret around and locked onto the Hammer's position. The enemy ship was a dark silhouette against the star field, its weapons ports glowing with charged energy. He fired. A ball of blue light, much larger than what his hand-held particle beam pistol produced, hurtled toward the enemy ship.

Missed! The Hammer banked hard to port, its pilot as skilled as Zhon. "Mallus isn't making this easy," Antel muttered. Before this mission, this would have been just another tactical challenge. Now, with Becky beside him, it was so much more—every decision a potential ending to the life they might have together.

The Black Cat rocked again as another hit struck their aft section. Warning lights bathed the bridge in red, and Antel could hear the whine of overtaxed systems.

"That last hit damaged the engines," Zhon reported, his voice tight with concentration. "We're down to seventy percent power, and the port thruster is stuttering."

Antel gritted his teeth and returned fire. The positron beam clipped the Hammer's shields, causing them to flare brilliant white before fading. Not enough to disable them, but it bought them precious seconds.

"They're adjusting their approach!" Antel said. "Zhon, get me closer to that satellite! We need to end this before they disable us completely."

"Copy that." Zhon spun the Black Cat toward their target, weaving between the Hammer's increasingly accurate shots. They were making a desperate run for the satellite, trading safety for position.

"If we use our last missile on the satellite, won't we be defenseless against the Hammer?" Becky asked. Her question wasn't just tactical. Antel could hear the unspoken concern about their survival.

Antel hesitated, just for a moment. The mission had always been to protect Earth's satellite network at all costs, but now the stakes felt painfully personal. Becky had entrusted him with her life, placed her faith in him to protect both her and her world. If they died here, Earth would lose its only defender.

But this was bigger than just the two of them. Billions of people below had no idea their fate hung in the balance.

"We take out the satellite first," he said finally. "Earth comes first. Billions of lives depend on it." He thought back to the beginning of the mission, when he'd been focused solely on military objectives and staying detached. How far he'd come since then.

Becky's expression softened. She nodded once, understanding the weight of the decision. "Then let's nail it on the first try."

The Black Cat shuddered as another hit struck their starboard side. Sparks erupted from a console behind Antel, startling Becky.

"Shields are down!" Zhon shouted. "If you don't take that shot soon, we may not survive to try again!"

Antel's thumb hovered over the launch button. The targeting system flickered between locked and searching, the jamming signal wreaking havoc with their electronics. In a matter of seconds, the satellite would pass within optimal range. So close that Zhon had to adjust course to avoid a collision.

His thoughts flashed to Becky's parents, to the promise he'd made to keep their daughter safe. To Becky herself, who had trusted him enough to follow him into space. To his fallen team members, who had given their lives for this mission.

"Firing!" Antel pressed the button. At this range, the jammer's interference would be minimal.

The missile streaked away from the Black Cat, its engine a brilliant white star against the darkness. Everyone held their breath as they watched it close the final distance to the satellite.

The explosion was silent in the vacuum of space, but the flash was brilliant enough to overwhelm their viewscreen filters. Debris from the destroyed satellite scattered in all directions like deadly confetti.

"We did it!" Antel's exhilaration was genuine. He turned to Becky, relief flooding his features. "Your planet is safe!" The mission had been his duty, but somewhere along the way, it had become personal. Earth wasn't just another world anymore. It was Becky's home.

Becky's face lit up with a mixture of relief and triumph. "One down, one to go," she said, nodding toward the Hammer that was still closing in on them.

The celebration was short-lived. A chunk of satellite debris, spinning end over end, slammed into the Black Cat's engine section. The impact wasn't violent enough to throw them around, but every system on the ship suddenly went dark.

"Power's out," Zhon announced grimly, his hands falling away from the now-dead controls. "Main power is completely offline. We're running on auxiliary only."

Antel's mind raced through their options. Without main power, he couldn't use the positron beam turret, their only remaining weapon. The Hammer was closing in for the kill, and they were helpless. His gaze drifted to Becky. Her presence here was because of him, because she trusted him. He couldn't fail her now.

"What if we shut down everything?" Becky asked suddenly, her voice cutting through his despair. "Make them think we're already dead?"

"What?" Antel turned to her, startled by the suggestion.

"Like playing dead," she explained, her academic mind working through the problem. "If they think we're just a drifting wreck, maybe they'll get close enough for us to..."

"That's brilliant," Antel breathed. "Zhon, kill all power except life support. Make it look like we're finished."

"Are you sure about that?" Zhon's voice was tight with concern. "If we drain auxiliary power and something goes wrong, we'll have no protection from the cold of space. Our suits only have so much life support."

Antel was already unstrapping himself from his seat. "I'm going to reroute auxiliary power to the positron beam. One shot is all we need."

"That's what we're using to stay alive," Zhon reminded him. "If this doesn't work..."

"One problem at a time, Junior Lieutenant." Antel understood the desperate risk he was taking. A year ago, he would have followed standard military protocol without hesitation. Now, every choice was weighed against what it meant for Becky, for Earth, for the future they might have together.

Zhon looked at Becky, uncertainty clear on his face even through his helmet visor. She met his gaze and gave him a confident nod. Even now, facing death in the void of space, she believed in their plan.

Antel rushed to the engineering section, pulling panels aside and exposing the ship's power distribution network. His hands worked quickly, rerouting power cables and bypassing safety systems. The work was dangerous. One wrong connection could overload the entire system.

"Weapon is powered," he announced as indicator lights flickered to life. "Zhon, you'll have to take the shot. I can't get back to the turret controls in time."

"Me?" Zhon's voice cracked slightly. "I'm a pilot, not a gunner."

"You're the best pilot I know," Antel said firmly. "And right now, you're our only hope."

The Black Cat drifted silently through space, all exterior lights dark. Only the faint glow from their helmet lamps provided any illumination. The Hammer loomed larger on their passive sensors, its bulk blotting out the stars.

Becky floated over to Zhon, placing a gloved hand on his arm. Whatever her fears, she'd pushed them aside to support their team. In the dim lighting, her determined expression reminded Antel why he'd fallen for her—that unwavering courage in the face of the unknown.

"You've got this," she told Zhon softly but firmly. "I believe in you. Antel believes in you, or he wouldn't have asked you to do it."

The Hammer's engines flared as it matched the Black Cat's trajectory. Zhon watched the targeting display, making microscopic adjustments to the turret's position. He would have to aim by sight since the jamming was still active, but that also meant the Hammer's shields might be down to conserve power.

"They're opening their docking bay," Zhon whispered. "They're planning to board us."

"Wait for them to commit," Antel advised. "They'll have to drop their shields before they can exit the ship."

The seconds stretched into eternity. Then, just as the Hammer's docking bay doors reached full extension, Zhon fired.

The positron beam lanced out from the Black Cat's turret, a brilliant blue-white spear of energy that struck directly through the Hammer's open bay doors. The beam punched through the ship's unshielded interior, triggering a cascade of explosions that tore the vessel apart from within.

The Hammer's destruction was spectacular—a brief, bright nova that lit up the void before fading to scattered debris. The shockwave rocked the Black Cat, but they were far enough away to avoid serious damage.

For a moment, the three of them floated in stunned silence, hardly believing they had survived.

The silence stretched for several heartbeats before Becky broke it with a jubilant shout. "We did it! We actually did it!" She was floating freely now, her arms raised in triumph before she reached out to shake Zhon's arm. "Incredible shot! I told you that you had it in you."

Zhon's smile was visible even through his helmet visor. Despite being a trained soldier accustomed to impossible missions, he appreciated her enthusiastic praise.

Antel exhaled slowly, feeling the crushing weight of responsibility finally lift from his shoulders. Earth was safe. Becky was safe. They had succeeded where failure would have meant the destruction of an entire world.

Returning to the bridge, Antel saw that Zhon had already helped Becky unstrap from her restraints. She pushed off from her seat with both legs, propelling herself toward Antel with enough force that they would have bounced apart if she hadn't immediately grabbed onto him.

"I wish I could kiss you right now," she said, her voice thick with emotion. Hugging someone in a spacesuit felt awkward and bulky, but the love in her voice transcended the physical limitations. "We saved the world, Antel. Together."

"I wish I could kiss you too," Antel replied, holding her as close as their suits would allow. He'd started this mission as a detached observer, duty-bound and professional. Now he was irrevocably connected to this world and the woman in his arms.

"Well, I hate to ruin the moment," Zhon interjected apologetically, "but we've got serious problems. We're completely out of power. Even auxiliary is drained."

"What's our status?" Antel asked, reluctantly shifting back into officer mode. The mission might have succeeded, but their personal survival was far from assured.

"Dead in space," Zhon reported grimly. "No power means no life support, no communications, no propulsion. We're essentially a metallic asteroid in orbit around Earth. And I can't even tell if our orbit is stable or if we're falling into the atmosphere. The computers are completely offline."

Antel noticed Becky's momentary look of alarm, quickly replaced by that determined expression he'd come to admire. Her resilience continued to amaze him. She'd evolved from a civilian caught in a conspiracy to his partner in a space battle, adapting to each new challenge with remarkable courage.

"Would it help if I got out and pushed?" Becky suggested with forced levity, trying to lighten the mood despite their dire situation.

Antel smiled at her attempt to maintain morale. "With all the explosions we've caused up here, it's only a matter of time before people on Earth spot us. When they realize the Black Cat is alien in origin, they'll move mountains to get a spacecraft up here within hours."

"How long do we have before we run out of air?" Becky asked, her question practical but tinged with underlying concern. They saved Earth, but might not live to see it again.

"We should be fine for a while," Zhon assured her. "Our suits can plug into the ship's emergency air reserves, assuming the tanks weren't damaged in the battle."

"So what do we do now?" Becky asked. "Radio for help?"

"The subspace radio is dead without power," Antel explained. He watched her process this information, saw her methodically calculating their options the same way she approached her academic research.

Antel took a deep breath and weighed their possibilities. "We need to repair the ship enough to limp back to Mars before we're discovered. If that's impossible, we may have to..." He couldn't bring himself to finish the sentence.

"We'll have to call NASA for help," Becky said for him. "Which would trigger an international incident when different countries race to capture us." She understood the implications perfectly. The irony that their success might lead to the very breach of protocol they'd fought to prevent.

"I better get started on repairs," Antel said, turning toward the engineering section. "With luck, we can restore enough power to get the engines running and make it to Mars."

"Wait," Becky called out. "Is there anything I can do to help?" Her expression was earnest, determined to contribute despite her lack of technical training.

Antel paused, considering. "Actually, yes. Help Zhon check the hull for damage. He'll show you what to look for. We need to know if it's safe to restore atmosphere before we can take off our helmets."

As Antel headed toward the engineering section, Becky called after him. "Where are you going?"

"Outside," he said, meeting her eyes through their helmet visors. "I need to see if I can get at least two of our engines operational." His determination was absolute. "We've come too far to fail now."

Hours passed as Antel worked methodically to restore power to the Black Cat's propulsion systems. The damage was extensive, but not irreparable. One engine was completely destroyed, which meant its opposite counterpart would also have to remain offline to maintain balance. But the remaining two engines, positioned on opposite sides of the ship, could potentially be restored.

Inside the ship, Becky followed Zhon methodically through every compartment, checking bulkheads and hull sections for micro-fractures or breach points. She applied her academic precision to this vital task, double-checking each area Zhon examined. Antel caught glimpses of her working with careful attention to detail, and felt a surge of pride at how seamlessly she'd integrated into their mission.

"I think we're clear," Zhon announced after completing their survey. "No obvious hull breaches. Once we get power back, we should be able to restore atmosphere safely."

"Excellent work," Antel replied, satisfaction evident in his voice. Pride swelled in his chest, not just for their victory over the Hammer, but for how they'd functioned as a team. Becky had become an integral part of their success.

Every minute the Black Cat remained in Earth orbit increased their risk of detection. If that space station's orbit happened to intersect with theirs, or if ground-based telescopes spotted them, Antel would have to craft the most convincing explanation in history to preserve their secret. He would probably have to reveal the truth about their origins, which wouldn't please the Empire, but they'd understand he had little choice.

Finally, auxiliary power flickered back to life. The lights throughout the ship wavered, dimmed, then stabilized. Zhon and Becky cheered when they saw the bridge systems come online. Air began hissing into the hull as the atmospheric processors engaged.

After several minutes, there was enough atmosphere for them to remove their helmets. Antel watched as Becky took her first breath of unfiltered air, her face filled with wonder despite the danger they'd just survived. As their eyes met across the bridge, he knew that whatever challenges still awaited them, they would face them together.

Chapter 36

The Black Cat drifted in Earth's orbit, its hull scarred from the battle with the Hammer and the satellite's debris.

"Rell, we need a damage assessment," Antel ordered, his voice tight with urgency.

"One second." Zhon reviewed the data logs from the ship's computers, which were thankfully running off auxiliary power just fine. "Main power is down. Both hyperspace and impulse drives are non-functional. No power is available for the particle beam weapons battery."

"How long will this auxiliary power last?" Becky asked Antel. "It sounds temporary."

"Good question. Rell, do you know?"

Zhon's fingers flew over the power readings display. "We have maybe six hours of power. Less if we run life support at full capacity."

"Well, that sucks," Becky said, her attempt at remaining calm betrayed by the tremor in her voice.

"Lieutenant," Zhon's voice crackled with sudden urgency. "I hate to bear bad news, but the long-range sensors just picked up multiple ships approaching Earth orbit. It's the strike force. They're moving fast."

Antel's stomach dropped like a stone. They had destroyed the Hammer and killed Admiral Mallus, but the strike force he had dispatched was still coming, unaware their orders were based on fabricated evidence.

"How many ships?" he asked, dreading the answer.

"A destroyer and three scout-class starships. They'll be in weapons range of Earth in less than two hours." Zhon's voice carried the weight of their implications. "Earth has no defense against that kind of firepower."

Antel exchanged a look with Becky. They both understood what would happen if they couldn't stop those ships. Earth's major cities could be reduced to ash within minutes, its satellite networks crippled, leaving the planet defenseless against a full-scale Rileean assault.

"We need to restore power," Antel said desperately. "Now."

"That's not going to happen without replacement parts," Zhon said, his disappointment evident. "The engine core took too much damage."

"Is the subspace radio still working?" Antel knew that now that the Hammer was gone, its signal jammer should no longer be active.

After running a quick diagnostic, Zhon nodded. "Yes, it's working on minimal power."

"Good enough for now." Antel moved to the communications panel with renewed determination. "At least we can warn them before they make a catastrophic mistake." Opening a channel to the lead destroyer, Antel transmitted: "This is Black Cat to the approaching fleet. Please respond immediately."

Static filled the speakers, then cleared into a crisp voice speaking in formal Intallan. "This is Commander Verun of the Rileean destroyer Vigilant. Identify yourself and state your purpose."

"This is Lieutenant Antel Ralnar of the scout ship Black Cat, reporting directly from Earth orbit," Antel replied, matching the formal tone. "Commander, you must abort your mission immediately. Admiral Mallus has deceived you about the true situation here."

"Lieutenant Ralnar?" Verun's tone sharpened with authority. "Our tactical briefing indicates you were killed in action alongside your expedition team. Admiral Mallus provided conclusive evidence that Earth forces attacked and eliminated the Rileean presence. He has also filed formal charges accusing you of violating the Standard

Protocol by aiding enemy combatants. Where is Admiral Mallus now?"

"Killed in action, sir," Antel said. "Along with his ship, the Hammer."

"Killed in action?" Commander Verun's surprise was evident. "Another Terran assault?"

"Sir, I request permission to present evidence before you proceed," Antel said, carefully avoiding the question since it was the Black Cat that had destroyed the Hammer.

For a moment, there was only static. Then Verun spoke with military precision: "Negative, Lieutenant. Prepare to be boarded for immediate arrest. If you are armed, secure all weapons. I am dispatching a shuttle while my task force proceeds with the authorized strike."

"Commander, please. Dr. Sallain and Admiral Mallus conspired to fabricate evidence against Earth," Antel pressed urgently. "Sallain coordinated the attack on our own expedition to justify this assault."

"Enough!" Verun snapped. "You expect me to accept the testimony of an allegedly dead lieutenant over the documented orders of a flag officer? Stand down and prepare for boarding. That is a direct order."

The communication cut off. Antel slammed his fist against the panel in frustration.

"They're not going to listen, are they?" Becky asked quietly.

"Military hierarchy," Antel said grimly. "The commander trusts rank and documentation over field reports."

Taking a deep breath, Antel reopened the channel. "Commander Verun, before you dismiss my report, I have one tactical question that may clarify the situation."

Silence. Then: "Proceed, Lieutenant."

"Did Admiral Mallus update the threat assessment level for Earth in your mission briefing? Because our months of observation show they remain at their previously assessed technological level."

Antel waited, then continued: "More importantly, sir, if Earth knew about your incoming strike force, wouldn't they be mounting some kind of defense? Are your sensors detecting any military mobilization, satellite repositioning, or defensive preparations planetside?"

The pause was longer this time. When Verun replied, uncertainty had crept into his voice. "Explain your reasoning, Lieutenant."

"Run a tactical scan, Commander. You'll find that Earth remains completely unaware of your approach. Their military assets are in normal peacetime positions. Should the Rileean Empire be conducting a preemptive strike against an indigenous population that doesn't even know we exist?"

The silence stretched for nearly a minute. When Verun spoke again, his tone had shifted. "Lieutenant Ralnar, I'm dispatching a shuttle to bring you aboard the Vigilant for immediate debriefing. You will surrender all weapons and submit to restraint. But I am temporarily suspending strike operations pending your testimony."

"Understood, sir," Antel replied, finally allowing himself to breathe.

"Strike force is altering course," Zhon reported from the bridge. "They're moving to intercept the Black Cat instead of proceeding to attack positions."

Antel took a deep breath and slowly exhaled. "Looks like we bought Earth some time."

The three of them had nothing to do but wait for the shuttle pod from the Vigilant to arrive and dock with them. Through the Black Cat's viewport, Becky watched in awe as the massive destroyer approached. The Vigilant dwarfed their scout ship, easily two and half times the Black Cat's length, with multiple weapon turrets bristling along its hull and launch bays that could house dozens of smaller craft.

"It's like a floating city," Becky whispered, watching the destroyer position itself parallel to their ship.

A small shuttle pod, sleek and angular, similar to the one she remembered from the ghost town encounter, separated from the destroyer's hangar bay and glided toward them. The Black Cat shuddered slightly as the shuttle's docking clamps engaged with their airlock.

"Time to go," Antel told Zhon and Becky, his voice tight with apprehension.

Zhon easily maneuvered to the docking port in the zero gravity. Antel helped guide Becky, who was still adjusting to movement in space. When the hatch cycled open, they were met by two armed soldiers in full battle dress, their particle beam rifles at the ready. Both wore the rank insignia of third-class servicemen.

"Which one of you is Lieutenant Ralnar?" asked the senior soldier.

Antel raised his hand to identify himself.

"By order of Commander Verun, you are to be taken into protective custody pending investigation," the soldier said as his companion moved forward and applied restraint cuffs to Antel's wrists, standard procedure, not aggressive, but unmistakably official.

"Follow us," the first soldier ordered.

"This woman does not speak Intallan," Antel said, gesturing toward Becky. "I may need to provide translation during the proceedings."

"Understood, sir," the soldier replied respectfully. "Inform her that all three of you will be escorted to Commander Verun for debriefing."

Antel translated quickly: "They're taking us to see the commander."

As they moved through the destroyer's corridors, Becky's eyes widened at the ship's scale. The passages were not just longer than the Black Cat's, but taller and wider, designed to accommodate large numbers of crew and equipment. Through observation ports, she could see multiple decks extending both above and below, each bustling with activity.

"This ship must be enormous," she whispered to Antel.

"If you think this is impressive, you should see one of our battleships," Antel replied with a slight smile, enjoying her wonder despite their circumstances.

They ascended through the ship's central lift system, passing multiple decks before stopping at the command level. Here, they were escorted to what was clearly an official briefing room, larger and more formal than anything on the Black Cat.

"It seems you have come back from the dead, Lieutenant," Commander Verun said without looking up from his datapad. "Our records show Mars Base lost contact with your expedition several days ago. Care to explain?"

Commander Verun was an imposing figure, tall and broad-shouldered with the bearing of a career military officer. His salt-and-pepper hair was cut in regulation style, and his brown eyes, framed by thick brows, missed nothing. His clean-shaven face bore the weathered look of someone who had seen combat.

"Admiral Mallus deployed a subspace jammer to isolate our expedition," Antel explained. "We couldn't contact the Black Cat or Mars Base until I managed to acquire a transmitter and send an emergency signal."

"And I was extremely fortunate to detect that signal through all the interference," Zhon added.

"I see." Verun's eyes remained fixed on his datapad. "And this civilian?" He gestured toward Becky.

"She is Rebecca Miller, sir," Antel answered. Becky recognized her name being mentioned.

Verun looked directly at Becky. "I asked her to identify herself."

"Apologies, Commander. She doesn't speak Intallan," Antel explained.

Becky started to ask Antel what was being discussed, but he quickly whispered, "Not now. Let me handle this."

She nodded, understanding the delicate nature of the situation.

"Very well, Lieutenant. Present your evidence," Verun said, finally setting aside his datapad. "Admiral Mallus provided detailed documentation of Earth's aggression. What contradictory evidence do you possess?"

Antel realized that testimony alone wouldn't be sufficient. Verun needed concrete proof. Then he remembered the phone footage.

"Becky," he said in English, "your phone. Do you still have the video from the battle in the abandoned town?"

"Yeah, why?" she responded.

"Can you find the footage from that night when the Rileean soldiers attacked us?"

"The ghost town, sure." She began scrolling through her phone, the pressure to find it quickly making her fingers less steady. Verun waited patiently.

"Here," she announced. "Got it." She held up her phone toward Verun.

Verun gestured for her to approach. The video played clearly on her phone screen, showing Rileean soldiers in combat gear exchanging fire with Antel and his team.

When the video ended, Becky returned to Antel's side.

"This is deeply disturbing," Verun said quietly, his expression grave. He turned to the soldier behind them: "Serviceman, remove the Lieutenant's restraints."

Over the next two hours, Commander Verun listened to Antel's complete account of events, interrupting only once to ask, "Is this the Terran with whom you've formed a personal relationship?"

When Antel finished his report, Verun leaned back in his chair. "We'll need to conduct a comprehensive investigation into this conspiracy. But our immediate priority is apprehending Dr. Sallain. He's still on Earth's surface with at least one co-conspirator."

"I've established contact with trustworthy individuals among the Terrans during my mission," Antel said. "With your permission, I'd like to return to Earth and coordinate their assistance while ensuring continued Standard Protocol compliance."

Antel knew he didn't really need to confirm their cooperation. They had already agreed. But he wanted to say goodbye before leaving Earth, possibly forever.

"Permission granted," Verun said. "I'll assign a support team." He paused, his gaze shifting to Becky. "The Standard Protocol complications will need to be addressed as well."

"I'll have the Vigilant's engineers restore the Black Cat to operational status," Verun continued. "Once that's complete, you'll return to Mars Base for mission closure and full debriefing. In the meantime, prepare the Horizon for immediate planetary descent. Locate and retrieve both Dr. Sallain and his remaining accomplice."

"Understood, sir," Antel confirmed.

"Dismissed," Verun said with military finality.

Chapter 37

"Dr. Sallain, Senior Lieutenant Tanron. Do you read me? This is Commander Verun of the Rileean strike force. Are you there?"

The commander waited several tense seconds, watching the chronometer on his console. Just as he was about to repeat the transmission, static crackled through the speakers.

"This is Senior Lieutenant Tanron. We read you loud and clear."

"Are you safe?" Verun asked, his voice carrying the authority of command. "We are about to commence our assault on the planet surface, but we need to extract you and Dr. Sallain first, on Admiral Mallus' direct orders."

"Oh, thank the Universe," Tanron's relief was palpable through the subspace link. "We've been waiting for word from the fleet. What are your instructions, sir?"

"I am sending you precise landing coordinates." Verun snapped his fingers and pointed at one of the ensigns, who immediately began transmitting the data. "You will rendezvous with the scout ship Horizon at these coordinates. They will extract you from Earth's surface."

"Understood completely. We are mobilizing now," Tanron confirmed.

Verun terminated the signal with a decisive gesture and turned to face Antel, his expression hardening. "Lieutenant Ralnar, take these two officers with you as backup. The conspirators expect a rescue.

They'll board willingly, believing they're being extracted by allies. Once they're secure inside the Horizon with no escape route, you arrest and restrain them. Then bring them directly back to me for interrogation."

"Understood, sir," Antel replied, appreciating the elegant simplicity of the deception. It would be completely unexpected. Their confidence in their success would become their downfall.

"Oh, and Ralnar..." Verun's tone grew more serious. "The Terran girl. Take her with you and resolve our Standard Protocol issue."

"Yes, sir," Antel acknowledged, though his heart began to ache with the weight of what 'resolving the issue' was going to entail.

Antel and his newly assigned team made their way back toward the shuttle bay. Along the corridor, he spotted Becky at one of the observation windows, silhouetted against the blue-white curve of Earth below, lost in contemplation.

"Becky, dear," Antel called softly.

"Oh, Antel, I didn't hear you approach. Isn't the Earth absolutely breathtaking from this perspective?"

"It truly is magnificent," he agreed, moving to stand beside her. "It reminds me of how Arkonus appears from orbital altitude."

"So what's our next move?" she asked, turning to study his face.

"Let's go get some bad guys," he said with grim determination. "We're descending to the surface and luring them into boarding our ship under false pretenses."

"You're not planning to make me wait here aboard the Vigilant, are you?" Becky searched his eyes intently. "Bad things consistently happen when we separate."

"Actually, the commander specifically ordered me to bring you back to Earth's surface."

"Um, that sounds rather ominous when you put it that way," she said, her brows furrowing with growing concern.

"Let's focus on capturing Sallain and Tanron first. We'll address the other complications afterward."

They proceeded toward the shuttle bay to transfer to the Horizon.

"We're not using the Black Cat for this mission?" she asked, noticing the different configuration of the vessel.

"No, that would completely defeat the purpose of our surprise.

They'd recognize the Black Cat immediately."

"Yeah, excellent point," she agreed. "I hadn't considered that tactical element."

On the bridge, Antel secured himself in the co-pilot's seat while Becky strapped into a position on the deck directly below with several armed soldiers, as the bridge could only accommodate two personnel.

"Ensign, initiate our descent," Antel commanded.

"Yes, sir," the pilot responded, his accent distinctly Virgranian. He was competent at the controls, though not quite matching Zhon's exceptional skill level.

The Horizon touched down at the identical coordinates the Black Cat had used as its primary extraction point. Antel knew this location wouldn't raise any suspicion with Dahnt and Tanron because it had been designated as the standard extraction site for all Earth missions. They timed their arrival for the pre-dawn hours, using darkness as cover.

The wait was mercifully brief. Dahnt and Tanron appeared so eager to escape what they considered a primitive, hostile world that they had positioned themselves nearby, ready for immediate extraction.

The moment the landing ramp descended, both conspirators strode confidently aboard, their posture radiating triumph. They clearly believed their retrieval by the strike force was a success.

According to the predetermined plan, the Horizon's crew sealed the ramp while the conspirators remained completely unaware of the trap closing around them. The instant the ramp locked into place and the distinctive hiss of the atmospheric seal echoed through the cargo hold, the soldiers drew their weapons in perfect coordination.

"Dr. Sallain, Senior Lieutenant Tanron," the ranking soldier announced with formal authority, "I am placing both of you under arrest by order of Commander Verun."

"What? Why?" Both conspirators reacted with identical shock. "This makes absolutely no sense!"

At that precise moment, Antel descended from the upper deck, his footsteps deliberate and measured. The cargo bay fell silent except for the hum of life support systems.

"Actually, it makes perfect sense to me," Antel said, his voice cutting through their confusion like a blade.

Tanron's face underwent a transformation. Confusion melted into rage as recognition hit him. He launched himself forward, only to be immediately restrained by two soldiers who had anticipated his reaction.

"YOU!" he screamed, spittle flying as he thrashed against his captors. "The Hammer should have reduced you to atoms! How are you still alive?"

"The Hammer failed," Antel replied with deadly calm, his gaze never wavering from Tanron's wild eyes. "Just like your conspiracy."

Tanron's struggles became more violent, his face flushing red with unbridled fury. "Do you comprehend what you've done? You've jeopardized the security of our entire civilization!"

"No," Antel stepped closer, his voice dropping to a whisper. "That's exactly what you and Sallain accomplished when you betrayed our mission and murdered our teammates."

Tanron's eyes darted around the cargo hold like a trapped animal. "Admiral Mallus will have your head mounted on his wall for this treachery!"

"Admiral Mallus is dead," Antel stated with brutal finality. "Destroyed along with his ship, the Hammer."

The blood drained from Tanron's face. For several heartbeats, he ceased struggling entirely, his expression frozen in shock. Then he resumed thrashing against his restraints.

"You're lying! That's impossible! You couldn't possibly have beaten them."

"How did you manage..." Dahnt began, his voice barely above a whisper. He had assumed the Black Cat was neutralized. "Where exactly is Admiral Mallus now?"

Tanron's hand began moving slowly toward his concealed sidearm, but the sharp-eyed ensign immediately spotted the motion. "Don't even consider it. Remove that weapon very carefully and hand it over."

Antel redirected his attention to Dahnt, who had maintained an eerily composed silence throughout the confrontation. "Dr. Sallain, I genuinely expected more from someone of your supposed intellect and integrity. You were entrusted to be our lead scientist, studying Earth to determine optimal contact protocols. Instead, you orchestrated a campaign to annihilate an entire civilization."

Dahnt straightened his posture, his expression hardening into defiant resolve. "I executed what was absolutely necessary for our security. Earth represents an existential threat that will only increase with time. The Council suffers from willful blindness."

"That decision was never yours to make," Antel said, his voice heavy with disappointment and barely controlled anger. "Our mission parameters were crystal clear: observe, analyze, and report, not judge, condemn, and execute. You've betrayed every principle the Empire stands for."

Dahnt's laugh was harsh and mocking. "We shouldn't be looking for new friends. We should be annexing this planet to ensure the security of the Empire. You're the one suffering from blindness, Ralnar. Your pathetic attachment to that Terran female has completely compromised your judgment."

Antel shook his head slowly, his resolve unshakeable. "No, Sallain. My relationship has given me clarity about what truly matters. Earth isn't perfect. Neither is Rilee, for that matter. We were sent here to learn and understand, not to destroy and conquer."

"Fool," Dahnt spat with contempt. "History will ultimately prove me right."

"I doubt it will," Antel replied. "We'll just have to wait and see."

With both conspirators finally secured, Antel personally applied restraint cuffs to their wrists, ensuring they posed no further threat. As he worked methodically, he couldn't suppress a deep sense of satisfaction. This represented a crucial step toward closing the chapter on the conspiracy that had threatened both Earth's survival and the Rileean Empire's honor.

With Dahnt and Tanron finally secured in custody, Antel experienced a profound sense of accomplishment, though he recognized his mission remained incomplete. He couldn't allow himself to fully relax. As Commander Verun had specifically stated, he still needed to definitively 'resolve' his Standard Protocol complications. By complications, he meant Becky. This was not going to be easy.

The morning sun had begun creeping above the eastern horizon, painting the sky in brilliant oranges and purples.

"Well, daylight has officially arrived," Antel informed his crew. "We're remaining groundside until full darkness returns before lifting off for the Vigilant. Standard operating procedure for avoiding detection." He turned to Becky with renewed purpose. "We have several critical communication tasks to complete."

Using Becky's phone, their first call went to Agent Navarro. He arrived about an hour later, his government vehicle navigating the rough terrain before he completed the journey on foot to their concealed landing site.

"Incredible," Navarro breathed, staring up at the Horizon in genuine awe. "Is this the famous Black Cat?"

"No, this is the Horizon," Antel clarified, "though they share identical design specifications with the Black Cat."

"Agent Navarro," Antel extended his hand, consciously remembering the Terran custom of handshaking during significant moments. "On behalf of the entire Rileean Empire and myself personally, I want to express our profound gratitude for your invaluable assistance. I'm fully aware you risked your entire career to help us."

"I'd rather risk my career than risk my entire planet," Navarro replied with characteristic directness.

"If there's anything you need to 'sanitize' in the official records..." Antel began, but Navarro interrupted with a raised hand.

"Antel, I believe you've more than earned the right to address me by my first name," Navarro said warmly. "Please call me Rafael from now on."

"I'm deeply honored by that gesture," Antel replied sincerely.

"And don't worry about the bureaucratic complications, mi amigo. I have everything completely under control."

"Could you possibly do me one final favor?" Antel asked. "Would you be willing to drive Becky and me to her parents' residence?"

"Absolutely! It would be my pleasure."

Chapter 38

Navarro's car rolled to a stop in front of Becky's parents' house, the engine ticking as it cooled. Antel sat in the passenger seat, his mind heavy with what he was about to tell Becky. She sat in the back, oblivious to the conversation that would change everything.

"This is where I leave you," Navarro said, shifting into park with a deliberate motion. He turned to face them both. "I'll do what I can to keep your secret safe. With Neil's confession making headlines, all the media attention will focus on his abuse of his Air Force position. With some luck, they won't dig any deeper."

Antel's voice remained steady despite the knot in his stomach. "Understood. Thank you, Special Agent Navarro."

"Hey! It's Rafael," Navarro reminded him with a slight grin. "We've been through too much together for formalities now."

"Rafael," Antel corrected himself, extending his hand with genuine warmth. "I hope we meet again someday." He watched Navarro drive away, disappearing into the Denver night.

As they approached the front door, the porch light flickered on in anticipation. Robert and Elaine Miller emerged quickly, their faces showing both concern and overwhelming relief.

Becky barely had time to brace herself before her mother's arms wrapped around her in a fierce embrace.

"Oh, sweetheart, we were so worried," Elaine murmured into Becky's hair, her voice thick with emotion. "You were gone so long. I kept imagining the worst."

"I'm okay, Mom," Becky said softly, meaning it. "Really."

Robert stepped forward, his gratitude evident as he extended a firm hand to Antel. "Glad to see you both made it back safely."

Antel shook his hand with appreciation. "I'm grateful for everything you've done for us."

Robert nodded and motioned them inside with paternal warmth. "Please, come in. You've earned some rest."

They moved into the living room, where the atmosphere felt charged with unspoken tension. Antel knew the moment had come—he couldn't postpone this conversation any longer. "We need to talk."

"That doesn't sound good," Becky said, her apprehension showing clearly. "That usually means we're breaking up." She tried to make it sound like a joke, but her worry was obvious.

The expression on Antel's face did nothing to ease her fears. He opened his mouth to speak, then stopped, the words catching in his throat.

"Antel, what's the matter?" Becky's anxiety grew with each passing second. "You're starting to scare me."

"Now that my mission here has come to an end..." Antel paused, struggling with what came next. The words felt impossible to say. "It's time for me to go back to Arkonus."

Becky's jaw tightened with stubborn determination. She crossed her arms. "And you expect me to stay here?"

Antel hesitated, torn between love and duty. "I love you, but... taking you away from your family, your planet, your entire life here would be asking too much of you."

"My life is with you now," she said with unwavering firmness.

"Becky, think about what you'd be giving up," Antel said, his voice soft but urgent with concern. "Your dissertation, everything you've worked toward. Your friends. Your future here on Earth."

"I've already thought about it," Becky countered with growing confidence. "I can study history anywhere. And with your people's technology, I could write the most comprehensive historical analysis of cultural exchange ever attempted."

Elaine's breath caught, and Robert's brow furrowed with deep paternal concern. "Becky, think about what you're saying," Robert urged with careful reasoning. "This isn't just a flight across the country. It's an entirely different world, with different customs, different everything. You won't know anyone there."

"I know," Becky acknowledged, turning to take each of her parents' hands. "I know what I'm giving up," she said, then looked directly at Antel, "but I also know what I'd be losing if I stayed."

"And what about us?" Elaine asked, her voice trembling with barely controlled emotion. "We may never see you again."

Becky's shoulders drooped under the terrible weight of that reality. "I know. That's the hardest part." She squeezed her mother's hand for comfort. "But if there's anything I've learned from studying history, it's that sometimes people have to make impossible choices for the future they believe in."

"Are you sure?" Antel asked, still conflicted about taking her so far from everything she knew. "It could be years, if ever, before we could return to Earth. The technology exists, but getting permission..."

"I'm very sure," Becky said, her voice steady with conviction.

Antel studied her face carefully, searching for any sign of doubt or hesitation. Finding none, he nodded slowly with thoughtful acceptance. "Then I'll request permission from Commander Verun."

Elaine wiped at her eyes and asked for a moment before disappearing into the master bedroom. When she returned, she held a delicate silver necklace with a small locket. "This belonged to your grandmother," Elaine said, her voice thick with overwhelming emotion. "If you're going, I want you to take this. So you never forget where you came from."

Becky swallowed hard as she took the necklace, her fingers trembling as a tear rolled down her cheek. "Thank you, Mom." She reached over and gave her mother a long, tight hug, then turned to embrace her father with equal emotion.

Antel turned to Robert with formal respect. "It's only a matter of time before the Rileean government sends the next expedition. They'll need help to reestablish a new Earth Outpost. I'll recommend you for assistance in establishing it."

"That means a lot," Robert said with deep appreciation. "Take care of my daughter."

"You have my word," Antel said with solemn sincerity.

The night sky stretched clear and star-studded above them. The mountain air felt crisp and clean in their lungs. Robert and Elaine stared in amazement at the black tower hidden in the secluded clearing among the trees.

The car came to a stop, and profound silence filled the space between them. Everyone stepped out slowly and walked closer to the Horizon.

"This is incredible!" Robert exclaimed, turning to Antel with genuine wonder. He found it difficult to tear his eyes away from the impressive vessel. To Robert and Elaine, this was their first real UFO sighting.

Eventually, Robert turned to Becky. Her face was beautifully illuminated by the ship's external lighting.

Robert spoke first with paternal reassurance. "You'll always have a home here."

Becky nodded, her eyes glistening with unshed tears. "I know."

Elaine pulled her into another fierce maternal hug. "Be safe. Be happy."

"I will," Becky promised with heartfelt sincerity.

Robert approached Antel. Instead of the expected handshake, he grabbed him in what he called a "bear hug." "I can't thank you enough."

Antel replied with characteristic modesty, "All part of the job."

Robert put his hand on Antel's shoulder with sincere paternal blessing. "Young man, I want you to know Elaine and I both trust you completely. We know you'll never break her heart. You have our blessing."

Antel felt overwhelmed by Robert's words—the man was entrusting his only child to him. "You have my word. She means the Universe to me."

With that, Becky's hand slipped into Antel's. Together, they walked toward the waiting ship.

The ramp lowered with mechanical precision. The pilot emerged, giving them a respectful nod of acknowledgment. "Lieutenant. Welcome aboard, sir," the young ensign said in Intallan.

"Thank you, Ensign," Antel replied with military authority. "Take this bag to the storage bays in engineering, and these two to my quarters." He pointed at Becky's two pieces of luggage.

The ensign snapped a crisp salute. "Yes, sir." He turned to one of the servicemen and passed along the order. The soldier efficiently gathered Becky's bags and carried them into the Horizon.

"Did you just order him to carry my luggage?" Becky asked with amused delight.

"The privileges of rank," Antel replied with a matching smile.

As they climbed the ramp, Becky paused halfway up, looking back at her parents one final time. For a moment, uncertainty flickered across her face—the enormous weight of what she was leaving behind suddenly crystal clear. She took a deep breath, steadying herself, then gave a final wave before continuing up the ramp with Antel.

Once inside, Antel called out with genuine concern for their safety, "You'll need to stand back to a safe distance before we can lift off. I hope to see each of you again someday. And on behalf of the Rileean Empire, we thank you for all your help these past few days." He offered them a solemn Rileean salute as the ramp folded closed with finality.

The ramp's clamps engaged with loud snapping sounds, followed by the distinctive hiss of the life support system pressurizing.

Becky leaned against Antel as they felt the ship begin to vibrate beneath their feet. "I can't believe I'm really doing this," she whispered, not in regret but in wonder.

"Are you afraid?" Antel asked softly, wrapping his arm around her waist.

"A little," she admitted with complete honesty. "But mostly, I'm excited. I'm ready for our new life together."

Antel kissed her forehead gently. "Let me show you to our quarters. You should strap in for liftoff."

As they moved through the ship, Becky absorbed every detail around her. This was just the beginning of her journey—a journey that would take her farther than she had ever imagined possible.

Epilogue

Becky carefully adjusted the camera's angle, tilting the small device until the viewfinder showed exactly what she wanted. The lighting had to be perfect: not too bright, not casting shadows across her face. She needed her parents to see her clearly when they received this message, to understand from her expression alone that she was truly happy.

The modest apartment she shared with Antel in Sillence wasn't spacious, but golden morning light streamed through the sheer curtains, illuminating floating dust motes that drifted like tiny stars across their living room.

She smoothed down her hair one final time and drew in a steadying breath before pressing the record button.

"Hi Mom, hi Dad," she began, her smile warm and genuine as she looked directly into the camera. "This message should reach you with the next expedition in approximately three weeks. I still can't quite believe it's been a full year since I left Earth behind. So much has happened here that I'm completely overwhelmed trying to figure out where to even begin."

She adjusted her position, leaning forward with growing enthusiasm. "But first things first. I want you to know I'm doing incredibly well. Better than well, actually. Antel and I have settled into life in his hometown of Sillence, which is this absolutely gorgeous city nestled in rolling hills and dense forests. It reminds me so much of Colorado, though the architecture here is completely unlike anything on Earth. I've been taking hundreds and hundreds of photos to send along with this message."

Becky raised her left hand toward the camera, displaying a delicate ring adorned with a stone that seemed to shift colors in the light: deep blues melting into silver, then flashing with hints of gold. "And yes, before you start wondering, Antel proposed to me last month! We're right in the middle of planning our wedding ceremony. The marriage customs here are fascinating and completely different from Earth traditions, but his parents have been absolutely wonderful and so welcoming to me. One thing I learned is that women here traditionally keep their family names after marriage. Actually, daughters take their mother's surname while sons take their father's. So I'll still be Rebecca Miller, carrying a little piece of Earth with me wherever I go."

She paused, her gaze drifting to something beyond the camera's view before returning with a touch of melancholy. "I wish more than anything that you could be here for the ceremony. We're planning to record every moment of it to send to you afterward. Maybe..." her voice wavered slightly, "maybe by then we'll have better news about when I might be able to visit home again. Since the last expedition didn't return much data because of all the scary stuff that went down, the next mission just got more important."

Becky reached beside her and lifted a sleek datapad, holding it up proudly for the camera. "Do you remember how worried I was about continuing my education? Well, I have incredible news. I'm now officially a doctoral candidate at the University of Granilest! They created a completely special exception just for me. Several professors from universities across Arkonus actually petitioned the Emperor directly to grant me a work and study exemption. Can you even believe something like that?"

She burst into laughter, shaking her head in continued amazement. "Being the only Terran on this entire planet has made me something of an academic celebrity. I have professors and researchers from every corner of Arkonus practically fighting each other to spend time discussing Earth with me. My background in historical studies has proven incredibly valuable. Understanding how Earth's cultures developed helps me explain our world to them, and simultaneously helps me understand their civilization better."

Becky lifted a can with strange, flowing script on its label and took a careful sip before continuing.

"My dissertation research focuses on comparative historical development between Earth and Arkonus civilizations. The university has been remarkably accommodating, especially considering I'm still learning to master Intallan. My accent is absolutely terrible, by the way, but Antel insists it's charming and makes me sound mysterious and alluring." She paused to laugh again. "I'm pretty sure he's just being sweet to spare my feelings."

Her expression grew more contemplative. "It's genuinely strange being the only Terran in this entire world. Sometimes I find myself desperately missing the simplest Earth things: the rich aroma of properly brewed coffee or a slice of pizza from that place downtown. But there are so many breathtaking things here too. Just last week, Antel took me hiking up to see the Ausfront Mountains during sunset. The peaks were absolutely magnificent, stretching endlessly like our Rocky Mountains back home.

"But you should see Arkonus's two moons in the sky. The first time I saw them, it was an incredible sight. I had tears because it was so beautiful."

"Oh! I nearly forgot to mention something important. The expedition planners for the next mission to Earth have been consulting with me regularly. I specifically recommended Sarah and Agent Navarro... I mean, Rafael, as primary contacts. There's an excellent chance they'll approve both Sarah and Rafael for the program since they're already fully aware of Arkonian existence and have proven trustworthy."

The distinct sound of their apartment door opening echoed from off-camera. Becky's face immediately lit up as she looked toward the sound. "Perfect timing. Antel just got home from work. He's been wanting to say hello to you both."

Antel stepped into the camera's frame, still dressed in his crisp red and black military uniform. He wrapped one arm protectively around Becky's shoulders and raised his other hand in a friendly wave. "Hello, Robert and Elaine. I want you both to know that I'm absolutely keeping my promise to you. Becky is not just surviving here; she's truly thriving in every way. You would be incredibly proud of everything she's accomplished."

Becky melted against his side, her complete happiness radiating from every feature. "We should probably start wrapping this up soon.

There are strict data transmission limits on these interplanetary messages." She pressed her hand firmly over her heart, her voice growing thick with emotion. "I miss you both every single day with an ache I can barely describe. I honestly can't say with certainty when I'll be able to visit Earth again, but I'm holding onto hope that it will be soon. The discussions about re-establishing a new research outpost on Earth are actively ongoing, and Antel believes I might be asked to help coordinate that process because of my unique position bridging both worlds."

She blew a kiss toward the camera lens. "I love you more than words can express. Please take care of each other until I can see you again. And Mom, I wear Grandma's silver locket every single day without fail. Having it close to my heart helps me feel connected to home even across the vast distance between worlds."

Becky started reaching forward to stop the recording, then suddenly froze with her hand halfway to the button. "Oh, and Dad? Don't start worrying about those grandchildren you keep hinting about in your messages. We're definitely not in any hurry, but..." her smile turned mischievous, "someday, I absolutely promise."

With one final, radiant smile that seemed to capture all her love and contentment, she reached forward and ended the recording.

A Request from the Author

If you enjoyed "Sentinel's Dilemma," I would be incredibly grateful if you could take a moment to leave a review on Amazon or your preferred book review platform. Reviews help other readers discover the book and are invaluable to independent authors like me.

Even a few sentences about what you liked make a huge difference.

Thank you for reading Antel's story.

---

https://gmgerstner.github.io/author

Coming Next: "Sentinel's Return"

One year ago, their attempt to study Earth to better plan a first contact failed. Now, with Becky's help, they can attempt first contact much sooner, but only after validating that her teachings about Earth were accurate and unbiased. Once confirmed, they can plan a safe first contact that prevents Earth's nations from panicking and fighting each other over alien access.

Lieutenant Antel Ralnar and Rebecca "Becky" Miller return to Earth as partners in love and mission, leading a nine-person alien team to complete what they started. Their objectives seem straightforward: verify intelligence assessments and prepare for formal first contact.

But when investigators close in on evidence from their first mission, Earth's military begins to weaponize alien technology, and the massive battleship Rilus is discovered in lunar orbit, the world again teeters on the brink of catastrophe. Earth's military prepares to fire on what they believe is an invasion fleet.

As external threats multiply, Antel and Becky's partnership fractures under pressure. With hostile forces closing in and their relationship crumbling, can they overcome their differences in time to prevent interplanetary war?

The future of two worlds and their love hangs in the balance.

About the Author

GEORGE GERSTNER has been building worlds since childhood, but it took a Master's degree in Physics and 25 years of solving real-world engineering problems to give those worlds the authentic scientific foundation they deserved.

When Gerstner tackles interplanetary travel or alien technology in his fiction, he draws on genuine scientific principles and his experience debugging complex systems, because whether you're troubleshooting code or designing a faster-than-light communication system, the logic has to work. His passion for tabletop role-playing games has taught him that the best stories emerge when characters face impossible choices, while his lifelong development of Arkonus, the fictional world at the heart of his novels, proves that some childhood obsessions are worth pursuing into adulthood.

"Sentinel's Dilemma" marks his debut as a novelist, though he's been crafting the universe behind it for decades. When he's not writing about first contact scenarios or the complexities of secret identities, you'll find him in Missouri, probably sketching out the next adventure for his characters or explaining to anyone who'll listen why the physics of space travel really matters in science fiction.

Acknowledgments

I owe a debt of gratitude to many people who helped bring "Sentinel's Dilemma" to life. To my beta readers who caught plot holes and helped refine Antel's character development, thank you for your patience with my imaginative ideas.

Special thanks to Dad, who, whenever I shared my ideas about alien worlds, would say, "You should write a book."

Finally, thank you to my family for understanding when my mind would drift off to explore storyline ideas and for supporting this dream from concept to completion.

Author's Note

The idea for "Sentinel's Dilemma" came from a simple question: What would first contact feel like from the alien's perspective?

Every sci-fi fan knows the classic scene: alien ship lands on the White House lawn, doors open, and out step visitors announcing, "We come in peace." But any species advanced enough for interstellar travel would probably be smart enough to avoid that mistake. A flashy entrance wouldn't just risk panic; it would inevitably trigger something worse: competition. Every nation, faction, and power group would fight for exclusive access to the newcomers, forcing the aliens to either choose sides before they understood what any of those sides actually stood for, or wait for the fighting to settle, and by that time, too much devastation could occur.

The smarter approach? Send observers who could blend in completely, learn the languages, understand the cultures, and map the political landscape before anyone knew they were there.

But what happens when your observer starts to care more about the people he's studying than the mission that brought him there? What happens when duty conflicts with the heart? That's where Antel's story begins...

While the Rileean Empire and planet Arkonus are fictional, I drew inspiration from real scientific theories and only "cheated" when necessary to break a few laws of physics, like faster-than-light travel and communication, that the story demanded.

www.ingramcontent.com/pod-product-compliance
Lightning Source LLC
Chambersburg PA
CBHW051954240626
47153CB00005B/1760